'I've done my bit, Fenwick. I've gone hungry, I've seen my wife and bairns sick. I buried one of them, just a few weeks since—'

'And where would you have been in those hard times, without the union? Who paid to bury your bairn, and get food when you were sick?' It was Adam himself who had been responsible for the administration of the relief fund in the Easington Lane area, so he knew very well what he was talking about.

'I paid into the fund last year. It was due to us.'

'You had more out of it than ever you paid in, Errington. You know that.'

'I gave more than money. I gave time, I gave all I had.'

'Aye, you did. So did we all. That's the reason we won. That's the reason we have to go on doing it. That's the reason you'll let down every single one of us, your brothers, if you turn your back on us now. Who will look after you in bad times to come, if not the union?'

'Maybe there'll be fewer bad times without the union.'

Appalled, Adam reached out and grasped his arm. 'Errington, think what you're doing, man!' But Errington shook off his hand and went into the house, closing the door behind him.

D0885146

Also by Helen Cannam

THE LAST BALLAD
A HIGH AND LONELY ROAD
A THREAD OF GOLD
A KIND OF PARADISE
CANDLE IN THE DARK

HELEN CANNAM

Stranger in the Land

WARNER BOOKS

A *Warner* Book

First published in Great Britain in 1992
by Little, Brown and Company
This edition published by Warner Books in 1993

Copyright © Helen Cannam 1992

The moral right of the author has been asserted.

*All characters in this publication are fictitious and
any resemblance to real persons, living or dead,
is purely coincidental.*

All rights reserved.
No part of this publication may be reproduced,
stored in a retrieval system or transmitted, in any
form or by any means, without the prior
permission in writing of the publisher, nor be
otherwise circulated in any form of binding or
cover other than that in which it is published and
without a similar condition including this
condition being imposed on the subsequent purchaser.

A CIP catalogue record for this book is
available from the British Library.

ISBN 0 7515 0130 1

Printed in England by Clays Ltd, St Ives plc

Warner Books
A Division of
Little, Brown and Company (UK) Limited
165 Great Dover Street
London SE1 4YA

For my son, Christopher, with love

Author's Note

Though the central characters in this novel are entirely imaginary, many of the events took place much as they are described.

I would like to express my gratitude to the staff of various museums, libraries and records offices in Weardale, Crook, Northumberland, Durham City, and Newcastle, for their help with my researches. I should add that any errors in the book are mine and not theirs.

Helen Cannam

People in the Story

Individuals who had some existence in history are marked with an asterisk.

Hetton people

Colliers in the union, and their families:

John Grey
Nan Grey, *his wife*
Matilda (Matty), *eldest of their seven children*
Jamie and Geordie, her brothers
Maria, *her sister*

Jack Marley, *friend of John Grey*

Adam Fenwick
Eliza, *his wife*
Ruth, *their daughter*

Mrs Raines, *Eliza's mother*

* Charles Parkinson, *delegate from Hetton to central committee of the union*
* Thomas Hepburn, *formerly of Hetton Colliery, now full-time union leader*

Colliers out of the union:
* George Allen
Samuel Raines, *Eliza's brother*
* John Errington
* George Holt
* William Steel
* Scott Steel, *his son*
* John Hepplewhite

Hetton Coal Company

* Arthur Mowbray, *senior partner*
* William Redhead, *partner*
* *Other partners*: John Burrell, William Smart, John Dunn
* Matthias Dunn, *consultant viewer*
* Thomas Wood, *agent*
* William Robson, *resident viewer*
* Mark Scott, *under-viewer, Isabella pit*
* Morgan Frazer, *overman, Isabella pit*

Weardale people

Tommy Emerson, *lead miner*

His sister Jenny
Rowland Peart, *her husband, former lead miner*
Mary, *eldest of their six children*
Emerson, *the second child*
William, *the third child*
Daniel, *the youngest child*

Joe Emerson, *brother to Tommy and Jenny*
Eve, *his illegitimate daughter*
Phoebe, *his wife*
Ralph, William and Esther, *their children*

Luke Emerson, *lead miner, cousin to Tommy*
Rebekah, *his wife*
Hannah and Ralph, *their children*

Sarah Craggs, *Ranter local preacher*
Anthony, *her brother*

Nathan Elliot, *lead miner, former partner of Rowland*

Lancelot Hall, *Rowland's cousin*

* Mark Dent, *lead miner*

Jacob Nattrass, *lead miner*
Margaret, *his wife*

Gideon Little, *lead miner*

 * George Crawhall, *agent for the Beaumont lead mining
   interests*

Others

Richard Trevenna, *Cornishman*
* Sir James Parke, *Assize judge*

Chapter One

'They're coming!'

Matty seized the bread from the oven and clutched it to her all the way back to the house, where she flung it on the table before her startled mother and then ran without stopping to the brow of the hill. From there she could see the road winding down into the valley and up again, and the men marching on it. Along the roadside, from every house and alley, women and children came running to wave and cheer, their voices mingling with the high brassy notes of the band and the joyous singing of the men.

Overhead the silken banners shimmered and rippled in the brisk March wind, blue and red and gold against a sky paling with the evening. Silver gulls wheeled far above the golden specks of celandines, bright on the new green of the roadside grass. Even this late in the day the sun was warm.

The winter was over, the long months of darkness and cold, the fear and suffering, the stench of disease and death. Pride and hope had returned to them with the spring. Matty stood on tiptoe, watching the column of men come steadily nearer, and felt her breath catch in her throat.

13

'Charlie Parkinson's in front.' It was her friend Eliza speaking just behind her: a thin fair young woman, baby in her arms, little girl clinging to her skirts. 'He wasn't there this morning. He must have met them at Boldon.'

Matty could just make out the lean black-clad figure marching below the foremost banner. He was not tall, but his dark hair marked him out, clinging close and smooth to his rounded skull under the high-crowned hat, and the way he walked, as if he owned the earth on which his clogged feet trod with so firm a step. Beside him, and a little behind, the other delegates – one for each of the pits at Hetton-le-Hole and North Hetton – seemed lesser men.

'Let's go down,' said Eliza. Matty took Ruth's small hand in hers and they ran together into the valley. There, the words of the men's song reached them, triumphant words composed last year, to celebrate their victory.

> *Still round our banners we shall stand,*
> *In love and truth combine,*
> *And children yet unborn shall sing,*
> *The lads of Wear and Tyne.*

Matty's eyes scanned the moving ranks, only a few yards from them now, slipped over the banners one by one, seeking blue silk, and words spelled out in fiery red. She knew what the words said. Last night she had run her hands over them, when the work was done, the last touches put to the flag the men from Blossom East pit were to carry to the meeting at Boldon Fell. 'What does it say?' she had asked Eliza, who had retorted, 'If you'd learn to read you'd not need me to tell you.'

'You know I want to!' Matty had protested. 'I've always wanted to.'

'Then come to Sunday School. Come on Sunday, or the next week. You'd learn sharp enough.'

She knew what her father would say to that. Yet – she wanted so much to learn. 'I'll come,' she had promised.

Now, she found the flag easily, with its lovely motto,

14

Brethren, dwell together in unity. Beneath it the men marched three abreast, an embodiment of the unity and brotherhood that had won them so much last year and sustained them through the long agony of the winter, and had now been renewed and strengthened at today's meeting, ready to face the storm that threatened all they had gained.

'There's Adam,' said Matty suddenly. She bent her head a little, so that the folds of her kerchief hid the colour rising in her face. Eliza's colour had risen too, and her eyes were lit with pride, but then she had the right, for the man whose fine blond hair caught the sun, drawing the eye from his slight figure and bandy legs, was her husband. Ruth jumped up and down and shouted to her father.

'Jack Marley's behind him,' Eliza said after a moment, and this time she turned to scrutinise her friend's face. If she saw any heightened colour now, clearly she attributed it (quite mistakenly) to the fact that Matty's gaze had moved to the tall handsome young man in striped waistcoat and ribbon-decked hat who walked behind the sober figure of Adam Fenwick.

'So what?' Matty tried to look as if she did not know the reason for Eliza's teasing tone. But even though (unlike most girls) she obstinately refused to be enchanted by Jack Marley, she could not prevent a lift of the spirits on seeing him. There was so much of the spring about him, its colour and brightness and hopefulness; and it was so long since there had been cause for rejoicing.

Smiling, waving, singing, the men passed, and the following columns, all in the same disciplined ranks. Eliza and Matty walked on with them, among the other women and children.

'Your Samuel stayed at home today,' Matty said after a little while.

'Aye, I heard.' Eliza's face grew shadowed. 'Has he said owt about it?'

'Not to me. Your mam says he got drunk last night and

wasn't fit to come. But he told my dad the other day, if they won't bind union men he'll leave the union.' It was so shocking a prospect that she lowered her voice as she spoke of it, watching Eliza intently as she did so. 'What would you do, if he did that? He'd be sure to fall out with Adam.'

'Then he'd fall out with me as well. I'd have nowt to do with a blackleg, even if he was my own brother.'

'Mam always says family comes first.'

'That's your mam speaking, not me. For me and Adam, it's right comes first. "A man's foes shall be they of his own household." That's what Jesus said.'

Matty stared at her with awe. Eliza looked calm enough, as if that terrible declaration could be accepted as a matter of course. She tried to imagine what it would be like to be set against your own family, and to be so sure of the rightness of what you did, but the effort was beyond her. 'What if your mam takes Samuel's side?'

'Matty, he's done no wrong yet, beyond getting drunk, and that's nowt to wonder at. There's no saying he'd go so far, even if the owners do what we think they will. But if he does, then he knows what will happen, and so does my mam. They would have to take what came to them.'

She looked troubled at the thought, but Matty knew that Eliza had already, on many occasions, opposed her mother's wishes, and those of her father too, before he died of the cholera last winter. She had done so when she became a Primitive Methodist – a Ranter – converted by an itinerant preacher one wild night of singing and preaching and praying near Sunderland; when she had followed the call to become an itinerant preacher herself and left home to wander alone yet undaunted among strange people in strange places, carrying her fervent message wherever the need called her; when she had wed her fellow preacher, Adam Fenwick, now returned to his old trade as a collier. Only two years older than Matty, her best friend since Matty first came to Hetton, Eliza was already, at twenty, far removed from her in experience.

The procession came to a halt at last, beside the beginnings of a waste heap on a muddy patch of open ground at the back of Brick Garth, where Matty lived. There, Charlie Parkinson raised his hands, closed his eyes and asked for a final blessing. Some of the men – Matty's father among them – fidgeted restlessly, as if conscious of the passing of good drinking time; but at least the prayer was soon ended.

Adam came over to his family, ruffling his children's hair, drawing his wife's arm through his.

'You should have heard Hepburn today, Eliza.' His eyes, Matty thought, were as blue as the sky over their heads, or the banner that she and Eliza had sewn, and as clear and shining. 'Truly he spoke as the spirit gave him utterance. He has never been better.'

Matty knew she was no longer wanted, though she doubted if Adam had even noticed that she was there. At home her father and brothers rarely talked of union matters to their womenfolk, and she loved to listen to Adam's talk; but more than that, she wanted to watch him and see the tenderness in his eyes, and feed her sweet wistful longing to be loved by such a man.

'Does he think the owners are out to break the union?' Eliza's tone was matter of fact, but her brown eyes were soft as she raised them to his face.

'We all think that. I've no doubt of it. But I know too they'll never do it, not while we stand together.'

'We'll stand together, Adam Fenwick.'

Matty glanced sharply round at her father, who had spoken so suddenly just behind her.

'We've come through hunger together, and the cholera, and we've not broken yet, not even bent. Never fear for us now.'

'I don't,' said Adam cheerfully – with reason, thought Matty, for if men so different as her father and Adam Fenwick could stand together through so many hardships, then no power on earth would ever destroy their unity.

17

Chapter Two

'Strangers,' said John Grey, coming to a halt.

The gas lights at the pithead threw an unhealthy pallid gleam on the faces of the men gathered beneath the walls of the engine house. They had a furtive look, Grey thought, as of newcomers unsure what to do, and not very sure either what sort of reception to expect. He knew he had seen none of them before.

Until lately there would have been nothing out of the way in that, nor anything to cause concern. Hetton was a new colliery, constantly growing as fresh pits were sunk, and almost its entire workforce had come into it, over the years, from other pits in Durham or Northumberland. But since the formation of Hepburn's union in the spring of 1831 – last year – strangers were looked at more warily. It was always possible they might be non-union men, deliberately brought in by the owners to take the jobs of union members, as had happened elsewhere.

Jamie, John Grey's eldest son – he was seventeen – studied the men. 'Maybe they're more of the Coxlodge men.'

Grey looked about him to see if there was any sign of a committee member – Adam Fenwick perhaps – in the subdued straggle of colliers walking to work in the frosty darkness, but he could see no one. Besides, it was cold, and Geordie, the younger boy, was openly shivering. They walked on, and by the time they reached the pithead the strangers were no longer there.

In a cabin near the shaft John and Jamie discarded their outer clothes, stripping to the drawers and shirt and shoes and stockings and cap all men wore at the coal face. Then, carrying bait and lamps and candle boxes, they were let down into the pit and set off to walk the considerable distance to their work places. Geordie parted from them very soon, without complaint but in silence, to take up his position beside one of the trapdoors used to control ventilation underground. He would sit there in the dark (no light was allowed, for safety reasons) for the next twelve hours, opening and closing the trap as required to keep the pit safe for the men, struggling against sleepiness and boredom and the terror natural enough in a nine-year-old. But it was one of last year's victories that he had only twelve hours to endure. Before the union fought for the boys, they had faced at least fourteen hours underground each day, and sometimes a good deal more.

His father and brother walked on, coming after some time to one of the cranes, where a group of men and boys had gathered: putters like Jamie, whose task was to push the loaded trams of coal from the face to the crane; hewers like John Grey and Jack Marley, pausing to snatch a few moments more of talk and relaxation, and to replace the candles that had lit their way so far with Davy lamps. John Grey saw that Adam Fenwick was there too, the fine bones of his face accentuated by the shadowy light.

'Do you know about the strangers?' he asked, enlarging on what he had seen.

'There were colliers came from Coxlodge, with our agreement, last week. But these . . . '

'Ask that man over there – he's from Coxlodge.'

Adam looked round at the two men coming towards

them, recognising the one pointed out to him as George Allen, who had begun work at the Blossom pit just last week. He went over to him. 'Do you know the men just come in? Where are they from? Do they belong the union?'

Allen opened his mouth and then shut it again. From somewhere in the darkness behind him a voice said, 'Allen doesn't belong the union.'

There was a silence. No one moved. Yet it was as if a great chasm had suddenly opened about George Allen. In spirit at least, his companions all recoiled from him.

He began to stammer out an explanation. 'I was in the militia when it all started. Then I was sick, oh, three months or more. I'd have joined if it hadn't been for that.'

The union had reluctantly agreed to the coming of the sacked men from Coxlodge, as a means of providing work for their fellow unionists without jeopardising their own position. Allen must have known that when he came to Hetton.

There was no softening in any of the faces gathered about him. Adam Fenwick's was icy in its decision and firmness. 'Get away home, Allen. You're to work no more this morning. We'll decide what's to be done when we meet this afternoon.' After that, he walked away, followed by most of the others. One man spat, deliberately, near Allen's feet as he passed.

Allen glanced at the man set to work with him today and saw him shake his head. 'Never think I'll work with thee.' And he too walked away, the glow of his lamp diminishing until the darkness swallowed it up.

John Grey nodded to Jack Marley and the two of them began to make their way to the place where they worked.

They had gone only a short distance when a sudden noise from behind made them turn. Left alone by his fellow hewers, George Allen had stayed where he was, uncertain what to do next. The putters – all young lads, like Jamie – had waited, watchful, until the older men had gone; and then they closed in on Allen.

20

John Grey halted, looking back at them, wondering whether to intervene. Jack Marley laid a hand on his shoulder. 'Let them be, man.'

'It's not the way Hepburn wants us to settle things,' said Grey, troubled. The lads had not moved again. They simply stood there, cutting off all Allen's hope of retreat, waiting.

'It's the way it always used to be done, when any man set himself against the rest of us.'

'Aye,' said Grey slowly. With some reluctance he turned and walked on, Marley with him. The sounds of scuffling, missiles being thrown, shouts and grunts, came to them through the darkness, but they did not look round. 'I did as much myself when there was trouble at Jarrow, the year before I came here. But – I'd never have believed it, but I reckon now we've got more by going Hepburn's way.'

'So far,' said Jack. They rounded a corner and could no longer hear anything, except muffled echoing noises that might have been quite innocent and were partly submerged in the sound of singing from the hewers already at work. 'But Hepburn's way's like to sink us now. There's one thing changed from last year, at Hetton anyhow – Dunn wasn't here then. He's not the man to listen to what we say to him, however fine the words. He's just waiting his moment to rid himself of all the best men. If we're to stop him, we have to make him see we'll not stand for it.'

'We made a start Friday.' Grey smiled with pleasurable reminiscence. 'You could see how sick he was, when they made him give up the bond to the delegates.'

Traditionally, the bond that set out the colliers' terms of work for the year was read out to the men (or to those who were close enough to hear it) some weeks before the signing – which, like the reading, had become a mere formality, a matter of each man's name being listed and then marked with a cross. But last Friday, when the binding opened, the union delegates had insisted on reading the bond through themselves, so that they could the more easily study the terms, prior to negotiating further. Mr Dunn, the coal company's chief viewer since last November, had been forced by the other colliery officials (in theory his subordinates) to give up the bond to Charlie Parkinson, and his chagrin on the occasion had been obvious to them all – the more so when the delegates had then gone on to raise objections to almost every clause.

'It's my guess that won't be the end of it. He'll be the more set to get his own way after this. And there are any number of ways he can do it . . . You know how long I spent stowing small coals Friday? So long I hardly made two shillings the day. And for what I get for it, I might as well have saved my strength.'

'Aye, and then you'd have had the overman down on you, because Dunn's on *his* back. Damn the man!' Each hewer was supposed to lay aside a certain quantity of small coals for every score sent up to bank, since there was at present little market for any but large coals. But the whole matter was a constant source of friction, as the amount of small coal cut necessarily varied more than the overmen or the viewer recognised, and the separating and stowing of it took time and effort that might otherwise have been used in getting coal for which the men would be paid at the full rate.

'It's my belief we'll have no peace in Hetton until Dunn's gone.'

'You could be right there.'

Nan Grey, tired and irritable as she always was in the first weeks of pregnancy, straightened slowly from the poss tub in which she had been pummelling the washing. She frowned at her eldest daughter, who was leaning idly on the yard gate. 'I'll want more water yet, Matty. Don't stand there doing nowt.'

Matty took a pail and scrambled down to the burn that ran through the little valley to the west of Brick Garth. Eliza Fenwick was already there, kneeling on the bank washing clothes, while near by on the grass her little girl played some kind of anarchic clapping game with the baby, their laughter wild and loud in the bright cold air.

Matty stooped to the water, just upstream from Eliza, who glanced round and then sat back on her heels, rubbing hands raw and red with cold on her skirts.

'I thought you were to come to Sunday School. I've been watching for you these three weeks.'

Eliza's words, only faintly reproachful, touched a sore point and Matty scowled. 'I would have come, but my dad said he'd thrash us.' She saw the brown eyes widen. 'You know what he thinks of owt to do with Ranters, outside the union, that is. And women reading too, come to that.' She did not add what her father said so often, and so disparagingly, about Eliza herself, *Teach a woman to read, that's bad enough – you make a rod for your own back. But a woman preaching! That's against nature.* The fact that, since the children were born, Eliza no longer went preaching made no difference at all to his opinion. She was already spoiled as a wife for any normal man. It was too late to mend matters.

Matty thought for a moment that Eliza might offer to teach her in private, but then she dismissed the hope. Eliza had enough on her hands, with a husband and children, and a home to run, and besides John Grey did not even like his daughter to call on the Fenwicks, for fear of contamination. *Next thing, you'll be looking down on your own, like that Eliza Fenwick . . .*

Eliza bent again to her washing, wringing out the garments and placing them in the basket at her side. 'You should learn somehow,' she said. 'It would open your eyes. It opened mine. It was the first step to liberty, for me.'

'Liberty', in Eliza's terms, meant conversion to the Ranter faith, which was not a prospect that greatly tempted Matty. That faith – so vital a part of her friend's life – was one of the few things about Eliza that was beyond her comprehension, much as Matty liked her and admired the strength and courage her faith gave her.

23

A small figure came running towards them from Brick Garth. 'Matty! Mam says where's that water!'

'Maria,' said Matty with resignation, and filled the pail and set out back towards the house, fending off her sister's self-righteous reproaches with an air of lofty unconcern.

At home again, Matty set the water to warm on the fire and then put her father's clean clothes ready near his favourite chair for when he was washed, and laid his place at the table. When he had washed and eaten, it would be the turn of her brothers, who worked longer hours than their father. They might be younger than she was, but they were working men, and took precedence in everything. Matty and her mother and her sisters would get their turn to eat when the men had washed and fed and gone out again, and not until then.

Their kitchen window looked out over a small yard to the raw brick walls of the other houses built about the court, a muddy, rutted area where toddlers played and women gossiped, and washing hung on lines, adding moisture to the rubbish underneath. Yet indoors everything shone and glowed with comfort. Rag rugs lay on the brick floor, a fine clock ticked solemnly in one corner, the table was covered with a spotless and brightly coloured cloth, the plates, laid on the table and stacked on the mahogany chest of drawers, were good earthenware, with even one or two china items; there were chintz curtains at the windows and two sturdy armchairs for the men to rest in at the end of the day, should they choose to stay by their own cheerful fireside. Copper cooking pots, well polished, shone warmly near the hearth, and a brass candlestick, double branched, stood ready on the table for when it grew too dark to see by the inadequate light from the small window. A good smell of mutton stew filled the room.

Matty went out into the yard to watch for her father's return. It was nearly midday and the sun for once reached into the court, giving it a more cheerful aspect. A pair of geese, waddling out of the opposite yard, reached the sunlight and suddenly shone so dazzlingly white that it hurt the eyes to look at them. A little girl bowled a hoop past them, setting them cackling noisily. Two women laughed together as they added more washing to what already hung there.

Then the noise of masculine voices broke into the feminine sounds of the court and a group of men emerged from the little alley at the top end, calling to their companions as they parted from them at one house after another along the row. Ahead of them, walking quickly, came Samuel Raines, Eliza's brother. He hurried past Matty, apparently without seeing her, and then disappeared into the house next door to their own. Her father came more slowly, small and stocky beside Jack Marley's tall figure. Matty stayed where she was, watching as they approached, and saw how Jack's eyes came to rest on her for a moment, dark and expressionless. Did he fancy her, as everyone seemed to think? Or was it as much a matter of wishful thinking on their part as the other idea they all seemed to have, that she fancied him in her turn? She could see no particular softness in his eyes – but nor would she have done, for if he did feel anything it would not be gentle or tender, but savage and hot and demanding, of a piece with his assertive masculinity. He looked away, and her father said, 'You'll be at the meeting today then?'

'Aye. Mind, I reckon I'd get better inspiration from a pint or two at Smith's.' He must have seen a hint of reproof in his companion's expression, for he added, 'I'll not risk a fine again, never fear. I'll save the drinking till after. But I tell you there are times I think I'll not stomach that pious abstaining crew a day more.'

'Aye, well, they're hardly to my liking, not in that. A drink never did a man no harm, which is more than you can say for that gnat's piss they call tea. But then I'd give up more than a bit drinking time, when I look at what they've done for us.'

'I wonder. If the owners stand together this time, what then? *Patience and perseverance!*' He spat expressively

25

on the ground. 'What are we to do – lie down and let the masters tramp all over us, just as they please? That's not my way, I tell you. That's the trouble with Ranters. All talk and no balls.'

'Tommy Hepburn, no balls— That's . . .'

'Why aye, he's got fire in his belly all right – for his preaching.'

'I've no more stomach than you have for preaching. No man calls me a sinner and gets away with it. But let him say I'm as good as the next man, with as good a right to freedom and dignity – then I'm with him all the way. That's what Tommy Hepburn's given us, and the other Ranters. There'd be no union without them.'

'They could kill it yet. They want telling, you don't win a war without blood.'

'Aye, but . . . Maybe this isn't the time for that kind of talk—'

They saw that Matty was listening to them and fell silent. Jack cast her a sideways look that was knowing without being particularly friendly. She ignored him and went inside, irritated at the whispered comment he made, which drew a burst of laughter from the other men. Shortly afterwards, her father came in, patting her cheek with casual affection as he passed.

His wife and daughters gathered round to see to his needs, pouring water for him to wash, holding towels ready, and clean clothes. Matty took his working clothes outside to bang them on the wall and shake out the worst of the coal dust. When she came in again her father was saying, 'There was trouble the day.' Matty folded the work clothes and put them away, as quietly as she could, so as not to distract her father from what he was saying.

'Was it the small coals again?' Nan asked, poised for sympathetic indignation.

'Why no . . . you know George Allen, moved in last week?' Nan Grey nodded. 'It came out he doesn't belong the union. He was set on by some of the putters.'

'Our Jamie?' There was a note of pride in her voice.

26

'Aye. They brayed him and stripped him, you know the kind of thing.'

'Was he hurt? Allen, I mean.' She sounded as if she rather hoped he had been.

'Not that bad. Plenty, though.' His tone indicated that the matter was more serious than his wife had supposed. 'He went crying to the overman, *he* called Mr Dunn, and now they've taken him to Houghton, before the magistrates.'

Nan Grey pressed her hand to her mouth. 'He'll say who did it!'

'If he saw. I'd guess he didn't. Besides, he's not been here long enough to know the putters by name. Mind, we can't be sure.'

'Then I'll call on him, as soon as he's home. Make him see, our Jamie's just a lad. A bit wild like, but there's no harm in him.'

Jack Marley came a little late to the union meeting, timing his arrival with care to be sure to miss the opening prayers, but early enough to answer when his name came up on the roll. True to his word, he had not been drinking. To have been fined once for coming drunk to a meeting had been enough for him. He took his seat noisily near the table at which several of the committee members – Parkinson and Fenwick among them – were seated. The roll was called, and excuses heard for those more prominent members who were absent; all but one.

'Errington's not here,' said Adam.

'Then,' said Parkinson, 'I ask that brother Fenwick call on him after the meeting, to know his reasons.'

Jack pressed his hands on the table edge, preparatory to getting to his feet. He had already drawn breath for what he wanted to say, when Fenwick stood up.

'Chairman, brothers, I've one matter to bring to the attention of the meeting today. It's not what the owners say in Newcastle that counts in the end. It's what happens here. And so long as Dunn is viewer at Hetton Colliery, then we're going to find our path blocked at every turn. I ask you, brothers, are we to be tyrannised over by an idol-worshipper, a Papist?'

There was a chorus of agreement, in which Jack joined as enthusiastically as anyone, putting aside his momentary regret at having his unspoken words seized on so exactly by a man he did not greatly like. Just to make his own point, he put in, 'I don't care if the bastard worships the sun, it's what he does to us that matters – and for that he's got to go.'

'Never mind that. I want to know what's to be done about Allen!' Heads turned to stare at John Grey.

Parkinson said, 'What about him?'

'I was coming to that later,' said Fenwick. 'We heard today, he's not in the union.'

Grey broke in impatiently, 'That's not what I mean. What if my lad's transported because of him?'

Fenwick looked puzzled. 'What has transportation to do with it? Allen—'

'You've not heard, then?' And he proceeded to tell Fenwick about the attack on Allen.

At the end, mouth set in a hard line, Fenwick said, 'So that's why your lad's not here. No wonder! He's played right into the masters' hands, him and the rest of them.' His tone was calm and quiet, but they could all sense the anger seething beneath the surface.

Parkinson said, 'Is Allen at home now?'

'So far as I know,' said Grey, looking a little puzzled. He did not mention that his wife intended to pay the man a visit. Women were not encouraged to interfere in union matters.

'Then one of us shall go to him, on behalf of the union, and offer him compensation for what was done. We must make him see it's in his interest to join us.'

There was a murmur of agreement from some of the company, but Grey said, 'What about my lad, and the others? If it gets to court—'

'If Allen's satisfied it won't get to court,' said Fenwick.

'Why should he be "satisfied"?' Marley demanded. 'He's a blackleg.'

' "Agree with thine adversary quickly",' quoted Parkinson. In the end, they all agreed that the move should be made, and the most diplomatic of their number was sent at once to call on Allen, with a purse of money in his pocket.

'And now, brothers,' said Parkinson, when he had gone, 'Mr Dunn and the committee meet within the hour. We'd best get to the rest of the business, or we'll not be through in time.'

When the meeting broke up Adam Fenwick went back to his house in Easington Lane to let Eliza know what had been decided and to pray with the children before bedtime. Returning soon afterwards to join the delegation to the coal company's committee, his attention was caught by a middle-aged man with a severe limp just turning into the road that led to Brick Garth. He knew the man well, for not only were they near neighbours, but they had both been among the most enthusiastic union members during last year's struggle, working side by side on the committee. He hurried after him, catching up with him just as he laid his hand on the latch of his door.

'You weren't with us today, Errington,' he said, kindly enough. 'Is owt wrong?'

Errington turned and stood looking at him for a moment, saying nothing. His expression had a certain blankness, almost as if he had no idea what Adam was talking about. 'I chose not to come,' he said at last, and then added abruptly, with a note of defiance, 'I'm done with the union.'

Adam studied his face, as if seeking some clue to so sudden and astonishing an assertion. 'Just when the union most needs you, Errington – I don't understand.'

'Don't you? Then you should. I can see the signs if you can't. The masters are out to break us. There'll be no fighting them this time. They won't let us win.'

'If we stand together they'll have no choice.'

'If we stand against them we'll be out in the streets, like

the Coxlodge men. They were just the first, that's all.'

'They've taken Coxlodge men on here, on our terms.'

'If you think that means owt, you're a fool, Fenwick. Let them think we mean to stand by the union and they'll sharp change their tune. Just wait till the bond's out, then you'll see.'

'If they see any of us faltering, before ever the terms of the bond are agreed, then they'll think we're weakening.'

'As we must, in the end. I'll not wait for that. I've had enough. I want to be free to get as much as I can for my wife and bairns, for myself—'

'At the cost of other men's jobs? To feed the greed of the owners?' With every phrase he seemed to hear Errington's voice, urging just these arguments on his fellow colliers through last year's struggle; always, with the same passion, the same conviction as Adam felt now. Yet today it was Errington's voice that was stubbornly disputing those very arguments.

'I've done my bit, Fenwick. I've gone hungry, I've seen my wife and bairns sick. I buried one of them, just a few weeks since—'

'And where would you have been in those hard times, without the union? Who paid to bury your bairn, and get food when you were sick?' It was Adam himself who had been responsible for the administration of the relief fund in the Easington Lane area, so he knew very well what he was talking about.

'I paid into the fund last year. It was due to us.'

'You had more out of it than ever you paid in, Errington. You know that.'

'I gave more than money. I gave time, I gave all I had.'

'Aye, you did. So did we all. That's the reason we won. That's the reason we have to go on doing it. That's the reason you'll let down every single one of us, your brothers, if you turn your back on us now. Who will look after you in bad times to come, if not the union?'

'Maybe there'll be fewer bad times without the union.'

Appalled, Adam reached out and grasped his arm. 'Errington, think what you're doing, man!' But Errington shook off his hand and went into the house, closing the door behind him.

Chapter Three

As it was a fine day, Matthias Dunn, chief viewer of the Hetton Coal Company, left his gig at the colliery at Moorsley, headquarters of North Hetton Colliery – where he was also employed as viewer – and walked down to the offices beyond Hetton village where he was to meet with the company's committee.

He never walked from one to the other without bracing himself for what he had to face. At North Hetton he was respected (at least by his employers) as the man of skill and experience he was, supported in all the decisions he took, all the innovations he attempted. At Hetton – well, he had known when he took up the post that the Hetton Company was notorious for the stormy relations of its partners, a mixed body of strong-minded entrepreneurs of varied backgrounds, very unlike the aristocratic owners of the greater part of the collieries of Northumberland and Durham. He should not have been surprised to find himself caught already between their warring factions. But it was beginning to take its toll of his nerves. He was not a man who easily weighed his words before speaking – he rarely needed to – but this afternoon he took the opportunity provided by the walk to plan what he would say to the committee.

From some way off he saw a group of men making their way purposefully towards the office from the other direction. Another union delegation, he thought wearily; just one more trial to contend with before he could turn his back on Hetton for the night. He began to quicken his pace, not wanting to confront them until he had to, and was pleased to reach the office door just as Mr William Redhead, one of the Company's partners, alighted from his carriage near by. Dunn liked Redhead, on the whole, if only because as a local man he seemed more concerned for the well-being of the colliery than simply the healthiness of his own shares in it. They went into the office together, talking of the progress of the Reform Bill through Parliament. Dunn, whose necessary support for Catholic Emancipation had given him reforming tendencies, expressed his hope that this time the Lords would refrain from throwing the bill out. Redhead agreed, but rather absently, and then paused with his hand on the inner door to say in a low voice, 'I should warn you, some of my partners want to insist that you reside at Hetton.'

'I thought I'd made my position on that plain enough,' said Dunn. He had no intention of leaving his comfortable house in a pleasant area of Newcastle to take up residence among a population which (at least as long as they were guided by such inflammatory leaders) would continue to hate him and all that he stood for. Besides, he knew of no other coal company or owner that would have made such a demand of its consultant viewer.

The other partners who made up the committee were already seated about the office table. As he and Redhead took their seats among them, Dunn looked round the room and knew he could not assume the support of any of them, with the probable exception of Redhead; there were even those who would oppose him as a matter of course, whatever he put before them. He felt a tremor of anger that he should have to face this added harassment in an already difficult position.

Once the initial greetings were over, Dunn cleared his

throat and began, 'I wish to express my dissatisfaction with—'

His words were lost in a confused noise from outside the door, which ended in a sharp knocking. The clerk, at a nod from one of the partners, went to open it, and half a dozen men stepped unbidden into the room. They formed the union delegation, Dunn recognised, arriving even before he had found time to put his other concerns before the committee – and led, as always, by Charlie Parkinson, his most bitter opponent. The man's hot brown eyes, bright and hard, rested insolently on the viewer's face. Dunn knew that even if Parkinson had been the most meek and biddable of workmen, he would still not have warmed to him. The Catholic viewer and the Ranter union leader were set apart by far more than disagreements about colliery matters. Dunn had heard Parkinson once, holding forth on a street corner, and had been uncomfortably aware of precisely what was meant by the half-caught reference to 'Babylon, the Mother of all Harlots'. It was in his blood, an understanding of hatreds three hundred years old, which recent changes in the law had done little to assuage.

Now, the man held out a scroll for the viewer to take. 'It contains our minimum demand,' Parkinson said. 'When that is met, then we shall discuss the terms of the bond, but not until then. We shall wait outside to learn your answer.' There was something approaching a sneer in his expression, Dunn thought, as the man turned away and led his fellows out of the room.

Dunn handed the scroll to Redhead, who unrolled it and studied it; and then gave a sharp exclamation.

'Did you know about this, Dunn?'

The viewer took the paper from him and read with incredulous eyes the sternly worded demand for the immediate dismissal of *the Papist Dunn*. The other men saw his colour rise, his eyes sparkle with anger. 'This is monstrous beyond anything!' He did not add, as he was greatly tempted to do, that it was precisely the kind of behaviour one might expect from men who had been led to believe that their every demand would be met.

John Burrell, the company's solicitor, took the paper and muttered the words over as he read. '*There is one obstacle to the peaceful . . .* so on, so forth *. . . the tyrannical procedures of the Papist Dunn* – disgraceful language! – *no man shall agree to be bound until Dunn quits Hetton colliery . . .* Shocking! Shocking!' He shook his head, and then passed the paper to William Smart, who sat beside him.

The man read it in silence and then said, 'It is indeed disgraceful. Yet—' Dunn looked sharply at Smart, who went on, 'It seems to me that you go out of your way to make enemies. Rather more flexibility, a readiness to — '

If Redhead had not intervened then, Dunn knew he would have made some quite unpardonable retort. 'There can be no question but that we refuse to treat with the men until they withdraw this outrageous demand.'

Fortunately the suggestion was accepted without opposition, and the clerk was instructed to draft a reply expressing the committee's disgust. 'And make it plain,' added Redhead, 'that every member of the present deputation must be ready to quit his house at the expiry of his bond. They at least shall not continue in our employment.'

Dunn, who had for some time now been advocating the sacking of the union leaders as the only means of bringing the bulk of the men to their senses, kept his gratification to himself. He looked round to make sure he had the attention of all of them, and then he continued, using the words he had rehearsed on his way to the meeting, which he felt were now more pertinent than ever, 'I did not set out with the intention of breaking the union, as such—'

'Ah, but you were privy to the decision of the coal owners' committee in January.' That was his namesake, Mr John Dunn, who had also been present at the coal owners' meeting, where a common policy aimed at destroying the union had been agreed.

'I was, and I am very clear that the owners must stand

together this time. However, my first concern here at Hetton has always been to encourage and support those men who work well and peaceably, and discharge those who are ill disposed. But it must now be clear to the meanest intelligence that this cannot be achieved whilst the union exists in its present form. We cannot allow ourselves to be ruled by our employees. I have kept you informed of the constant quibbling I have met with whenever I have tried to enforce your wishes. Some of you may have heard of the ill treatment of a hewer underground today, the poor man having the temerity to be out of the union. The colliers must be brought to see that only in rejecting their delegates can they hope to make an honest living. Until now we have been hampered by the terms of the bond. But when the bond expires we shall be free to take whatever steps are necessary.'

'If you mean grovers – lead miners – that was tried last year,' said Smart.

'In very small numbers, and only above ground – and without conviction, for you dismissed them the moment the delegates protested.'

'We'd already lost more money than we could well afford. Any further interruption would have given our rivals an overwhelming advantage. We had to agree with the union, and quickly.'

'If I may say so,' Dunn returned as politely as his irritation would allow, 'the advantage you gained was very short lived. You will never be strong while you allow yourselves to be ridden over in that way.'

Smart was about to make a further retort, but Redhead said quickly, 'Let us hear what you propose.'

'I ask that every man bound be required to renounce all allegiance to this union or any like it.'

'Can we do that – legally, I mean?' Redhead asked.

'We should have to word the undertaking carefully, that is all,' Burrell said.

'Do you really believe lead miners are going to be competent to do the work?' There was a sneer in Smart's voice.

'I have spoken to viewers at those collieries that have already taken them on, and they are entirely satisfied with them. Their work is not vastly different from that of a collier, and they are said to be intelligent and independent minded – we'll have no union foolishness from them. If we can induce them to come in sufficient numbers to keep the pits going, I think nothing but good can come of it. Mark my words, the colliers have only to sniff the threat that other men will take their work from under their noses to see reason.'

'They are inclined to believe that no one else can do the work as they can,' said Redhead.

'I'm aware of that. But a little revolution directed by ourselves will soon teach these boastful aristocrats of the coal pits that they have overreached themselves. When lead miners are getting coal as efficiently as any pitman, and a good deal more peaceably, they'll sharp see the error of their ways. The more if their bellies are empty.'

They were interrupted at that point by someone coming with a message. There was a whispered conference between Dunn and the man who brought the message; then the viewer said, 'I had hoped to report that the putters responsible for the assault this morning had been arrested.'

'The warrants were issued,' said Redhead. 'Has Allen still not given the names?'

'He claimed, as you know, that he was not sure who his assailants were, his lamp being out. But we know from the overman which lads were putting in that place this morning. We intended to jolt Allen's memory, once he'd had time to consider. Unfortunately, when I called on him this afternoon he showed a marked unwillingness to witness to the events at all.'

'Has he been got at?'

'So it would seem. He maintained that it was no more than a minor incident of no significance, and he wished to forget about it. His wife claims the union sent a man to pay him "compensation". "Hush money" might be a more appropriate term.'

'Then what do we do?'

'That is our difficulty. It seems he's gone. Either from fear for his own skin, or because the union has spirited him out of our reach – that was the message I had just now. So, unless we can lay hands on him again, we've lost our witness . . . I shall, of course, do what I can to find him. Meanwhile, I suggest we apply the warrants, using what information we have, and prepare to do our best to convince Allen he must appear, when we get him back. If we can't convince him, then the law must make him. It is imperative that he appears in court to give a full account of what was done to him.'

Generally Matty went to bed long before her father and Jamie came home at night, but this evening she felt restless, unsettled by a confused mixture of excitement and discontent.

Her mother retired to the handsome mahogany bed in the front room, which she shared with her husband, and the baby, when there was one. Matty was left to bank down the fire with coal dust; once that was done she went outside and wandered along to the end of the row, and then down into Elemore Vale, across the burn where she had talked to Eliza this morning and on to the highest point close to the towering waste heaps of Elemore Colliery.

It was a still night, cold and clear; there would be a frost again before dawn. The blackness of hills and fields and woods was broken everywhere before her by points of light. Here and there the unnatural gleam of gaslights marked a pithead, contrasting with the red flickering flames of the intermittent fires that burned on the waste heaps. Strung along the road, saffron squares glowed from the windows of houses, all the way down from Hetton village on the far hillside, spreading briefly in a cross at Four Lane Ends and then on again up the slope to her right along the line of Easington Lane. The light caught the gleam from a puddle or picked out the black swaying figures of men staggering noisily home from public houses. Snatches of singing – not all drunken – reached her, and shouts and laughter, a child crying, a dog barking on and on, all muffled a little by distance, merging into one general night-time sound, familiar, ordinary. It seemed to have been the background of her life for as long as she could remember, here and in other pit villages where the Greys had lived, following the best-paid work from colliery to colliery. But then her memory of the years before they came here had grown dim. She had only been ten when they moved to Brick Garth, and it seemed as if all the thoughts and feelings of her life had been packed into the years that followed; as if before that time she had not had any kind of separate existence, as if what made her Matty Grey and no one else had not yet come into being.

It had been a strange day today. In many ways so ordinary, filled with the tedious washday routine that seemed to leave no time for what she was doing now – simply looking and feeling and thinking – and offering no excitement or pleasure or satisfaction, it had yet brought all kinds of threats for the future. She did not share her mother's relief that George Allen had disappeared. They would find him, she was sure, and then Jamie would be hauled before the court, with who knew what consequences. She and Jamie, being closest in age, fought constantly, and at times she thought she hated him, but the thought that, because of what happened today, he might be sent to the other side of the world was terrible. Yet at the same time she found herself almost envying him. She had seen ships at Sunderland and wondered what it must be like to be a sailor, as her own grandfather had been. She thought she would love to travel great distances, to see strange places and meet strange people and face unknown, perhaps unknowable, excitements and adventures. But then it was not she who was threatened with transportation, but Jamie. To be left behind wondering what had become of him would offer no excitement at all.

That was the trouble with her life, that it was lived on

the edge of an excitement that was just out of her reach. The most she could look forward to was to marry one day, very soon, and bear children and watch them grow, while day after day, week after week, year after year, she went on doing the things she had always done. Meanwhile, the men in her life, facing daily danger underground, had all the excitements of the union struggle to fill their hours above ground, excitements from which she, as a woman, was deliberately excluded. She had no wish to be a man, but she wished very much that she had something of a man's control over her life.

She looked up into the velvet darkness of the sky, pricked out with the clear pure points of the stars around the moon's thin crescent, veiled here and there by smudges of smoke from the chimneys of the colliery rows; and suddenly all her half-formed discontents were swept away in a great flood of feeling. She could not have put the feeling into words. She only knew she was alone on her hill with the stars above and the earth spread out beneath her, so that she could, for a moment, believe it was all at her feet, at her command. She was happy, in a wild sad way, full of a yearning for something unknown and never experienced, something that perhaps she would never know. She wanted to fly, to float away, up and up among the stars, away from the small tedious everyday things of her life, from the people and places she knew so well, to something new and strange. She wanted magic and adventure and mystery. For a moment she almost believed she *had* floated away, that all she wanted was just within her grasp . . .

And then she realised that she was no longer solitary on the hill, for a number of black shapes were coming towards her up the slope from the west, lighting their way with a lantern: a group of men coming over the fields from Moorsley, she supposed. She turned quickly and began to hurry back the way she had come, but the men had already seen her and one of them called out, 'It's Matty Grey – I'll swear it's Matty Grey!' Then she made out the powerful outline of Jack Marley, in front of the

40

rest (few pitmen were as tall or straight of limb). She gave a shriek, half laughing, and began to run. She had no particular reason to be alarmed or to run from him, but she felt her heart thudding faster as she went, quickening the more as he too broke into a run. She shrieked again, but always in fun, because only prim and pious girls took a man's playfulness in bad part. Near the house, running faster than his companions, he caught her up, and pulled her into his arms and kissed her with a fierceness that left her at last in no doubt of the strength of his feelings for her. He smelt of ale and tobacco, but he was not, she thought, very drunk; he had always carried his drink well. She did not much care for the kiss, but she giggled a little breathlessly before pushing him from her and running on again, still laughing. She was glad when she had the door safely closed behind her.

But once upstairs in the bed she shared with her sisters she wondered if her submission to that kiss had somehow committed her to something more than, at present, she wanted to give. She supposed she would like to be wed and have a home of her own, and she knew no one more desirable as a husband than Jack Marley – or no one who was single, that is – yet . . . It would be as well, she thought, to keep out of his way for a time, just so that he did not think himself sure of her.

A week later, William Robson, one of the two resident viewers of the Hetton Coal Company, and thus subordinate to Matthias Dunn, a situation which he (having been with the company far longer) greatly resented, set out to seek workers in the lead dales.

He started before dawn, for he had more than thirty miles to ride, and the roads were not of the best, particularly once the far side of Durham city. He knew Sunderland well, he had been often to Newcastle, and even, once, to London, but he had never travelled so far west before, into the high wild Pennine hills that fringed Durham County on its borders with Yorkshire and Cumberland and Northumberland.

He did not reach his destination that first day, for close to the small scattered hamlet of Crook his horse cast a shoe, and he was forced to seek shelter, of a kind, in a damp and dismal inn. Next morning, he had to find a smithy before setting out again, and by the time his horse was shod it was pouring with rain. He was greatly relieved, at the end of a miserable day, to reach the township of St John's Chapel and the shelter of the King's Arms, standing solid and square on the market place, where there was a good fire and good ale and a comfortable bed. He decided that he would leave the start of his mission of recruitment to the following day.

Chapter Four

About a mile to the west of the King's Arms, while William Robson was sitting down to a substantial breakfast, two young men walked away from Short Thorns public house in a sober mood.

They had left their partners to drown their sorrows at Short Thorns after calling at Newhouse, headquarters of Mr Thomas Beaumont's recently inherited lead mining interests. The house was in the process of being substantially enlarged, hinting at a prosperity wholly belied by what they had heard from its occupant, the Weardale agent Mr George Crawhall.

'I have taken on all I can at Burtree Pasture. If you wish to continue in your ground at Sedling, then you may do so, but I am unable to raise the price above thirty-two shillings a bing.'

It was the price they had been offered last year, for each eight hundredweight of lead raised at Sedling mine. During the year they had lived, as did all lead miners, on the thirty shillings a month advanced to them from their potential earnings; only to find, at the recent annual pay, that they had raised too little lead even to cover the scanty lent money. Now, strictly speaking, they owed the company money. They had consoled themselves with the thought that they would seek a ground at Burtree Pasture mine, where the lead was much easier to get, but Mr Crawhall had dashed that hope for them. Everyone else wanted to work at Burtree Pasture, of course, and some had to be disappointed; so it was their old ground at Sedling or nothing. They had not yet decided whether to take it.

As they walked up the hill away from both public house and mansion, Luke Emerson repeated what he had said to Mr Crawhall. 'There's not lead enough in the whole of Sedling to make us a living at that price.' Then he went on, 'And the lent money won't keep a man and his family. There have been times this past year when I've thought we'd starve.'

'It'll scarce keep one man, I know that,' said his cousin. 'It wasn't so bad when you could go to the parish for help. That would always see us through.'

'Aye. I heard it was Mr Rippon's doing that was stopped.' Until recently, when the income of a working man fell below subsistence level, the parish authorities had made up the difference, but now Mr Cuthbert Rippon, magistrate and owner of Stanhope Castle, had exerted pressure on the overseers of the poor to end the practice.

'It's against his free trade principles, I suppose,' said Tommy.

'More likely he's thinking of his own pocket,' Luke suggested cynically.

'Aye, well, the poor rate must hit men like him hard. There are few enough wealthy landowners in Weardale to pay it.'

'Don't you ever think badly of anyone?' Luke demanded with a wry smile.

Tommy looked a little sheepish, but defended himself. 'Men do sometimes act from good motives,' he asserted. 'But what does it matter why he did it? It doesn't help us know what to do. The worst of it is, if there was some hope of a bit more at next year's pay we might just get by.

But the tradesmen know as well as we do there'll be few of us clearing the books again, with rates as low as this. There's not going to be much credit for any of us to keep us going in the mean time. But what else is there?'

'I don't know,' said Luke gloomily. 'The Quaker Company's paying forty shillings lent money, but they're having to lay men off too.'

'There's the Nent Force Level – they want labourers for that.'

'Not any more. I asked last week. And the farmers have all the men they need now, the way things are.'

'The only other thing is the collieries.'

'Why aye. I thought of that. But it means flitting. Maybe not as far as Canada, but I've no wish to leave Weardale at all, not if I can help it. I think Rebekah would sooner starve . . . Be thankful you've only yourself to feed, that's all I can say.' Then he saw the look on Tommy's face. 'What's up?'

'I was thinking, that's all. There were times last winter I thought I'd be keeping all my sister's bairns as well.'

'When Rowland was so bad? Aye, I thought it too. But he's well now, isn't he? You said he was back at work.'

'Aye, he went back last week, but he's not fit to go underground any more. He's convinced he'll get back to what he was, once the summer comes, but in the mean time he's at Greenlaws, on the washing floor. And you know what the pay's like there. He gets no more than the boys.'

'Aye,' said Luke. 'I'm sorry it should have come to that. He's a good man.' Then he grinned and added, 'For a Ranter.'

Luke's family had always been Methodists, but of the older Wesleyan persuasion, whose Conference had expelled the Primitive Methodists many years ago for their insistence on holding camp meetings, against Conference policy. Most Wesleyans still looked askance at the activities of the Ranters, but Luke was too close to his cousin for there to be any but the most good-humoured banter between them about it. They had been shoulder

45

fellows from the time when Tommy, at eighteen, had first joined his cousin underground. Six years of constant working companionship had forged a deep friendship out of what was already a strong family affection, though on Tommy's side it had initially been marked by the respect of a youngster for an experienced miner five years his senior. Now that they were equals in skill, the difference in years no longer mattered.

They reached the point where the road levelled out, running eastward above the valley. To their right they could look down on the line of the river Wear, its banks wooded in places, or edged by gentle green pasture and meadow, the whole landscape on either side scattered with the little stone houses of the lead miners, grouped in hamlets or townships or, on the steeper slopes that ran up to the fells, standing alone, because the land there offered less of a living. Since Tommy had first started work as a washer lad fourteen years ago, the number of houses had grown amazingly, so that there was now no land that someone had not tried to cultivate, except where nothing would ever grow.

But then for some years lead prices had been high and the Beaumont company had explored new veins and even reopened old ones, attracting ever more men to come and work the mines. They had been good years. Few had made a fortune, but most had lived well, by Weardale standards. Then suddenly, four years ago, without warning, the price of lead had tumbled, and then continued to fall until it had reached its lowest point for fifty years. Now many of the houses were empty, falling into ruin, the land rapidly reverting to bracken and heather and coarse moorland grass; and others, though lived in, were almost as silent, with the terrible haunting quietness of hunger. Tommy who, as a Ranter local preacher, did his best to minister to those in need, was becoming only too familiar with the sufferings of his neighbours; familiar enough to know how near he was himself to the possibility of disaster.

And now he had to go home to Jenny and see the look

46

in her eyes as he told her what they had learned at Newhouse today . . . He came to a halt, just where a path ran down the slope of the dale to St John's Chapel. Luke looked round at him. 'What's up?'

'I'm away to see Joe,' he said. 'You coming too?'

Luke looked regretful. 'Why no, I'd best not. Rebekah's expecting me home. She'll have dinner ready.' He grinned. 'You'll just time it right at Joe's, with luck. I'm told he has meat to his dinner every day.'

'Most days anyway,' agreed Tommy. His elder brother, no longer a lead miner, had done well for himself. He had married the only child of one of the more well-to-do farmers in the dale, and on her father's death everything had come to them. Joe had dreamed from boyhood of breeding galloways, the sturdy ponies used in the dale, and for some years now he had been doing precisely that, with reasonable success.

Luke hesitated a moment, then said, 'Maybe it's best if we let things be for a day or so. They may seem clearer then. At those prices, I can't see there'll be a rush for anyone to take our ground.'

'No,' Tommy agreed. 'We'll give it a bit more thought then.'

He was in time for dinner at Well House, where Joe lived – cold roast beef such as he had not eaten for months, accompanied by the tempting aroma of fresh brewed ale. 'You'll not have the like of this at home!' Joe said, waving it towards Tommy, who quickly slipped a hand over the mouth of his tankard. Joe shook his head. 'My own brother turned abstainer! I never thought it would come to this!' He had gone through this ritual every time they met, ever since the day when Tommy, concerned by the debilitating effects of drink on his fellow working men, had been won over by the growing temperance movement.

But whatever their differences, Joe was as always warmly welcoming, urging him to eat his fill and then, after dinner, despatching his children back early to

47

school so that the men could talk in peace. He offered his own favourite fireside chair to his brother and then proceeded to ask after everyone at White Lea and to recount all his own news and then, as generally happened at some stage, to tease Tommy good-naturedly about his continuing lack of a wife. 'Why now, our Tommy, don't tell me you're frightened of women!' – 'Of course not! I just haven't found one I want to marry.' – 'Not even Sarah Craggs? She's bonny, for a preacher.' – 'Sister Craggs is just that, my sister in the Lord,' Tommy had replied, rather stiffly, at which Joe had teased him all the more.

Through his blushes and his indignation Tommy had been aware that there was some truth in what Joe accused him of; except that it was not women he feared, so much as the feelings that tormented and disgusted him when confronted with a woman he found attractive – a category that did not include Sarah Craggs. Those shameful feelings bore no relation to the holy and reverential love that he knew should mark the affections of those who were sanctified, and he preferred, whenever possible, to avoid situations where they might come upon him. He knew better, of course, than to say that to Joe, who would have laughed uproariously and probably made some coarse and offensive comment on the subject.

Nor did he, after all, as he had intended, put his more pressing problems before his brother. It was partly that to do so might seem like begging for help, something he would not dream of doing. But more than that, he was by no means sure that Joe would be able to offer him the kind of sympathy and advice he most needed. He loved Joe deeply, but whenever they met he would find himself wondering what he had in common with this quick-tempered, good-hearted, hard-drinking horse breeder. He considered the matter as, much later, he walked back along the river bank towards St John's Chapel. At any other time, in normal circumstances, he would have turned first for advice to Jenny's husband Rowland, who had been his friend and brother and guide for almost as long as he could remember. But this time Rowland himself – or rather, his precarious state of health – was part of the problem. Besides, he knew that Rowland would only have told him to pray about it and wait for a sign; which he would do, of course, but what he most wanted was some more practical advice.

On the way home (it was growing late by now, nearly supper-time), he called to borrow a book from a friend at St John's Chapel. It seemed more than a coincidence that, as he turned to go, his friend nodded towards a neatly dressed stranger crossing the market place and said, 'A chance for you there, if you've a mind to go as a collier. He's from the Hetton Coal Company, seeking men.'

Tommy looked at the man with interest; he had come to a halt by the door of the King's Arms, where two others had accosted him. Tommy recognised one of them as Mark Dent from Westgate, some kind of distant relation of Joe's wife, Phoebe, and more to the point the brother of a Ranter minister. Like Tommy himself, the Dent brothers had been converted by 'the Apostle of Weardale', Thomas Batty, during the great revival of 1823. But whatever Mark Dent might choose to do, Tommy had never had any inclination to leave Weardale, still less to work in a colliery. Now, faced with an opportunity to do both those things, what Mr Crawhall had offered them this morning seemed suddenly to be a good deal less easy to resist than he had thought.

Feeling more cheerful, he set off in the direction of the bridge that crossed the river at Burnfoot. Rounding the corner by the school he saw ahead of him two men deep in conversation. One was broad and sturdy, the other a small frail-looking man in a tattered plaid, leaning heavily on a stick. He appeared to be in a state of some agitation, anger even, for his thin fingers were quivering against the knob of the stick, as if itching to give emphasis to what he said, if only his strength had allowed him to stand unsupported, and the words burst from him in a wheezing disjointed fury, between bouts of

49

coughing. As he came nearer, Tommy could make out something of what he was saying: ' . . . I told them it was nowt but dark superstition and blasphemy . . . a slur on the very name of God!'

The other man, who had heard him with increasing impatience, frowned sharply. 'Come now, Brother Peart, you go too far! You'll be denying next that we any of us have need of God's mercy.'

'You know I don't deny it . . . Nor that his judgement will be terrible, on those who choose to walk in the dark . . . But the cholera is no part of his judgement . . . '

Tommy smiled to himself as he slipped past them. Rowland had not seen him, nor would he while he was so engrossed in his argument. Sometimes even Tommy wondered if his brother-in-law did not occasionally take up a position simply because he enjoyed the combat. Certainly he seemed unable to accept the opinions of others with equanimity. There had been many such battles as this in the past years, punctuating Tommy's life, causing greater or lesser difficulties for the household, depending on the magnitude of the matter at issue. Tommy could not remember ever having thought that Rowland was in the wrong, but he had often wished he would not so readily persist in his opinions against all the odds. It had often been hard on Jenny, forced to take sides and stand against her neighbours and friends. That Rowland, who never doubted her loyalty, did not seem to mind what effect his actions had on her was no help at all.

The sun was low over Burnhope Moor by the time Tommy had crossed the river and climbed the hill and made his way through the hamlet of Side Head, where Luke lived. Beyond Side Head, he came at last to White Lea, a long stone building set just beneath the brow of the hill, looking across its own steep field to the southern slopes of the dale. He pushed open the door and stepped into the austere but spotless kitchen. Jenny was pouring warmed milk on oatmeal for the crowdy that was to be their supper, as it had been their breakfast many hours before. Mary, her eldest child, a slight twelve-year-old with her mother's eyes, was setting the table, while her brother Emerson, practising on his fiddle upstairs, filled the house with the vigorous strains of 'The Keel Row'. When his schoolteacher had given him the instrument four years ago it had been on condition that he played only holy music, but fortunately the Ranters liked to set pious words to the most popular tunes. William, the second son, home like his brother from their day's work as washer boys at Level Gate mine, was supervising the hand washing of the three little ones, with much noise and splashing, at a pail in the passage outside.

'I couldn't make up my mind if it was a good sign or a bad that you'd not come in yet,' said Jenny with a smile, scooping the cat from the settle so that Tommy could sit down near the fire. Then she added, 'You've not seen owt of Rowland, I suppose? He should have been back by now.'

'I passed him in Chapel, disputing with Joseph Walton,' Tommy said. 'From what I heard, Brother Walton must have asked why he stayed away last Wednesday. So of course Rowland was telling him . . .'

'Aye, that sounds like Rowland,' said Jenny, imagining the scene. The day of fasting and penitence against the cholera had been a national affair, for the most part rigorously observed by all denominations. Mines and shops had closed, churches had been full. Tommy, in spite of his reservations, had done what he saw as his duty and attended the converted byre at Side Head that served as a Ranter chapel. Joe, so he had learned, had put in a rare appearance at the parish church, with his wife and children. Only the Peart family had stayed at home. Now Jenny added, a little wearily, 'Why can he not accept things peaceably, like other men?'

'Would you have wed him, if he'd been like other men?' Tommy returned, and she smiled ruefully. She had not, after all, gone blindly into marriage, and she knew that, even with hindsight, she would make the same choce again were she to be faced with it tomorrow. She had

51

never supposed that life with Rowland would be comfortable or easy. Sometimes, indeed, it had been very uncomfortable. As a matter of course they provided a friendly lodging for any itinerant Ranter preacher passing through Weardale, but Rowland was as likely to extend the same warm hospitality to anyone he thought was in need, whether a homeless neighbour or a vagrant of unknown origins. Jenny remembered one old man who had stunk appallingly, and had left the most dreadful soiling on her kitchen floor, so that it had taken days to banish the smell; and another, younger man, given supper and a bed by the fire, who had disappeared while they all slept, together with the bag containing the month's lent money, just paid to Rowland that day. They always had more than their share of wanderers begging at the door; word had got around that there was a sure welcome at White Lea. Even when Rowland was at work, Jenny would never have dared turn anyone away, for fear of his wrath were he ever to find out. Besides, she was sufficiently in sympathy with him to share his belief that it was better to be taken in a hundred times than to risk turning away one person who was genuinely in need.

'And what of you?' asked Jenny then. 'What happened this morning?'

Tommy told her what they had heard at Newhouse, trying to soften it as much as he could. He did not want to worry her until he had to. 'We're thinking about it,' he concluded. Then, to distract her, he told her he had been to see Joe.

'Was Eve there?' she asked after he had given her Joe's news, such as it was.

He cast his mind back, recollecting with an effort the dark sullen face among the laughing company of Joe's other children, home from school for their dinner. 'Aye, she was.' But last night she had been at White Lea, he remembered. 'You sent her off to school this morning then?'

'Aye, but I couldn't be sure she'd get there. You know what she's like . . . I wish I knew the right of it. We never hear owt but her side of things, and you know how sharp bairns are to cry, *It's not fair!* I'll have to get to Joe's some time and see him about it, and Phoebe.'

Eve was Joe's daughter by a girl he had loved long ago, who had died at the child's birth. A few months older than her cousin Mary, she was a difficult child, always at odds with her stepmother and half brothers and sister; as a consequence of which she spent almost as much time at White Lea as she did at home.

The crowdy was ready in the bowls, the children gathered about the table, hands washed, and still there was no sign of Rowland. Jenny, tired of waiting, a little frown gathering on her brow, went to watch from the door; and the next moment gave a cry of dismay. Rowland had come into sight at last, where the road curved up from Side Head; but only a little way along it he had come to a sudden halt and sunk down on the bank. Jenny cast a swift anguished glance at Tommy. 'See to the bairns!' she cried. And then she ran.

Rowland was still sitting in the same place when she reached him, coughing and retching into his handkerchief with such violence that he did not seem to know she was there.

She sat beside him and put her arms about his convulsively shuddering body and waited until it had subsided into the quietness of exhaustion. Then he raised his head, and she saw the blood on the handkerchief before he had time to slip it back into his pocket, not the usual smear of blood, brightening the black spittle that most lead miners brought up from time to time, but a torrent of redness that drenched the white linen. Their eyes met, and they both knew what it meant, a knowledge that had been with them for months now, perhaps even for as long as they had known one another, as something inevitable, inescapable. Only Jenny had not looked it full in the eyes until now, when she saw it in Rowland's.

'The strength will be given,' he said after a moment, his voice faint but steady.

And if that could be given, why not go further and give

the rest of it: restored health, years together as man and wife, lovers as they had been from the very first? But she knew it was a question she could not, must not ask.

She stifled the protest that rose in her, though it took shape all the same, toned down to a sad complaint. 'I don't want to need it.'

He put out his hand to brush her cheek. 'Wanting has nowt to do with it, hinny. Thou knows that.' Then he said, 'Here, give us a hand.' She stood up and stooped matter-of-factly to help him to his feet, putting his stick into his hand, and then she gave him her arm to lean on at the other side and they walked slowly, with frequent stops, up the hill to the house.

Usually the children ran to the door when Rowland came home, each one eager to be the first for his embrace. Tonight, Tommy restrained them and they stayed at the table, watching with round anxious eyes, abnormally silent, while their mother led the gaunt shambling figure of their father to the settle by the fireside. Tonight it was Uncle Tommy who asked for a blessing over their meal before they ate.

'Is there owt to be done?' Tommy asked, when the meal was over and the children had said their evening prayers and gone upstairs.

Jenny shook her head. 'I can get Rowland to bed.'

'I can get myself to bed, when I'm ready,' Rowland put in. He smiled at Tommy, his haggard face briefly transformed. 'I'm better now, as you see. But thank you.'

He did not look very much better, though his breathing had returned to its usual laboured regularity and he had not coughed for some time. But all Tommy said was, 'Then I'm away to see Luke. I promised to call on him.' It was not true, but he knew he must speak to Luke tonight; and perhaps take other steps, afterwards, that might set him on a path he did not want to take. What had happened this evening had made that much clear.

He lit a lantern and left the house and Jenny went up to settle the children. As she climbed the stairs she heard

54

them talking, their voices soft and solemn. They were sitting together on one of the beds, apparently listening to something Mary had been saying, though they fell silent as their mother came in and gazed at her with a gravity that she found alarming.

Trying to be cheerful and normal, she hurried them into the two beds that nearly filled the room, boys in one, girls in another, and then bent to tuck them in. As she reached him, Emerson said, 'Mother, how old is Father?'

Startled, she straightened, smiling a little. 'Thirty-eight,' she said.

She was the more surprised at the boy's look of relief. 'That's all right then.' She watched the colour return to his face. 'Mary says he's going to die. But in the Psalms it says, ''The days of our years are threescore years and ten.'' That's seventy, so he's not nearly that.'

Jenny stood there, quite still, looking down at her son. What should she do? Smile reassuringly, kiss him and go? Or destroy his precarious source of comfort? He was eleven years old, mature enough to face the truth, as he would have to before very long. Yet . . .

She looked up and saw Mary watching her with eyes as bleak as a November sky, and she knew Em's reassuring calculation had not convinced his sister. In the end, she simply bent and kissed them all, one by one, and left it at that.

Downstairs again, she found that Rowland was disinclined as yet to go to bed. He was not hungry either, he told her, so she sat down near him with her knitting, as calmly as if everything was entirely normal. After a moment he took something from his pocket and held it out to her. 'Here, Jenny.'

She opened her hand, and three coins fell into it; two shillings and a sixpence.

'My wages,' he said; there was, Jenny noted, an ironic tinge to his voice. 'For six days' work, with an addition for the bit hotching I did today. They've been generous. Make the most of it.'

'I don't understand.'

'I shall get no more. I'm not going back.'

Jenny looked at him, her hands stilled on her lap. His meaning reached her, yet she did not want to accept it. She sat there with her mind shut against it, waiting for him to say more. It was a little while before he did.

'I thought it best to tell them before they told me. I think today they meant to. So I got in first. I cannot do it any more.'

'No,' she said. 'I know that.' As she did, though she had not realised it until now. It was a knowledge, unrecognised as such, that had been with her ever since he had been so ill last winter. Then, she had told herself it was just a cold, settling on a chest already weakened by the shortness of breath common to most lead miners. It had brought fever and a persistent cough, lingering rather longer than usual. But then he had suffered similar attacks at some time each winter for several years now, and with the summer healing had always come and he had been able to work again. Only this time she had known in her heart it was more than that, and now at last he had acknowledged it too. They had to face together the fact that his working days were over.

She forced a smile. 'So I'll have you under my feet all day, for good.' She reached out and took his hand.

He folded his other hand about hers and looked at her with great tenderness. 'I'll do what I can to help. And when the bairns are at school we shall be just the two of us again. I shall like that.'

She thought, *Why do we lie like this, why pretend that what's coming is something we might have chosen, something good, when we both know it's not? I've never before felt I dared not speak the truth to him. It's come between us as nowt else has ever done, this thing we cannot say out loud.*

'Mother.' Jenny looked round. Mary stood in the doorway, her usually grave face more serious than ever. Jenny waited for her to go on, wondering how much she had overheard. A good deal, it would seem, and she had understood too what had not been said, for she came to stand beside Jenny and burst out, 'Mother, I shall seek work. I can go as a servant. Then I can give you all something. And you won't have to buy things for me.'

Without looking at him, Jenny sensed Rowland's dismay, but she said only, 'Thank you, my lass. We'll keep it in mind. Though we hope it won't come to that.' But it would, as she knew only too well. They might be able to put it off while Rowland lived, if the last months were not dragged out too long, but after that they would all have to accept that every one of them who could earn something must do so. They would have no choice about it.

'Maybe I'll try my hand at schoolmastering, like old Isaac Graham,' suggested Rowland.

Jenny saw their daughter's face light up. Isaac Graham was a Ranter local preacher who ran a little school in his house at St John's Chapel, which the children attended in preference to the Barrington School, where tuition was dependent on the pupils worshipping at the village church every Sunday, something that Rowland's scruples would not allow. Graham had been a lead miner until the inevitable shortness of breath had forced him to retire and make a living by less strenuous means. But he had been retired now for the best part of ten years, without visibly growing any more infirm. Mary clearly found it reassuring to think that her father's state might be no worse than that of the schoolmaster; which was, Jenny supposed, what Rowland had intended her to think. Jenny wished she could have consoled herself so easily.

'Off to bed now, lass,' she said, drawing the girl into her arms for a kiss. 'You'll not be up for school in the morning.'

Mary went to kiss her father, clasping her arms tightly about his neck as if she did not want ever to let go of him. 'If you have a school, Father, we can go to it.'

'Why now, there's a thought,' he said lightly. 'But does thou really think I'd choose to plague myself with such an unruly pack of bairns?'

She giggled and soon afterwards went happily back to bed. Her parents began to make ready to go to bed themselves in the box bed against the far wall of the kitchen.

It was then that Jenny realised that Rowland was not after all prepared to allow the things they had left unsaid to come between them, for he took her hand and knelt on the floor, drawing her down beside him. Then, her hands in his, his eyes closed, he murmured, 'Dear Lord, thou knows what dark paths lie before us. Not our will but thine be done. We know thou art present with us, a light unto our feet, though we walk through the valley of the shadow of death . . . '

When he had finished they knelt there in silence for a little longer, gazing at one another, though Jenny could not see him clearly for the tears that were in her eyes. He kissed her gently. 'My dear brave Jenny. I wish you could be spared this.' She clung to him, and then she did weep, openly, while he held her.

She lay awake for a long time that night, listening to Rowland's difficult breathing as he sat beside her, propped nearly upright, because he could breath more easily that way. So her father had sat in his last weeks, with all the pillows in the house at his back, and even then fast losing the painful, exhausting battle to draw air into his ruined lungs. She knew, starkly, that it would not be long before Rowland was as her father had been, as so many lead miners were in the final weeks of their short lives. He would stay at home now, doing what light work he could about the house and the smallholding until the morning came when he could no longer get to his feet. Six weeks, they said, from the day a man took to his bed with the miners' disease; it had not taken her father so long as that to die. She had known from the moment she married Rowland that this was the likely price they would have to pay for their years together, had accepted that there was no reason why they among all others should be spared. But now it was nearly upon them she found she did not accept it at all.

And meanwhile there were six young mouths to feed, six healthy appetites as yet uncurbed by the rigours of work. True, Em and William worked in the summer months as washer lads and brought home a tiny sum to help the family income, but it was not even enough to feed the boys, let alone the rest of them. There would be something from the parish too, now it was clear that Rowland was wholly unfit for work, but that would provide no more than the barest necessities, at best.

She wished she shared the certainties of Rowland's faith, for that would have made it so much easier. But all she had ever done was to follow where he led, now and then catching a glimpse over his shoulder of what it was that drew him so unhesitatingly on. Perhaps she was just too practical, too bound up in the need to love and care for the people around her, to want to look beyond them to some other world; especially when this world had, until now, provided all the happiness she could ask for.

She had thought Rowland was asleep, but suddenly she felt his hand reach out, seeking hers, and then close about it. 'The Lord will provide, Jenny,' he said softly, as if he had read her thoughts. Did he really believe that, she wondered, or was he trying to convince himself of it as well as her? She thought the first was more likely, yet who knew what doubts and fears must be troubling him tonight? If he was not afraid for himself, as a loving father and husband he might not find it so easy to keep his fears for his family at bay.

'Aye,' she said, since there did not seem any more appropriate response. 'What time is it – can you see?' They peered at the tall clock, trying to read the face by the faint glow from the damped-down peats in the hearth.

'About two I think,' Rowland said after a while.

'Tommy's late.'

But almost at once they heard his step outside the door; and then he came in, pausing just inside to remove his clogs and put out the lantern.

'We're awake,' Jenny said, as he began to tiptoe across

59

the room. She sat up. 'Have you been at Luke's all this time? Have you made up your minds what to do?'

Tommy sat down on one of the benches at the table. They could not see his face because it was turned towards them, against the firelight. He said, casually, 'There's a man at Chapel seeking colliers for the pits at Hetton.'

'To break the union, I suppose,' said Rowland. There was something in his tone that made Tommy fidget a little.

'I don't know much about that,' he said cautiously.

'What do you know?' Rowland demanded, his voice so stern that it was easy to forget he was a sick man. Tommy felt like a small boy again, on the edge of being rebuked for some misdeed.

'This Mr Robson said the colliers got all they asked for last year, when they formed the union. He was in favour of that, he said. They had the boys' hours cut to twelve a day, and a promise that they should all have their wages in money and not goods, and then the wages were raised. There were other things too that I can't bring to mind at present. But though they've got all they could reasonably ask for, they've refused to end their union. They threaten any man who wants nowt to do with it. They've said they'll none of them be bound unless the owners acknowledge the union.'

'Bound?' put in Jenny.

'Colliers agree a bond with their masters, to work for a year on those terms. Something like our quarterly bargains, I guess. But Mr Robson said if we went there we'd not be bound, not at first.'

'You're thinking of going!' Jenny exclaimed.

Tommy nodded and was about to continue when Rowland put in, 'To take the places of union men thrown out of work.'

'You didn't hear what Mr Robson had to say.' Tommy sounded hurt that Rowland should think he would take such a step unthinkingly. 'There've been any number of outrages from the union men. They want to dictate to the owners in everything. Their leaders even said that the man in charge of the colliery should be dismissed, because he tries to make them work harder than they like. They dropped that, when the owners stood firm, but it hasn't stopped them trying any other way they can to obstruct the working of the pits. They say no man must work longer than it takes to earn four shillings a day—'

'I'd have thought that was plenty for any man. Most of all for one who couldn't hope to make more than seven and six a week if he stayed here.'

'That's not the point. If they work such a short time they don't bring up enough coal to supply what's needed. So naturally the owners want to bring in men who make no such conditions.'

'Naturally!' said Rowland sarcastically, but Tommy persisted. 'It's only a few of the colliers who are so obstinate. Once the leaders are gone, Mr Robson says the rest will go back to work as quiet as lambs.'

'If it's only a few, how come the coal owners need to bring men in from Weardale?'

'The pits are expanding. They're new pits, most of them, with new seams being opened every day.' He paused, then turned to his sister. 'Four shillings a day is the least I'd make. I don't need that to live on, so there'd be plenty to spare for you, Jenny. Luke would go too and he says I could lodge with them – there's a house provided for those who want, rent free, with coals too.'

'What about your other partners?' Rowland asked. 'I can't see George Lowes wanting to flit at his time of life.' There were two other men in Tommy's partnership, Luke's older brother and George Lowes, who, at sixty, was one of the oldest working miners in Weardale.

'They did talk of going in with the Featherstone brothers from Ireshopeburn. But things aren't so hard for them. George says if he was in our shoes he'd not think twice about it. He says colliers have it easy, compared with lead miners. The conditions of work are good, the hours not long, for hewers at least. The coal company has a surgeon if you're sick—'

That reminded Jenny of something she had heard. 'Isn't it Hetton where the cholera's so bad?'

'That was months ago. It's over now. Besides, men who live good clean lives don't get cholera.'

'Not you too!' put in Rowland, at which Tommy looked startled.

But before he could respond, Jenny went on, 'Coal pits are dangerous.'

'So are lead mines—'

'Not with explosions. You don't get fire damp in lead mines. There have always been more lives lost . . . '

Tommy shook his head. 'Not since they brought in the Davy lamp. And the Hetton Coal Company's pits are very new, with no expense spared to ventilate them well.'

'I see the agent had a fine tongue on him,' said Rowland sharply.

'Maybe,' said Tommy with dignity, though Jenny thought he had reddened. 'I think I can judge the truth of what he said for myself. Besides, what choice is there?'

'There's always a choice, always.'

'There's no future for me here, and there's Jenny too . . . '

'What have I to do with it?' she demanded.

Tommy chose his words with care. 'You're going to have need of money, you and the bairns, all of you – for food and clothes and schooling. It's only right I should help. You've cared for me all these years.' His eyes moved to Rowland. 'Like a father, an elder brother. I can never repay you for what you've given me – food and clothing's only a small part of it. But now I want to do the bit I can to give you something back.'

'The best you can give me,' said Rowland, his voice harsh in its breathlessness, his body vibrating with anger, 'is to show that you have learned the lessons I tried to teach you. That means more than any amount of money.'

'I have learned that a man need never go hungry while there's work to be done. That my brain and my hands are to be used to the best of my ability—'

'That it's right to let yourself be used as a tool in the hand of tyranny? That other men's misfortune is your opportunity? That justice is nowt, set against the chance to earn more than the next man? No, that's to turn it all upside-down. Justice is more than bread, more than a roof over your head. What's the use of all your education, if it hasn't taught you that?'

'To serve God better?'

'You serve God best by serving your fellow men – is that not the first thing you were ever taught?'

'So I am doing.' He almost said: *It is what Jenny needs. You're in no state to help them. You have no right to reproach me.* But he did not say it, for he knew it would be unpardonably cruel, as it was cruel even to think it, of someone who had given him so much. But he was hurt, terribly hurt. It was hard enough to stand by and watch the suffering of those he loved, without having his wish to help thrown in his face. He had never before found himself in disagreement with Rowland over anything and he hated the feeling, the more because he sensed that Rowland too was hurt by it. 'I'm away to my room,' he said abruptly, and took a candle and marched up the stairs.

Rowland, agitated, began to cough, and at the end burst out, 'You know what he meant, don't you?' The words were half whispered, harsh, cracking.

'He meant it for the best,' Jenny said, her voice soft and slow and calm.

'What he calls best. What I think's nowt to him. I have no right to a say. I cannot do owt for you or the bairns any more.'

What could she say to that? The note of self-pity was so unlike the Rowland she knew and loved so well. But then who knew what depths they were both of them to pass through in the coming months, taking them into places and feelings they had not dreamed of, even in their worst nightmares? She searched her mind desperately for the right words, for something that would bring him comfort and reassurance. That he had done so much already, that he had helped make Tommy what he was? But there was no comfort in that, when Tommy was so clearly set on a course that was wrong, at least in Rowland's eyes. That he did it for Rowland, still more for Jenny, only made it worse. And she could not undo the words Tommy had spoken, nor deny what was unspoken and yet so clearly implied.

'It will all turn out for the best,' she said at last, conscious that she sounded as unconvinced of that as indeed she was.

Rowland did not even bother to respond to that remark. 'He must be told we shall take nowt from him, ever,' he declared.

She did not protest that for the children's sake she might be forced sooner or later to disobey him. She could at least spare him that humiliation.

Tommy had come home from Luke's – and from their later visit to Mr Robson at the King's Arms – convinced that all the signs pointed him in one direction. It could be no mere coincidence that the coal company's agent should have arrived in Chapel just at the moment when what he offered was most needed; even before Tommy himself had realised it. And Luke had agreed more readily than he had expected that they should investigate the possibilities of the collieries, perhaps because his wife had seen only too clearly that the alternative for their small family was hunger. Yet now, faced with Rowland's bitter disapproval, Tommy no longer felt so sure of himself. Could he have misread the signs?

Once in his room he set the candle on the table and took his Bible in his hands and knelt down and prayed with great concentration; and then, his eyes still closed, he opened the book at random. He waited a moment longer and then opened his eyes and let his gaze fall on the page before him, marking the exact spot with his finger. *Whatsoever thy hand findeth to do, do it with thy might* . . . He felt his heart lift. It was plain then, so plain that even Rowland would have admitted the truth of what he saw. God had shown him unequivocally that the path on which he had set his feet was the right one.

The next morning he told them calmly how he had been confirmed in his decision, and then he put on coat and hat and set out for Side Head, to call for Luke and go with him to the King's Arms to make the necessary arrangements.

Chapter Five

At Hetton, the colliers who had not been bound for the coming year were legally obliged to leave their houses by 20 April. But 20 April was Good Friday, and Matthias Dunn was prevented by religious scruples from carrying out evictions on so solemn a day. Accordingly, it was not until early on the Saturday that he and the other colliery officials set out with the support of a mixed band of special constables and soldiers to remove the first twenty families from their homes.

The soldiers had been there for three days already, two squadrons of hussars and an infantry detachment, patrolling the streets, keeping watch on the colliery offices and the wagonways and the pithead winding gear, anywhere that might prove a focus for trouble. They provided an escort, too, for the ten pitmen who alone, out of a workforce of thirteen thousand men, had agreed to be bound. John Errington, once so strong a voice in the union, was one of them. He limped to the Blossom pit (he had suffered a severe leg injury in an accident some years before) with an escort of red-coated infantrymen, while his former friends jeered and shouted at him from a distance. Even Samuel Raines, never more than a lukewarm union man, had his own military escort for his daily walk to and from the Isabella pit at Elemore. They were, of course, far too few to be of any use once they got to work, but to show how greatly they were valued the company provided them with firearms so that they could take their part in protecting their own and the colliery's property.

With a view to ensuring a more permanent means of keeping order, Matthias Dunn had applied for help to the new London police force, and an inspector and seven constables had come north and set to work to train a body of forty local volunteers. They had no control over the quality of the volunteers, for they had to take all who came forward and even then had difficulty in bringing the force up to strength. Like the people they would have to face in any conflict, the special constables had to be drawn from the pit villages of the area, and it was hard to find men willing to set themselves so openly against their fellows. In the end the local magistrates were reduced to releasing a handful of petty criminals from Durham Gaol to make up the numbers. Most of the existing regular constables – like Robert Kellet of Easington Lane, a collier and a union man himself – would have nothing to do with policing the evictions.

The first men to be turned out were, of course, the union committee members, in particular those who had presented the petition demanding Dunn's dismissal. John Grey, being in neither category, might have escaped, but his son's involvement in the assault on George Allen had marked him out. The fact that, when the matter had at last come to court, the lads had been declared innocent, made no difference. Dunn at least had been sure of their guilt. So, soon after dawn on that chilly spring Saturday, John Grey, his pregnant wife and their two sons and five daughters were evicted from their house.

The previous Saturday, at a massive meeting on Black Fell, north of Chester le Street, Tommy Hepburn had prepared the colliers of the Tyne and Wear for the coming ordeal. Some coal owners tolerated the union and had bound their men without difficulty, and these men agreed with enthusiastic cheers to subscribe to a fund to maintain their less fortunate brothers. For the rest, eviction would come sooner or later, and to them Hepburn spoke again for patience and good order.

At Hetton that Holy Saturday his words were heeded. The soldiers were not called on to intervene, nor the constables; there was no need for them. When the knock came each evicted family walked in silence from its house and stood at a distance, still saying nothing, while precious possessions were flung out into the street. John Grey might be fuming, but he was outwardly submissive, and so – warned beforehand – was every member of his family. Adam Fenwick was silent too, and his wife and their little girl, young as she was, though the baby cried and had to be rocked to sleep in his mother's arms. Charlie Parkinson, also turned out, strode into the cold wind with his head high and his eyes bright with unspoken rage, and then slipped away to report what had happened to the central committee of the union in Newcastle. Their neighbours looked on in silent sympathy, knowing that it was only a matter of time before the same thing happened to them, unless they were to follow Errington and Raines and Holt and Hepplewhite and Steel and the other marked men into disgrace and betrayal.

By the end of the morning the evictions were finished and Dunn and his officials and the constables went away, leaving a detachment of soldiers to keep watch from a distance, in case of trouble. Adam Fenwick marched to the waste ground behind Brick Garth and there turned to face the rows and alleys, scattered with heaped furniture and little knots of men and women and children. Then he raised his eyes and hands to the sky and called in a loud voice, 'You hear the cries of your children, O Heavenly Father – avenge them, as you avenged the children of Israel! Destroy their oppressors as you destroyed the armies of Pharaoh in the Red Sea!'

After that, he organised a group of men to take some

of the furniture to the Ranter chapel in the front street, for temporary storage; some of the families could also be accommodated there, though room had to be left for worship and class meetings. Otherwise, neighbours and friends opened already overcrowded houses to the home-less women and children, and the men arranged between themselves to keep watch over the furniture that could not be stored.

A pleasurable mixture of pride and rage swept Matty that day; rage that anyone should do this to them, pride that her family should be among the first to be singled out. As she helped to carry their belongings from the narrow alley at the front of the house to the open ground to the south, where there was more space, she looked at Samuel Raines's house and wondered what could have made him set himself against his neighbours. Oddly, his house had a more deserted look than the cleared houses, with their doors and windows thrown wide and a scatter-ing of rubbish and small objects on the thresholds, dropped by the men on their way out. No one had seen any sign of Mrs Raines or her son today, not even the twitch of a curtain. The shutters were firmly closed and only the faintest blur of smoke rose from the chimney. Matty thought perhaps they hoped that no one would remember they were there. What must Samuel Raines be feeling now, as his neighbours suffered for the unity and brotherhood he had betrayed? Was he ashamed? He ought to be, she thought, ashamed – and afraid too. Whatever the union leaders might say about leaving the blacklegs alone to suffer the misery of their self-inflicted isolation (not to mention their own guilty consciences), Matty knew quite well that men like her brother and Jack Marley would not be content with so passive a retri-bution; or not for long.

Jack Marley's widowed mother offered shelter to Nan Grey and her children. Usually a strong and determined woman, Nan was prostrated by the eviction, being over-come with tearful exhaustion the moment the officials left. Matty, conscious of her responsibilities, went with her to the Marleys' house, relieved to find that Jack was not there. She saw her mother settled in a chair by the fire with a comforting cup of rum and then made sure the younger children had something to occupy them while she went back for the more valuable items of furniture – the smaller ones, at least – which Mrs Marley was willing to take in.

Her father was watching their belongings, crouched beside a fire he had lit, concentratedly cleaning his pipe. She arrived at the wrong moment, for Jack Marley was just reaching the fire with a pail of coals, from his own supply, Matty supposed. John Grey spared his favourite daughter an affectionate nod, and then grinned up at the young man to whom he hoped, one day soon, to give her in marriage. He pulled a stool from the stack of furniture beside him. 'Have a seat, lad.' Then he reached out and tapped his pipe on the nearest surface, which proved, on Jack's surprised examination, to be a pile of books.

'These yours then?' Jack knew that (like him) none of the Grey family could read.

Grey gave a chortle of laughter. 'God, no! Some fool'll be missing them, I reckon – or maybe not.' He gave his pipe another tap on the edge of the piled volumes. 'Use for them at last,' he said cheerfully, and began to refill the pipe.

'Aye – what was it Hepburn said – *Knowledge is power*? Why, think what a difference it would make to have his circulating libraries to hand the day!'

'Build a house from them maybe!' The two men laughed.

Matty had heard a good deal since last Saturday of Hepburn's scheme for colliery libraries, which her father had put down to a momentary fit of madness, natural enough in a Ranter; in his opinion it had spoiled an otherwise stirring address. She wished Adam was by to defend him. *Knowledge is power!* It had a fine ring to it. What power would be put into her hands, if she had books and could read? She could not imagine, but her spirit seemed to soar at the very thought.

She carried an armful of cooking pots back to the Marleys' house. To her regret Jack went with her, the grandfather clock slung across his shoulder, carried as easily as if it weighed no more than the pick he used for work. 'May as well give you a hand,' he said. She was relieved that he had nothing more to say after that, for he walked in silence all the way to the house, where he set the clock up in the only unoccupied corner (facing his own clock, at the other side of the front room) and then hovered around for a time, saying and doing nothing in particular, until the quarrelsome clamour of the place reached such a level that he fled.

Matty could not blame him. The squabbling of the children irritated her too, and her mother's whining misery, played on enthusiastically by Mrs Marley, who enjoyed a good moan. She could feel no sympathy with their mood, for her anger at what had happened today was a fierce and positive thing, enlivened by pride in the rightness of what the men were doing in the face of such certain hardship; and even more by excitement. In the old days, so she had always understood, the women had been as active as their men when disputes arose between them and the owners, often first in the line to riot and destroy, to teach strike-breakers a lesson or demand fair wages. Tommy Hepburn was right, of course, to speak against the old way of doing things, as last year's success had proved. Eliza had explained it all to her, and she could see the sense of it. And for all her anger, for all that she was a part of it, she had been moved herself by the silence and dignity of the victims at this morning's evictions, which had clearly baffled and exasperated the colliery officials. They had been made to look foolish, with their unnecessary troops of soldiers and constables, standing idle for want of any provocation.

The trouble was, that this new way of doing things left very little for a woman to do, except support the men in her life. And Matty had no men in her left, except her father – and Jack Marley, if she chose. She had no wish to stay dutifully minding her sisters in an overcrowded house, listening to the complaints of two unhappy women while, outside, the men whose courageous fight had brought them all to this were preparing to watch through the night hours, planning and facing together with cheerful conviviality the sufferings that lay ahead.

It was not until much later in the day, when her mother was safely in bed (Jack's bed, Matty realised) in the garret bedroom, the younger children beside her, that Matty felt free to slip out into the dusk, led by the light to her father's fire.

Several girls of about her own age were out there too, lingering on the fringes of the firelight, exchanging jokes with the men, or simply giggling and whispering and nudging one another, to give emphasis to shared gossip. Matty stood with them, but made little attempt to join in. Instead, she watched the men about the fire, listening to their talk. They had been drinking for some time now, and the patience and dignity with which they had faced the evictions were being steadily washed away. All the resentment, suppressed with such difficulty, came boiling to the surface. The talk grew more and more angry, the threats against the blacklegs ever more imaginative, and especially against John Errington, whose treason was the greater because he had once claimed the greater loyalty to their cause.

In the daylight, the heaps of personal belongings had looked pathetic, untidy, even sordid; the men about them, for all their dignity, merely colliers, like all the men she knew; the fires that warmed them just drifts of faint smoke over pale flickering flames. Now, in the dark, the scene was transformed, made strange, dramatic, awesome even. Matty gazed and gazed, trying to see it all with such clarity that it would stay in her mind for ever. She rejoiced in the sense of danger, the knowledge that today something had happened that must bring a great change into her life. It might not last. Some day soon she might find herself thrown back into the old orderly, predictable routine. But tonight she could believe that anything was possible, that her life would never again return to its old tedium and that each one of them out here in the dark had taken a great step into the unknown.

She saw all that caught in the great circle about the fire, in the angry faces, with their deep shadows and hard flame-lit angles. There was Jack Marley, the noisy boastful centre of the group, dark and strong-boned and fierce, her brother Jamie, his face still soft and rounded, like a child's, her father's sombre features, warmed by the gentle glow of his pipe, all the other men, sitting on boxes or stools or simply on their hunkers on the bruised grass, the girls, soft and whispering in the shadows behind them, as if they had no part to play but to watch and comment and perhaps, if required, bring drink or food to sustain the heroes of the night. And beyond them, spreading outward, the light flickered and died away into the dark, scarcely reaching the houses, soon losing itself in the blackness of alleys and the open spaces that stretched into the distance. Here and there, far off, the darkness was broken again by other fires, blossoms of light against which black shapes moved, coming and going, with firewood or news. Smoke, tinged with rose and gold, hovered over them, softening and hazing the sharp brightness of the stars in the night sky. It was a scene of magic and strangeness.

She heard someone come up behind her, and then Adam Fenwick's voice spoke softly, making her jump. 'Have you nowhere to go, Matty?'

She looked round at him, glad that the darkness hid her deepened colour. 'Aye, but they're like cats in a sack in that place. I'd sooner be here.'

'It's getting rough, lass. You'd best get indoors.'

She tried to imagine that his concern was deeper and more personal than it would have been for any other girl, but she knew from the direction of his gaze that his remarks had been addressed almost as much to her companions as to herself. 'Where's Eliza?' she asked, trying not to let her disappointment show.

'Seeing to the bairns,' he replied, though where and

73

how he did not say. Matty supposed that someone had taken them in.

'I'll be safe enough,' she said. 'My dad's here, and my brother.' But Adam had already moved away, concerned for someone else's needs.

Matty realised soon that he had been right; things were getting rougher. About the fires the men grew noisier, there were shouts and snatches of aggressive singing. From one of the other fires a burst of shots came sharp and sudden, fired randomly into the night. Someone came to their own fire with a musket in his hand, and she saw it passed from one to another of the men. Yet she did not take Adam's advice. Curiosity kept her there, and a sense of excitement that was stronger than the tingle of fear she felt. The fear was even, in an odd way, rather pleasant.

Her brother Jamie had the gun in his hand now, was fingering it lovingly, moving this part and that, examining it. She saw Adam go to him. 'Give us that, man Jamie, before you take someone's head off with it.'

Jamie grinned. 'Aye, Errington's head – isn't that what it's for?'

'I wasn't fearful for Errington,' Adam said good-humouredly. 'He'll not come near us. But the way you handle that it'll be one of us gets it.'

'What do you know about handling guns?' Jamie asked, a little derisively.

'A good bit more than you,' said Adam.

'Show us then.'

Jamie handed the gun over, a marked sneer on his face. Then he watched, scorn turning rather reluctantly to wonder, as Adam carefully and meticulously checked the loading and priming of the musket and then levelled it, and then without warning fired into the sky. The sound hurt Matty's ears, and she pressed her hands to them. There was a little silence afterwards, then Adam said, 'Now it must be put away for safe keeping. I'll see to that.' He walked away into the night, the gun on his arm.

'That was a trick to get it from us,' Jamie grumbled.

'Maybe,' said John Grey. 'Mind, he was right about one thing: he knows about guns.'

'What use is that?' Jamie demanded. 'He'd never shoot with it. He's got ice in his veins, not blood.'

'He doesn't let his blood rule him, that's all,' said Matty, leaping swiftly to Adam's defence. 'He knows violence won't serve, in the end.' She was aware, as she spoke, of Jack Marley's eyes watching her, bright with mocking amusement, as if she were a child chattering idly about things she did not understand.

It was clear that Jamie was simply contemptuous of such witless female intervention. She was surprised that he deigned to answer her at all. 'Then he's a fool. It's worked before. It's the only thing that has worked. What's so different now?'

'What, like when you set on Allen?' she demanded sneeringly. But her brother refused to revise his opinion.

'He got what he deserved. He learned his lesson.'

Matty had been surprised how quickly her brother had got over the fright of his court appearance. Did he remember how she had found him snivelling in the alley the night before he went to Durham to appear in court, little more than two weeks ago? She was tempted to remind him of it now, but she knew it would be unforgivable to shame him in front of his friends. She found herself almost regretting that the case had collapsed so quickly, faced with the difficulty of identifying lads seen only dimly, deep underground. But no, it would have been terrible if her brother had faced transportation, and that would certainly have been his fate, had he been found guilty, as they had all expected beforehand. 'Well, English justice is still the best in the world,' John Grey had commented afterwards, as if he were an expert in such matters.

It was after dark, while Mrs Raines was smothering the fire for the night with coal dust she had brought in before the house clearing started, that there came a knock on the front-room shutters. It was a faint and tentative tapping, not the ferocious banging that she might have expected, but even so she jumped, and then stood quite still in the middle of the kitchen, one hand to her heart, which was beating with a wildness that set her shaking. Samuel had only gone out a few minutes ago; she knew he would not be back yet. Besides, he never came to the front of the house, especially not tonight when the alley was dark and deserted and enemies might be lurking on every corner; nor would he have tapped on the shutters like that, even though she dared not leave the doors unbarred for him to come and go as he pleased.

She waited, and the tapping came again, a little more persistently this time. She moved to the door that led into the front room and slowly, softly pushed it wide, and then listened again, just to one side, in case whoever was at the window could see through the cracks in the shutters. She heard someone walk to the front door, and then a voice whispered sharply, 'Mam!'

Relief made her tremble weakly, and it was a moment or two more before she had the strength to go and unbar the door to her daughter.

Eliza stood there, unsmiling, wrapped up so closely that only her mother could have recognised her. The baby was clutched in her arms, the little girl clung to her skirts, wide-eyed and frightened. She stepped quickly inside and Mrs Raines barred the door again.

'You've seen sense then,' she said, as they went into the kitchen. 'You'll come and stay here.'

Eliza shook her head. 'Nowt's changed, Mam. I go with Adam, and neither he nor I will ever take shelter where Sam is . . . I know he's out,' she added. 'I'd not be here if he wasn't.'

Mrs Raines sat down unsteadily by the fire, shaken by the realisation that the house was so closely watched by hostile eyes; for she had to recognise that even Eliza's eyes were hostile. Ignoring the effect of what she had said on her mother, Eliza went on, 'It's the bairns—'

Mrs Raines, appealed to in the only way that could

have broken through her fear, stood up again and came to her daughter and reached out to take the baby. 'You want me to mind them. Have no fear, that I will. It's not right they should be out in the cold all night.'

'Aye well,' said Eliza, 'if Samuel has his way, there'll be more bairns out in the cold before the month's out. I'd have kept them by me, but you know how weak Ruth's chest is. It might make my courage fail. So we talked it over, Adam and me . . . '

'So you're here.' Her face was soft. 'I'm glad you still think of your mam first, in trouble.'

'There's one thing,' Eliza said. 'I don't want them keeping company with Samuel.'

'How can they help that, living in the same house?'

'Send them to another room when he's here, or outside.' She could see that her mother was dismayed, so she added fiercely, 'Mind, I mean it, Mam. I don't want my bairns mixing with blacklegs.'

'Maybe you should have thought of that before you brought them here.' Then she seemed to glimpse a similar regret in her daughter's eyes, for she said quickly, 'But I'll do as you say, I give my word. If you can swear your friends will let us alone.'

'We don't fight with bairns, even if the masters do,' Eliza said sternly. 'No one will touch the house. Besides, our weapons are peaceful ones.'

'Tell that to George Allen,' said Mrs Raines. 'And the rest of them.'

'Allen's in the union now. He'll be let alone. Besides, you know none of it was of my doing, or Adam's. Though they brought it on themselves, when all's said and done.'

'Aye, well, don't let's quarrel.' She gazed at her daughter in silence for a little while, then said with deliberate casualness, 'Will you stop for a bit and have some tea?'

Eliza shook her head. 'My place is with Adam. But I'll come now and then, to see the bairns.' She looked down at them, and for a moment her steadiness wavered. She bent and hugged them both for a long time, and then, on impulse, kissed her mother too, and then she let herself out again by the front door and disappeared into the night.

If their small numbers made profitable work impossible, the newly bound men at Hetton found greater difficulty still in occupying their leisure hours. They could not, of course, seek drinking companions at the public houses where they used once to go to talk and play cards or throw quoits or join in a game of pitch and toss, for they would have been attacked the moment they set foot in any of their old haunts. So, instead, they occupied furtive corners of the soldiers' favourite drinking places, where they could never quite feel at home. As a result, their meetings were not very cheerful or convivial. They drank to keep up their courage, and talked, but they had little in common apart from their situation and their talk was mostly of weapons and strategies, as if they were living in a state of war; as in effect they were. They went nowhere without the firearms and ammunition supplied by the colliery storekeeper, for they knew that some of the union men had weapons of their own, if not many. Even yesterday there had been the sound of shots late in the night, after they were in bed; and yesterday no man had yet been thrown out of his house.

That night, after a day that had been more than usually difficult, Samuel Raines and John Errington and a father and son of the name of Steel went after work to the house of George Holt at the western end of Brick Garth, where another returning collier, John Hepplewhite, lodged. They lingered there for an hour or two, drinking while they cleaned and loaded their weapons and tried to turn their minds to some cheerful subject, to no avail; whatever they talked of, somehow it always seemed to come back to the events of these past days, and what was to come. They were conscious that staying too long in one place laid them open to possible attack, since it gave time for the aggrieved union men to discover where they had

78

gathered. Besides, Hepplewhite and Holt were supposed to be on duty tonight, patrolling the streets with two other bound men. So, around midnight, they set out for their own homes, Hepplewhite going with them to see them safely on their way. Samuel and Errington each had a pistol, as had young Scott Steel. Hepplewhite had been supplied with a sword, which he seemed a little unsure how best to carry. William Steel shouldered a musket, and, having once been a soldier, assumed the leadership of their little group as they set out warily through the dark streets, trying to find a way that avoided the most shadowed corners, the hidden alleyways near the most hostile houses, or the angry groups about the watchfires. 'We'll see thee home first,' William Steel promised Errington. After all, he lived furthest from Holt's house, almost in Easington Lane, and had to pass one or other of the watchfires whichever route he took.

The men reached a clump of bushes that fringed the road just where it rose a little, giving a clear view from the summit of a fire and the street beyond it. 'Get down and watch from there,' said William Steel, and his son and Hepplewhite and Raines slid behind the bushes, peering out just enough to see what was happening. They watched the other two men walk on to the highest point, and there Steel too halted, exchanging some words they did not hear with Errington, before the lame man limped off alone, towards the fire that barred the path to his home. Steel stood watching him, his musket primed and ready in case of need. They all saw Errington reach the fire, and then pass it, at a safe enough distance. A shout or two followed him, but no one stirred from the fireside, no one moved but the halting figure of their companion. Then he disappeared from view into the darkness between two rows of houses.

Steel turned to retrace his steps; the men in hiding got to their feet.

A musket shot rang out, sharp and sudden and very loud. The watchers froze where they stood.

Then they ran to Steel, straining to see. About the fire

all was quiet, and in the darkness beyond it nothing stirred. Someone left the group by the fire and began to walk their way. They retreated quickly and slid down again behind the bushes, watching in terror, listening until the steps passed them and they were alone again. It was quiet now, with only small distant harmless sounds breaking the stillness; a dog barked somewhere, a child cried and was hushed to sleep, a song was begun and abruptly broken off. 'They've been firing all night,' Hepplewhite said, soothingly. 'I've heard three shots before this. That one was a bit close, that's all.'

'Aye, just someone fooling on,' agreed Samuel. But they were uneasy all the same. They kept together as they walked softly home, looking about them all the way, not convinced that they were safe even when they had barred the doors behind them.

Matty and her friends heard the shot, and one of them gave a little shriek of mock terror. Jack Marley and Jamie began to run to the next fire, about fifty yards away, from which the shot seemed to have come. As they neared it, another shot rang out.

John Grey was on his feet. Matty knew that the next moment he would turn to her and order her to watch their things, while he followed the others. She grabbed the arm of the girl nearest to her. 'Howay now – let's go!' Clutching one another, laughing yet frightened, the girls ran off, arms linked, towards the other fire and the black shapes gathered about it. Matty thought her father called after her, but she pretended not to hear.

The men at the fire were talking animatedly, some clearly pretty drunk, but there was no sign that anyone had been hurt, no sign of alarm. Nor were there any weapons, that she could see.

She looked about for a familiar face. She knew all the men there by sight of course, and some a little better than that, because they drank with her father or brother, but none of them was well known to her, except her brother and Jack Marley. With the other girls, she hovered once again on the rim of the firelight, watching and listening. 'Who was shooting then?' she asked Jamie, when she managed to edge closer to him.

He shrugged. 'No one saw. A blackleg maybe.'

Two of the men – one called Turnbull, the other Anderson – rolled drunkenly past her and on into the blackness of one of the alleys. Then Adam Fenwick appeared from roughly the same direction, stepping into the firelight as casually as if nothing untoward had happened.

'Where's the gun?' Jamie asked him.

'Put away, for safe keeping.'

'Did you see owt?'

'I heard a shot or two, that's all. From this way, mind. It's quiet over there.' He gestured with his head back the way he had come. 'I thought Turnbull had a gun.'

'Aye, but that was an hour since.'

'Blacklegs fallen out maybe,' said Jack.

It grew quieter. Some of the men left the fire, others settled into groups, talking and drinking. Matty wondered where Eliza was and what she was doing. She and her friends were the only women at the fire.

Before long, Turnbull and Anderson came strolling back, Turnbull reaching out an arm in one smooth, instinctive movement to take a flask of rum from another of the men. 'There's someone in the ditch over there, near the oven,' he said, and tipped his head back to gulp from the flask. Then he lowered it again and wiped his hand over his mouth. 'Anderson thinks it's Errington.'

'Let him lie then,' Jack Marley growled; while Adam demanded, 'Is he hurt?' He sounded more curious than concerned; but then like the rest of them he saw Errington only as a traitor.

Turnbull shrugged. 'Can't tell. Too dark. He wasn't stirring.'

'We'd best let Kellet know,' Adam said, with a certain grim reluctance.

The constable might be a reliable union man, but even

so it was some time before it could be agreed that he should be sent for, and then the two men despatched to fetch him might as well have saved their breath. 'Couldn't make him hear,' they said when they returned.

'None so deaf as those who won't hear,' said Jack, grinning.

At that moment someone came running into the firelight from behind and grasped Matty's arm so suddenly that her heart missed a beat. Then she saw it was her sister Maria. 'Matty, Mam's poorly. You've got to come. Where's our dad?'

George Holt and John Hepplewhite, patrolling with their companions in separate parts of the township, were careful to keep to the safer streets, away from the evicted men and the watchfires. Some time around three in the morning their paths crossed, and they split from their companions and set out on a cautious patrol of Brick Garth itself, which until then they had avoided altogether.

By now it was quiet. The watchfires burned low, the few remaining watchers huddled close to them – the night was cold – their voices murmuring in the stillness. Holt and Hepplewhite made their way cautiously by a roundabout route along the rows, keeping clear of the darker alleys, veering away at any distant glimpse of a fire, diving for cover when (as happened twice) anyone came near.

They came at last, just short of Errington's house, to an alley a few yards from where Hepplewhite had last seen him; and there, in the deeper shadow cast by the corner of a half-built house, they saw the black shape of a man lying in the gutter. They did not dare look any closer, but all the way past him their eyes stayed on the motionless figure, in a kind of horrified fascination. Once round the corner they halted. Holt, shaking, whispered, 'Was it Errington?'

Hepplewhite nodded. 'I think so.'

Together, without further word, they broke into a run

and did not stop until they had reached the colliery office, where they roused the soldiers on picket duty.

Errington had two musket wounds in his chest. He had clearly been dead for some while.

About that same time Matty's mother finally miscarried of the baby she had been expecting. Matty, sitting at the bedside, heard the news of Errington's murder being shouted in the street outside by a group of men passing the house. One of them gave a faint cheer, and then a sterner voice said, 'Whoever did it was the instrument of the Lord.'

She was not sure, but she thought it might have been Adam who spoke.

Chapter Six

If you pull a plant up by its roots, it dies for lack of
nourishment; that Tommy knew full well. And now it
was happening to him. His roots were in Weardale,
dug deep into its earth, nourished by its hill and burns, by
its people, by its harsh climate and its simple faith. He
was not even sure if, now that the time had come, he
would be able to drag his roots wholly free of this place,
as he must do if he were to set out on the new life that had
been marked out for him. He was trying to do so, forcing
himself to take the steps that must lead to his going, but it
was agony, almost more than he could bear. The small
things he was doing now – taking books one by one from
his shelf, to bundle them together for tomorrow's
journey, folding his few clothes – seemed to require all
his strength, all his powers of endurance. It was like
doing things in a nightmare, so slowly, fighting all the
time against some inner or outer power that sapped his
strength and his energy. He could feel the reluctance
dragging at him, as if a part of him still hoped that he
might suddenly see that he need not do this after all, that
the sacrifice was not required of him.

It was not as if he were the only one who had no

stomach for his going. Rowland did not want him to go, had never once during the past month failed to tell him how much he hated what he intended to do; Jenny did not want him to go, nor did the children. It was only his own conviction that this was where his duty lay that made him press on, in the face of Rowland's anguished disapproval and Jenny's hurt. Why then should he not stay? He would only be praised for changing his mind; they would receive the decision with joy and thankfulness, wrapping him round again with all the love and warmth that had been withdrawn from him since he had told them what he planned to do.

He went to the window and looked out over the dale in the last of the evening light, at the darkening slopes of Black Hill and Chapel Fell, and the far line of Harthope: the scene on which his eyes had looked every day since he was born. He had never been away from White Lea, not even for one night. Why go now, when everyone he loved most opposed it; when in going he might never see any of them again?

But he knew why, of course. It was stark, simple, unavoidable: God had shown him that this was the path he must take. And if God commanded it, then no power on earth must be allowed to stand in his way. There was no living to be had here, and his sister would need his help, all too soon. The path was as clear as it was cruel and hard. He had to take it.

He turned back to his packing and finished the joyless task and then poured out his grief to the God who had imposed it on him; and then he lay down on his bed. He had not slept at all by the time Jenny came to wake him for the journey.

For Jenny the morning of Tommy's departure came almost as a relief, bringing hope of an end to the strained and unhappy atmosphere that had filled White Lea ever since he had made his decision. Rowland had not become any more reconciled to what Tommy was doing, and Jenny knew that his anger and bitterness soured a life already made difficult by failing health. The news lately reaching them, that the Government in London had fallen and the country as a whole was in a turmoil that, it was said, might even lead to revolution, had made it all worse, though to Tommy, uninterested in politics, the state of the country as a whole was a matter of supreme indifference. 'Can't he see?' Rowland had exploded through violent coughing. 'It will all be swept away – centuries of injustice, in one great flood. Those who swim against it will perish.'

As for Jenny's own feelings, they were in a turmoil too, confused and at odds with one another. She was angry with Tommy for being so blind; yet common sense, warring with principle, told her that he could not stay in Weardale without the means to live, for most certainly she and Rowland could not afford to keep him. On the contrary, she recognised that she might one day be very glad of what help he could give her. Yet she was ashamed of that knowledge, because it put her, in spirit at least (she did not, of course, speak of it to anyone), at odds with Rowland – she who had always been so loyal to him in everything. And she was sad for Tommy, because she knew it was only his sense of duty took him away, and yet he had received no thanks for it, no hint of any understanding. She would miss him too, because he was her brother, for whom she had cared from infancy; yet at the same time some small part of her was glad that for the first time since their marriage she and Rowland and the children would have the house to themselves, for however short a time. She was ashamed of that feeling as well.

Each conflicting emotion only added yet another twist to the great tight agonising knot that had been growing within her during the past weeks, until sometimes she felt she must explode into a horrible cataclysm of grief and rage, screaming to the heavens for what they had done to Rowland and to all of them. Yet she would not explode, could not even weep the little inadequate tears that might have brought some release. She, above all, had to be strong, to carry the burden of the family with courage and even cheerfulness, as far as she could. So she held all her feelings pressed down inside her, where they seemed only to fester and burn, more and more every day.

It was still dark when they gathered in the kitchen for that last breakfast before Tommy's departure. The children were still sleeping – they had made their farewells last night – but Rowland insisted on dressing and coming to sit at the table with them, though he ate little and said even less.

'I'll come to Side Head with you,' Jenny said, when Tommy had finished eating. 'You'll need help with the carrying.'

Tommy took his coat and hat from the settle and put them on. Then he went to stand beside Rowland. 'Whatever our differences, you know I shall always think of you as my best friend and brother.' He held out his hand.

There was, momentarily, a hint of a thin smile on Rowland's face. Breathing heavily, he got to his feet and took Tommy's hands in his. 'That thou'll always be, whatever comes.'

Jenny felt the tears spring to her eyes, moved – and relieved – at the gesture of reconciliation. Tommy said, 'Let us ask for God's blessing,' and they all three knelt down. He closed his eyes and raised his hands. 'We are heavy of heart, dear Heavenly Father, that we must be parted this day. But you know our needs and our weaknesses. Send down thy blessing on us all, and especially on the journey that lies before me, and the new work that I shall undertake. Let it be to thy glory . . . ' The prayer went on for some time, and at the end there was a little silence.

Then, just as Tommy showed signs of getting to his feet, Rowland suddenly spoke. 'Dear Lord, thou was always on the side of the poor and the oppressed. Open our brother Tommy's eyes to see how he has strayed from thy path, and set his feet safe upon it again.'

There was something so obstinately contrary about the intervention that for a moment Jenny almost exploded into laughter; but only for a moment. The next instant she saw the hurt on Tommy's face and felt a flash of anger. Why, at this last moment, could Rowland not just this once have left the matter alone? He had – goodness knows he had! – expressed his opinion to Tommy at every available opportunity during the past weeks. She had hoped so much that her brother would be allowed to leave without one final twist of the knife in the wound. It was possible – they must all recognise it – that he and Rowland would never meet again after today. For him to carry this with him as his last memory would be bitter indeed.

She noticed that Tommy's voice did not echo the 'Amen' at the end of the prayer and that when he rose to his feet again, after a prolonged silence, his expression was grim. She thought there might even be a hint of tears in his eyes, but the candlelight was dim and the daylight had scarcely begun to slide into the dale. The only comfort was that, just as Tommy started towards the door, Rowland came and embraced him, this time in silence. For a moment they clung together like children seeking comfort; and then Rowland stood back and watched as Tommy, with Jenny at his side, set out down the hill.

At Side Head Jenny's aunt and cousins had come out to see Luke on his way, and Anthony and Sarah Craggs were there too. The brother and sister were Ranter lay preachers, like Tommy, and, owing their conversion to Rowland, had a special affection for all those connected with him. Joe was not the only one to see rather more than that in the liking Sarah had for Tommy, though Tommy was quite sure they were mistaken. This morning he thought that even Joe could have observed nothing more than friendship in Sarah's manner as she came to say goodbye, cheerfully, with words of encouragement and a brief prayer. If she shared Rowland's disapproval of what he was doing, she did not say so, for which he was grateful. 'I shall miss you,' he said, and knew it was true.

Jenny saw Tommy's belongings packed on the cart,

88

dwarfed by the piles of household goods among which they nestled; and then she waited as the last of the packing was done and Luke helped his wife and children onto their rather precarious seats amongst the luggage, and they were ready to go. Jenny turned to Tommy. 'Here,' she said, and pressed something into his hand. He looked down and saw a small piece of quartz, glittering in the early light, the crystals pure and pale as the mist along the river. Once, it would have been part of a lead vein, deep in a mine. 'To remember with,' she said, and he found he was not able to say anything in reply. Then she kissed him, and the little group moved off, Luke leading the pony, Tommy walking beside him, and all those left behind wept and waved and called as the cart rattled unevenly away.

Tommy said nothing as they went, thankful that Luke, too, seemed disinclined to talk. The murmuring of Rebekah and the children, the occasional sniff that punctuated it, formed a sombre background to the first part of the journey. Tommy looked about him as they went, thinking all the while of what this place meant to him, of what he was leaving, and conscious that, with every step, all that made him what he was, all that he cared about in this world, was being torn up and thrown aside. Every inch of the landscape was filled with memories, with sights and sounds that linked it with every stage of his life, day by day. Here were found all the people who had, for good or ill, influenced and guided him. Of them all, only Luke would stay with him; every other person he cared about was being left behind, to remain a part of the earth that had nourished him, from which he was now so ruthlessly uprooting himself.

Here, they passed the head of Jacob's Ladder, the steep hill path that led to St John's Chapel, down which in his early years he had skipped daily to school; and some way further on they reached the cart track that veered off suddenly, sharply, in an eastward direction, not far from Level Gate mine, where Tommy had first started work as a washer boy at the age of eight. They descended the hill, the cart rattling on the stony track, and he gazed at the river in which the boy Tommy, the boy he was sloughing off with all the rest of his life, had played; the shallow places, the deep pools for bathing, the stepping stones, and the bridges on which to stand and watch the water rush in spate after the spring thaw. On either side rose the hills he loved, on which he had roamed at holiday times, the wooded denes that cut through them, where he had climbed trees and hunted birds' nests and splashed in waterfalls; places he knew so well that they were a part of him, as much as his breathing and his blood.

They came to the level floor of the valley and the road led along the river bank, on to Westgate, the place that was perhaps the most sacred to him of all, even more than White Lea; for in this village and on the desolate eastern slopes of Chapel Fell that ran down to it, so many preachers had moved and inspired him: men and women like 'Praying Johnny' Oxtoby, Jane Ansdell, above all Thomas Batty, 'the Apostle of Weardale', whose preaching nine years ago had fired him to take the final leap into faith and salvation; though it was Rowland, of course, who had prepared the way.

Here their party was joined by a handful of miners from Chapel, some with their families, and a slightly larger group from Westgate itself, among them Mark Dent and two other convinced Ranters; they were all destined, like Luke and Tommy, for one or other of the pits in the Hetton area. Several of the remaining Westgate Ranters had come to sing their fellow worshippers on their way with a hymn. Its warm and hopeful sound echoed in Tommy's ears, lightening his spirits a little, overlaying the bitter memory of Rowland's final prayer. As they set out again, the Ranters continued to sing, though more raggedly now from the emotions of parting.

Just beyond Westgate, Well House stood square and prosperous-looking on the northern slope of the dale, sheltered with fine trees and set in fertile pasture. A drive wound from it down to the road, and by the solid gate-posts Tommy saw, with a leap of the heart, that Joe was waiting for him. He broke into a run and reached his brother well ahead of the slowly moving carts.

Joe clapped him on the shoulder and said gruffly, 'Make thy fortune, lad. And take care of thyself.'

Tommy had been surprised at Joe's reaction to his plans, when he had at last found the courage to tell him of them, only two weeks ago. He had not expected the bitter accusatory tone that Rowland used towards him, but he knew well enough that Joe had led a strike in Weardale in his youth, which was why he had never worked in the mines again since; and he had supposed that he too would disapprove of what his brother was doing. But it was quite clear that either Joe had mellowed with the years, or he regarded the colliers' strike as quite a different matter. 'Why,' he had said, when Tommy expressed his surprise, 'if the colliers are so foolish as to put their jobs at risk, then you should take your chance. You have to eat, man.' Tommy had been glad of his approval, but a little uneasy too; it smacked too much of the compromising pragmatism of which Rowland so disapproved.

'They wanted more men anyway,' he had said quickly. 'Hetton's growing every day. They have the deepest pits there have ever been, well over one thousand feet underground.'

Joe had whistled, moved to an exclamation he knew Tommy could not approve. 'Dear God! I knew they'd got through the magnesian limestone, but I somehow never thought it'd be that deep. How the hell do the colliers get down there?'

'By shafts, I think.' Tommy had not in fact given the matter very much thought at all, and at that moment he had felt a certain inner quailing at the prospect. There were shafts in lead mines, but access to them was almost always by means of levels, long passages running slightly uphill into the ground. It was only once inside the mine that shafts were needed to reach the lower levels, and then the deepest of them was unlikely to be more than about twenty fathoms – a mere one hundred and twenty feet. What would it be like to drop, by some unguessed-at means, thousands of feet into the earth, into a shaft so deep that its base was many fathoms below sea level? He had been glad when Joe asked him about that more congenial aspect of his future prospects, the pay. That too had brought an astonished whistle.

'What gowks the colliers are, turning their noses up at pay like that. Make the most of it, lad – and good luck to you!'

This morning, Joe had a parting gift for his brother, a fine gold watch that made Tommy catch his breath with amazement.

'Get you to work on time,' Joe said, through Tommy's stammered thanks. The gift, and Joe's affectionate fare-well, set Tommy on the next stage of his journey feeling cheered and more hopeful than he had for a long time. If Joe approved of what he was doing, then surely, in the end, Jenny and even Rowland would come round too?

'This isn't how I thought it would be,' said Luke in an undertone, on the last stage of their journey.

'Nor me,' said Tommy. He tried not to think of all that Rowland had said. He must not think of it, for he had made his choice and he had to believe it was the right one. But a coldness crept through him with every step.

The soldiers had been waiting for them on the second day of their journey, lined up in ranks outside an inn at Rainton Gate. Tommy had stared at them in amazement, not realising at first what they were doing there. There had been some signs of unrest in Durham City as they had passed through, noisy groups on street corners and posters everywhere demanding reform, but nothing approaching the imminent revolution that Rowland had hoped for, nor anything requiring a military presence. Outside the city, there had been even less to cause disquiet. He could only suppose that they had chanced upon some kind of military exercise, a view shared by

Luke's children, who had laughed and chattered with delight at the unexpected entertainment.

Then they had seen that Mr Robson was among the handful of men waiting with the soldiers, and at a shouted command the troop had marched towards them and fallen into line on either side of the little column of carts and walking men and women, and Tommy had caught Luke's eye and they had glanced at others in their party and seen the same unease on every face. Then he had turned to the soldier nearest to him, a broad red-faced man. 'What's all this for?'

The soldier, scarcely looking round, had shrugged. 'Just in case,' he said. Then he added, 'There was a man murdered Easter weekend, in Hetton. He'd left the union. They've got some of those who did it. But last week I was in the escort for his coffin, at the funeral. The union men cheered when it went by.' Tommy shivered at the horrible story. It was hard to believe that there could be such wickedness; and harder still to grasp that they themselves might in some way be caught up in it.

Then they came to the fringes of Hetton. The roads themselves were empty, clear of any human or animal, except for the incoming Weardale contingent and the soldiers; but, further off, along alleyways, on higher ground looking over the road, on the far banks of streams, people had gathered, men and women and children. They stood in a long single line, very still, watchful, the only movement the bright wind-blown banner of a ribbon or an apron or a cravat, the restless fidgeting of a baby in its mother's arms. They stood in that grim stillness as the first of the carts came into view, and the second, and the third, their eyes intent upon them. And then, as if at some hidden signal, the whole watching mass rippled into life from its nearer end, on and on as far as Tommy could see. Arms waved, fists shook, children jumped up and down in unrestrained fury; a chorus of shouts and jeers burst out, swelling quickly into one great long angry roar. Stones were thrown, and some fell not far short of the cavalcade, landing with such force that they sent a shower of dust spurting up as they dug themselves into the road. Once, a detachment of soldiers marched off to deal with a stone-thrower, though in what way Tommy did not see; the line of watchers neither bent nor broke. He had not expected the soldiers, still less had he expected this bitter reception, and it shocked and chilled and appalled him. He had never in all his life heard anything like it, but he knew well enough what it meant. The hatred was tangible, like an icy blast blowing at them from all sides.

Hetton-le-Hole was a once-small village with a nucleus of stone cottages at its heart, built on a ridge and backing onto a stately mansion that faced away from them, over a wooded valley. But now in every direction houses spread out from the centre, tiny stone hovels smelling of damp, cramped brick rows running down onto the low-lying ground at the foot of the hill. It was to these last that Mr Robson despatched the Westgate families, under guard; they were to be employed by the North Hetton Company, at Moorsley Colliery. Tommy and Luke were among those who continued on the road to the south, soon rising steeply again.

It was growing dark, but still the figures watched them pass, shouting their hate into the night. Their voices carried over the roofs of the low mean cottages that lined the road, over the stinking open drains that fronted them, over dark and sluggish streams, waste tips and wagon-ways, the whole desolate landscape in which, in this light, there seemed nothing left of the green loveliness of spring.

They were told that the place to which they were brought at last was called Brick Garth, which seemed fair enough, for that accurately described it: set on the brow of the hill, it consisted of a series of brick rows built at angles to one another, the houses larger than some they had seen, but stark and functional. Work was still going on here, for one or two of the rows were incomplete, the houses only begun. Through the chill of misery that had so firmly fastened its grip upon him, Tommy found one small crumb of comfort, which he shared with Luke as they passed along the lane that led to the houses. 'Look – over there. A Ranter chapel. That's home-like, for some of us anyway.' His voice sounded hollow, echoing into the silence of their little party, and Luke said nothing.

A man they were told was Mr Thomas Wood, the colliery's agent, led the way, paper in hand, and despatched each household to its new address. His manner was brusque and unwelcoming, and Tommy felt more unhappy than ever. He was glad when they came to the house that was to be theirs and the officials moved off, leaving them to unload the cart. The house was simple enough – two cramped rooms downstairs and a garret bedroom above – but adequate, with just enough space for them all, though there was no garden and the stench from outside came in even through closed doors and windows. They set to work quickly to make it habitable, unloading the cart, lighting the fire (there was ample coal), making beds, setting stools around the table. And then, before Rebekah prepared their evening meal, they gathered in the kitchen and Tommy led them in prayer, calling for God's blessing on their new life in this place. After that he felt better. God had never denied a blessing, not once in all his life. He would not fail him now.

Tommy fell asleep that night to the ominous tramp of patrolling soldiers; and a few hours later was woken, abruptly, by a sharp hammering on the front door.

He lay dazed for a moment, trying to remember where he was and why, listening for any sound, familiar and reassuring, that would tell him what he should do next. He heard a child cry downstairs, but it was no voice he recognised; a cat mewed outside, and the hammering came again, further off, a few doors away. There seemed to be a great swell of subdued noise, as of a vast population stirring from sleep, doors banging, feet clattering. He remembered then, and his spirit, hovering uncertainly, fell again into depression.

They had been told they would be woken in time for

work; they had to be at the Isabella pit by four. It was still dark, but Tommy supposed it must now be about three. He groped for the candle he had put ready on the floor and lit it, and then rolled off his mattress and dressed. By the time Rebekah and Luke came yawning into the kitchen he was already stirring the fire to life to heat water for a breakfast they none of them much wanted.

The soldiers were lined up again to escort them as they gathered for the walk to the pithead, though this morning they saw no one watching; but then it was scarcely beginning to grow light. The march of military feet echoed between the houses, an emphatic rhythm underlying the less orderly clatter of their own clogs on the road.

At the pithead they were met by Mr Mark Scott, underviewer at the Isabella pit. Mr Wood was there too, and it was he who spoke to them first, rather as if he despised them, Tommy thought.

'You grovers, you think you've come here for easy money. You think what waits for you down there' – he gestured towards the gaslit shaft – 'is just like your snug safe little mines at home. Well, I tell you, you couldn't be more wrong. Maybe you think life was hard in Weardale. Wait till you get down there, lads, and you'll see you didn't know you were born. Now, a true collier, he knows the dangers, he's born knowing it, he can smell when owt's wrong. But you've still to learn, and some of you are going to learn the hard way, with your lives. Coal pits are for men, and if any one of you isn't man enough for hewing, then he'd best get off back home this minute, because there's no place for him here.'

He then handed them over to Scott for a demonstration of the Davy lamp, which, they were told, must be their only light in certain parts of the pit. Scott was earnest and businesslike. 'Once near the face, never let the air get to naked flame. You do that, and you'll have the whole pit blown up. That'll not just be your life but those of all your marras. If the flame burns blue, turn down the wick and get out – let someone know.'

They were supplied with candles as well as lamps, and tools – though many, like Tommy and Luke, had brought their lead mining tools with them and set them out now to be inspected, to be reassured that some of them at least would serve them just as well here.

After that, they stripped to the shirt and drawers in which they were to work, leaving their outer clothes where they were shown; and then they were ready to begin.

Tommy had tried not to wonder what the descent into the pit would be like; but the thought of it had lurked as a great dread somewhere at the back of his mind. And now the moment had come. They passed a group of buildings from which the ventilation climney rose against the sky, and rounded the corner by the great mass of the engine house, from which came the wheezing of the steam engine that powered the machinery of the pit. The gaslights, augmented by the first grey dawn light, showed the black opening in the ground, below the elaborate tangle of the winding gear – a shaft perhaps eight feet wide, divided in two by a wooden partition to allow one side to be used as a ventilation shaft, with a great flat chain running into the other side to carry men and coals to and from the pit.

In the lead mines what shafts there were – small homely holes in the ground, compared to this chasm – had rungs at either side on which the miners climbed down. Here, each man was expected to *ride the loop* in the chain, and by that precarious means to be lowered into the depths. The only thing that stopped Tommy from fleeing from the place in horror was pride; he would not so shame himself before his fellows. His heart beating furiously, his face, he knew, as white and drawn as those of his companions (he was not then alone in his fear), he watched the man in front of him step forward and slip one leg through the loop, and then hold tight to the chain before, with a jolt, it moved off and swung him into space above the chasm. Then it was Tommy's turn to attach himself to the next loop and feel himself swaying over nothingness, as men climbed in above and the chain slowly, shudderingly, descended.

Down and down into blackness they went, rattling and swaying and terrified. After the first moments, during which they still had a little light to see by, Tommy had a strange sensation, as if he were not falling at all but being pulled rapidly up. He lost all sense of time, all feeling, except the desperate urge to stay alive, clinging to the chain, until he was safely on firm ground again.

At last he felt a change in the air, a slight lessening of the darkness from somewhere beneath his feet, a renewed sensation of descending; and he knew that the descent was nearly at an end. Looking down, he could see that the first man had already reached the faint gleam where the shaft ended. He felt the chain jolt and shudder, pause and then clank on again, heard the sounds of men trying to clutch again at normality; and then he too was climbing onto solid ground, feeling bewildered and cramped, and looking about him.

They were met by Morgan Frazer, the overman – cool, blunt, neither friendly nor warm – who instructed them to light their candles, set in lumps of clay, as were the candles they used in the lead mines. Then he ordered them to follow him, along a passage much like one of the levels in a Weardale mine, except that it sloped downwards rather than upwards.

They picked their way along the rails that ran through the level, deep into the mine, their feet splashing in the water running in a little stream towards the drainage pump they could hear working away in the distance. That was familiar too, and the constant dripping from the roof of the level, and the far-off echoing sounds of voices and machinery. But there were differences, one of which Tommy noticed very soon.

'They were right about the ventilation,' he said to Luke. 'When you think how deep we are – I can't recall any mine in Weardale with air as fresh as this, not once away from the day.'

They passed a crane, standing motionless by a row of

empty wagons harnessed to a pony minded by a silent and solitary man. Then they came to more cramped passageways, where they had to walk constantly bent. The overman ordered them to put out their candles and light their lamps.

The walls gleamed in the candlelight, but there was no smell of wet stone, no sparkle of quartz, nothing but black coal and the smell of coal. It gave Tommy some idea of the richness of this seam for so long too deep to work, that the whole place seemed formed of it.

He had expected to find the pit already bustling with activity, for he presumed that the local colliers would have started work while the new men were being given their instructions. But apart from the man at the crane they saw no one, no sign of activity, and when they came to the frequent trapdoors Morgan Frazer had to open and close them himself. 'We're short of trappers,' he said. 'We'll take boys on sooner than usual, if you have any about five or more. Tenpence a day, they get for the work.' It was a princely sum, set against the fourpence a day earned by washer lads in Weardale, but Tommy felt shocked at the thought of any child so young working in this darkness. Luke, having heard beforehand that there might be work for little Ralph, who was just five, had said no son of his would start work so soon, but Tommy wondered if he was now tempted to change his mind; he hoped not.

At last Frazer halted. 'This is where you'll be working,' he said. All they could see were yet more low passages running away into the blackness behind him. 'I'll set you on and then come by and see how you're shaping.'

It had already been explained to them that the coal was cut in sections – bords – leaving great pillars of coal intact to support the roof, until a large area was finished; after which the pillars themselves would be worked, back from the furthest point. Now, Frazer led each man to the bord where he was to work, and spent a little time explaining how to cut the coal, how to make sure small coals were put to one side and only larger round coals used to fill the wooden corves that waited nearby; how to mark the corves to show which man had worked the coal, so that he could be paid accordingly; how to lift the full corves onto the trams, for transporting to the crane. It was some considerable time before Luke and Tommy were given their places, in adjacent bords.

Tommy's place was scarcely three feet high, so he had to work on his side, struggling to see by the inadequate light of the Davy lamp as he made vertical cuts with his pick at either side of each section of coal (*kirving*, they called it), before undercutting (*nicking*) to allow the coal to fall away. Sometimes, they had been told, gunpowder would be needed, but not as often as in the lead mines, for fear of explosive gases. It was not long before he grew uncomfortably hot, the sweat mingling with the damp from the coal around him, drenching the few clothes he wore.

Now and then Luke called to him, sharing exasperation or triumph as the work progressed. 'How do they think we can see what's small coal and what isn't in this light?' he complained. Then, 'They should have set colliers to work with us, just at first. They'd have saved time in the end.'

At that moment Tommy heard someone come up behind him. He looked round and saw that Morgan Frazer was there. The overman said, with a note of some irritation in his voice, 'Why man, there are no more than half a dozen hewers at work in all the Hetton pits. What could they do among all you strangers?'

Tommy eased himself into a sitting position. 'We were told there were very few for the union.'

'Were you? That's as may be. I'm no reader of men's minds, to know who's for and who's against. All I know is there are hardly any have come out of it. What cause would we have otherwise to bring in unskilled men?'

It was a question to which Tommy, with that now familiar chill growing in him, could think of no adequate reply.

*   *   *

It was clear that someone had lived in the house before, but on moving out had not troubled to leave it clean for its new occupants. As the growing daylight showed up the grimy corners, Rebekah Emerson found herself itching to set to work with a scrubbing brush. But first she had to find water. Luke had brought in enough last night to wet the oatmeal for this morning's crowdy and to make a little tea, but that was used up now and she had forgotten to ask him where he had fetched it from. She looked out of the window.

The view was not encouraging. At home (could she ever think of anywhere but Weardale as home?) her kitchen window looked out on trees and meadows, on sheep and cattle grazing, the river and the fells. Here, there was only a drab yard and brick walls and mud; and a large elderly woman hanging out washing behind the adjoining house.

She instructed the children to watch the baby and seized a pail and went out. 'It's a grand day,' she said with a forced cheerfulness; a quick glance to her left, where the court was open to the muddy land beyond, allowed a glimpse of blue sky and sun.

The woman turned and looked at her with some suspicion. 'Aye,' she said, without smiling.

'Where can I get water?' Rebekah asked, persevering.

The woman made a gesture with her head. 'Over there.' It seemed that she was indicating some point beyond the furthest house in the opposite row, but Rebekah could not be sure. She could see no sign, from here, of any well or pump. The woman picked up her basket and went back into her house. After a moment, Rebekah set out in the direction the woman had indicated, on past the ends of all the rows, to where the ground rose a little and fell again to the foot of a waste heap, where ran a small muddy burn, from which she filled her pail.

As she walked back to the house, she studied the scene before her. There were hills here, but insignificant, set against those she had left behind, and more deeply scarred by workings and spoil heaps. Along the line of Easington Lane houses straggled, but there seemed to be no one about, except a group of soldiers talking together on a corner by Brick Garth and a horseman riding purposefully north on the road. Smoke curled from one or two of the chimneys in the rows, but it was quite clear from here that most of the houses were empty, only just built perhaps and waiting for more men to come from the lead dales. On the land to her right there lay a scattering of rubbish, and blackened circles where fires had been, as if some kind of camp had recently been set up there. Gipsies, perhaps, she thought. But, if so, they had left no other trace. It all looked very desolate and deserted.

She tried hard not to think of what she had left behind. Side Head was a small place, with few inhabitants, but she knew everyone there, and her mother and sisters and brothers all lived within a few miles of the place. There was always someone she could go to when she wanted advice, or simply companionship. Here, she did not even know those who had come from Weardale very well and there were few women among them. She bit back the tears that filled her eyes, swallowing through a harsh lump in her throat. She had never in all her life felt so alone.

To keep homesickness at bay, she set to work with her scrubbing brush, angrily scolding the children when they got in her way, splashing water around so vigorously that she had to make several journeys to the stream, but once every inch of the house was clean she felt better. After that, she began to rearrange the furniture to what she hoped was its best advantage, taking great care over the placing of each item. The house still looked very bare, which would not have mattered at home, where the windows gave all the colour and distraction anyone could ask for. But here, Rebekah felt, the rooms needed more than the very simplest furniture, so as to help them all forget the cheerlessness outside. Of course, Luke would be well paid for his new work and very soon they would be able to afford things they had never dreamed of owning until now, such as ornaments and pictures.

She was gazing at one of the walls considering the matter when a sudden happy sound caught her ear; the chatter of children. It came from outside, to the front of the house, and Ralph and Hannah had heard it too, for they slid down from the stools on which she had placed them out of her way and ran to the front door. She went with them and looked out. A little girl about her daughter's age was kneeling before the door of the adjoining house, poking in a puddle with a stick, while she chattered away to a baby seated against the doorpost behind her. Rebekah watched as her own children went hand in hand towards the little girl.

The children studied one another with the solemn curiosity of small things, and then Ralph crouched down at the further side of the puddle and said something Rebekah did not quite catch. Before long, all three children were playing happily together. Rebekah stood in the doorway watching them and hoped that soon the woman of the house (their mother she supposed, though she looked a little old for it) would come out too and prove more friendly than she had seemed at first.

Once, Rebekah heard a voice from inside the house calling to warn the child not to get dirty (a little late for that, Rebekah thought, with a smile), but no one came out. Instead, a young woman suddenly came in sight, approaching down the alley; and the little girl looked round and saw her and then gave a shout – 'Mam!' – and ran to meet her. She was about Rebekah's age, a slight fair woman with a sweet face. For the first time that morning, Rebekah felt hopeful and almost happy. Children were a great bond, she knew, and this was clearly the little girl's mother. She smiled, ready to greet the woman. Ralph and Hannah stood up, watching too.

The young woman came to a halt, frowning a little. She drew her little girl in to her side and looked at the Emerson children, and then her eyes moved to Rebekah and the hostility in them made her catch her breath. Her

103

own ready smile wavered and she stood open-mouthed, speechless.

The woman crouched down facing her child, holding her arms firmly, so that their eyes were on a level. Then she spoke with great clarity, her voice full of all the solemnity of a parent warning a child of a terrible danger. 'Ruth, those are stranger children. The strangers have taken our houses and the bread from our mouths. You must never, never play with stranger children or talk to them. You must pretend they are not even there. You cannot see them or hear them. Remember that, always. Promise me that you will.'

Rebekah wondered how much so young a child could understand, but Ruth listened, grave and round-eyed, and then she nodded. 'Yes, Mam. I promise.' And then her mother took her hand and they went into the house next door. An arm scooped up the baby from the step and the door slammed shut.

Rebekah, feeling as if someone had just tipped a pail of cold water over her, stepped back from her door, out of sight. She was trembling. A moment later her own children came in; Hannah was crying. Rebekah gathered them into her arms and rocked them.

By the end of a week, life had not grown any easier for the Weardale families. For the men, the first shift in the pit had seemed interminable, as if a lifetime had passed while they were underground. Yet when they had emerged it was scarcely midday, with several hours of daylight before them. After four more days, no better than the first, Tommy wondered if he would ever get used to the work or learn to take a pride in it, as he had in the lead mines. At present he was concerned only to do what he had to do as well as he was able, with the conscientiousness of one who walked in the light, but that did not make him like it any better. He told himself that when he had learned the special skills that coal mining required of him, it would be different. It would take a little time, that was all.

It would take longer still, he suspected, to grow used to the presence of the soldiers. Or would there come a day when they were no longer needed, when no angry crowds would gather to jeer the Weardale men home from work? Mercifully, they were left alone once they had reached their houses, perhaps because the soldiers patrolled the adjoining streets, keeping a constant watch on all who came and went.

There should have been compensations. On arriving at Hetton, the Weardale men had been given an advance on their wages, enough to keep them going until their first pay, in a fortnight's time; and it was more than most of them had ever earned in a month. Rebekah explored the shops in Easington Lane, braving a chilly reception in some of them, and spent a good deal of the money with what seemed to her a prodigal recklessness. They had meat on the table most days, and luxuries they scarcely ever met with at home. Unfortunately, Rebekah, accustomed to making crowdy and not much else, had no idea how to cook such a variety and abundance of food and Tommy very quickly found himself longing for Jenny's cooking. His sister might not often have the means to provide anything more than crowdy, but whenever she did cook more luxurious food – at Christmas, when Joe made them a gift of meat or game – it was always wonderful. He had no idea what she did to it that was any different from anything Rebekah did, but there was no comparison; Jenny was, he supposed, quite simply a better cook.

Rebekah was miserable too, given to sudden bursts of weeping and complaints that she missed Weardale and her friends and family. Luke did his best to comfort her, and so did Tommy, but it did not help any of them to feel more cheerful.

There was one thing that Tommy kept in his mind, like a fire in a cold place, to warm and cheer him: the thought of the little Ranter chapel just beyond Brick Garth. A worn notice outside the chapel had indicated that a preaching meeting was held on Sabbath mornings, and so on that first Sunday morning Tommy woke with a sense of happy anticipation and dressed with care and went to call for a number of others who were of his persuasion – Jacob and Margaret Nattrass and their children, and Gideon Little, who lodged with them – and then they set out together along the alley. They had not gone far when they found their path barred by a soldier, who asked them where they were going.

'To chapel,' Tommy replied.

'I'd not advise it,' the man said. 'We can keep them from coming down here, but if you go across there we can't guarantee your safety, not today. Let well alone, that's what I advise.'

Tommy glanced at the faces of his companions, who seemed as surprised and puzzled as he was. 'No one shall keep us from worship,' he said firmly.

'Then say your prayers at home.'

'What can we have to fear in God's house? He is with us.'

The soldier shrugged and let them pass, with an expression which indicated that, faced with such foolishness, there was little he chose to do about it.

'Maybe some of the worst of them have attacked the chapel,' Jacob Nattrass suggested as they approached the corner.

'Maybe,' agreed Tommy; but he was not afraid. He believed firmly in what he had just said to the soldier: the Lord was with them in this. He could not be otherwise.

It was obvious that the meeting for worship was about to begin, for the chapel door stood wide and a group of men and women were making their way in. Tommy could not remember having seen any of them before – by now he knew the non-union colliers of Brick Garth by sight, though none had yet spoken to him. As Tommy and his companions approached, one or two of the people looked round and then said something to those beside them, and the group came to a halt. Those who were already inside came back out again – to make the newcomers welcome, Tommy supposed; until he drew a little nearer and saw on

106

their faces the stony, watchful look with which the Wear-dale men were already depressingly familiar after the best part of a week at Hetton.

'Maybe that soldier had a point,' said Gideon Little.

'They're Ranters, like ourselves,' Tommy said, as if that could not fail to reassure him.

The group parted to let someone through, a slight young man about Tommy's age, with blond hair and a fine-boned face at odds with his misshapen body. Tommy liked his looks. Resolutely ignoring the severity of the young man's expression, he smiled.

The young man spoke, his voice as cold and clear as his eyes. 'Go home, strangers. There's no place for you here.'

Tommy continued to walk steadily forward. 'There are no strangers in the kingdom of heaven. Not strangers, but fellow citizens. We come only to worship God.'

'There is no place in the kingdom for those who set their faces against Him and blaspheme against the Holy Spirit. Go home, before you fall into that sin.'

'Let us pass, brother. We come in love.'

It was the wrong thing to say. There was a rumble of anger from the group behind the fair man.

'It is not love, to take the bread from the children's mouths. If you choose to go, then go in peace . . . ' He raised a hand, and his voice took on a new power and ferocity. 'But if you stay, then be ye warned: Ye shall have not peace but a sword, for ye have ploughed wicked-ness, ye have reaped iniquity; ye have eaten the fruit of lies. Therefore shall a tumult arise against you and all your fortresses shall be spoiled, and the mother shall be dashed to pieces upon her children. And ye will say to the mountains, cover us; and to the hills, fall on us – for the great day of His wrath is come; and who shall be able to stand?'

There was a long silence, while the two men looked at one another, blue eyes at blue eyes, two men who now understood one another perfectly, for they spoke the same language. Tommy shivered, and then quietly turned and nodded to his companions, and they walked away, back to where the soldier, his expression knowing, had been watching the exchange.

As they went, Jacob Nattrass burst out angrily, 'To think that Ranters should come to this!'

'Aye,' said Tommy slowly; he was trembling still from the shock of it. 'I pray God will open their eyes to the error of their ways.' But he remembered as he spoke where he had last heard something like those words, and he seemed to hear them again, a mocking echo of his own.

Behind them, the group by the chapel were singing, heartily and loudly,

> *Long, long, may Hepburn live;*
> *Long may our Union last;*
> *May God our souls receive,*
> *When all our toils are past.*
> *O, may we all to heaven ascend,*
> *And reign, with Christ, the Pitmen's friend!*

Chapter Seven

It was very early, but Tommy had been woken from a fitful sleep by the baby crying downstairs and he knew he would not sleep again tonight. Already the anxieties and doubts and miseries of the past weeks were crowding in on him again, going round and round in his mind.

Last Sunday he and his fellow Ranters had gathered in Jacob Nattrass's crowded living room and he had led their worship as best he could, trying to give comfort and reassurance and to turn their minds from the bitter little scene outside the chapel, but he knew that his words had brought them no more than a fleeting consolation. As for himself, he had gone home again knowing how much he still needed to examine all that had happened to him during the past days, and make sense of it, and seek God's guidance through the equally difficult times that lay ahead.

The working hours were not so long as to prevent him from thinking, and he had tried, day after day, to set aside some time to read his Bible and ponder its message to him. At White Lea it had not always been easy to find such moments, when there were so many tasks on the land to take his time when he was not at work. His long-held ambition to teach himself the Bible languages of Hebrew and Greek had made only very slow progress over the years. But here, he had thought, he would have ample time. Now he was dismayed to find that he could hardly even concentrate enough for prayer. Though he had the garret room to himself, the floor was very thin, as was the roof, and he never seemed able to be really quiet, night or day. There was always the noise of children, of talking and pots clattering and scolding voices, not just from downstairs but from the houses on either side and all the others that surrounded the court. The noise was growing too, for every few days another contingent of strangers would arrive to take up residence in Brick Garth, the most recent being a group of colliers from Wales, marked out from the rest of them not simply by a difference of accent but by their own sing-song language. The lead miners looked on them with considerable suspicion; but then none of the disparate groups working in the Hetton pits mixed readily with any other. The non-union colliers hardly spoke to the lead miners – who came from Teesdale and Swaledale as well as Weardale – the colliers from Derbyshire and Yorkshire kept to their own groups, and none of them had any time for the Welshmen. Tommy, accustomed to the closeness and warmth of home, found it all rather depressing.

But that, of course, made it the more imperative that when the Weardale men met again for worship they should find the strength and refreshment they needed in this place of exile.

And now Sunday was here again, and in a few hours he would be leading their worship and trying, by prayer and singing and inspired words, to bring them a sense of God's love and the joy of His presence. Yet how could he begin to do so, when he himself was possessed by such a turmoil of doubt and anxiety?

He got up and dressed and crept downstairs, his Bible in his hand, to find Rebekah sitting by the kitchen fire, harassed and weary, rocking the baby in her arms in an attempt to soothe him without disturbing Luke any further or waking the other children. She showed little interest when he told her he was going out. He did not even consider talking to her of what was on his mind. He had tried, once, to talk to Luke, but his cousin seemed unable to understand his unease, though he was angry enough at the behaviour of the union men.

It was still dark, the deserted streets lit only by a fitful moon. Tommy had no idea where he was going. All he knew was that he needed the solitude and the tranquillity that he had sought so often and found so easily on the fells in Weardale.

He crossed the waste land behind Brick Garth, down into the little valley, across the burn and then up again, taking a long route round Elemore pit so as to escape the attention of the soldiers on picket duty. They might be there for his protection, but their presence was part of his unease, so that he wanted to avoid them tonight. It was only when he was stumbling in the dark over the fields beyond the pit, walking without any conscious aim simply where instinct took him, that he began to turn his mind to his troubles.

He saw now that he had been blind as to the consequences of his coming to Hetton. He had accepted the assurance of Mr Robson that few of the colliers supported the union, and it had been a terrible shock to find that it was quite untrue. Rowland would have told him it was only what he ought to have expected, not with any gloating *I told you so*, but in sorrow that it should have taken all this to show Tommy what his common sense should have told him. Rowland had known it well enough, Tommy saw that now. And what of the other things Mr Robson had told him, so earnestly, so convincingly? Had they been any more true?

If they were not, did that make Rowland right? Did it mean that Tommy had been mistaken in thinking it was God's will that he should come here? In Rowland's eyes the colliers had a right to form their union, by law and according to natural justice, and the opposition of the coal owners was something that must be resisted, as the action of tyrants. But in one thing Tommy knew that Mr Robson had not misled him: the colliers in the union were guilty of the most appalling brutality in their treatment of those who opposed them. For that very thing, a man had died in this place, only a short time ago. Tommy was quite sure that if it had not been for the soldiers their own lives would have been in danger too. Even Rowland could not have approved of that.

Yet two things had become clear: the vast majority of the Hetton colliers (and, from what he heard, the colliers of the whole Tyne and Wear district) supported the union – and among their number were Ranters like himself, who sought guidance, as he did, from the same Bible, the same prayers and hymns and emotional meetings for worship. Could so many be wrong, could so many men of his own faith have come by an identical path to such a very different conclusion . . . as indeed Rowland himself had done?

But no, being in the majority did not mean you were right. In fact, it was more likely to be a certain sign that you were wrong. The truly holy were like salt, like a candle flame, something small and precious and set apart, in the world but not of it, giving savour to the mass of everyday life around them. The saints had always been few in number, even though their aim must be to convert the world. As for the Ranters, he knew even from his experience in Weardale that individuals, seeking God together, could still come to quite different conclusions, each convinced that God had shown him alone the right way. It was one of the paradoxes to which he had as yet found no satisfactory answer. After all, Rowland had almost always found himself in a minority, set against the others; it was simply that until now Tommy had never been one of those others.

But what was hard for Tommy was to hold fast to his convictions when faced, not with simple disagreement, but with such naked hatred. He was not used to hatred. He was not even used to mere dislike. He had never given

112

the matter much thought, but if asked he would have supposed that most people liked him well enough. They certainly treated him as if they did. More than that, he knew that many people loved him deeply. He accepted that love the more readily because he himself found it easy to love. He did not think he had ever hated anyone and his dislikes had generally been passing things, based on a transient incident, ending with it. In his experience evil was something he read about, not something he faced in his daily life, except perhaps in his own thoughts and impulses. He had always found it difficult to think ill of anyone else. Until, that is, he came to Hetton.

Now he had come face to face with men who would kill to get their way; he had heard the hate in their voices and seen the hurt it could bring. No, it was right that, faced with men of that kind, the coal owners should bring in more pliable workers from elsewhere, men who would be grateful for high wages and good working conditions. After all, what right had the colliers to jib at their terms of employment, when in Weardale and the other lead dales families were starving for want of a living wage? They had a legal right to belong to a union, certainly, but no right to terrorise those who would not join them. It was for that, of course, that the coal owners would not employ them.

Scarcely knowing where he was going, he stumbled in the dark through little knots of trees, over streams, down hills and steeeply up again and then down. Once or twice he was brought to an awareness of his surroundings by some obstacle or the need to make a decision; to leap a burn, take one route or another at a crossroads, extricate himself by a hasty retreat from a patch of brambles into which he had inadvertently stumbled.

He did not know how long he walked, but after a time, as his thoughts began to clear and fall into a reassuring pattern, he came more fully to himself and realised that it was beginning to grow light. It was grey and cheerless still, a world drained of colour and warmth, but he found himself far away from colliery rows and pit heaps and wagonways (at least he could see none), at the top of a steep wooded bank running down to a stream, as yet out of sight in the early morning shadows.

Even in the greyness, the tangled growth of ash and hawthorn, beech and alder and willow shimmered with a fresh and luminous green, and underneath celandines shone, and great drifts of wood anemones. The little valley was wider and shallower than a Weardale dene, more open to the sky, yet there was enough about the scene to make him think of home with such force that he could almost imagine that, at any moment, Jenny or Joe or Rowland or one of the children would come walking up the slope towards him.

Feeling a lift of his spirits and a boyish wish to explore, he turned under the trees and followed a muddy little path that wound its way through them. He felt as if he were the only man on earth, alone in this place, startling birds into flight, sending small animals scuttling away from him through the undergrowth. He walked slowly, looking about him and drawing long deep breaths of the damp sweet air, with its scents of earth and rotting leaves and crushed undergrowth. As soon as it grew light enough, he decided, he would find some spot within sight of the burn and sit down and read his Bible. In this place, he was sure, he would come easily to a sense of God's presence. Already, looking back the way he had come, he could see the first faint rays of the sun reaching the edge of the wood.

The valley floor was level and curved its way through the trees, following the course of the stream. It was, he realised, when at last he caught a glimpse of it, a small insignificant stream. Babbling gently on its way, it had none of the tumultuous impetuosity of the Weardale burns, with their rocky shelves and splashing waterfalls and deep brown pools, but it was clear and silver in the morning light and he wanted to walk beside it. So far, however, the path had continued more or less at the same height, some way above the burn. He was looking for a suitable gap in the trees, not too steep and slippery for his

Sunday shoes, when he suddenly realised that he was hearing some quite unexpected sound. No, sounds – happy human sounds, laughter, a child chattering, the clash of cooking pots. Turning a corner, he had a clear view across to the far side of the valley, where, on a wide grassy space a little above the water, a tribe of gipsies had set up camp. Makeshift shelters, fashioned, in a cheerful and chaotic patchwork, from branches and waste materials, wood and all kinds of cloth, formed a rough crescent about the area, facing the burn and the morning sun, and before them women were already lighting fires, while their children played about them. One or two men, early risers, looked on from the doorways of their shelters, smoking their first pipes of the day. The scents of woodsmoke and tobacco reached him even here.

It was a picturesque enough scene and a happy one, and Tommy had no particular aversion to gipsies, who were God's children like all humanity; but this morning he did not want human company. He turned and retraced his steps for some way, until well beyond all sound of the camp, and then he slowed his pace again, letting the renewed quietness close about him. Soon afterwards, he saw the path he had been looking for, descending steeply to the burn. It was very slippery in places, but he made his way down it, clinging now and then to tree branches for support.

Once at the bottom, the path ran on beside the burn and he followed it in the direction that led away from the camp, though it was less well-marked here, half-covered at times with encroaching undergrowth. The sun was flooding the valley, and he realised it was growing late and he had little time left. It was, then, the more urgent that he should find the place for quiet reflection that he was seeking. He pushed his way past a particularly bushy hawthorn, and then, abruptly, stood still, a confusion of feelings running through him.

The space by the water's edge was occupied already, by a gipsy girl. She knelt on the bank, very close to the burn so that she could bend over it to splash herself with

115

water, gasping a little as its coldness touched her warm body. She was stripped to the waist.

Tommy had never before seen a woman even partially undressed. He knew he ought to flee the scene at once, but he was terrified that the slightest further movement on his part would betray his presence to the girl and somehow make things worse. So he stood there, colour rising in his face, unable to help himself, and took in the slenderness of her body, the small firm curves of her young breasts, the rosy nipples, the damp shining darkness of her hair falling against the flawless olive skin. And he felt as if his whole self had suddenly exploded into fire, as if he was burning, burning in a furious combustion.

Then she looked round, and he started; and she stood up just as she was, her face alive with amusement at his consternation. Horrified that he should have been seen, that he should have stayed even for a moment, that this should have happened at all, he turned and fled; and promptly tripped on a root and fell flat on his face.

He heard a gurgle of laughter behind him and then, when he did not move, approaching footsteps. Next, he heard her voice just above him, all concern. 'Are you hurt?'

He did not know what to answer. In his shame he wanted just to lie there, face down, until she went away – and indeed, he was shaken by the fall and could not easily have moved for those first moments. Then, slowly, he raised himself and even dared to look at her, blushing furiously as he did so. 'I — I am sorry.'

She looked briefly relieved, and then laughed again, merriment lighting her dark face. She had, he was thankful to notice, fastened her bodice, and looked modest enough, if a little showy. But he could not remove from his mind the memory of what he had seen. 'I did not mean . . . I . . . ' What could he possibly say that would be any kind of excuse, or make things right again? He decided that he could only remove himself from her with as much dignity as possible. He scrambled up; and then felt his ankle give way. Pain shot through him, flooding him with nausea and dizziness. He sank down again.

'You *are* hurt.' She sat beside him. 'Howay now, let me see.'

Her hands were small and brown and quick – and soft too, gently probing his ankle above the shoe, slipping up under the edge of his dark Sunday trousers so that he shivered and felt more dizzy than ever. She rubbed his ankle in a way that soothed it wonderfully and yet was thoroughly alarming. 'I've only twisted it, I think,' he said, conscious that his voice sounded strange and breathless.

She made him move his foot this way and that, and then agreed that it was unlikely to be anything much. 'Wait now.' She ran to the burn and took the apron from about her waist and soaked it in the water, and then came back and tied it about his ankle. It felt blessedly cool, the wetness seeping through his thick stocking. 'Rest a bit, then you'll be able to stand on it.' She sat there looking at him, and then laughed again. 'Your face, just then! I didn't think anyone would come.'

He was appalled that she should even think to speak of it again. It was hardly the talk of a modest woman; but then gipsy women were not, presumably, given to modesty. She was every inch the gipsy too, a tiny slight creature in clothes a little too bright, with the exotic, foreign look of her kind, the heavy dark hair, the oval face and olive complexion, the long nose, the lustrous dark eyes, the sparkling earrings dangling from her small ears. Her close scrutiny of him only increased all the curious unfamiliar impulses that had been set up in him on first seeing her, and he knew enough to recognise sensations that a pure-minded young man, his heart given to God, ought not to feel; sensations from which he ought to flee with all speed. If only he had not been so foolish, so clumsy . . .

She smiled, showing white even teeth, and it was worse than ever. He saw her through a kind of haze in which her features alone stood out, the pretty red mouth, full and soft about the white teeth, the glowing eyes that never left his face.

She moved away suddenly and stooped to pick something up from a bramble patch. It was his Bible, dropped there when he fell, momentarily forgotten (which was further cause for shame). She dusted the earth from the worn leather cover with its gold printing, fading a little now. 'Is it a Bible?'

'Aye.' He took it, thanking her quietly. Presumably she could not read. 'I was seeking the Lord's help for what I am to preach today.' To say that, so gravely, was to remind himself of the seriousness of his purpose, of where his thoughts ought to be. Already his breathing was steadying a little, coming under his control.

'You're a preacher then?'

'Aye.'

She looked at him with renewed interest. 'A Ranter?'

He nodded.

'Like Adam and Charlie Parkinson. And Tommy Hepburn.'

At his questioning look, she shook her head wonderingly. 'Where are you from, that you've not heard of them?' He was about to answer her question, when she went on, 'Tommy Hepburn's the union leader. He was a hewer at Hetton till last year. He's a great man, even my dad says, and he's no great liking for Ranters. But then better a Ranter than a blackleg. Adam's my friend Eliza's man. He's in the union too.'

A blackleg. Like Tommy Emerson. He shivered, as suddenly cold as he had been hot a moment before. And then he realised what else her words implied. He stopped himself just in time from saying, 'You're not a gipsy then,' suspecting that she might be offended by the suggestion. 'So your dad's a pitman?' he asked instead.

She nodded, and there was a new bitterness about her mouth. 'He was. They won't bind union men. But you must know that!' Whether or not she saw any response in his face, she went on, 'We used to live up at Brick Garth, Easington Lane – then they threw us out to make room for the strangers. I live over there now.' She gestured in the direction of what he had taken to be a gipsy encampment.

'In the wood?'

'Aye. We went to neighbours first, then they turned them out too. So we made tents by the road. Then they said that was against the law . . .'

Tommy remembered how Rowland used to condemn the harshness of the vagrancy laws, and felt more uncomfortable than ever.

'So we came here, and no one's moved us on yet. The woods belong Hetton Hall, but it's empty. We live as best we can, on what we can get. The other union men give something, if they're in work. Mind,' she added, 'we're not too hard up to give bread to a friend. You could come back with me. Mam's getting breakfast.'

He shook his head, trying not to let his dismay show. 'No, I'm expected at my lodgings.' *My lodgings, in Brick Garth, Easington Lane*, his mind added mockingly. 'But thank you. You are kind.'

'Have you far to go? I could see you home.'

'It's not far,' he said, having in truth no idea at all how far he was from what he had not yet learned to call home. He realised with a little shock that she had more right than he to give it that name. 'I'll manage.'

'I'll help you up to the top then. It's wet; you might slip.'

It felt strange, strange and alarming and wonderful all at once, to be hobbling up through the trees with her arm about his waist; her hair, scented with woodsmoke, so close to his nostrils. It took them some time and she talked as they went, asking him about himself, questions he fended off as best he could. He did not even tell her his name, except that it was Tommy. She was Matilda Grey, she said; and, just as he was thinking that the quiet subdued name did not suit her, she added, 'My dad named me for a ship he saw once, in Sunderland. But they call me Matty.' That, he thought, suited her much better.

Anxious to avoid the personal and with his own doubts and anxieties full in his mind, he asked her about the strike, though he took great care to make it seem as if he was someone who knew nothing of it, wanting only to inform himself. He was swiftly dismayed by the passion with which she answered him, her vehement support for the union case. 'Charlie Parkinson says there'll be a revolution any day now, and all working men will join together and live as equals with the masters!' The words rose into the soft spring air, astonishing and disturbing from so young and lovely a girl. Once, into the torrent of her fervour, Tommy said tentatively, 'But did I not hear that a man died?'

Her eyes burned with indignation. 'Maybe one of his blackleg friends killed him, in a quarrel. They don't like each other much. They only stick together because they're all traitors.'

'Do you believe that's what happened?'

'I don't know. If a union man killed him, then it's no more than he deserved, dirty blackleg that he was. He was with us last year, when we fought to make things better. It was the union did all that; we'd have got nowt without it. Then at the first sign that there's a price to be paid, he goes crawling to the masters. Can you wonder we hate blacklegs? The masters will go all lengths to break the union. They've spent hundreds of pounds bringing strangers in to take our jobs, and soldiers to keep us from getting our hands on them. But they know right well that if we all stick together, then we shall win. They can bring in all the strangers they like, but they still need skilled hewers to get the coal up. You have to be born to it, to do it well, and lead miners aren't. Even hewers from other pits in the south – they don't understand Durham coal, not like our men do. But every single man who leaves the union to save his job, he makes our fight the harder. Not,' she added quickly, 'that the leaders want violence. They don't. Tommy Hepburn's spoken against it, and all the other leaders, especially the Ranters, like you. But there are some too angry to be held back.'

'Do you not think it tarnishes your cause, to use violence?'

He was almost surprised when she nodded. 'Aye, maybe. That's what Adam says, and he's right. Not that they don't deserve the worst, but it gives the masters a reason to use force against us – and it makes it look as if they're right to fight the union, when they're not. It's not against the law to be a union man – why should anyone be turned out of his job for it, I'd like to know?'

At the moment of turning onto the woodland path, Tommy had believed his mind was made up, that he knew what he thought of the situation at Hetton. Now, faced with this lovely angry girl, everything seemed to be turned upside-down again. He suddenly saw it with her eyes, and from that vantage point it all looked very different, as simple, as much a straightforward matter of right and wrong as Rowland had said it was. He began to wish he had not questioned her and was glad when, after a pause (they were climbing the steepest part of the bank), she asked abruptly, 'Have you ever taught reading?'

'I've taught bairns, in the Sunday School, now and then,' he admitted.

'Then you know how to? I wish I could learn!'

'Is there not a Sunday School at Hetton?'

'My dad doesn't hold with women reading. He says it gives them ideas above themselves. He can't read himself, so he doesn't see the use of it.'

He imagined the possibilities it might open up, were she to ask him to teach her to read; and then he realised how precarious were these first hesitant shoots of friendship. If she were ever to know what he was . . . ! He was surprised that, as yet, she had not apparently begun to guess the truth.

For the moment her thoughts were still on her own aspirations. 'Do you think women should read?'

'I think everyone should read, and write, and get all the learning they can. We have our gifts from the Lord, and it's for us to make the best of them. Besides, if you can't read, you can't know the Bible.'

121

'No,' she agreed, a little doubtfully.

At the top of the bank they halted. 'I can get on by myself now,' he said. 'Thank you.'

'Why, it was my fault,' she said, grinning.

He coloured again, looking down, and then exclaimed and began to unwind her apron from his ankle. 'You're forgetting this.'

'Keep it on,' she said quickly. 'Just till you get home. You can bring it back tonight, if your ankle's better. If I'm not here, hang it on this tree.' She touched a nearby hawthorn, newly broken into leaf. 'Mind, I might just be passing. About dusk, say. That's if you haven't to be going before then.'

He was momentarily puzzled by that last remark, until he realised that she must take him for an itinerant preacher, passing through the district to keep a preaching appointment; which explained why she had not questioned his being here. He had no intention of putting her right on the matter. He recognised too, with alarm and even some disapproval, that she was making an assignation; but he also knew, as he stammered his goodbyes, that he would come back here tonight even if he had to crawl.

He hobbled away into the sunlight, heedless of the pain in his ankle but very conscious indeed that she was still there, watching him from the shadow of the trees. He was as far as ever from knowing what he would say at worship this morning, but he no longer cared. Words would come, and for now there were other things on his mind.

She must have been waiting, there by the tree under which they had parted this morning, but a little behind it, so that she should not be seen until she chose. She stepped out to greet him as he came, limping a little, towards her, and only then did her assurance slip into a hint of shyness. She smiled and said nothing, and it was Tommy who spoke first.

'Your apron,' he said, handing it to her; his voice was

122

shaking, his face flushed. Then he fumbled awkwardly inside his coat and brought something out. 'I picked these. To thank you.' And, colouring still more, he held out a bunch of primroses, a little bruised. They were hardly much of a gift for a girl who lived in the woods, surrounded by spring flowers, but he had not been able to think of anything else to bring.

She took them as if they were the most precious gift she had ever received and stood gazing at him, clasping them to her breast, her colour high and her lips parted in a dazzling smile. The next moment, there in the dusk, she stood on tiptoe and kissed him, swiftly, yet enough for him to feel the touch of her lips on his cheek as if they burned him, marking him for ever.

For just a moment he hesitated, holding his breath from surprise, shock, wonder. All the wild, hot sensations of the morning churned inside him, and then without conscious thought he reached out and pulled her near. He had never done this before, but he needed no telling to hold her in his arms and bring his mouth down on hers. He felt her arms go about his neck, warm and eager, her whole body press closer, moving against him. Fire exploded through him, a fierce blaze taking swift hold of every part of him, whipped into frenzy, beyond control . . . but he knew he must control it, he must somehow take hold of himself, for his sake and hers.

It was agony to tear himself from her, though he moved back only far enough to look into her face; he still had his arms about her, he could feel the ragged warmth of her breath.

'I love you,' he whispered, and then wondered that he should have made so momentous a statement to a girl he had only seen for the first time this morning; and almost at once knew that he had done so because, simply, it was true.

Matty smiled to herself as she made her way back through the trees towards the camp. She was trembling with a mixture of joy and wonder. She had never in all her life felt like this, so happy, so sure, yet so carried out of herself and ready to let things take her where they would. All the little passions and loves of her past seemed now to have been trivial foolish things, shrivelled to nothing; even her blushing girlish attachment to Adam. They had all been shadows of what had happened to her now, so suddenly and so completely. There was no room left in her thoughts for anyone but Tommy. She whispered his name to herself as she found her way in the dusk, by instinct rather than by sight; she would have walked as blindly even in full daylight. 'Tommy . . . Tommy . . .'

Sturdy and broad-shouldered, yet with a soft sweet shyness that showed he was not much used to women; blue eyes, more clear and innocent even than Adam's; thick waving light brown hair that fell, a little unruly, over his forehead . . . If all her longings, all her desires and hopes and dreams could have taken human shape, then she knew that shape would have been Tommy's. She halted suddenly and shut her eyes and remembered how his kiss had felt, how strong and warm and yet gentle his arms had been about her, how all of it had set her on fire. She hugged herself, living the moment again, and the one that had followed. *I love you.* Could love come so swiftly? Of course it could, for it had seized her too. When, at what instant, had it come to link them so surely together? She thought over everything that had happened . . . At first sight, standing there, hot with embarrassment, watching her, he had just been a man, taking her by surprise, though not alarming even then. She had not felt threatened in any way; not as she had felt threatened when Jack Marley watched her washing, as he had begun to do so often that she had been driven to seek an unaccustomed privacy, to escape from him. But it had not been like that when Tommy found her.

It was a little after that, as she sat back on her heels and laughed at him and saw how he looked at her – she thought perhaps it was then that the spark had been struck. She remembered that she had felt as if her whole inside was turning a double somersault. She knew that the fire lit today would never go out, as long as she lived. She knew almost as surely that he felt as she did.

'I shall come again this time tomorrow, if I can,' he had whispered as they parted. She loved his voice, soft and deep, its speech slower than the sharp liveliness of Hetton speech; she wondered again where he came from. She knew Ranter preachers could be sent from any part of the country to work in another district. Tomorrow she hoped she would be able to learn more of him; today, whenever she had asked any personal questions, she had somehow found that they were talking of something quite different. But he would answer her tomorrow, because he too must want them to meet again, and she supposed he would be moving on soon to another village or town. This morning when she had returned to the camp she had looked for Adam, to ask him about the preacher (an itinerant preacher, not a local preacher, like Adam himself) who was planned to preach at one of the local chapels today, but Adam had already left for his own preaching appointment somewhere over Sunderland way. He should be back by now and she would seek him out the moment she reached the camp.

I love you . . . I love you. The words sang in her head as she went on again, smiling to herself like an imbecile, lost in a foolish world of her own, far from hurt or bitterness or anger or from the everyday squalor of life. It was almost dark, but a fire glowed inside her, lighting her way, warming her, transforming the universe.

She crossed the burn, leaping it with a new lightness of step; she felt as if, with just a little more effort, she would be able to fly. She ran on along the bank, emerging from the trees into the space where the camp fires burned, a bright warm space in the dark woods; but not as bright or as warm as what lay inside her.

It was a moment more before she realised that something had happened, some disturbance that sent people hurrying to and fro in agitation, voices shouting in anger. She stood still, trying a little dazedly to look out from her joy and understand what was going on; and to care about what seemed so far away and unimportant.

Someone came running from the firelight towards her, a black shape, distraught, skirts and hair flying.

'Oh Matty – Matty! They've got Adam!'

It was Eliza, uncontrolled as Matty had never seen her before, her white frightened face smudged with tears. 'Someone told them he was seen with a gun, just before Errington was shot.' Her voice soared off into a desperate wail of anguish. 'They've taken him – Adam! He's charged with Errington's murder!'

Matty put her arms about her and held her, and Eliza sobbed and sobbed, while the cold and the dark crept in again to her friend's sweet secret world.

Chapter Eight

Rowland had been gone about half an hour. Jenny had watched him ride away on their elderly galloway and tried not to feel anxious, though she knew she would not be at ease again until he returned. She hated any moment spent apart from him, now that every second was precious.

But it would be some hours before he returned, and there was work to be done, for she refused to let any but the most essential tasks keep her from spending time with him, so that by now she was well behind. This morning his absence gave her an opportunity to catch up a little. She went into the house reluctantly, for it was a beautiful soft May morning, trails of mist milk-white along the river, the sun already warm, the air filled with the sounds of calling curlews and larks and the rattling and rippling and rushing of burns and waterfalls and the slower river.

Since Tommy had left, a strange kind of tranquillity had settled over the household at White Lea. There were even times of real happiness, intense and sweet enough to banish the shadows for a while. It was perhaps partly because of the awareness, never quite absent, that this was likely to be Rowland's last spring that it seemed so

127

especially lovely. Every shared moment was the more precious because of its fragility, to be savoured to the full, lingered over. Every small thing seen or smelt or touched or tasted was to be enjoyed and observed with senses heightened by the knowledge of its transcience.

Certainly Rowland's improved health had a great deal to do with it too. Jenny knew that the improvement could not last; that it had more to do with the fact that he was no longer at work and could rest when he needed to than with any more fundamental cause. There was also the fact that Tommy had gone, so that the bitterness of their disagreement could be put aside; and that the weather was warm and dry and Rowland was able to spend much of each day outside, helping with the lighter tasks, like milking the cows or planting potatoes. But she was able for a good deal of the time to put that knowledge to the back of her mind and take each day as it came.

There were bad days too, of course, not simply when Rowland's cough was worse or he had overtired himself the day before, but also because he was liable to sudden violent swings of mood, one day full of apparent energy, talking of the future – *next year, when the bairns are grown* – as if he fully expected to have one; the next, plunged into anger or a depression so intense that Jenny would know he had retreated into some dark world beyond her reach. The only consolation was that these sombre moods did not, on the whole, last long. Oddly, they did not seem to bear much relation either to external events (though his hopes of revolution had dwindled, as the despised Reform Bill passed smoothly into law), or, still less, to his state of health. He was as likely to be optimistic on the days when Jenny at least could see how painful his breathing was, as on those when he seemed rather better.

For some days now one of his buoyant moods had carried him along, sweeping Jenny with it too. They had gone for walks together (she had only with difficulty, and considerable tact, prevented him from walking too far for his strength), eaten meals out of doors, sometimes

128

taking bread and cheese up onto the fell, while Rowland talked cheerfully about anything but his illness and its implications. At weekends and after school the children came too, or he would play with them, or tell them stories, or ask Em to accompany him on the fiddle while he sang to them, as he often used to do in his spare moments. Last Sunday he had even fulfilled a preaching appointment at Side Head for a preacher who had been taken ill – his first for several months – and this morning, as once or twice lately, he was on his way to visit a former member of the class he used to lead, who still valued his spiritual guidance. At least today he had agreed to ride, since Joshua Wearmouth lived two miles from White Lea and that was no longer a negligible distance for Rowland.

Jenny had got no further than fetching stool and pail for the milking when she saw that she was not after all to have the uninterrupted morning's work she had expected. Coming along the road was the grey plodding shape of a donkey, bells and ribbons on its harness, with an exotic-looking figure walking jauntily beside it. As he came nearer, she could make out the broad-brimmed plumed hat set at the back of his head, the glossy black ringlets falling to his shoulders, the dark lean hook-nosed face, the gold earrings, the coat of rich green velvet. She remembered now that someone had said he was in the neighbourhood. She smiled to herself, a little ruefully, and waited outside the door for him to reach her.

He came to a halt before her and took off his hat and bowed. 'I swear you're lovelier than ever, Mrs Peart.' His lustrous black eyes sparkled at her.

'You're ahead of yourself,' she returned, laughing. 'I didn't expect you so early.'

'How could I bear to wait a further minute before seeing you? For you, I have turned my whole route upside down!' He clasped long eloquent hands to his bosom and his eyebrows rose and fell to the lilt of his words.

She laughed again and tried, through a constant flow of teasing banter, to bring him to the point of his visit, which was to sell her something from the bags and cases carried by himself and his donkey. Or rather, his intention was to tempt her to make some more frivolous purchase, alongside the small necessities with which he regularly supplied her; in this case soap and a length of linen to make handkerchiefs. 'It's no use wasting your flattery on me,' she warned him cheerfully. 'I haven't another penny to spare.'

'Pay me next time?' He tipped his head on one side.

She did not want to think about next time. He called only about every six months, and in six months' time . . .

She kept her cheerful manner until he had gone and then she went back to her neglected tasks, trying to distract herself with vigorous activity.

There was one other interruption that morning. A beggar called not long before midday, claiming to have spent last night in the open somewhere near Stanhope and not to have eaten since. He had a shifty look, which she did not much like, so she did not press him to accept more than some tea and crowdy and a brief rest beside the fire; besides, she did not want any extra guests at this time. Fortunately, he spoke of going on to Alston, so she wished him good day and stood watching as he walked down the hill.

He had just reached the road when she saw the galloway come trotting into sight. She stayed where she was, just outside the door, and saw Rowland draw rein to talk to the beggar. She held her breath until man and pony had moved off again, in opposite directions – she knew Rowland's capacity to encourage the needy to accept his help, even when they had not actually asked for it.

The galloway turned up towards the house, her sturdy hooves clattering on the stones that scattered the track. Jenny could see now, with relief, that Rowland sat relatively upright still and that he looked cheerful, with more colour in his face than usual.

He drew rein by the byre door and slid down and began to unharness the pony. Jenny went to help him, while the animal tossed her head, eager to go and graze in the field behind the house. They released her and together carried saddle and reins to the byre, and then Jenny slid her arm through Rowland's. 'Did you eat at Wearmouth's?'

'No, and I'm hungry.' He gazed over the dale at the green loveliness of the spring day. 'It's a shame to go in. Let's eat out here.'

She brought food out, and they spread his plaid and sat on it at the top of their hay meadow, just outside the low wall that bounded the paved area in front of the house.

Despite his admission of hunger, rare enough in itself, he did not eat a great deal, but she had long ago ceased to let that worry her; no lead miner had much appetite after his first year or so underground. Afterwards they lingered on in the midsummer heat, enjoying the warmth on relaxed limbs, content to say little. It was a long time since Jenny had known quite this sense of well-being. She lay back on the plaid and gazed up at the cloudless sky, conscious of small stirrings of desire, insignificant enough at first but growing soon to a persistent longing ache that set up its own tensions in her body and ended her tranquillity. It was a long time since there had been any intimacy of that kind between her and Rowland, not since before last winter's illness, but she accepted without question that her own need was something that must be suppressed and ignored, most likely for the rest of her life. It was trying, but not of any great importance, set against everything else. She thought perhaps it was time to go indoors again and return to those neglected tasks.

Rowland stirred beside her, and she turned her head and reached out to stroke his cheek. He smiled and edged nearer, and there was no mistaking what she saw in his expression. She caught her breath, and then he sat up and bent over and kissed her, slowly, his mouth moving over hers with a hunger that was no less real for being tentative and hampered by his laboured breathing. Her lips opened to his, though she kept her own desire in check, fearful of

131

extinguishing the little flame by too demanding a need. Soon, she felt his hand slide under the crossed white folds of her tucker, on beneath the neck of her bodice, to come to rest caressingly on her breast. She reached up to draw him nearer.

For a long time they lay there, kissing, gently aroused, sharing all the little tender caresses that they knew gave the most pleasure to the other, sometimes pausing to say some small loving thing or laugh softly, before going on again. In the end, Jenny knew they would come together, out here, in full view of anyone who happened to come walking up from the road. And she knew she did not care. Nor would she have dreamt of warning Rowland to be careful not to exhaust himself. All that mattered was that they should share this time of gentle intimacy and slowly growing passion, and the contentment and peace that followed it.

Afterwards, as they lay still and happy in one another's arms, she rubbed her nose against his and said softly, 'Good thing no one came.'

'No one comes on Fridays.'

'Except the pedlar . . . ' She laughed at his expression of alarm, not quite serious. 'It's all right. He was early this time. He came while you were out.'

'He must have known.'

Jenny could see how tired he was now, but she had no regrets and knew he had none either. They had shared many moments, many hours of passion in their married life, but Jenny did not think there had been any quite so lit with such a glow of sweetness and joy, or so precious to her as this.

That morning, early, Joe Emerson's favourite mare had foaled. The event entirely disrupted the usual routine at Well House, for Joe had been up most of the night with the mare and his jubilation made itself felt the moment the tiny creature (*a jewel of a filly!*) tottered onto its trembling spindly legs under the urgent nuzzling and licking of its mother. He came in from the byre and called to everyone to come and admire the new arrival (Eve, not summoned by name or look, stayed in the house), then he gulped down two tankards of ale, ate a huge breakfast and went back outside again, with a parting instruction thrown at the rest of the family to see to the other beasts.

His wife, irritated by a broken night and the prospect of extra work, scowled at her stepdaughter, who was standing dreamily by the window, gazing down at the distant view of the river and the gentle green meadows that fringed it. 'Eve, get out and milk the cows. There's no time to stand around doing nothing – why do I always have to tell you? What have we done to deserve so idle a lass, I'd like to know?'

Eve glanced round, catching a glimpse of her two half brothers disappearing quickly upstairs before their mother's eye could fall on them, and then moving on to their sister, sitting at the table trying to prolong the eating of a slice of bread and butter for as long as possible. As Eve looked at her, Esther stuck out a well-crumbed tongue. Eve returned the gesture. Then she said, 'Esther's not doing owt.'

' "Anything", not "owt",' said Phoebe sharply. Eve deliberately favoured the more earthy speech of White Lea when in her stepmother's hearing. She despised Phoebe's pretensions to respectability – as if she was somehow better than Aunt Jenny or Uncle Rowland or her father! 'And don't answer me back. You can see Esther's not finished her breakfast. Get on now, or it'll be time for school and you'll not be finished. I don't want . . . ' But with rebellion in every line of her body, every swaying movement of her limbs, Eve had already gone.

She did the milking, though hampered by teasing from her half brother Ralph, who came to the cow byre out of his mother's way. If their father had not been so pre-occupied, Eve knew he would not have got away with such idleness, but there was nothing she could do about it. Telling tales of her stepmother's children only got her into trouble, whatever the rights or wrongs of it.

133

After that, she slipped out by the front door before her stepmother could find something else for her to do, and ran across the two adjoining fields to a lane that led down to the road, parallel to their own drive but out of sight of the windows of Well House. Then she slowed her pace, wandering dreamily on in the sunshine, through Westgate, where she avoided the little school, in case the other children were on their way there by now. She could hear the bell ringing for the start of lessons. She should have been there herself, but she hated school. Once safely past, she took the path that led along the river to St John's Chapel.

The market place was already busy, but not cheerful in spite of the sunshine. Groups of men stood talking gloomily by the doorways of public houses where they could no longer afford to buy anything to drink. Most of them had little or no work and no prospect of any. Not that Eve was remotely interested in them. She could have taken a more direct route to White Lea, up by Middle-hope burn, but she had deliberately chosen to come this way for a purpose of her own. She crossed to the far corner, where Jacob Todd's grocer's shop stood neat and trim, and then walked very slowly past it, peering in through the well-stocked window.

To her disappointment, the owner himself stood behind the counter, very upright, deep in grave conversation with one of his customers. Eve walked on slowly, past the shop and into the lane behind, filling in time in the hope that when she came back again Jacob Todd would have been replaced by his wife.

She had known for as long as she could remember that the grocer was her grandfather, but he had never forgiven his daughter, even in death, for the error that had led to the conception of Eve, and never since had he given any sign that Eve was anything to him at all. He had only one daughter, so he always maintained, and she was eminently respectable, married to another of the village's shopkeepers, who, like her father, was a pillar of the Wesleyan Methodist chapel.

But when Mrs Todd was alone in the shop, it was another matter. Meeting Eve in the company of others, Mrs Todd was apparently as oblivious of her very existence as was her husband. But whenever no one else was by she would stop and talk to the girl, with great affection, and even press small gifts into her hands, sweets perhaps, once even a little china doll, which Eve still treasured. She did not wholly understand the depth of concealed emotion that she released in her grandmother, but she knew she was of great importance to the old woman. She liked that feeling.

Her welcome at White Lea, when she reached there some considerable time later, feeling a little sick from the number of sugar mice she had eaten, was not what she had hoped it would be. As she came up the hill she could see her uncle and aunt walking towards the house, their arms about one another. Aunt Jenny's cap had fallen off and her hair had tumbled down her back, soft waves of light brown hair like a girl's. They did not look round and soon afterwards disappeared inside. But a moment later, just as Eve reached the house, Aunt Jenny came out again. Her cap was firmly back in place, the hair pushed tidily away under it, and she looked a little disapproving.

'Shouldn't you be at school, Eve?'

'I hate school,' said Eve emphatically. She heard her aunt sigh, though she did put an arm about her and lead her into the kitchen, where Uncle Rowland was dozing on the settle by the fire.

'School is important,' Aunt Jenny went on.

'But they call me, all the time. And pull my hair, and nip me.'

Her aunt stroked her dark hair. She looked as if she was thinking of something quite different, perhaps not of Eve at all. 'Have you told your father?' she asked at last.

'He never listens to what I say.'

'Of course he does.' She turned suddenly and took Eve by the shoulders. 'I tell you what, my pet. I have to see your father about something this afternoon. We can go

135

together and I'll tell him about school and we'll see what he says.'

Eve bit her lip. 'Can't I stay here tonight?'

She could hardly ever remember Aunt Jenny refusing her such a request before. Now she said, 'Your uncle's very tired and needs to rest — ' At that she glanced at him with an odd little smile, which he returned, holding her gaze for quite a long time, in silence. Eve was curious about it and wondered if it had anything to do with her. Were they mocking her in some way? It was not what she would have expected, but then nothing seemed quite right today.

'No,' her aunt went on. 'You must go home. I'll come with you. Maybe you can come and stay another time.' That *maybe* was daunting too, but Eve recognised the firmness in her aunt's voice. She accepted an offered drink of milk and then the two of them set out, back to Well House.

Eve, not wanting to confront her stepmother any sooner than she had to, led Jenny to the byre, where Joe was still standing proudly watching the foal. It was clear, however, that Phoebe had already complained to him about Eve, for he gave her enough of his attention to rebuke her severely for her behaviour and despatch her to the dairy to help her stepmother with the cheese-making.

'That's no way to turn her into a willing worker,' said Jenny, when Eve had gone.

'I've tried every other way. They none of them work,' said Joe. 'Is that what you wanted to see me about? Because you can save your breath.'

'Only partly. There were other two things. One I promised Eve I'd say.'

He looked impatient, but said rather grudgingly, 'You can tell me on the way. Let's go in.' He led her out of the stable and across the yard.

'You know she's unhappy at school?'

'I know she's off on the fell or Lord knows where every chance she's got. It's a waste paying good money for her to go. If she wasn't so useless at home she'd have left school long since, but what would we do with her at home all day?'

'She could still get some benefit from schooling. She hasn't learned all they can teach her. Maybe she should try somewhere else.'

'Jenny, I haven't time to go seeking out other schools for Eve. If that one doesn't suit, then she can come home and give Phoebe a hand . . . But that's enough of that. What was the other thing you wanted to see me about?'

He held the door open for her to enter the kitchen. She stepped inside. 'The rent,' she said. 'You must have wondered what was become of it.' She held out the bag taken from her pocket.

Joe recoiled as if it contained some deadly insect. 'You can't think I'd want it from you, the way things are now! I only took it before because Rowland would have it that way.'

'That hasn't changed.' Joe did not know it, and she hoped he never would, but the whole tale that Rowland insisted upon paying rent to his brother-in-law was a complete fabrication. Jenny had invented it (more by hinting than deliberate lies), as a means of persuading Joe to accept money from them for the house and land at White Lea. It was not so much that she felt it right that they should pay her brother for the use of what was after all his property, but rather that she wanted there to be nothing that might, at some future date, lead to rancour or ill will between them. As it was, Joe and Rowland did not always see eye to eye, and Joe could at times be less than tolerant of what he saw as his brother-in-law's eccentricities. Unfortunately, Rowland would have been perfectly happy to live rent free at White Lea, since that left more of their spare income (such as it was) to be used in what he saw as God's work. It was only Jenny's insistence, using her own supposed feelings on the matter, that had made him agree to pay rent. Fortunately she had managed (largely by emphasising to each of them

137

the pride and sensitivity of the other) to keep the two of them from talking of the matter together, and they did not guess her part in it at all.

'Maybe not,' Joe said now, 'but other things have. Besides, look about you. Can you really think we have need of your money?'

She did look about her then, at the warm kitchen, with its polished furniture, the fine clock, the good crockery set out on the table, the gleaming copper pans, the flowered chintz curtains, the general air of prosperity. Her own kitchen was as clean and comfortable as she could make it, but there was a shabby austerity about it that told of their poverty. No, Joe did not need the rent; but they had need of every penny that came their way. She realised now that she had brought the money with her today not from any of the scruples that had made her pay it in the first place, but because to do so was somehow to behave as if nothing had changed.

Joe misread her hesitation. 'If you want to spare Rowland's feelings, say nowt to him about it. Let him think it's been paid. God knows you'll have need of it soon enough.'

'I'm sure.'

'You have the feeding of Eve often enough. Think of it as a help towards that.'

'Aye. Thank you.'

She accepted Phoebe's invitation to take tea with them in the spotless parlour, with its piano and sofa and elegant little writing desk. She was longing to get home again, but good manners and sisterly affection compelled her to stay. She had never really warmed to Phoebe. She was a good housewife and mother – to her own children at least – and she clearly made Joe happy, but there was something complacent and self-sufficient about her that repelled Jenny a little. Today, however, she was in a confiding mood, for when Joe left them together she leaned across her pretty polished tea table and said with refined coyness, 'We are looking forward to a happy event, in September.'

Irritated by her manner, Jenny deduced that Phoebe was pregnant again. She offered her congratulations, and then fell abruptly silent. After what had happened today, was it possible that she too . . . ? Then she dismissed the idea. She had not conceived since Daniel was born, five years ago, though until comparatively recently she and Rowland had been as passionately loving as ever. She had long ago concluded that something had happened to prevent her falling pregnant again, and was thankful for it. Six children were quite enough.

She made a few more observations about the weather and was glad when the tea was drunk and the pleasantries done with and she could go home to Rowland.

Eve watched her go from an upstairs window: Aunt Jenny, a small neat figure, warm and kindly. Not like *her* downstairs, the woman she had to call mother, though there was, as far as Eve was concerned, nothing of the mother about her. Eve had, after all, spent her earliest years at White Lea, at least until her father married, and often after that, when it suited those concerned. But where was her home? At White Lea, where they always made a show of welcoming her, or here, where no one ever seemed pleased with her, whatever she did? She knew where she would have preferred to live, if she could have made a choce. Yet even there, even at White Lea, she knew she did not really belong. They were a family, Aunt Jenny and Uncle Rowland and their children, the more obviously since Uncle Tommy left. She could never be a part of them, not as each one of them was a part of the whole.

She did not even have a name of her own, to mark her belonging. She was generally known as Eve Emerson, but she knew quite well that, as her parents had not been legally married, she should really have borne her mother's maiden name: Eve Todd, as her mother had been before her. Sometimes she wondered what it would be like if she were to assume that name, what Jacob Todd, severe in his respectability, would think of it. But she wanted to belong to Jacob Todd even less than she wanted to belong to anyone else.

That was the worst of it. She was not anyone's child, not really. Mothers loved their own children and put them first, whatever they did, whatever the circumstances. So Aunt Jenny put her own bairns first, and her stepmother hers. But Eve had no mother, and she was first to no one. At best, she was only a second thought, however loving a one. It was not the same.

At White Lea the children were back from work and school by the time Jenny reached home and Rowland looked more tired than ever, though he was cheerful enough. 'Sister Craggs called while you were out,' he said, while behind them Mary took command of the preparation of supper.

'What did she want?' It was clear from his tone that it was a matter of some importance.

'There's to be a camp meeting in August, when the hay's in, on Chapel Fell.'

Jenny hated it when anyone looked ahead, however short a way; and August was two months off, a vast distance in the present abbreviated time scale of their lives. In previous years Rowland had always been first among the organisers and preachers at the camp meetings in the dale, but it was obvious that all that would be beyond him now. Yet he sounded as happy at the prospect as usual, clearly looking forward to it. She was trying to think of the right thing to say, to show that she shared his pleasure without holding out any unrealistic hope that he would take part in the event, when he added, 'There'll be a love feast the next day, the Sunday.'

'Then I'll get some spices when I'm next in Chapel,' she said cheerfully, while her heart sank even more. She enjoyed the ordinary worship in Side Head chapel, for she loved the unrestrained singing and the lively preaching. But the other Ranter activities – camp meetings, love feasts, even the weekly class meetings – left her with an acute sense of inadequacy. There was something intensely competitive about them, as each man and woman eagerly sought to lay claim to the most sinful past, the most sudden and dramatic conversion, the greatest hardships faced for the sake of the faith. Rowland had no need to compete, for everyone agreed that he had been a terrible sinner in his youth and that the change in him had been exemplary. But Jenny had no spiritual drama to lay before her neighbours, not even a hint of a conversion experience. She made delicious spice cake for the customary tea and she was good at keeping the youngest children occupied with simple Bible stories, but in every other way she was out of her depth, a failure even.

Then all thought of her own deficiencies left her, because Rowland said, casually, almost as if it were an afterthought, which she knew it was not, 'I told Sister Craggs I was moved to preach at the meeting.'

Jenny stared at him, a frail and exhausted man slumped at the fireside. By August, at best he would be weaker still. Only a blind optimist could hold out any hope that in two months' time this man would be able to stand for hours on the open fell and preach to a great crowd. That he might do it at all was beyond belief; that he should do it effectively was utterly impossible.

But she knew that Rowland was convinced that he would be there, so she stopped herself from saying, 'You can't do that!' or even, 'We'll wait and see how you are first.' Instead, she kissed him and said, 'That's something good to plan for.'

Chapter Nine

After work, Tommy washed in the water Rebekah had heated for their return and put on clean clothes, and having eaten what he could of the meal – half burnt, half raw – set out to call on Mark Dent.

His plan was to suggest to the other young man that the two groups of Weardale Ranters – Mark's companions, living on the edge of Hetton village itself, and the smaller number at Brick Garth – should meet together for worship on Sundays, if that could safely be done. Since they were none of them able to worship in any of the chapels in the district, it seemed a sensible solution; not simply sensible, either, for Tommy and his few friends felt particularly solitary when they met together. Joined with the others to form a larger congregation, they might be able to recreate something of the warmth of a Weardale meeting for worship, with all its noisy, chaotic fervour.

But he was conscious that his reason for going to the village, though real enough, was more than a wish to see Mark Dent. If that excuse had not been to hand, he would have found another – any excuse he could think of

142

– to escape from the house. It had never been a comfortable place, but lately the atmosphere had grown increasingly miserable, for from the moment he and Luke stepped in the door Rebekah kept up a continual litany of complaint. Tommy sympathised with her. She was desperately lonely, missing friends and family, and she faced daily hostility from the woman next door and even more from the younger woman who called there sometimes. At least he and Luke had a fair number of friends and acquaintances within reach, and a sense of purpose in coming here. Rebekah had the house and children to care for, but no land to tend, as she had at home, and little in the way of chapel activities, though, unlike the Ranters, the Wesleyan Methodists had been welcomed readily enough at their local chapel; if there was sympathy for the union there, it was not officially sanctioned.

In a way, Tommy thought, Luke's wife had come between his cousin and himself as he had not thought anything ever could. It was only at work that they talked with anything like the intimacy of the old days (once at home, Luke was too busy trying to placate Rebekah), and even then Tommy found that he was still unable to make Luke understand his unease at the situation in which they found themselves. Luke's own unease was all for Rebekah; as far as the work went, that was simply a job to be done and a means of keeping his family fed, neither more nor less than that. On leaving Weardale, Tommy had consoled himself with the thought that he was at least bringing one of his closest friends with him. Now he began to feel that in coming here he had finally lost that friend. The move had changed them both and they had begun to grow apart.

Oddly, Luke seemed to be as blind to Tommy's sudden happiness as he had been, and still was, to his cousin's anxieties. But then, when he was not with Matty, Tommy had troubles enough to temper any excess of happiness. He did not care for the work any more than he had done at first. The descent into the shaft still terrified him –

more than ever since last week, when two men had fallen to their deaths from the chain while their own shift was descending; every time he came near the shaft now he seemed to hear again their despairing cries as they fell. Recently, there had been an explosion not far from where he and Luke were working, followed by a brief but terrifying fire. Nothing very much, they had been assured by Samuel Raines, with just a hint of malice (he must have seen their apprehension), but a man had died. All because some fool had lit a candle in the wrong place. In fact, accidents, large and small, seemed to be a daily occurrence – a child kicked and severely injured by a horse he was driving; a man crippled by a roof fall, because the deputy had failed to check that sufficient timbers had been used for propping; a fire in the hay stored underground for the ponies, which mercifully had resulted in no more than a few minor burns for the horse-keeper . . . Then, though Tommy's skills as a hewer were improving, he missed the sense of control he had in the lead mines, the confidence that he knew exactly what he was doing and why, that he had all the skills required of him to do the work.

But then, thinking about it as he walked down the steep hill from Brick Garth, that was true of other aspects of the work, and for the most part it had little to do with his lack of skill. Even in the shaft . . . In the lead mines, the men descended, when necessary, by means of rungs, a laborious process in which every step was, consciously or unconsciously, a deliberate move, carefully made; not like the shaft here, where all they could do was cling tightly to the chain and allow themselves to be dropped into the earth. A collier's life was all like that, he thought. In some ways the work might be easier – the coal was extraordinarily light to shovel into the corves, once cut, at least for men used to the great weight of lead ore; and the good ventilation made it possible to breathe easily even in the deepest parts of the mine, so that they were at last free of the nausea and headaches and lassitude which they had thought were inseparable from mining; and no hewer had to do more than cut the coal and fill the corves – after that, others saw to the business of getting the coal to bank (he must learn not to say *out to the day*). But lead miners at least had the illusion of control over their working lives, for they had to use their skill to bargain for the place in which to work, choosing it according to their estimation of its geological potential, arguing for a fair price on the basis of their own estimation of the costs of raising that particular stretch of lead. It might sometimes be an illusory control, in that the masters always had the final word, but the colliers had no say at all. Traditionally, Tommy had discovered, the hewers simply drew lots for the sections of the pit where they were to work each quarter, leaving even that to chance . . . He began to see that it was only by banding together to fight their case with the strength unity gave them that they could take control of their lives.

He had come back again to the inevitable obsessions; as how could he not, when with every step he was watchful, not for angry colliers (the dispossessed men and women no longer gathered daily on the hills to watch them pass), but for Matty. He did not really think she would walk openly along this main highway that linked the colliery settlements, but wherever he went that possibility lurked in his mind, as a constant anxiety. They had been meeting every few days for four weeks now, and he had still not told her the truth. It was becoming progressively more difficult to evade her questions and so far he had succeeded only by giving her occasional little scraps of unrevealing information – references to Jenny and Rowland, for example, without saying much more than who they were and what he felt for them – and by refraining from putting her right when she drew mistaken conclusions from what he said or did not say. 'You'll be posted here for a fair few weeks,' she had said at their second meeting, commenting on the fact that he was not, apparently, about to move on elsewhere. 'Eliza was sent to Yorkshire for a long time, when she was preaching.' At which he had simply asked a question about Eliza, which she had been happy enough to answer at some length, apparently taking his lack of any other response to her remark as acquiescence with its chief assumption. That was one thing that made it easier for him to keep things from her: she talked very readily, and all he had to do was listen, with an occasional sympathetic or interested interjection. She talked artlessly, with a confiding trust that he loved, about her hopes and dreams, about little things in her daily life, her feelings for her family, about the pitman who fancied her but had no hope of success (it hurt Tommy to think of him), about all kinds of things, just as they came into her head, an inconsequential jumble of anecdotes and aspirations and hates and loves and fears, with all the freshness of an unspoiled observing mind.

But then he loved everything about her. During the four weeks since their first meeting he had lived for their trysts beneath the tree. Memories of the previous meetings, anticipation of the next, filled him with a glow of happiness beyond anything he had ever experienced before. They were never together for very long, but there would be time enough for them to walk a little way or sit under the trees, while they talked and laughed and said tender loving things to one another and, of course, always, before they parted, he would put his arms about her and kiss her. It was then that her warmth and impulsiveness would frighten him a little, because he was conscious that she had no wish – perhaps saw no need – to control what happened next, and if he too had allowed things to take their course . . . It was not that he did not want to. Indeed, it was becoming increasingly hard for him to keep a check on his own feelings, as he knew he must, for both their sakes.

Yet, oddly enough, he no longer suffered pangs of conscience because of those feelings. They were so overwhelming, yet so much greater than simple physical arousal, that he recognised them for what they were and was glad: love was after all more than passion and desire and need, more than affection and friendship, more even than the sum of all those parts. It was the one simple yet overwhelming fact that had transformed his life as – thank God for it! – it had hers. Sometimes he had to stop in his tracks and close his eyes and breathe his gratitude to God for what He had so generously given: the amazing gift of Matty's love. He was aware, with great humility, that he was given not only this love, but the opportunity, through it, to win Matty for his faith. Already, gently prompted by him, she had ceased to wear earrings, and beads about her neck, and had begun to dress more soberly. He rejoiced in the little signs that God's grace was already at work in her, because vanity was of the devil, and he had never been able to endure the prospect that anyone he loved – or indeed anyone at all – might be condemned after death to torments too horrible to imagine.

Only one thing spoiled his happiness: his knowledge of its fragility, based as it was on what he had to recognise as deception. He could only hope and trust that by the time she learned the truth (as she must, sooner or later) their love for one another would be so deep that it would be proof against any disclosure, however dismaying.

It could only be strengthened by what he was to give her today. It was no conventional gift from a young man to his sweetheart, but it was one he was well qualified to give, which would mean more to her than anything else he could think of. At their last meeting she had said to him suddenly, 'If you're staying a bit, you can teach us to read.' Though it had been nearly dark, he had seen how her eyes shone at the thought and felt the eagerness that held her poised beside him, holding her breath for his answer.

He had resisted his first impulse to agree warmly, delighted that he had it in his power to give her what she wanted so much. He had learned now to hesitate, always, and consider the implications of anything she asked, before answering her, for fear of disaster. 'I should like that,' he had said, very carefully. 'Mind, you said your father would not approve.'

'I can come to your lodgings. He'll never know.'

He had felt cold at the very thought that she might find out where he lodged. He had looked down at his hands so that he should not see the longing in her eyes, while he considered the matter. He had said slowly, 'It's too noisy there. Too many people.' That at least was true. And then he had seen what to do and, happy to give way to his most loving instincts, he had raised his eyes to her face. 'Mind, I could teach you here. I reckon the weather will hold a bit yet and the days are long. We can be quiet here, and we'll know the moment anyone comes. I can bring all the things we need.'

She had flung her arms about him and pressed kisses at random all over his face, and delighted little cries had burst from her; and they had agreed that at their next meeting – today – the lessons would begin. He would go on to the wood from Mark's house, and his pockets were heavy with the materials he had brought with him, his Bible and paper and a pencil, and a slate such as children used at school.

Matty had not said anything to Eliza about Tommy. The day they had met she might have done, in the first flush of her joy, but Eliza's terrible news had prevented that, and since then she had felt she could not flaunt her own happiness in the face of her friend. When Adam was free, then she would, she told herself, though every time the thought came to her she felt a little tremor of fear that Adam might never be free, that he might . . . No, that was too dreadful to contemplate, under any circumstances.

Six men had been taken into custody for their supposed parts in the murder of John Errington, though later one of them had been released. John Turnbull was among those in Durham Gaol awaiting trial. Matty remembered him coming drunk to the fire to say he had found Errington's body; she knew from things her father said that he was quarrelsome when drunk, which happened often; she remembered Adam saying he had been seen with a gun.

But then so had Adam . . . Yet she knew, as they all did, how strongly Adam had always spoken against violence. It was impossible to imagine him setting out deliberately to shoot another man, even one he hated as much as John Errington.

'If they knew Adam, they'd know he couldn't have done it, not ever!' Eliza had cried again and again, as if she had somehow to convince Matty too of Adam's innocence. As she need not, of course – except that, uneasily, Matty remembered that voice speaking into the night after Errington's death. *Whoever did it was the instrument of the Lord.*

It had sounded very like Adam; and only a Ranter would use those words. Yet would a man who had done the deed himself make such a claim? She thought not. She wished now that she had challenged Adam with it afterwards. If he had approved the deed, as the words implied, that was a long way from his frequent pleas for peace and order, though it was not of course a proof of guilt. But she was afraid that in a court it would go against him and she hoped that she had been the only one to hear the words. Fortunately, none of those in authority, investigating the case afterwards, had thought to ask her what she had seen or heard.

One day she repeated the words to Eliza, implying that the speaker had been some other Ranter. Eliza said, 'The Lord makes use of many unworthy instruments. He can turn evil to good.' Where that left Adam, Matty was not sure. But she had no doubt at all that Eliza believed with utter conviction in his innocence.

But she knew Eliza was afraid, horribly afraid. She had lost weight and her eyes were red-rimmed and sunken with sleeplessness. Matty and others of her friends urged her to go and stay with her mother and the children, rather than remain in the rough tent she had shared with Adam, which must seem so empty now. But she would not go. Her place, she asserted, was here, because it was what Adam would have wanted; besides, she still refused to seek shelter in the house where her brother lived. By agreement with the local Ranters, she took over her husband's preaching appointments and that seemed to give her a consoling purpose. But it would be nearly two months before the case came to court, and Matty could only guess at the fear that haunted her.

The news that Jack Marley brought back to the camp one day did not help matters. It was a hot day, even here where the full force of the heat was softened by the June foliage overhead, still with some of its young freshness about it. The air was full of the heavy scent of the hawthorns, their blossom lighting the wood about the camp, where the women, Matty and Eliza among them, gathered on the banks of the burn, engaged in various domestic tasks, washing clothes, mending, preparing vegetables, knitting. Jack came strolling over, pausing to take a piece of apple (rather dry and shrivelled after long storage) from those his mother was peeling. 'They've got a magistrate now,' he said casually.

Eliza looked at him. 'What are you saying?'

'In Jarrow. Fairless, they call him. Attacked as he rode home. He's not expected to live.'

'They' must be the colliers, and 'got' clearly meant beaten up, or some such thing. Eliza shivered. 'Do they know it was a pitman did it?'

'They've arrested someone. A union man, name of Jobling. There's one thing, they'll do their best to find him guilty. If he is, there'll be no mercy for him. And if Fairless dies, as they think – well . . . ' He made a rough gesture to indicate a noose tightening about his throat.

Eliza said nothing then, though she did not need Jack Marley to tell her what fate a convicted murderer was likely to meet, whatever the standing of the man he killed. Later she and Matty walked into Hetton to buy a few necessities with the small sum of money the younger girl had earned the previous week, weeding for a local farmer. As they reached the first houses of the old village, Eliza said suddenly, 'Matty, if they've just arrested that man, they'll bring him up before the next assizes.'

'With Adam and the rest?'

'Aye.' They looked at one another. Matty's father was fond of praising English justice, and often tried to console Eliza with his belief in its impartiality. But an assault on a magistrate was a grave matter and must change everything. Whether he lived or died, no one before these assizes could expect mercy. There would be one sentence only for men found guilty of assault or murder, and jurymen only too ready, in the angry mood of the times, to convict even where doubts remained; the more especially if the accused were union men or, worse, their leaders.

Matty slipped her arm through Eliza's. 'Adam's innocent. They can't find him guilty. It wouldn't be justice.'

'When have pitmen ever had justice?'

'My brother got off. And he *was* guilty.'

'That was different. That was months ago. And it wasn't murder.' Matty felt a tug at her arm and, looking round, saw that Eliza had come to a halt. There was a look on her face that her friend had never seen there before, a kind of intense white hatred. She was looking at something or someone at the end of the lane that led down the hill to their right, and Matty followed her gaze; and then froze where she stood.

The man walking briskly round the corner below was Tommy, without any doubt at all. She would know that easy yet upright walk anywhere, and the square set of his shoulders, and the thick light hair falling to his collar beneath the brim of his hat. She felt her colour rise. Then he disappeared from sight, and she heard Eliza let out her breath in a great sigh. She was shaking.

'I never thought I would hate like this!' she burst out. 'I could kill them with my bare hands.' She turned and held on to Matty, as if she needed help in controlling her murderous impulses.

But Matty, through her bewilderment, was aware of the beginnings of a horrible unease. 'Who? What do you mean?'

'Blacklegs. Like that man – Emerson, they call him. He's got Jack Marley's house, him and a whole pack of Emersons. I've seen him when I've been at my mam's. He came to chapel that first week – as if his kind had any place but in hell! If it wasn't for them — ' She broke off, suddenly aware of some change in her friend. 'Matty, what is it?'

It was shock, a shock so complete and so intense that she could not for the moment move or speak or think or feel. She simply stood there, open-mouthed, cold, her breath held. Eliza gave her a little shake. 'Matty!'

Slowly, Matty got Eliza's face into focus again. It looked full of concern, but Matty was not interested in sympathy. The blood was beginning to flow again, her breathing resumed, unevenly, too quick. She was shaking even more than Eliza had, just now.

A blackleg. Tommy. Her Tommy. The man she loved. And he had kept it from her.

Perhaps he had not done it deliberately. Perhaps he had not known who she was, or that she would mind.

Of course he knew. How could he not know? They had talked of the strike, she had even told him where she had once lived. And he had not said, *Why, that's where I lodge.* Of course he had not, because he did not want her to find out.

He had not lied, not in so many words, or not that she could remember. But that made no difference. He might as well have done: the effect was the same. He had deceived her.

There was only one reason why he had kept the truth from her. He loved her so much, and he knew that if she ever guessed the truth he would lose her.

And because of that she had been lured into going with a blackleg, kissing him and putting her arms about him. She had filled her thoughts with him, every waking moment, and when she slept too; he had stolen her heart. He had led her into a most terrible betrayal, one that in anyone else she would have found beyond forgiveness. As it was in her too, but it was not herself she would not forgive.

Feeling was flooding back and it was agony. She knew that in a moment she would scream with it. She tore herself from Eliza and ran back the way they had come. On and on she ran, far into the wood where she knew she would not be heard or seen, down the slope and along the narrow path until she came to a place where dense undergrowth barred her way and screened the burn. She forced her way to the water's edge and there she tore off all her clothes and flung them into the water and jumped in with them, splashing herself all over, pummelling the clothes as if they were soiled, rubbing her skin, scouring every last trace of his touch from all that was hers. And as she did so she shouted, 'You black lying bastard! I hate you, I hate you!' And then she sobbed and sobbed, shouting her hatred out through her tears until she was hoarse and her body red and shivering from the icy water. And at last she pulled on her clothes again, wet as they were, and went back to the camp to dry herself and put on the brightest and most showy outfit she possessed.

Mark Dent was surprised to see Tommy at his door, and alarmed too. He ushered him quickly inside and pushed the bolts firmly shut again behind him. 'You should take more care,' he said. 'It's not wise, coming all this way alone.'

Tommy smiled faintly, unconcerned. 'I've taken no harm so far. If it's dark I go by the back roads and keep an eye open. In daylight no one's going to set on me.'

'I wouldn't be too sure. The soldiers can't be everywhere, and the constables are useless. Two Welshmen were beaten up last week, coming back from a public house.'

'Maybe they quarrelled with someone.'

'Maybe,' said Mark sceptically.

But when Tommy told him the reason for his visit he agreed with the suggestion happily enough and then made tea for them both – he shared the house with two other men, so there was no woman to wait on them. There was a moment's silence as they sipped at the tea, Tommy contented at the success of his visit and even more at the thought of the meeting that would follow in an hour or two, not far from here, under the tree on the fringe of the wood.

Mark sat bent forward on his stool, the cup cradled in his hands, looking into it with great intentness, as if he were some gipsy fortune-teller seeking inspiration. At last he said slowly, 'You know, Tommy, I don't much like what we're doing here.'

Tommy, not grasping at once what he was talking about, stared at him. 'Such as what?'

Mark raised his head and looked across at Tommy. 'I came here in good faith, like you did, I don't doubt. We were told the pits needed more men, and the strike hadn't much support. We were led by the nose. Used.' He gave a faint wry smile. 'Mind, I seem to be the only one to see it like that.'

'No,' said Tommy. 'No, you're not the only one.' He felt warmed and cheered by a sense of relief and of affection for this man who was putting into words the things he had been unable to make anyone else understand. 'I know just what you mean.'

'I tried to see Tommy Hepburn when he was here the other week – you know, the colliers' leader. They've made songs about him.'

'I heard.'

'Aye, well, he hadn't time to see me, so they said. One of the Hetton delegates, a man they call Parkinson, he said they wished no ill to any man, but they'd have nowt to do with blacklegs. I told him I wanted to hear the union men's side of the story, but all he said was to go back where I came from and let the colliers run their own affairs. Still, there we are. Maybe I can see their side well enough without any help from him.' He gave a rueful half smile. 'I'd even thought I might join the union, if their arguments convinced me.'

'You'd have been thrown out of work for it.'

'Why aye. But it seems it's not a sacrifice I'll have to

make, for they won't let strangers in. You have to be Durham born and brought up a pitman to join, so I only qualify for the half of it.'

'What will you do then? Go home?'

Mark shook his head. 'There's nowt left for any of us in Weardale. We all know that. And I like the work here well enough, if it wasn't for the rest of it. It's well paid too. Better that than going overseas. No, I shall see it through now, because I can't see I've any choice. But one thing's sure. No one's ever going to use me like this again. Never.'

'Mind you, when all's said and done, a man was murdered. And every one of us goes in fear of being set upon. Or so we should, if we were wise,' Tommy added with a smile. 'When I think of that, I think maybe we're in the right after all.'

'It's only a few men use those means, and the leaders are dead set against it. But you know yourself how men can be driven to violence, when everything's against them. Why aye, there've been bad things done on the colliers' side, but look at the other side of it. The owners are using troops and starvation to force the men to give up what by law they have a good right to do. There's no getting away from that. Or from the fact that we're in the middle of it, fools that we are.'

'I'm sure.' Tommy did not add, as he might have done, that there had been less excuse for him than for the rest, because he had been warned very clearly, by Rowland, precisely what he was doing . . Yet had he not been shown that he must do it? Could he have been mistaken about that clear sign?

He stayed talking until a glance at his watch warned him that he risked being late for his assignation with Matty. He took his leave then, in a more grave and thoughtful mood than before. But after only a few steps of the way to the wood the happiness returned to him.

Matty was waiting for him, but this time she had not come alone. 'There's a blackleg been pestering me,' she had said casually, that afternoon, to her brother and Jack Marley. 'He's the one that's got your house. So I said I'd meet him the night.' Her face had been very grim and cold and hard, her voice tight and clipped. They had grinned and exchanged glances, and she knew they would do what she wanted. They halted a few yards behind her, out of sight, while she stood very still beneath the creamy hawthorn, watching for him.

He saw her and came to a halt, colouring as he always did, even after all this time. From guilt, perhaps, she thought now. She did not smile or move, but he did not seem to have noticed any change, though last time she had run to hold him.

He put up his hand to his hat, removed it, smiled his tender, shy smile. Any moment some loving phrase would come from that smiling, treacherous mouth.

She spat full in his face.

She saw the smile freeze and vanish. She saw the utter disbelieving astonishment that replaced it.

'Blackleg! May you rot in hell! May the pit bury you alive, you and every stranger that's taken the bread from our mouths!'

And then she turned and ran from him, back into the trees. A moment later she heard the shouts and the blows. She halted, fighting an urge to go back and cry to them to stop. Then she remembered what he had done and how much she hated him and she walked on, sobbing. He deserved the very worst they could do to him.

It took Tommy a long time to get home, when the two men had finished with him. He was not even sure if he would have got home at all, had not he stumbled on the wagonway just as the colliery locomotive was puffing towards him with its train of coal wagons, rattling on their way to the coast. Two soldiers came to his rescue, just in time, and helped him on the last part of the journey. They questioned him as to what had happened and tried to get him to go and lay a charge against his attackers, but he said he had not seen them at all and had no idea who they were; which was true, as far as it went.

Rebekah, opening the door to him, did not recognise him at first. Then she gave a cry of dismay and called Luke. They got him to bed and sent for the surgeon.

It was some days before he was fit to go to work again, but though the broken ribs and the bruises healed quickly enough, the deepest wound lay untouched, beyond the reach of any surgeon's skill.

As for Matty, she heard the young men's account of what they had done to Tommy with a fixed expression, showing no emotion, not even perhaps the satisfaction they expected; but then they were too pleased with themselves to need her approval.

Later, when they had gone to toast their success in a public house, she crawled into bed and cried herself to sleep. Yet even in sleep there was no escape, for she dreamed she was in Tommy's arms and they loved each other and she was happy; and then she woke again, and remembered.

Chapter Ten

At haytime – usually towards the end of July – every school in Weardale closed so as to free men and children alike to help with the mowing. This year there were fewer men working, fewer children in the dale, fewer families left with hay to mow, and the crop was ready about a week earlier than usual, but in every other respect it was the same as always.

At White Lea the only adult fit to get in the hay was Jenny. The apparent remission in Rowland's illness had come to an end just before haytime with a particularly severe spell of fever and coughing and breathlessness that had forced him to spend some days in bed. He recovered enough to get up again, but though each morning he would seem a little better, a few hours later he would be struck down once more with shuddering bouts of fever. He ate next to nothing and Jenny thought she could almost see the flesh falling away from a body already too thin. That he should help with the mowing was out of the question.

Unfortunately, Joe had considerable hay meadows at Well House and no time to spare to give them a hand, and the same could be said of many of their neighbours.

Once, those with little or no land of their own would have turned out to help at haytime, but the landless families had been the first to leave the dale when hard times came, and the burden of getting in the crop now fell on far fewer people. Those who could do so promised to give a morning or afternoon at White Lea, once their own hay was in, but Jenny was unwilling to put off the mowing until she had help, knowing how quickly the weather could change.

She had everything to do, though the children exerted themselves uncomplainingly, taking on as many as possible of the routine household tasks while their mother swung the scythe through the two White Lea hay meadows, which seemed to have grown to vast proportions. The first morning, Rowland ignored her protests and took the other scythe and tried to help, but he scarcely had strength to lift it and the least exertion set him coughing again. He went back into the house in a black and bitter mood, so withdrawn that for the rest of the day neither Jenny nor the children could get anything but the briefest angry retort from him. Jenny was in any case too weary to make the effort needed to try and console him. She felt resentful and angry herself that he should be so difficult, just when she most needed his loving support. Very little indeed would have made her lose her temper and perhaps say something unforgivable, so she spoke to him as little as possible. She knew she was being unfair, but she was too tired and miserable for fairness.

That night as they knelt to pray, he said at the end, 'Dear Lord, forgive my anger,' and she added, 'and mine too,' and then he kissed her and told her he was sorry. They got into bed and lay in silence, holding one another, trying to find again the closeness they had lost through the day. Jenny had known there would be hard times ahead, but she had not thought that anything could ever seriously drive them apart. Now she felt afraid. She knew she could not endure it if, as Rowland's life slipped away, she were to find herself cut off from his love too.

Next morning they rose from a bed drenched with his sweat and while she hung the bedding out to dry (there was no time to wash it today) and the children prepared the breakfast, Rowland sat on the bench outside the door and stared out over the misty whiteness of the dale.

Jenny could see that yesterday's black mood was still on him, to some degree at least. But she was not yet too weary to try and reach through it, in the hope that today might be better. She went to him and was about to speak when she saw that his hands were clasped and his eyes closed, as if in prayer; though if it was prayer, then it was of no cheerful kind, for his face was drawn, his expression anguished. She turned to go, but his voice caught her. 'Jenny!' She sat down beside him and he took her hand, saying nothing.

'Is it bad today?'

'No worse than usual.' Then, after a silence of some length, he said, 'I find it hard – to be so useless.'

'I know,' she said, stroking his hand.

'If I thought it would end soon . . . '

She felt as if a knife had twisted in her heart, but she only said with apparent cheerfulness, 'It's good just to have you near, even if you're doing nowt.'

He shook his head at that, as if he did not believe it. When he spoke again his voice was hoarse and ragged. 'I don't want . . . I wish . . . It's hard . . . ' And then in a great angry outburst, 'Why did this have to happen?' He broke off, his head bent, and she felt how he shuddered.

'Love—' She broke off, helpless. If he with his certainties shrank in the face of suffering, what was there that she could say?

'It's not,' he went on after a moment, 'that I fear death. When it comes, I shall be ready, glad. But there is so much I wanted . . . And the dying, what lies ahead . . . '

He broke off then, and his gaze sharpened. 'Someone's coming,' he said. Jenny saw a figure emerging gradually from the mist, a large fair man walking with a slow yet purposeful step up the track towards them, and did not

160

know whether to be glad or sorry that he had chosen this moment to arrive.

When he came near enough for recognition, Rowland said in surprise, 'Nathan!' There was a genuine warmth and pleasure in his voice.

Nathan Elliott had been Rowland's partner for many years at Guinea Grove, where he had mined for most of his working life. He was also one of Rowland's converts, and had occasionally paid them a visit, but since he lived at Lanehead, some way further up the dale, they did not see him a great deal and Jenny knew him only slightly.

'I thought maybe you could do with a hand,' he said quietly. A slow smile spread over his face, transforming its square, rather severe features. 'Not having any hay of my own to mow . . . '

Jenny could have hugged him, but she contented herself with the warmest thanks she could muster. 'Take some breakfast with us first, then the dew will be off the grass.' They went inside, and she sensed that Rowland's dark mood, like the mist, was already dispersing.

It made a great difference, having Nathan to help with the mowing. 'You're worth three of me,' Jenny told him with a laugh when they paused for the food and drink brought out to them by Rowland half-way through the morning. 'A dozen of me,' Rowland added.

Jenny liked Nathan. He was a man of few words, but gentle and courteous, and it was clear that he and Rowland had long been the closest of friends. During the breaks in the work the two men sat together and she could see how their talk, slow and quiet though it was, cheered Rowland and drove back the last of his bitterness.

While they sat in the shade of the trees at the afternoon break, they had another caller. The children, untroubled by the heat, were chasing each other noisily over the cut hay, when Mary suddenly stood still and shouted to the others. The adults looked where she pointed. 'Oh dear,' said Jenny with a sigh. 'Eve.' She rose to her feet and went to greet the child.

Nathan glanced at Rowland, who explained, 'Our niece. She's a troubled bairn.'

'Aye well, she's come to the right place then.' They watched as Jenny met her and then walked back up to the house with her, listening attentively to her agitated talk. The other children, at a gesture from their mother, had resumed their game.

The two men were silent for a time, until Rowland said, 'Do you know what I miss most, now I've left off work?' Nathan looked at him questioningly and he went on. 'Coming up to the day, at home time. The colours.'

'Aye,' said Nathan. 'Even that . . . ' He gestured towards the lovely green valley spread before them and then broke off, as if he had no need to explain any further; as he had not, for Rowland knew what he implied. They both knew how intense the colours seemed on coming out of the mine, how sweet the air, how dazzlingly beautiful the landscape, a beauty unequalled by any seen with more accustomed eyes.

Then Rowland said, in the tone of someone who has just made a discovery, 'That's what I'm seeking!' Seeing his companion's puzzled look, he added, 'For the camp meeting.'

'You preaching there then?' asked Nathan in astonishment.

'Why not?'

Nathan did not answer, but once again he was understood, though Rowland made no comment either and simply went on to talk of something else until Jenny came out again to resume the mowing.

Eve had been close to tears when Jenny met her on the track. 'They hate me, Aunt Jenny, I know they do!'

'You know that's not true, my pet. Your father loves you very much.'

'He loves her more, and her bairns. I'm just in the way. I can see it.'

When she had left school for good – a change that at

the time had pleased her greatly – Eve had known that a condition of her leaving was that she should help her stepmother about the house. It was an arrangement that had very quickly turned sour. The two had found it hard enough to agree when they were together only outside school hours, but when every minute of the day was spent under the same roof it became impossible. Jenny had only heard Eve's side of it, since she had not seen Joe or his wife lately. Eve, on the other hand, had escaped several times during the past weeks to the refuge of White Lea. Until now Jenny had always, as gently as possible, induced her to go back home again, urging her to greater courage and patience. Jenny had not wanted her at White Lea during those precious days when she and Rowland were alone there together. But now that the children were on holiday from school and the house was busy all day Eve's presence would no longer be such an intrusion and, besides, it was clear that her unhappiness had increased.

So the girl stayed and joined the rest of them in the fields. She was willing enough at first, but her interest in any task quickly faded and she would wander away or (worse) hang around the others, hindering them, until scolded for her behaviour, gently enough, by Jenny or Rowland. Fortunately she never seemed to resent correction by either of them, as she did that by her father or stepmother.

As it happened, it was one of their own children who gave Jenny most trouble that day. It was growing late, the sun already set, and the younger children had gone to bed. Mary and Eve and Em lingered outside on the bench, talking together in soft voices. Jenny could hear them as she made up the fire – even on these hot days there was need of a fire – and tidied the kitchen, scattered with the debris of the day. On the settle, the men sat quietly, resting in the evening tranquillity.

It was broken suddenly by shouting from outside – Em's voice, Jenny thought – and running feet. She looked out and saw only the two girls, standing by the bench, their expressions unreadable in the dusk. She went

163

to the door. 'Where's Em?' There was no sign of him now.

'In the byre,' said Mary. She sounded a little embarrassed.

'Did you fall out?'

There was a silence. Jenny decided it would be easier simply to find Em, so she made her way to the byre. She could hear him sobbing somewhere in the dark at the far end of the building. She followed the sound to the stall where, in winter, the galloway was housed, and halted there. 'Em!'

The next moment he had thrown himself at her, weeping uncontrollably. She held him close, stroking his hair and trying to make out the disjointed words of accusation that burst out between sobs, 'The Bible says . . . ! The Bible cannot lie . . . ! He's got to get well . . . !'

There was a stool somewhere around, she remembered, so she groped for it and sat down, holding her son's thin body in her arms. 'Was it something Eve said? Or Mary?' she asked when he had quietened a little. She could feel him nod vigorously.

'You said the Bible was right . . . about threescore years and ten . . . '

She had almost forgotten the incident. Certainly, if asked, she would have said that by now Emerson no longer clung to its delusive consolation; that he had realised the truth long ago. But she had never actually talked to him about it; as she should have done, she thought now, with remorse.

'*I* didn't say it, Em,' she reminded him gently. 'You said it. Maybe I should have put you right. You know the psalms are just fine songs. Songs aren't always true in every word. Sometimes they tell about what should be, not what is. You see, I think God means that His children should all live until they are old, but this is a fallen world and very many things don't happen as God would like them to, because of sin . . . '

'Father's not sinful!'

'We're all sinful, even Father sometimes. But I didn't

164

mean his sin. It's the greed of men, wanting riches from getting the lead, wanting to have more than other people, more than their share. That's what's made him ill.'

And it was that Rowland had always thought he could change. She remembered how in the early days he had tried to inspire others to join with him in fighting the injustices of the miners' lives, recognising that he could not do it alone. But his neighbours had heard only a spiritual message, failing to see what to him was obvious, that the Gospel reached into every part of life. Now, facing death, he must realise it was too late, for him at least. And meanwhile, the colliers of the Tyne and Wear had united as the lead miners had never done; yet Tommy, Rowland's friend and brother, was allowing himself to be used as a tool for the destruction of what they had achieved. It was no wonder Rowland was bitter about it.

In the silence Jenny heard an owl hoot from somewhere in the trees outside, and a mouse rustle through the straw near her feet. Em said, mournfully, as if he knew it was a vain hope, 'I wish Father would get well.'

'So do I, Em, but I know it can't be, not in this life. We have to be brave and help each other . . . And pray,' she added, not because prayer had, as yet, helped her very much, but because that was what Rowland would have said.

Later, she told Rowland what had happened, and the next day he found a moment to talk quietly to his son. She was glad of it, because Em seemed calmer afterwards, if unusually subdued; and because, if there had ever been a time for pretence, it had long been over.

Nathan stayed at White Lea until the hay was all safely dried and stacked in the byre, which up to then had been his bedroom. Then he took his leave as quietly and unobtrusively as he had come and went back to the house where he lived with his aged mother, and his new work at Burtree Pasture, which was shared with a partner who would never be to him what Rowland was.

A few days after the hay was safely in, Jenny made her weekly trip to St John's Chapel to collect what was due to them from the poor rate. It was little enough, and it had already dwindled a good deal by the time she left the village, for she owed money at one or two of the shops there. Once, she had been able to run up debts without anxiety, as all lead-mining families did, knowing that at the annual pay she would be able to settle them. Now she dared not risk owing more than the very smallest sum. So there would be no new shoes yet for the children, though Em's clogs were far too small and Mary not yet grown enough to pass hers on to him. They had gone back to school for the time being, but she knew that very soon that would have to stop too. Isaac Graham charged very little for his lessons, but he could not be expected to teach the children for nothing. She thought fleetingly of Tommy's earnings, but pushed the thought aside. While Rowland lived she would accept nothing from her brother, unless the only alternative was starvation. A brief letter from Hetton had told them little, except that he was well. She wondered if his views on the rights and wrongs of what he had done had changed at all.

As she approached the place where their track met the road, she saw someone coming towards her from the direction of Middlehope burn, and a moment later realised it was Joe. She smiled delightedly. 'Are you coming to White Lea? It's so long since we've seen you.'

Joe gave her a quick hug. 'Aye, I thought I'd look in. How's Rowland?'

Her smile faltered. 'Rather worse I think.'

'Poor Jenny.' His arm tightened about her shoulder. 'Has Eve been with you these past days?'

'Do you mean to say you didn't know where she was?'

'Oh, I wasn't worried. If she's not at home she's always over here.'

'One day you may be wrong . . . Joe, that's something I must talk to you about.'

He halted, frowning a little. 'Not again, Jenny.'

'She's very unhappy at home, you know.'

He shrugged impatiently. 'She's no need to be. She wanted to leave school. If she doesn't like it now she's got her way, that's too bad. She should be more biddable. You can't imagine how difficult she is sometimes. Or maybe you can. You see plenty of her.'

'She needs to be sure she's loved, that's all.'

'She'd be easier to love if she'd act a bit more lovingly.'

'Oh, I know it's not easy, Joe. Not for you; still less for Phoebe, with her own bairns to care for. But you loved Eve's mother so much. For her sake—'

'Aye, I know, but then she was— Why, Eve may look like her, but she seems to have nowt else of her mother in her, barring the name.'

'I think she has. It's only that you don't let her show it. Remember how unhappy your Eve was at home.'

'She'd good cause to be. Jacob Todd used to beat her. I've never laid a finger on Eve, not once. Not that I've not been sorely tempted, mind. Sometimes I think I can't do owt right for any of them. Give Eve a bit more love, and Phoebe says I'm neglecting her bairns. Give *them* more love, and Eve goes off in a huff. And Phoebe has to check her, you know. She can't be let get away with it. But then she takes it badly. What can I do?' When Jenny did not immediately reply, he asked suddenly, 'You don't mind her coming to White Lea, do you? Sometimes I think it's for the best all round. She must be a good help to you, when you've so much to do.'

That from him, when one of his most frequent complaints was of her laziness! But Jenny only said wearily, 'No, I don't mind.' But she did mind, very much, especially now that her own children were back at school and work and Eve was a constant demanding presence about the house; when she ached to be left alone with Rowland. On the other hand, Rowland himself had said more than once, 'If she needs us, then we can't turn our backs.'

They walked slowly on towards the house. 'You'll be giving the camp meeting a miss then,' Joe said after a moment.

'What makes you say that?'

'Why, Rowland won't be fit to preach this time. Not that I ever saw what good he thought it did.'

She ignored that last remark. Fond though Joe was of Rowland, he had never had much sympathy for his religious views; perhaps in some ways he still regretted the loss of the wild youth who had been his boyhood friend. All she said was, 'He means to go. It does him no harm to think he'll be there. But no, I don't think he will.'

'If you do go, send Eve home first.' When she looked surprised, he explained, 'I don't want her out there on the fell getting up to God knows what.'

Jenny stared at him in astonishment. 'What do you think could happen to her?'

'All I know is the fell at night with all the riff-raff for miles around is no place for a young lass. What you let your bairns do is up to you and Rowland. But Eve's staying safe at home with us.'

Jenny could not remember ever having seen this side of her brother before. That many respectable people were offended by camp meetings and doubted their morality was something she was well used to. But Joe, whom no one had ever called respectable – that he should disapprove was astonishing. For a moment she even laughed at him. But it was clear he meant what he said, and in the end she agreed soberly enough. She did not in any case think it at all likely that the question would arise.

Joe stayed for some time, adding his jovial noisy presence to the family meals, teasing his daughter in a gently affectionate manner that seemed to please her, at least once she was reassured that he had not come to fetch her home, and then sitting downstairs with Rowland while Jenny supervised the children's bedtime. Fortunately, Eve was accepted by her cousins as one of the family, fought with and loved in equal measure.

When Jenny came downstairs again Joe was clearly ready to leave. She went with him to the door, and they stood just outside in the soft twilight. She saw that her brother's expression had become very grim.

'Do you know what someone said to me the other day, talking of Rowland? – ''Whom the Lord loveth He chasteneth.'' All I can say is, I wouldn't use anyone I loved like that.' He sounded enraged.

She said nothing and after a moment he asked softly, 'How can you bear it, Jenny?'

'What else can I do? Besides, we always knew it was likely. He was a miner, like Father and Uncle Ralph and all those others.'

'The price of lead!' said Joe bitterly. 'If it was a thousand pounds a ton it would be too cheap.'

'Aye, well, there it is.' They said goodnight and she went back into the house and closed the door.

She had mending to do still, but Rowland was very tired so they knelt down together and then he went to bed, asking her to read to him as she often did when he was too exhausted to do it for himself. She took his Bible from where he had left it on the settle.

'Read Proverbs thirty-one.' He closed his eyes. 'From verse ten.'

She found the place and began to read, without at first noticing what passage it was.

'*Who can find a virtuous woman? for her price is far above rubies* . . . ' She caught her breath then, and stole a glance at Rowland, but his eyes were still closed, his face expressionless, so she read on. ' . . . *She seeketh wool and flax and worketh willingly with her hands . . . She riseth also while it is yet night, and giveth meat to her household . . . She considereth a field and buyeth it: with the fruit of her hands she planteth a vineyard . . . She perceiveth that her merchandise is good: her candle goeth not out by night . . . Her husband is known in the gates, where he sitteth among the elders of the land . . .* ' She gave a sudden gurgle of laughter.

Rowland's eyes flew open. They rested on her face, intent and questioning.

'What an idle layabout – while she does all the work!'

'Why, hasn't that always been the way of it?' He grinned, looking suddenly much younger, almost himself again, though his eyes had a certain gravity in them, warm and tender. 'I know what I owe thee, what I've always owed,' he said quietly, the smile gone.

She laid the book aside and knelt by the bed and put her arms about him, and his closed around her. She laid her head on his hollow chest and felt the warmth of his body – too warm, damp with sweat – the unfleshed bones and the difficult breathing; heard the bubbling rasping sounds of his struggling lungs and the muffled thud of his labouring heart; felt his hands move, caressingly, on her back and her hair. Then he bent his head to kiss her, gently and slowly. 'It is not all on one side,' she said then.

'Not always – but now . . . '

'Not even now,' she returned, and she knew that it was true, though she would have found it hard to say in what way. She moved back a little to look more easily into his face. 'There must be ways I've been a disappointment.' She meant: in not having been won over in a passionate moment of conversion, as she knew he had hoped would happen one day. And perhaps, too, in being unwilling sometimes to support him to the limit of what he wanted in some action he undertook.

He was silent for a little while, pondering the matter, perhaps considering his reply. She knew he had understood her. Then he said at last, hesitantly, 'What we expect, or want – it's not always given . . . for good reason, mostly . . . No, I've never been disappointed, not in thee. Not that . . . surprised, sometimes. Made to think . . . Always, most of all, amazed – no, awed – that thou should love me so . . . that, above all, this should have been given me.'

'And I,' she whispered, 'have never ceased wondering that thou should love me.'

They held one another then for a long time in silence, very still, with no more need of words.

Chapter Eleven

Tommy blinked as he slid from the loop onto firm ground beside the pit shaft, though it was dull enough out here in the late July afternoon, the sky heavy and grey, hinting at possible thunder to come. In Weardale this moment of coming out from the darkness after each shift underground had always had something magical about it, right up to his last day in the lead mines; and even here the ill-used landscape looked dazzlingly green and lush and fertile, for the first few minutes at least.

It was the closest he came to magic now, and it was a short-lived and inadequate thing, more significant for what it brought to mind than for what it offered in itself: a tiny moment when the drabness of his existence retreated a little and he could recall that he had known a richer life than this, and might even again one day, though at present he found that hard to believe.

The days and weeks had done little to lessen the pain, a pain so acute that he could scarcely bear it even now, a clear month and more since Matty had spat in his face and cursed him. He had lost her, the girl he loved; lost her completely in the most appalling circumstances. He was not sure that she had deliberately engineered the attack upon him, but he had no doubt she had approved of it. Oddly, miserable though he was, he could not find it in himself to blame her. For had he not deceived her? Worse, in deceiving her, he had put at risk not only his love but any influence for good it allowed him to have upon her. Hating him as she must do now, she would inevitably hate all he stood for, even perhaps his God. That thought only added to his misery.

Luke plodded beside him in silence. Lately he had begun to suffer from severe indigestion, brought on, Tommy supposed, by too much rich food badly cooked. It was a wonder he had not suffered that way himself, but perhaps a broken heart was anguish enough for one man. He thought he would even have welcomed indigestion, because it might have made the other pain hurt less, by contrast.

Rebekah had the water hot and the meal (unfortunately) on the table the moment they had finished washing. They began, dutifully but without enthusiasm, to eat, but Rebekah did not sit down with them, as she usually did; Luke liked to have the whole family at table together. Instead, she stood by the table watching them, not even making a pretence at being busy.

'Sit down, lass,' Luke said at last, with a faint note of impatience. 'Your dinner will be cold before you've started.' And not improved for that, thought Tommy, who was trying to concentrate on more wholesome things while he shovelled the greasy unappetising mess into his mouth.

'Luke,' Rebekah said at last, 'Margaret Nattrass says two of the Welshmen at Hetton are down with the cholera.'

Both men stopped eating. They glanced at one another. Then Tommy said, 'I was there yesterday. No one said owt of it.' He tried to sound reassuring, but he could feel his heart beating fast. For some days there had been rumours that the sickness – so virulent here last winter – was breaking out again, though no one they knew had shown signs of ill health.

'Why, it's true for all that,' said Rebekah. She turned to Tommy. 'I don't want you going over there again. We must keep to ourselves. It's the only way to be safe.'

'Let's find out if it's true first,' Tommy said, 'before we start frightening ourselves.'

Rebekah, trembling, sat down suddenly. 'It'll be too late, when we know for sure!' She swung round on her husband. 'I wish we'd never come here. I wish to God we hadn't!' She began to sob wildly. The children, sitting either side of their father pretending to eat, stared at her wide-eyed.

Matty told herself that Tommy had been wiped out of her life. All that mattered to her now, with a single-minded dedication, was the union struggle and the lives of her family and friends. When her mother commented that she looked pale and thin and was not eating properly, she was surprised, because she had not really noticed it for herself. When she could not sleep – which was often enough, the more because she feared what she might find in her dreams – she occupied her time in thinking of Adam and the other men in prison, of Eliza and her anguished wait (she had been to see Adam once, but it was a considerable journey and she could not easily afford the bribes that were needed to ensure admittance to the gaol). Matty was glad when the time came for the trial.

Her parents did not want her to go to Durham. 'You stay here and help your mam,' her father said, as he made ready to go.

'Eliza needs us,' Matty said firmly. 'She has to have a woman with her.'

'There are plenty of Ranter women to go with her.'

'I'm her friend. It's me she wants there.'

'So she can put more of her stupid ideas into your head? No, she's a bad enough influence as it is.'

'The more of us there are in court, the more they'll see the union's still strong.'

173

'That's men's business. It's our fight. The best thing our womenfolk can do is stay quiet at home, with their mouths shut. That's what Tommy Hepburn says.'

'He only said it because some women were causing trouble and getting the union a bad name. I shan't do that.' When that did not sway him, she tried coaxing, which often worked; but today he was immovable. He patted her cheek, and then said,

'Now hold your tongue, canny lass. That's my last word. You stay here with your mam and the bairns.'

In the end, Matty had Jack Marley to thank that her father allowed her to go. He had been called as a witness for the defence, as had her brother Jamie, but where Jamie was openly nervous, Jack was nonchalant and clearly saw the whole affair as a perfect opportunity for furthering his cause with Matty. When her father said she was not to go, he made his disappointment plain. John Grey, who wanted Jack as a son-in-law, softened at once. Matty did not much relish the reason for his change of heart, but she accepted it quietly enough, resolving to keep as well clear of Jack as she could. She had already repelled his advances twice since she broke with Tommy, and told him in no uncertain terms that she wanted nothing to do with him. But he was not easily repelled, and she knew he had not given up all hope of her – or any hope, perhaps. He clearly believed she was playing with him for some deep purpose of her own, perhaps to inflame his passions the more; which was unfortunately the effect her actions seemed to have upon him.

They set out before dawn on the Monday, so as to reach the city before the assizes opened, walking the five miles along roads crowded with marching or riding troops.

Matty had never been as far as Durham city before. Until now, Sunderland had been the only large town she knew, and it was a long time since she had been there, in the days when her maternal grandparents were still alive. She found the bustle of Durham bewildering, and the size of the place; there were soldiers everywhere. The party

174

from Hetton, noisy until they reached the outskirts of the city, quietened as they descended the hill by Gilesgate and Claypath and crossed the market place, most of them a little awed by the watchful military presence. Jack Marley, keen to show that he was not one to be subdued by a few soldiers, walked close behind the young women, talking to Jamie and his other friends in a loud voice that was clearly designed to impress Matty.

'Cuthbert Skipsey's murderer's coming to trial this week, in Newcastle,' he said, as they left the market place by means of Fleshergate, where high houses overhung cobbles stinking with blood and offal thrown out from the adjacent butchers' shops. Matty retched, and then quickly pressed one end of her shawl over mouth and nose; Eliza did the same.

Cuthbert Skipsey, as every union man knew, was a collier from Chirton, north of the Tyne, who had been unwise enough to intervene in a dispute between a group of special constables and some union men. Trying to restrain the violent behaviour of a constable named Weddell, he had laid a hand on the man's shoulder, at which Weddell had shot him at point blank range. The constable, of course, maintained that Skipsey had assaulted him.

'Well, we'll soon know what kind of justice there is for union men,' John Grey said. His faith in English justice had begun to waver a little during the past weeks.

They stepped aside to avoid an ox, being led along the street for slaughter. As they descended the slope that ran down to Elvet Bridge, they could hear its frightened bellowing, an ominous undercurrent to the clatter of their feet. Matty shivered. All that slaughter, the talk of murdered men, the stink of rotting meat and blood – she wished they had not marked the path that led to the court where Adam's life would be weighed in the balance. Beyond the bridge they came to Old Elvet, a wide pleasant street lined with comfortable town houses; yet the stench of death seemed to follow them and hang about them still, and the noise of the doomed ox.

The Assize Court was surrounded by dense ranks of soldiers, on foot and on horseback. Matty, awed, had not thought there could be a building so massive, so dominating those around it that even the respectable town houses looked small and mean. You could, she thought, have slipped a whole colliery row beneath its great pillared façade. Yet, glancing to the right of it, the eye went at once across the encircling river to the vast towers of the cathedral, and its attendant castle set on the fortress rock of the city, and at once the Assize Court itself seemed to shrink to insignificance.

More soldiers were marching along the street, pushing everyone back against the house walls; and soon afterwards a file of coaches rumbled past, the sunlight catching the heraldic crests that decorated them and the glossy coats of the horses. They came to a halt in a long row before the court. One by one the dignitaries descended, to step in scarlet robes and vast wigs between the ranks of soldiers towards the pillared entrance: His Majesty's Justices of Assize, Sir James Parke and Sir William Bolland, the High Sheriff of the County, and, taking precedence over them all, embodying in his dignified person the special powers of the County Palatinate of Durham, the Right Reverend Lord Bishop William Van Mildert, in full episcopal splendour, with a train of attendant clergy and officials.

The watching crowd clearly enjoyed the spectacle. There were appreciative comments, eager pointing out of this detail and that and, even when the comments were less than respectful, an enthusiastic relish for the unaccustomed splendours of the scene. The assizes brought a welcome interlude of colour and excitement to otherwise harsh or uneventful lives. Yet Matty found herself filled with dread. It was indeed a spectacle such as she had never imagined in all her life, but the fear she felt at seeing it was not only to do with the knowledge that Adam awaited his fate somewhere within the grim damp prison walls behind the splendid honey-coloured façade of the court. This, she saw with sudden chilling clarity,

176

was not just a grand spectacle: it was a display of power. A warning, even.

Most of the time Matty took words for granted, not thinking much about their meaning. She had sometimes thought about the word 'power', because it was used so much in her hearing, by men like Adam and her father, talking of their struggle. *Power* had always brought certain images into her head – Mr Dunn and the other colliery officials, turning the pitmen from their houses; the special constables watching at street corners, patrolling the streets; the soldiers escorting the blacklegs to work; the strangers who had taken the very bread from their mouths. And power, too, was what working men and women gained when they got learning and dignity (*Knowledge is power*, Tommy Hepburn had said); it was what the colliers had in their hands, since they joined together to form the union, a new and exhilarating power marked by little concessions, here and there, which otherwise they could not have hoped to gain.

Now she knew that power meant none of those things. Power – real power, in its only true meaning – was displayed here before her eyes, in the towering splendour of cathedral and castle and court, in the impressive robed figures of the Bishop and the Judges and the endless ranks of lesser court officials. Without them, Mr Dunn and the soldiers would have been powerless. Behind the scenes, hidden from the eyes of mere Hetton colliers, this greater, more terrible power directed and decided, gave the orders, spoke for life or death, moving the lesser men like puppet masters pulling strings.

Matty felt suddenly very small and weak and insignificant, like an ant about to be crushed by a passing foot. The colliers thought that by means of their union they had begun to take power into their own hands, but what were they – what was she or Adam or any of them – against these men? No more than insects, left alone as long as they crawled busily over their little ant heaps, causing no trouble; but let them dare to try and sting the great ones and they would be crushed remorselessly. Even

Tommy, she saw suddenly, was no criminal, but a victim like the rest of them, a mere tool in the hands of the powerful. If the power these men held was indeed impartial, as her father had thought, then it offered a last hope to the poor and the oppressed, against the lesser tyrants who ruled their everyday lives, but if her father was wrong, as some instinct had long told her, then it was greatly to be feared. For it was a power so vast and so entrenched that only an explosive upheaval, a revolution, could ever hope to overturn it. She had feared for Adam before. Now she dreaded what was to come.

They had some difficulty finding a place in the public gallery of the court, not because there was such a great crowd clamouring for admission (though there was), but for the simple and unexpected reason that the court officials had decided to limit the number of those to be admitted. Each man or woman was looked over with suspicious eyes, questioned, pondered over; and even then, most of them were turned away. Matty was not sure how she and Eliza came to be admitted – perhaps they looked harmless – but they found their way in at last, taking up their places where they had a good view of the ranks of robed figures, Bishop and Judges, on the bench before them. There was one consolation for their difficulty in getting in – Jack Marley was among the many left to fume helplessly outside.

One by one the members of the Grand Jury were sworn in – twenty-two gentlemanly Justices of the Peace, some of them colliery owners, so Eliza whispered to Matty. Then the senior Judge, Sir James Parke, solemnly addressed the jury.

'Gentlemen,' he began, his gaze sweeping the entire courtroom before settling on the jurymen, 'I look forward with very painful interest to the discharge of your duties and mine on the present occasion, on which we are called upon to administer criminal justice; not merely on account of the number of cases, which is unusually great – I believe I may say unprecedentedly great – for this county, but because I perceive there are so many acts of violence against the person, in which the lives of several of our fellow creatures have already been lost; and if the evidence to be adduced brings home the guilt of the accused, the lives of others of our fellow creatures must be sacrificed also . . . '

Matty shivered. Adam's life was among those that might be lost before the court had ended. She laid her hand over Eliza's and felt her friend close her fingers about it.

'Gentlemen,' the Judge continued, ponderously, emphatically, 'there is besides a very painful feature in the contemplation of the cases which are contained in this calendar. Almost every act of violence – I believe I may say, directly or indirectly, every act – may be attributed to the combinations amongst workmen, which have prevailed for a long time in these counties, to a greater extent, I believe, than in any other part of England.'

Struggling to grasp the meaning behind the long words, Matty knew that her father had been wrong: this man was not impartial, nor on the side of the colliers. When he spoke of 'combinations' he meant the union, Matty knew, and she wanted to shout out her indignation at the unfairness of what he was saying. Did he not know how many acts of violence there had been in the old days, before unions were allowed? Did he not know, as she did because everyone said so, how peaceful the colliers had been since the union began – peaceful, that is, until the masters set out to destroy it, because it had made them give up so much? It was only anger and despair at what was happening to them that had made the colliers turn to violence again, because the masters left them no other way.

' . . . Gentlemen, these combinations are so dangerous to personal safety, and so injurious to the peace and welfare of society, that sooner or later they must be put down. I hope, by the proper administration of the law as it stands, this great object may be effected.'

And *this great object* was what the masters wanted too: the destruction of the union. What could a few poor

179

colliers do, faced with such formidable opposition? Matty thought, gloomily, that the Judge would probably think the hanging of a union man or two a small price to pay for what he wanted.

She did not say precisely that to Eliza when later, back in their rented room, they talked over all they had heard, but she tried to explain something of what she had felt this morning.

'I don't doubt they wish they'd never made unions lawful,' her friend agreed bitterly. 'But they've found a way round it: make the men so angry that they resort to violence, then declare that unions are evil. Who could disagree with them after that?' Then she broke out in a howl of anguish: 'Oh, Matty, what hope is there for Adam, before such a Judge!'

Their cramped and squalid lodging house was at the unfashionable end of Old Elvet, the haunt of prostitutes and gamblers and pickpockets, a warren of disreputable inns with a nightly din of drunken brawls. But rooms were hard to find in Durham in assize week, and it was close to the court and enabled those who could gain admission to be in their place early each day. Eliza did not attend again after that opening ceremony, not until the Wednesday when the two murder cases were to be tried; but Matty, filled with a fascination that combined awe and horror and simple curiosity, would miss none of it, even though it meant going to the court alone, more than once, to the dismay of her father. Fortunately, he was so eager himself to make the most of his absence from his wife's watchful eye that he was less vigilant than he might have been of his daughter. He and Jack and the other men gave up trying to get into the court and instead spent each day sampling the many other sources of entertainment offered by Durham in assize week.

On Wednesday, however, all those who had come from Hetton went to the court very early, to queue until the doors were opened. 'They've got to let us in,' said John Grey with conviction. 'It's our marras in there.' But the scrutiny at the door was more stringent than ever, and

Matty and Eliza were the only ones of their party to be allowed in. Matty would have crowed with triumph, except that Eliza was in too tense and sombre a mood for triumph.

Almost all those admitted to the court today were quite clearly not colliers but respectable citizens, troubled by rumours of unrest and civil disorder, which had continued even though the worst fears of imminent revolution had gone with the restoration of Lord Grey's Government, whose moderate parliamentary reforms had now passed smoothly into law. Alarmed by months of newspaper reports of arson and rioting in other parts of the country, they feared that these evils might well spread to Durham if the pitmen were not put in their place; which happy result they hoped the court would achieve. Across the gallery, Matty glimpsed the neat, self-assured figure of Matthias Dunn, come presumably to witness the latest step in the humiliation of the union. Not far from Matty, a large man was denouncing riotous pitmen in a way that made her want to hit him. But she was too fearful of being thrown out to do more than glower at him, unseen, over the head of his substantial wife.

The Judge took his seat and the first case was called; and the collier William Jobling was brought into the dock, to be accused with laborious solemnity that he did 'wilfully and maliciously beat and wound Nicholas Fairless, Esquire, of which beating and wounding he lingered and died'. Matty was familiar now with court procedure – the case for the prosecution, supported by witnesses, then the case for the defence, with its opposing evidence; the Judge's summing up, biased according to which side put the better case (which was almost invariably the prosecution), and then the jury's decision and, sooner or later, the sentence. She prayed that the men accused today would have an eloquent counsel for the defence, for it seemed from what she had seen so far that there lay their only hope, whatever the evidence.

One after another the witnesses stepped up to the bar and told how they had seen the magistrate (on his way to Jarrow to help keep order at the colliery there) being violently beaten with a stick and a stone, by one Armstrong, who was still at large. They differed only in the part they claimed Jobling had played – some said he had held the man down while Armstrong hit him; others that he had protested at the violence and then run away. The blood-stained stick, a gentleman's cane with a polished rounded end, was shown to the court, and Matty felt the shudder of horror that ran through the crowd. She was sure then that Jobling was doomed. As to whether he was guilty or not, she could not tell. She had heard the Judge say again and again that the jury must be convinced of a man's guilt to find against him, and she could not see how, on the evidence they had heard, they could be sure of Jobling's guilt. Except that the victim was a magistrate, and Jobling a union man . . .

The gentlemen of the jury clearly had no doubt. They were out less than a quarter of an hour before they delivered their verdict. Then Mr Justice Parke placed the black cap upon his head and they heard the dreadful words with which he pronounced sentence. Even at this solmen moment he could not resist a reference to the *perversion of moral principle* for which the union was to blame. He condemned Jobling to be hanged in two days' time, after which his body was to be exposed in chains, unburied for ever, on Jarrow Slake, where the crime had taken place, as an awful warning to others. Like a dead crow on a fence, Matty thought grimly.

As the prisoner was led from the court, he turned to the crowd and cried out, 'The Lord preserve you from such as this!'

Afterwards, Eliza began to weep, and so did other women in the gallery; there was even a general murmur of dismay at the ferocity of the sentence, with its final cruel twist. Matty knew that Eliza was right to believe that no pitman could expect mercy from this Judge.

The court adjourned then, though Matty and Eliza

stayed where they were, fearful that they might otherwise lose their places. Eliza, her nerves stretched to the limit, alternately chattered wildly or sat in a tense silence, her hands tightly clasped before her, her eyes staring at the empty dock.

At one o'clock the court resumed, and into the dock stepped the five men from Hetton, and there was Adam, looking thin and pale and shabby, and the other four men who until such a short time ago had been Matty's neighbours, drinking with John Grey, playing at quoits with Jack Marley. It might even have been her brother there, Matty thought, had Adam not made the fatal decision to take the gun from him. She saw Adam glance once at the public gallery, seeking Eliza perhaps, though he did not seem to find her and almost at once returned his gaze, sombre and direct, to the Judge facing him.

For Matty now all sense of drama evaporated. There was only terror in the words of the accusation, that John Turnbull and Adam Fenwick did shoot John Errington with intent to kill him, and George Strong, John Moore and Luke Hutton did aid, counsel and abet them. This was real life, something in which those she loved had a vital part to play, and from which they might not emerge with their lives. Yet it was the by now familiar process that unrolled before her; the witnesses called (this time most of them known to Matty and Eliza), the confused and differing stories – who was seen with a gun when and where, how many shots were heard, what was done afterwards. The colliery surgeon gave his report of the dead man's injuries, and at that point Matty learned for the first time that two shots had been fired at him. 'It is my view,' said the surgeon, 'that the shots were fired from two guns. And that the persons who fired must have been very near the dead man.'

It all took a very long time, partly because the various stories were so complicated and confused and contradictory that the questioning of the witnesses went over and over each point, until even Matty, who had been at Brick Garth that night, began to wonder if they were

183

talking of the same few hours, or even the same familiar streets and alleys.

It was late in the afternoon before the three witnesses against Adam had all given their evidence. The first, called early in the proceedings, was the blackleg William Steel, who told the whole story of the fateful night, as he claimed to remember it, and hinted at Adam's part in it. He had already described Errington disappearing from sight beyond the fire, the sound of the shot – only one, he claimed, and that very loud – the watch from behind the bushes. Then he went on, 'It was ten minutes past twelve. As we went home, I looked over my shoulder, and there was Fenwick running from the alley near the oven.'

'You are sure it was him?' prompted counsel for the prosecution.

'Quite sure, sir. There's no mistaking his hair, and the way he walks.' Matty saw how heads turned to stare at Adam, whose hair, even after months in gaol, still had something of its old sheen.

'Tell the court if he had anything in his hand.'

'He had a musket, sir.'

After that a woman, whose husband was one of the bound men, took the stand and described how, earlier that same day, Adam had called for vengeance on those responsible for the evictions. It was hardly evidence, but it was damning enough, for those hearing it in the court. Matty sensed their hostility.

Then, to a shocked indrawn breath from his sister, Samuel Raines was called to the stand. 'I didn't know!' Eliza murmured in horror. Matty understood enough of the law to realise he would have had no choice but to come today, once the summons reached him. On the other hand, he must first have given the authorities information of some kind, or they would not have thought it worth bringing him here. But it was clear that now he wished he was anywhere but in the stand, so close to his brother-in-law, with his sister's eyes upon him. Stumbling, reluctant, he had little to say; but that little

184

was more than enough. 'I was lying in my bed, sir, about three in the morning. I heard shouting outside. They were saying Errington was dead.'

'Was any voice known to you?'

His head bent, he answered so softly that the man had to repeat the question. 'Fenwick's, sir.'

'And what did he say?'

There was a long silence, during which not a sound could be heard in the court either. Then Samuel said, 'I can't be sure . . . I think it was, *Whoever did that was the instrument of the Lord.*'

The murmur that went round the court was appalled and chilling.

The case for the prosecution was over, the light was failing in the court. Discreet figures crept about the room and successive candle flames sprang up, high on the walls, along the desks of the clerks and lawyers, near the stands for witnesses and accused, in glowing tiers about the Judge's bench.

Counsel for the defence stepped forward and called the accused men one by one to the stand, each of whom denied his guilt. They heard Adam's voice, firm and clear and unafraid, 'As God is my witness, my lord, and as surely as I shall speak on the dreadful day of Judgement, I swear that I am innocent of this crime.'

The defence made moves to call two witnesses on behalf of Hutton and Moore, but at that point the Judge intervened: the evidence against them had been so unreliable that in his opinion there was no case for them to answer. Matty saw the relief on the faces of the two men as they were led from the court. But Adam and the other two were still there, as much in danger as ever.

Jamie was called before long, looking so cowed and frightened that at first Matty did not recognise him. He told how Adam had taken the gun from him and gone away, he did not see where.

'Did he give you any reason for taking the gun from you?'

'So I should do no harm with it,' said Jamie. 'To put it

away.' But he sounded so shifty that Matty was sure no one would believe so innocent an explanation.

After that came the inevitable question, which had been put to each witness in turn, and Jamie's answer, 'I belong the union, sir, since last year.'

Jack Marley followed him and confirmed with rather less than his usual assurance that Adam had not been seen again by anyone until after Errington had been shot, but that by then there was no sign of the gun.

A statement made by Adam at the time of his arrest was read, too, claiming that he had taken the gun to the chapel and locked it away for safety. It was there that it had been found at a later date, but that of course proved nothing.

There was little more evidence after that. Joseph Love, a grocer from Easington Lane whose kindness during times of hunger had made him a true friend of the union, spoke for the good character of Strong and Fenwick, as did a number of others; other witnesses spoke for Turnbull.

It was nine o'clock at night before the Judge began his summing up. He spoke with great gravity, underlining the seriousness of the crime and the heinousness of the actions the union had led men into, and then he emphasised the ambiguous and contradictory nature of the evidence. Apart from Turnbull, Fenwick and Strong, two other union men were known to have had guns that night, and the dead man's friends had also been armed; it was for the jury to decide whether or not any of those in the dock before them had fired the fatal shots or played any part in the murder. There was more than a hint, Matty thought, that he believed Strong to be innocent. 'If, gentlemen, there is any doubt of his guilt, then you must find for the defence.'

As for the other two, he reminded the jury that it was Turnbull's story against those of the prosecution witnesses, and he gave the strongest of hints that he would choose the latter, without hesitation. At the same time, none of the evidence on Adam's behalf proved the impossibility of his having committed the crime, and his own statement was the only evidence that he had not. He was, then, in a similar case to Turnbull, with one damning distinction: 'Remember well, this man not only belongs to that combination of colliers which has been so fertile and lamentable a source of crime, but he has from the outset been one of its most vociferous and active supporters.' It was that above all, Matty thought with bitter despair, that would take him to the gallows.

The jurymen filed out and the door was closed and the court erupted into a murmur of speculative conversation. Somewhere, far off, a clock struck eleven. Eliza sat with head bent and eyes closed and her hands clasped tightly in her lap. Matty knew she was praying. It did at least have the merit of giving her something to do, though Matty was not sure of its usefulness. Could God really be on the side of men like Adam, when all the power was ranged so openly in the hands of the Judges and the Bishop and the Army?

They were coming back – *Already*! Matty thought, her heart beating fast. She felt sick, and horribly, chillingly, sure of the verdict the jury had reached.

Silence fell on the crowd. There was a moment or two of rustling, while men robed in silks and furs rearranged themselves and assumed a suitable posture.

'Gentlemen of the jury, have you reached a verdict?'

The foreman rose and cleared his throat. There was a tiny pause, a holding of the breath, and then he spoke firmly, 'We find the accused severally not guilty, my lord.'

There was a tiny terrible moment when Matty did not believe what she had heard, could not take it in. She was aware only of a gasp of astonishment rising from those around her. Then Eliza gave a sob and Matty turned jubilantly to hug her. She glimpsed the colour rising in Adam's haggard face. From somewhere across the court-room a great moan broke out, protesting and dismayed. Looking round, she saw Matthias Dunn rise furiously to his feet and push his way angrily from the court that had so profoundly failed him.

'There is justice then!' Eliza said in a voice made hoarse with emotion. Her eyes were full of tears.

'Aye, even for us,' Matty agreed. She wondered if they would ever know who had killed Errington; on the whole, she hoped not.

Then Eliza rose and elbowed her way to where Adam stood with the other accused men, looking rather dazed, as if he dared not yet move too far from the dock from which he had just been released.

Somehow, they made their way outside, and there, before the torchlit entrance to the court, Adam knelt down, Eliza at his side, others of his friends kneeling too, quite unconcerned at the minor obstruction they were causing. Then he gave thanks, aloud, for the miracle of his release.

Turnbull and Strong and their friends hurried to the nearest public house, to celebrate in their own way. As for Matty, there was nothing for her to do but go back to the lodging house and snatch what sleep she could. Eliza and Adam had no need of her any more.

The next morning there was one thing only to detain them in Durham: four men and a woman, found guilty earlier in the week on various charges of assault, were to be brought before the Judge for sentencing, after which the court would move on to Newcastle, where the assizes should already have begun. This time none of the Hetton party was admitted to the court, so they waited outside, their presence expressing their sympathy with the prisoners, one of whom was a Hetton collier.

It did not take long, and the soldiers were already clearing a way for the Judge's carriage when news was brought out that the Hetton man was to be transported and the other three hanged for their crimes.

As if to emphasise the point, every word their informant spoke was underlined by the hammering of nearby workmen, constructing the scaffold on which William Jobling was to die tomorrow morning.

'Let's go home, sharp as we can,' said Adam.

As they came within sight of Hetton village they passed a funeral procession making its way to the parish church at Houghton-le-Spring. 'A stranger, dead of the cholera,' said Jack Marley with a note of satisfaction. 'That'll get them off our backs.'

'We had our fill of the cholera last winter,' said John Grey. 'I thought it had done with us.' The sickness had gone through his entire family, and he had lost his youngest son because of it.

'We'll take no harm this time,' Adam pointed out. 'We had our dose then. But the strangers haven't come across it before. They're in for a bad time.' There was no trace of regret in his voice at the prospect. They all knew that the cholera was a more terrifying enemy than the most angry pitman.

Tommy Hepburn came to Hetton two days later, from Newcastle Assizes, where he had been present at the trial of Cuthbert Skipsey's murderer. The constable, Weddell, had been found guilty, as was inevitable with such a weight of evidence against him. He had then been sentenced to six months imprisonment.

Chapter Twelve

The day of the camp meeting arrived and Rowland was as determined as ever to go. Jenny had humoured him whenever he talked of his plans, conscious that it gave him a purpose and made him believe he still had something useful to do, but she was quite sure that when the time came he would see that it was impossible.

He was daily growing weaker and she believed that it was only his iron determination that dragged him out of bed in the mornings. Once up, he spent most of the time on the settle by the fire, reading or dozing or talking to whoever was in the room. He no longer attempted any outdoor work, scarcely even venturing as far as the bench outside, except on the hottest days. But on one occasion when, hunting for scraps of material with which to finish a hooky mat she was making, Jenny took his plaid from where it lay on top of other garments in a chest, he had said, 'You'll have to wait a bit to put that in your mat, hinny. I'll be wanting it yet.'

She had smiled at the pleasantry, though she had not been much amused by it. The children had laughed, except for Eve, who had stared at him with wide frightened eyes, as if she had read into the remark more than it had actually said, and been taken aback by it.

On the day of the camp meeting Rowland was clearly worse, for the fever of last night still hung about him and he looked exhausted and desperately ill. But he insisted so firmly that he would be on the fell tonight, as promised, that Jenny gave up trying to convince him otherwise. All she said was, 'Then you'd better get some rest,' and he had taken her advice without question, which disturbed her even more.

Eve had a miserable morning. Yesterday, to her dismay, her father, leaving nothing to chance, had come to White Lea to take her home with him, away from the contamination of the camp meeting. He had been deaf to her objections and pleas, brusque to Aunt Jenny, and had then made his way back to Well House at a vigorous striding pace that showed Eve (panting to keep up with him) only too clearly that he was annoyed with her.

This morning she had been despatched to help Esther and her stepmother with the shopping at St John's Chapel, where she was dismayed to see that Jacob Todd's shop was unmistakably empty, its windows shuttered, a little scattering of dust and last year's leaves gathered already, unswept, by its once busy doorway. She had said nothing about it to her stepmother, but back at Well House sought out her father (he was outside, breaking in a colt) and demanded, 'What's happened to Todd's shop?'

Her father glanced at her with some impatience; he did not like being interrupted in so pleasurable and delicate a task. The colt continued to circle him at the end of its long rein. Eve had to jump aside as it passed. 'Not enough business in Chapel these days, I suppose. I heard they've got a new place, in Newcastle or somewhere.'

Eve did not move. So they had gone, and Mrs Todd who she thought had loved her so much, had not even tried to say goodbye! It was quite clear to Eve now that her grandmother had never loved her at all. Quite why she had given her all those little treats Eve did not know, but it did not really matter; adults were unpredictable beings. What mattered was that she was not loved by the one person to whom she had thought she was of real importance.

'What are you doing, lass, standing there in my way? Get back in the house. I'm sure there's work to be done.'

She went, stung still more by her father's tone.

It was not the end of her troubles, on a day that proved to be miserable in the extreme. Her stepmother, clearly displeased to have her back at Well House, nagged and scolded more than usual and kept her constantly busy, largely at the tasks she most disliked. Her half brothers and sister were as unwelcoming as their mother, and teased and tormented her with an enthusiasm only sharpened by the weeks of her absence.

About supper-time she escaped for long enough to go and stand just outside the front door of the house, where it was quiet and no one, at this moment, could see her.

She stood watching the traffic on the turnpike road that ran along the floor of the dale. It was much busier than usual today. There were not many carriages (there never were in Weardale), but a fair number of small carts, many riders and a growing throng of men and women and children making their way on foot towards Westgate and the little road that led over the river to the eastern slopes of Chapel Fell.

Eve sighed, wishing she could have gone with the Ranters to the camp meeting. She had never been to one – by chance, she had never been at White Lea at the right time before – but she had heard all about them from her cousins and they were quite clearly memorable occasions. This one was to be at night too, and that made it the more exciting a prospect. She toyed briefly with the idea of slipping down the hill and making her way to the meeting ground, in spite of her father. But she thought better of it, not because he would be angry (as he certainly would), but because Aunt Jenny and Uncle Rowland would be displeased too, knowing what her father's instructions had been. They were very firm about obedience to parents. It was, she thought with regret, their greatest defect.

She was intent upon watching a small family, following them with her eyes along the whole length of the road, seeing how the children ran and skipped beside their parents, catching snatches of their singing as they went; when all at once her stepmother flew at her from inside the house, grasped her arm and slapped her.

'You idle useless girl – I told you to get the table set, and here I am with supper ready and not a spoon, not a plate on the table!' She found herself shaken and flung into the kitchen, striking her head on the door frame as she fell through it. 'Now get on with it this minute!'

Shocked, dazed, her arm hurting from the grasp, she turned on the woman. 'I hate you! I hate you and your horrible bairns! I wish you were all dead!'

'Eve!'

She had not seen her father coming. It was quite clear that he had heard every word she had said to his wife. The worst thing was that he did not burst into a rage, as – shrinking a little – she expected, but simply looked at her as if she were some unpleasant mess in which he had accidentally trodden, and said with icy disapproval, 'Never let me hear you speak like that to your mother again. Never. You are a wicked unbiddable girl. Now go up to your room and stay there. There will be no supper for you tonight. And you'll not come down tomorrow or any other day until you've begged your mother's pardon for what you've just said. And your brothers' and sister's too.'

Eve stared at her father. She saw severity, anger, coldness; but not the merest trace of love, or even of liking. When Aunt Jenny scolded her, or Uncle Rowland, they sounded sad about it and their eyes were kind. There was no kindness in her father's face. Did he love her at all? Fathers were supposed to love their daughters, but when had she last seen love on her father's face? When, indeed, had she *ever* seen love on her father's face, for her? She could not remember, now she came to think of it. She had received tenderness from Aunt Jenny, from Uncle Rowland; now and then, a little off-handedly, from Uncle Tommy. But from her father – no, she could not remember when he had ever smiled at her, seemed glad to see her coming, praised her, all those things he did so readily, so easily for his other children.

She gave him one last long look, and then turned and walked away, very upright and steady. She did as she was told, and went up to her room and closed the door. It was the one advantage this house had over White Lea, that here she had her own room – but what consolation was that, when she had nothing else?

Rowland had asked Jenny to wake him at five. When the time came, she stood by the bed fighting a strong sense of reluctance. He had fallen asleep at last about an hour ago, and it seemed foolish in the extreme to drag a sick man from his bed to keep an appointment on a windy hillside. But she knew that he would be angry with her if she failed him now, so she gently shook him awake.

He woke to a fit of coughing that went on for some time and left him blue-lipped and exhausted. Jenny laid a hand on his forehead and felt how hot it was, and saw how the sweat filmed his skin, how deep-set his eyes looked in their shadowed hollows. She did not think she had ever seen him look so ill. But it was not until he began to get out of bed and she saw how much of a struggle every move was, how every small gesture seemed to set him coughing, that she said gently, 'Get back into bed, love. I'll tell them you're sick.' She tried to ignore the little voice that said, *He will not get up again, not ever. This is the end.*

He shook his head, though it made him cough the more. 'No. I'm promised to go.' He smiled faintly at her expression. 'The strength will be given.'

That phrase again. She felt choked by it, unable to say any more, even to protest that in his condition he would never make the camp, even on the galloway, still less find strength to speak to all those people. In any case, she knew from years of experience that once Rowland's mind was made up, that was it; no power on earth could sway it. There was perhaps some comfort in knowing that in this at least sickness had made no difference.

'Help me, hinny,' he said. 'I don't want to be late.'

She helped him dress and put her arm about him as he struggled to his feet. It was ridiculous, madness, to think he could make it onto the fell tonight! Yet she kept her protest to herself, helped him to sit down and drink some tea (he would not eat), and then wrapped him in his plaid – 'You see,' he said with a grin, though his voice was little more than a whisper, 'I said I'd want it yet.' Then she supported him (how thin he was, all bone, his strength gone!) out to where the galloway waited. The animal was small, sturdy and patient, but it took some time to get Rowland onto her back.

The sun was low as they made their way down the hill into the depths of the dale. They crossed the river at the ford at Westgate, and then followed the track up the farther side, onto the lower slopes of Chapel Fell, already shadowed with the coming night. Here they came up with others going the same way, scores of them, full of excitement and anticipation, many with no motive stronger than curiosity or a wish for excitement, even some who had quite clearly come only to mock the proceedings or meet a sweetheart. Jenny heard someone comment in passing that there weren't so many making their way onto the fell as there used to be in the days of the great revivals, but then, as she pointed out in reply, there were fewer people in Weardale now. Not that she cared much either way; she was not interested in the success of the camp meeting, only in how it affected Rowland.

Some of the travellers were singing as they went, lively Ranter hymns, full of warning and fear and hope. On their way to past camp meetings the Peart family would have sung too, led by Rowland in his clear musical tenor. But tonight he was silent, requiring all his strength to sit relatively upright on the galloway. The children, subdued themselves because of it, talked little as they went, and Jenny merely watched her husband with anxiety and wondered again how he could think he would be able to play any part at all tonight.

The track wound steeply up, on and on as the darkness grew. Around them, people lit lanterns or torches, and the lights bobbed and flickered in the growing night. A cold little wind pulled at their clothes and hair, and they leaned into it. To their left, the land dropped steeply to the Swinhope burn, its sound heard fitfully, chattering among the black shapes of the trees that fringed it. To their right, there was only the bleak black outline of the fell, treeless, empty, scoured by the wind.

Then, a mile or so further on, they saw outlined against the last fires of the setting sun, whipped by the wind, the flapping shape of a flag, marking the spot, and the wind-shivered flames of torches, and lanterns flickering yellow and rose on the faces of men and women and children gathering about the stands prepared for the preachers. Singers were already pouring their warning song into the night, full and strong and fervent, swelling all the time as the crowd grew.

> *Stop, poor sinner, stop and think,*
> *Before you further go,*
> *Can you sport upon the brink,*
> *Of everlasting woe?*

It was as if the whole world was encompassed in the lantern-lit fellside, and below it a dark pit lurked, hidden from view by the night, but into which at any moment the unwary might fall for ever.

Here and there a man or woman stepped onto a stand and began to speak, praying with anguish or ferocity, crying out to the listeners to think of the fate that would be theirs if they did not here and now recognise how sinful they were, how much in need of salvation, yet how utterly unworthy of it. From the crowd, cries of agreement broke out, and other prayers, echoing or vying with those of the preachers, and through it all the singing continued from all sides. Jenny halted at the edge of the crowd and helped Rowland from the pony. She left Em to tether the animal in the place set apart for that purpose, and walked with Rowland towards one of the stands. Beside it, on a stool provided quickly by someone nearby, he sat down, still silent, still with that look of utter exhaustion.

Near them, Sarah Craggs, who had been calling with passionate longing for God to bring all those before her to repentance, moved on to speak directly to them, sometimes by name, fiercely urging them to a sense of sin. Around her stand, some stood silent, but many cried out, groaning, sobbing, wailing their agreement. A man fell to the ground calling out, 'Help me! Help me! I am lost!' The praying group gathered around him, their calls for divine aid rising into the night. Sarah stepped down from the stand and came to join them. The singing swelled and grew, and the praying. Others fell. The night was filled with the sounds of singing, shouting, weeping, wails and urgent pleas.

Then the first man rose to his feet, tears running down his face, forming long gilded rivulets in the lantern light, his arms raised. He cried, 'Hallelujah!' and all at once Rowland was on his feet too and went to embrace him and lead him to the stand; and then he himself climbed onto it, not slowly or hesitantly, but leaping up as if all the vigour and strength of his youth had suddenly returned to him. Near him, the singers caught up the man's word and a new hymn rose into the night, its chorus ecstatic,

Hallelujah, hallelujah,
Hallelujah to the Lamb!

Rowland spread his arms wide, black against the sky, and joined in the singing, his voice almost as clear and true and strong as it used to be.

Welcome, welcome brother Christian,
To a rich and heavenly place;
Enter in thou new born creature,
Christ is here, there's nothing sweeter.
  Hallelujah, hallelujah,
  Hallelujah to the Lamb! . . .

Hands, and hearts, and voices raise
To the God of all our praise;
He that sends us light from high:
There let all our wishes fly.
  Hallelujah, hallelujah,
  Hallelujah to the Lamb!

Then with a gesture Rowland silenced the singing (though snatches of other hymns came to them from other parts of the ground), and into the little pool of quiet his voice broke, husky, trembling yet resonant. 'Aye, brothers and sisters, He sends us light, for God is light, and in Him is no darkness at all . . . '

The faces raised to him were already rapt, attentive, while behind them new faces were caught in the torch-light as others came softly to hear, perhaps remembering past times when Rowland's voice had captivated them, when his words had seemed to answer some need or longing within them. For a moment even Jenny forgot that he was sick, ceased even to be awed by the astonishing transformation. Beside her, the children were silent, enthralled.

'You look around; you say, *How can that be?* For here, now, even in this place, we are in darkness – the darkness of night, which our puny lanterns can scarcely disperse.

'Why yes, brothers and sisters, we are in darkness! But it is a darkness against which this night is bright as the sun on the brightest day.

'My brother miners' – his voice now was warm and intimate, soft and yet heard by every one of his listeners – 'you know how it is at the forehead of the mine when your candle goes out. You know that blackness, the darkness you can touch and taste, so dark it is, so complete. The little candle flame goes out, and there is nothing, nothing for the senses to take hold of, just the dark. It stifles you, presses on you, shuts out everything. You don't know where to go in safety, for there is nowt to guide, nowt to show the way.' His hands gestured, as if he too were lost in the dark, groping his way, fearful of falling.

'So is our life, wrapped in the darkness of sin. We think we live, we think we know joy and happiness, we think we have light. But while we live in sin we are as in the deep places of the mine, where we cannot see our way, nor hope to miss the shafts and sumps that open beneath our feet, the treacherous water, the crumbling rock that may at any moment fall upon us. We are lost in the depths, adrift in darkness, cut off from hope, from our comrades, from any help. We know only fear and misery and loneliness.

'What can we do, dear brothers and sisters; how can we break free? We can blunder on in that darkness, knowing that we shall surely fall. We can cower in terror, helpless and hopeless, too fearful to move, to act, to live. Or, brothers and sisters, we can reach out for the only light that can bring us hope and relief and joy; the only light that can show us the true path, that can light our way and lead us where we ought to go.' Behind his head the moon was rising, round and brilliant, and they could almost imagine that he held some of its light clasped in his raised hand.

'Reach for that light, dear brothers and sisters. Reach out from your sin and darkness and terror, take hold of it, that tiny flame of hope. It will grow in strength and power, it will warm and guide you. You will see the dangers that lurk in your path, you will see them clearly and step aside in time. For that light, dear friends, is Jesus, and He shines in love, He calls us in love.

'He calls each one of us – you – and you – ' His hands gestured out towards this one and that among his listeners. 'And you – and me – and you. No man or woman or child is outside his love, beyond the reach of his light.

'But do not think that once you have reached for the light, that is the end of it. No, dear friends, it is only the beginning, the first step in a new life, a new understanding. Hold the light high, and what do you see? Not just the dangers, the pitfalls – but more than that, the light shines out from your clasping hand onto the faces of your brothers and sisters, your companions in life's journey. For it shines for them too. Try to shield it from them, try to clasp it close to you, away from their outstretched hands and their longing eyes, and you will stifle it. Your light will go out and you will be as alone as ever you were, and as lost. Can you keep it to yourself? Try and see – walk carefully on, shield the light from the wind – ' He cupped one hand over the palm of another, as if shielding a flame. 'Your flame is safe, aye, maybe it is – but you cannot see to right or left, you cannot see your brother's hand outstretched in need, you cannot see your sister's eyes red with weeping. What does that matter, you think, for *I* am safe, I shall reach the end of my journey, unharmed, unsullied, untouched? But no, my friend, you are wrong. You are so anxious to keep the light for yourself, that it no longer shines out to show you the way. You no longer see what lies before you. Before you know it the pit has opened in your path and you are as lost as ever you were.

'For we do not, we cannot, pass through life alone. We are all loved, each one of us. Think what that means . . . If our brother and our sister are loved as much as we are, then we must share the light with them, share that great love we have been given. The light of Jesus is not *my* light, or *your* light, it is the light of the world, the light of the whole world, given for every part of the world, for every living man and woman. When the day comes that every human creature opens his eyes to the light and reaches for it and lifts it high, then, on that great day, the darkness of sin will be banished, and hunger and war and oppression and hate and fear will vanish from the earth. There will be no more masters and servants, no more rich and poor, only simple men and women, brothers and sisters in Christ, equal in His love and His light. Make no mistake, my brothers and sisters, we are called, each one of us, to walk towards that day, and to strive for it, with all the power that is given us, every gift that we have. That is why the light is given, not for our safety alone, but that we may work together to bring God's light to all his creatures. It may be that we are small and weak, it may be that we have only a short time allotted to us, but what little we can do, that we must do.

'So, dear brothers and sisters, hold the light high and clasp the hand of your brother and your sister, and walk forward together, in loving union one with another, striving always to care for the lonely and the oppressed, to feed the hungry and comfort the sad. Hold your light high, and do not fear that the wind will blow it out. Take no thought for yourself, think only of what you are called to do, and your light will not perish. It may be that none of us here tonight will live to see the day of justice transform the earth, but do not falter, do not weaken. Do what you are called to do, with the light of Jesus to guide you, and His spirit to give strength to your arm, and your light will grow and the darkness will fall from you. And then at last, when your earthly life is over, you will come to that place which is the pattern of all our earthly hopes and all our dreams.

'There, my dear friends, in that place, you will see at last, with eyes unclouded. There, before you, will be revealed the full glory of His perfect day, where there is only light and joy and singing, where there is no sin, no pain, no hunger, where justice and peace and brotherhood reign in perfect harmony and shine in the rays of His perfect light.'

There was a tiny interval of silence, into which the resonance of Rowland's voice seemed to echo on, as if he were still speaking. Then, suddenly, the men and women about the stand reached out to link arms with one another. The hymn broke out again, triumphant and joyful, and they all sang, swaying to the music.

> *When we reach that blissful place,*
> *We shall with our Jesus feast;*
> *We shall with Him happy be,*
> *Sing to all eternity.*
> *Hallelujah, hallelujah . . .*

In the joyous clamour no one saw that Rowland had stumbled from the stand into Jenny's arms. Whatever had given him strength to speak so long, so eloquently, had left him now. He was scarcely conscious, his breathing harsh and painful. Jenny sent Em for help, and Nathan Elliott and Rowland's cousin Lancelot Hall came and wrapped him in blankets and carried him to a cart, and then they set out down the hill, Jenny and the children walking silently beside the vehicle.

They had just crossed the river when someone came running towards them from the far side, his lantern swaying wildly. The spasmodic light lit furious features that Jenny did not at first, in her distress, recognise as Joe's. He halted before her and burst out, 'After all I said, I never thought this of you! I trusted you!'

Jenny stopped the pony and stared at him, not understanding any part of his incoherent words. He did not seem to have noticed the men who were with her, or what lay in the cart.

He stepped forward, lantern high, and swept its light over the little group. 'Where is she then?'

'Who?' demanded Jenny.

'Why, Eve, of course!'

Still she stared at him. 'She went home with you. Yesterday.'

It was his turn to stare. Then, slowly, he began to realise that something was wrong, that they were not simply returning early from the camp meeting, as he had supposed. Jenny said, 'Rowland's bad. We can't stay.'

He looked again at the cart and the swathed form lying

there, and then he stepped back. 'I'm sorry. I didn't
know. She's gone, that's all.'

Jenny said no more. Scarcely looking at him, she led
the pony on up the hill. At White Lea, Mary helping her,
she put Rowland to bed. It was almost impossible to
believe that this frail exhausted figure struggling for
breath had only a short time before spoken with such
passion, so movingly.

The strength had been given, for just long enough; and
now it had been withdrawn. It was over. He had spoken
for the last time. All that remained to him now was the
weeks of his dying.

Chapter Thirteen

'If he doesn't love me, then I'll do what he wants,' Eve had thought, alone in her room on that Saturday afternoon. 'I shall go away, and he will never see me again. Then maybe he'll be sorry. He'll realise he loves me after all. Perhaps he'll weep. Or drink to drown his sorrow and his shame.'

She sat on the edge of the bed, quite still, her hands clasped in her lap, listening to the sounds from downstairs. The family at table, clearing away, the children laughing as *she* put them to bed . . . Her father going to say goodnight to them . . .

She heard quietness settle over the house, sat on while the light dwindled into dusk. Downstairs, they would be seated either side of the fire, her father one side, *she* on the other, perhaps talking, more likely silent. They seemed to talk to one another much less than Aunt Jenny and Uncle Rowland; sometimes they seemed like two quite separate people, living two quite separate lives, though when her father's friends came round, Well House was much noisier and more lively than White Lea.

She stood up. Outside, the deepening night was silvered with moonlight, soft and still; inside, it would soon be too dark to see what she was doing. She pulled on her cloak, slipped off her shoes and held them in one hand, and then, very softly, crept out of the room and down the stairs, pausing often to listen for any sound that might warn her that someone was coming. She heard their voices, briefly, exchanging some remark in the parlour. Light rimmed the door, though here it was dark, very dark. She had to feel her way across the hall to the kitchen, and then through it to the passage beyond, to the back door. She unbarred it very slowly and carefully, fearful of the least sound, and then pulled it open and slipped out into the night.

She paused just outside the door to put on her shoes and then crept across the yard and out into the lane. There she stood still for a little while to allow her eyes to grow accustomed to the dark, and then she set out steadily down the hill. She knew precisely where she was going. No one would think to find her there. She would live like a wild thing, on what she could find. And if she were to starve, then what would it matter? No one would care. Perhaps they would even be relieved that she had gone.

The entrance seemed very black in the night, a gaping mouth. She could see nothing beyond it, just that deep intense blackness. She slid one foot forward, and then hesitated. Most lead miners took a stick when they went into a mine, to help feel their way. She remembered Uncle Tommy talking of it once.

There was a small group of trees near the level mouth and she went over to them and felt around until she found a stick – rather small and thin, but better than nothing – and then she went back to the entrance and, feeling her way along the stonework with one hand, edged slowly inside.

She swung the stick in front of her, bending a little so that it swept the floor, striking the wooden rails of the wagonway. With her other hand she felt the wall at her side, cold wet stone, roughly cut. She heard her feet splash in the water running along the level towards the

205

entrance; her shoes were quickly soaked right through, chilling her.

Soon she felt as if she had been walking for hours; she must, she thought, be miles into the hillside. Then she turned and looked back the way she had come and saw the faint outline of the level mouth, deeply blue. She had come hardly any distance at all. She resisted a momentary impulse to turn round and retrace her steps, as quickly as she possibly could, and turned resolutely back and on, into the blackness. Next time she looked round, it was as black behind her as in front. She halted, struck with terror. Would she ever be able to find her way out again now? She was lost, shut in by the dark, alone, entombed alive. She almost screamed.

Then she bit her lip, and gulped, and drew a deep long breath and forced herself to go on. After all, that was what she wanted, to be lost for ever, so that they would all be sorry for what they had made her do.

Soon she lost all sense of time or distance. She felt as if she had been doing this for as long as she could remember, feeling her way with the stick, following after with a slide of each foot, slowly, first one and then the other, stubbing her toes often on the rails or a protruding piece of rock. Her feet were wet, her clothes growing colder and wetter with every step. Drops of moisture fell cold on her hair and trickled down her neck. She knew, though she could not see, that her hands were slimed with thin mud. The air smelt stale, filled with the odours of wet rock and earth. The little movement of wind that had followed her from the level mouth had gone now. There was no sound except the splashing of her feet, her anxious breathing; when she halted she could hear only the drip drip of moisture from the roof and, further off, distantly echoing, the faster falling of water – a ventilation fall, perhaps, or some underground stream. She ceased to think of anything, for it took all her concentration to feel her way forward, to force herself to keep going.

She was brought suddenly to a halt. Her stick hit rock,

she put her hand forward and felt a great wall confronting her. Surely she could not have reached the end of the level? She felt to the right, felt the rock curve round in front of her; then to the left, and there was no curve, only the wall extending on beyond her reach. Puzzled, she felt with her feet, nearly tripping on a rail where she had not expected one to be. Then she realised why: the level took a turn to the left. Very carefully, she felt her way round the corner, until she was once more going straight ahead along its length.

On and on, with little change; here and there a turn in the direction of the level, a change in the air to tell her that another level ran into it at a right angle, or that a shaft opened into it to one side, for then her hands felt nothing except, perhaps, the platform on which waste material or lead ore waited for transport to the day. In doubt, she took what felt the clearest route, as far as she could tell.

What made her stop again she did not quite know. It was not the stick, for that gave her no warning. But she halted all the same, and gently pushed forward with her foot. The earth was drier here, with no water running upon it. She kept her hands firmly on the walls, and slid one foot on; and then felt it extend into nothingness.

She drew it back sharply, her heart beating in wild panic, throbbing in her ears. Fear dried her mouth, tingled cold down her back, to the roots of her hair and her fingertips. She knew, with certainty, that there in front of her was a sump, one of the downward shafts that gave access to some lower level at who knew what depth. It might not extend the full width of the level – most probably did not – but without light, alone, she could not tell how wide it was, still less how deep; she could not tell if there was any way past it in safety.

She stood there for a very long time, feeling as if she were perched precariously on some tiny portion of solid ground with emptiness around her into which at any moment she might fall; waiting until the terror subsided enough for her to think what to do. And then she slid backwards, feeling every inch of the way, until she came to one of the places where the width of the level and the multiplicity of rails on its floor told her there was a passing place for the wagons; and there she sank down against the wall and sat very still, hugging her knees, her face bent onto them, her eyes closed, trying to find some warmth, some comfort, trying to shut out the blackness and the nothingness and the fear.

Perhaps, for a time, she fell asleep, for all of a sudden she jerked her head up and opened her eyes, fully expecting to see some sign that dawn was near; and was shocked rigid by the intensity of the darkness, before she remembered. It was then, trembling and cold and frightened, that she began to whimper.

Like the darkness, time stretched endlessly on, without form, with no boundaries to mark it, no contrasting point of any kind to tell her how long she had been there. She thought she fell asleep again more than once, but she could not be sure. She knew she was hungry. She was certain now that she was going to die here, and that would not even serve her purpose, because no one would ever find her or know what had become of her. For a long time she shivered with cold, until she grew drowsy and dozed again. Once, she heard something scampering past her. It might have been a rat, but she could not tell and simply held her knees more tightly, pressing her skirts close about her ankles.

For hours and hours she must have sat there, with the constant drip drip of water in her ears, and the more distant splashing, and after a time all kinds of odd breathings and groanings and rustlings that might have been real or might have been imagined. She slept and woke and slept and woke and still she dared not move. Her mind grew numb, like her limbs, with nothing to take hold of, there in the dark.

A noise broke into her sleep like a thunderclap, and this

time it was real, jolting her into terrified wakefulness. She sat there, listening, her eyes peering into the blackness, trying to discover what it was.

A muffled rumbling came nearer, growing louder, its echoes rolling over her and then on into the depths of the mine. It seemed to go on for a long time, with other, sharper, noises shooting out intermittently around it. Then it stopped. In a way that was worse because she imagined some kind of fearful monster lurking there in the dark, halting to watch her with eyes that could see as hers could not.

Then she did see something, faintly, in the distance: a tiny yellow point of light, very far away. She held her breath. An eye? One of those dancing flames that hovered over marshy places but disappeared when you went near, leading you on to a horrible death?

It was a candle, and a man carried it. She could see his face now, glowing behind it. There was another man beside him, just visible as they came nearer. She could hear the tramp of their clogs, the click of their sticks on the rails.

She did not know whether to be glad or afraid, whether to call out or draw further back into the space behind her in the hope that they would not see her.

There was no escape, for they had reached her, and the one with the candle halted with a catch of his breath. He almost dropped the candle. 'By God, there's a lass here!'

The other man took the candle from him and peered closer. Eve shrank back. She did not recognise him as anyone she knew and in the flickering light his face looked grotesque and threatening. 'It's Joe Emerson's lass – the one they've been out seeking all weekend.'

'Aye, I do believe it is.' Eve tried to stand up, feeling it was a safer way to face them, but her legs crumpled under her and she fell down again. She felt strong arms fold about her. 'Come now, lass, let's get you back to your father. Why, you're soaked through!' They fussed about her, wrapping her in their coats, and then one of them lifted her and carried her back through the dreadful passageway, the other holding the candle to light their way.

They passed other men, and her rescuers called out to let them know what they'd found. They drew aside into a passing place, like the one in which she had hidden, to allow a galloway to go by with his train of wagons (that, she realised, was the first noise she had heard). The rock that arched overhead looked very ordinary in the candle-light.

She was astonished to find how short a time it was before the tiny pale outline of the level mouth appeared in the distance and then grew larger, until at last the daylight overpowered the candle flame; and then, suddenly, they were outside and she was blinking in the light. The air felt cold and clear and pure, the world looked dazzlingly green, as she had never seen it before. She saw flowers everywhere, and a sky so amazingly blue that it hurt to look at it.

She was taken to the forge that served the mine, where there was a hot fire, and they brought her rum that ran fierily through her and made her cough, and the men hovered over her, all rough concern. Someone had gone to seek her father, they told her, as if that offered re-assurance. He'd been worried sick; out since Saturday night hunting her, with half Weardale to help. It was now Monday morning.

He would be furious with her for causing such trouble. She imagined his anger, and the tears began to trickle from her eyes, so that one of the men put an arm about her and made soothing noises, sounding just a little embarrassed.

Her father came, all too soon, his strong shape filling the little doorway. She managed to get to her feet to face him. But only for a moment, for he swept her into his arms and carried her out into the light, scolding her, but tenderly, his voice rough, not with anger but with relief and love. Out there, a considerable number of men and a handful of women cheered as they saw her. After a few dazed moments, Eve realised they must be the 'half

Weardale' who had joined her father in searching for her.

On the way home, carrying her triumphantly on his back, he said, 'What made you do it, hinny? You could have been killed. A mine's no place for a lass, without light or a guide.'

'I know,' she said, shuddering at the recollection, but already imagining how she would tell Mary and Em about it when she saw them next.

Nearing Well House she wriggled suddenly, and then slid off her father's back. He looked down at her.

'Can I go back to White Lea, Father?'

He shook his head, suddenly sombre. 'No, my pet. Your Uncle Rowland's taken very bad. Aunt Jenny has plenty on her hands just now.'

She went with him, but there was a weight inside her, doing its best to crush her relief and happiness at being found and being alive and being loved.

But it was not quite all over. To her amazement even her stepmother gave her a hug – rather a brief and half-hearted one, but a hug nevertheless – before sitting her down to a vast breakfast. The rescue party crowded into the kitchen round her and enjoyed their own noisy celebrations.

No one, for today at least, talked about doing any housework, and Esther and Ralph and William plied her with eager questions and heard her story with wide, envious eyes.

Chapter Fourteen

'Ah, Dunn! Good day to you!'

Matthias Dunn, emerging from the colliery office on his way to the Isabella pit, shaded his eyes against the sun and looked up at the elderly, dapper figure of Arthur Mowbray, founding partner of the Hetton Coal Company, who was just dismounting from his horse.

'I understood the committee was not to meet until this afternoon,' said Dunn.

'I have undertaken to receive the union delegates again before then, if you recall,' said Mowbray.

Dunn, fighting irritation, pointed out that he had not been told of this development.

'Ah, I see.' Mowbray looked momentarily embarrassed, then explained smoothly, 'They wrote requesting a meeting. It seemed politic to accede to it. . . But I am glad to have met with you. There is a matter on which I would like your opinion before I confront our union friends.' He gave a heavily ironic emphasis to the last word.

Dunn would have liked to say that he was too busy to give up his time to employers who failed to keep him informed on the most vital colliery concerns, but recognised that would hardly be in his interests, in the long run. Instead, he explained that he had been on his way to the Isabella pit to check a repair to the pulley on the winding gear, which had come adrift the previous day, necessitating the temporary closure of the pit. 'I required them to let me see it before entrusting any of the men to it,' he said. 'So work is held up until then.' He hoped that Mowbray would at once recognise the dedication and conscientiousness of his viewer, and feel some compunction about the treatment Dunn had to endure.

Mowbray nodded approvingly, but merely said, 'I shan't detain you long.'

They went indoors and once the door was closed behind them, Mowbray showed Dunn the letter he had spoken of.

Dunn read it and then said, 'It gives nothing away. Have you any reason to hope they might have come to their senses at last?'

Mowbray smiled faintly. 'Who can say? But I do believe that by now they must be as heartily sick of the dispute as we are . . . Hepburn's here, you know. I passed him on my way.'

'That may be to our advantage.' After last year's success, the union members had appointed Tommy Hepburn as full-time leader and adviser, as a result of which he had left Hetton well before Dunn came there in November, returning only occasionally to give advice. The viewer had only met him twice before, and then briefly, but he had quickly gained a considerable respect for the man. Many of the other union leaders he regarded as self-seeking rabble-rousers – Charlie Parkinson in particular, whom he detested as a dangerous subversive – but there was something about Hepburn that compelled respect, however reluctantly.

'I have considerable hopes that they will prove to be more flexible than in the past. There are some of us who are most anxious for a settlement.'

'Of course,' said Dunn, 'though not at any price. On our terms, not theirs.'

'Perhaps. But it has been put to me that if there were a way in which we might come to some accommodation with them, while maintaining at the very least the appearance of having retained the upper hand, then it would be greatly to our advantage.'

'Last year's tactic,' said Dunn dismissively. 'I suppose that's Wood's view.' His relations with the colliery agent had reached breaking-point some time ago, over Wood's refusal to treat the stranger colliers with the consideration Dunn felt was their due; further, Wood had publicly and insolently disagreed with Dunn on the matter. The two men never spoke now, and Dunn had told the partners that Wood must go. They were, unfortunately, taking rather longer than he would have liked to set the matter in motion. It was clear that Wood had friends among both the lesser officials and the partners. Dunn had not thought Mowbray was one of them.

'I have not sought Wood's opinion in the matter. No, it is Redhead's view. He is convinced that so long as we continue to rely on the stranger pitmen, we shall fall ever further behind our rivals, until in the course of time we shall be producing so small a proportion of the coal shipped for sale that we shall face certain ruin. He is not alone in his opinion, I may say.'

'There are some capital hewers among the strangers,' Dunn pointed out. 'The Derbyshire men in particular. As for the rest, it is my belief that the majority of them will prove, in time, to be every bit as good as the old pitmen. What is more, I anticipate far fewer difficulties with them in introducing innovations into the colliery.' He wished he could say the same of his employers, who constantly resisted his suggestions for change; unfortunately, replacing them with new blood was not open to him.

'I think Redhead would differ with you there. He is of the opinion that men not born to the work, or trained to it from their earliest years, can never be expected to attain the skills and knowledge required for the most effective production of coal. Consequently, he takes the view that we should make terms with them, insisting only upon one further condition.'

'And that is?'

'That they drop their ruinous insistence that hewers work only until they have earned four shillings in the day. Under such conditions, we shall never be able to compete with our rivals, as we must do if our enterprise is to survive. Of course, the men will claim that there is a limit to the quantity of coals required by the world at large, and that to raise more will only flood the market and lower prices. My view is that, in such a case, then Hetton coals must be first on the market, at the most competitive rates. The policy of restriction renders that impossible. So, of course, does the inexperience of the stranger hewers.'

Dunn considered his reply with unusual care, speaking at last without any audible trace of the exasperation he felt. 'In my opinion the single essential condition for the future profitability of this company is that the union be broken. So long as it retains its hold over the men, then there can be no hope for present or future peace. If we do not remain firm now, we shall bitterly regret it in the future – as, I fear, we must already regret that we did not stand firm last year, at the outset. But we cannot continue to allow ourselves to be dictated to by those who should be our servants, not our masters.'

By the time he left the office Dunn thought he had convinced Mowbray of the wisdom of what he urged, but he could not be sure. That was the difficulty with his employers. They would listen to his advice – sometimes – and then do quite the opposite, even on occasions giving instructions on colliery business behind his back. Since he was supposedly employed by them to manage the colliery, that created endless difficulties.

He made his way quickly to the Isabella pit, where he found that the pulley was once more working perfectly. He gave instructions that the pit should be opened again, in time for the recently revived second shift; but the incident brought to mind quite another problem, which was troubling him with increasing frequency. An accident in the shaft – a fire, the failure of machinery – could be very serious indeed, and at other collieries had often cost lives, especially when there were insufficient alternative shafts to offer a means of escape. He was haunted by the fear that something of the kind might happen in a pit under his control. He had plans of the colliery workings at home. Tonight, he decided, he would study them and see what could be done to make them safer, perhaps by providing access between different pits within the coal company's property. Whether or not the committee would listen to his arguments, when he had them ready, was another matter, which he must face when he came to it.

But before that there would be this afternoon's committee meeting to attend. He was not looking forward to it. He was, of course, a little apprehensive as to how Mowbray would deal with the delegates; but, whatever the outcome of that meeting, he knew that it would be tranquil indeed compared to the gathering of the company committee, with its inevitable squabbling and carping, and the niggling criticisms of himself which had become only too familiar.

Tommy, laid off because of the damage to the Isabella pit, sat trying to read by the kitchen fire, against the constant background of Rebekah's complaining and Luke's harassed attempts to soothe her. At least this morning it was quiet outside. Last night there had been a gang of youths running through the alleys of Brick Garth, shouting abuse. Fortunately nothing worse had happened than a broken window three doors away, because two of the special constables had put in an appearance; but such incidents were becoming more common, perhaps because the authorities assumed the worst was over, now that the strangers were settling in and entire rows of the colliery houses were occupied by them. The strangers now took care to go in groups, or at the very least in twos, when making their way through the streets after dark.

216

'He should be at school, you know. At home he would have been—' Rebekah stopped, suddenly listening. The yard gate had squeaked open, and now feet clattered quickly towards the house. When the knocking came on the door there was a moment of silence while they all three looked at one another. Then Luke went to answer it.

Jacob Nattrass stepped into a room made the more welcoming by relief, though he was clearly too agitated to notice it. He did not even look at Luke.

'Tommy, my wife's very sick. Will you come and pray with us?'

Tommy went with him at once to the house on the far side of Brick Garth. The sick woman lay on a bed soaked and stinking with all that had drained from her body. He had never seen anyone look so horrible before, her fair skin darkened to a dusky purplish colour, dried up and wrinkled, as if she were some ancient corpse; though she was clearly living still, her eyes deep sunken in her gaunt face, watching him with misery and terror. He knelt down at the bedside, wondering where, in all his sense of horror, he would find words of prayer.

He had not even begun when behind him one of the children cried out. He turned. She was clutching her belly, bent on the ground in agony. The distraught father caught her up, comforting her, questioning her. When Tommy turned back to the bed again, the mother was dead.

Two hours later, the little girl died, and then her infant brother. Jacob himself sickened that night, though by the morning he was showing signs of recovery. By then, Tommy, who had stayed to pray as best he could in the intervals between his clumsy and inexperienced attempts at sick nursing, knew well enough what the disease was, if only because no other neighbour had come to offer help. He heard the whisper as he went home. 'The cholera,' a woman said, drawing back from him as he passed. 'It's the cholera.'

Word had reached Luke's house before he did. By the

time he got there, Rebekah was clutching her children in her arms, weeping in a state of shuddering terror.

Tommy Hepburn, meeting with the Hetton union committee before the appointment with Mr Mowbray, was quietly confident of their prospects. 'They've had a poor return on the great sums they've laid out bringing strangers in. It's my belief, if we say nothing of it, they'll quietly drop their objections to the union, just to have skilled men back in the pits.'

'Just like that?' Adam asked, incredulously.

'Why no, they'll require some small gesture, to save face.'

They discussed the various items on which they might make concessions to the company. Afterwards, Adam asked, 'What if they'll give us nowt?'

'The collieries vote tonight on an all-out strike. If they vote in favour, that'll sharp bring the owners to their senses.'

'In my opinion it should have been done at the outset,' said Parkinson.

'It looked as though we'd have no need of so strong a measure. And we must have the sanction of the members first. But far better we get what we ask from the owners today.'

'Mind, if Hetton gives in, will the other owners follow their lead? Kenton, Coxlodge, Waldridge . . . ?'

'Aye, in time, they will. They were forced to last year.'

Hepburn, not now being a Hetton man, stayed in the background while the committee members met Mowbray, though he was ready to give advice if he should be called upon.

It looked as though he had been right in his belief that the company was eager for a settlement. In fact, Mowbray declared at once, in the strongest terms, that such was his wish. The sticking point, he implied, was the union insistence that earnings must be limited. If that were to be abandoned . . .

It took some time and a good deal of heated discussion, but in the end the delegates agreed to give way on that point. Mowbray observed, with some asperity, 'A pity it could not have been settled so amicably at the outset. A deal of trouble and expense would have been avoided, on all sides.'

The union delegates curbed any impulse to make a sour retort to that remark. They knew they had lost face to a considerable degree by conceding almost everything the owners had demanded; but so long as the one vital point still stood, then they could afford that lesser humiliation.

They moved on to examine one by one all the terms of a possible agreement. Most of them had already been discussed, at earlier meetings, and all had previously been agreed upon – except one, which stood out starkly among the rest: every man bound to work for the company must make an undertaking not to belong to the union.

'That's been a condition of employment for some months now,' Mowbray pointed out, when Adam exclaimed at it.

'Maybe, but that was when you were taking on strangers.'

'The more then that we should insist upon it from men who have for so long held out against us. Take note, it requires only an undertaking that no pitman will enter into any association that interferes with the terms of his agreement with his employers. For example, a simple friendly society, concerned solely with the mutual support in sickness and death of its members, would be entirely allowable under those terms. It is not unions as such to which we take exception, but those that interfere with the free movement of trade and the regular supply of labour. In essence, we ask only for a restoration of the correct relationship between masters and men.'

'So you'd have us slaves again!' retorted Charlie Parkinson, with great bitterness. 'We've had our taste of liberty, since the union won it for us. We'll not lightly put ourselves in shackles again.'

'As you please. Remain free to starve, by all means. I would not be the one to interfere with that freedom.'

In the end, Parkinson glanced at the others and, together, with a scraping of stools on the flagged floor, they rose to their feet. 'Let the Lord decide between us,' he said. Then they turned and left the office.

Outside, he said to Hepburn, 'They are as hard of heart as ever. Our hope now must be in a general strike of the whole coalfield.'

Ten days after the first outbreak of cholera at Brick Garth, on his way home from work, Tommy left Luke to go on alone and turned aside to call on three or four of the neighbouring houses, to see what he could do for the cholera-stricken families.

The Nattrasses had only been the first to sicken in Brick Garth. Each day, others were added to their numbers; often, when calling to pray at one house, Tommy would be told of another family that had been struck down. Whether asked to go or not, he would then call on them, to offer what assistance he could give. Sometimes they wanted practical things, like shopping, water fetching, a fire lit, food brought in for those who were still well enough to eat. More often, they wanted his prayers, since that seemed the only thing that offered any hope of recovery from a sickness that struck so suddenly and with such devastating swiftness. Most of all, he thought he brought comfort simply by being one of the few people not too frightened for simple neighbourliness. By now most of those he visited were strangers even from his viewpoint – families from Wales or Cornwall or Derbyshire, with strange accents but the same terror in the face of catastrophe.

Today he did the various errands that were asked of him, lingered to pray in a house where the wife's elderly mother had just died and undertook to make the necessary arrangements for the burial. After which, weary and hungry, he went home.

There he found not a bright fire and the doubtful smell

of Rebekah's cooking, but a hearth full of cold ashes and the room scattered with boxes and baskets half filled with the family's possessions. It was clear at once what was happening, but he stood in the doorway and stared, until Rebekah looked up, silently, and then Luke came in from the front room.

'We're going home,' he said, abruptly, without a smile.

'I see that,' said Tommy. Still he did not move.

'Jacob Nattrass is coming with us. He says there's nowt left for him here. But at least he's over it. We're not waiting until you—' He broke off, his eyes suddenly avoiding Tommy's. Had he been about to say, *Until you bring it home with you one day?* If he had, he thought better of it, saying instead, 'You should come too. There are more sick every day. We're better off in Weardale. Sooner eat grass than die like that.'

Tommy stood looking at him in silence for some time without seeing him, trying to gather his own thoughts. Should he go with them? He had learned quickly enough that his reasons for coming here had all been wrong. There had been many occasions in the past months when he had wondered if he ought to leave, especially since Matty had turned on him. Was he now being offered a way out, even though no apparent purpose had yet been served by his leaving home in the first place?

He thought of what he had been doing today. Those families would not be going back to whatever part of England or Wales they thought of as home, or not yet at least, for they were too sick to do so. Was it right that all who were still healthy should run away in terror?

He knew the answer. 'I'll not come,' he said. 'If there was ever work to be done here, then that time is now.'

Luke coloured a little. 'It's the bairns—'

'I know,' said Tommy. He did move then, closing the door behind him, and came to help Luke with the packing, though as if his hands were moving independently of the rest of him. He was too abstracted to notice how

Rebekah shrank away from him. 'But I have no bairns. No one at all.'

'What of Jenny—'

Tommy shook his head. 'Don't think I've not thought of her. But I see that my work is here.'

And so is Matty, said a little voice in his head, though he repressed it at once. In any case, it was beside the point; she was lost to him. Much more significant, he knew with certainty that it was God's will for him to stay. That, he saw now, was why he had been brought here in the first place – not for all the sensible worldly reasons he had laid before Rowland, but for this, that he might serve God by serving his suffering fellow creatures in their time of need. *Whatsoever thy hand findeth to do, do it with thy might.* There had been some ambiguity in the message, necessarily, because only time and circumstance had made it clear, but now it all fell into place. It was that which, haltingly, inadequately, he tried to explain in the long letter he wrote that night to Rowland, for Luke to take back with him.

He gave Luke a package too, containing all that he had saved from his pay since coming to Hetton. 'That's for Jenny. Wait till you're alone with her before you give it her. She may not take it. In that case, put it by for the moment, until you find a better time – when she has more need of it and won't say no.'

He was glad that Luke knew him well enough to understand what he implied, without his having to underline it further.

They left next morning, before daybreak. Tommy stood alone in the little house, stripped now of almost every stick of furniture, all but his own tiny store of belongings, and felt suddenly unbearably alone. His conviction that he must stay burned low in the darkness of that early hour. Loneliness oppressed him. He was so very far from all those he loved, two days' journey, cut off by a choice that was not his own, from which there was no going back.

*　　　*　　　*

The camp in the wood had shrunk considerably since the May morning when Tommy had first come upon it. Some of the families had found more permanent shelter elsewhere, others had gone to wander the roads, seeking work where they could. Matty wondered how long it would be before the rest of them also melted away.

This afternoon, as usual, the remaining men had gathered at one side of the clearing, to discuss union matters. Their disappointment at the failure of the negotiations had been quickly followed by a majority vote against an all-out strike. The working colliers had no wish to give up their jobs, particularly when they might consequently be hauled before the courts for breaking their bonds. Worse than that, many of them were now growing restive at the obligation to give funds weekly to support their workless brethren. Some had even refused outright to contribute any more.

Matty, hovering near by in the hope of catching something of what the men said, grasped little more than that their mood was one of general gloom. She knew that some of the families in the wood were already wavering in their loyalty, muttering amongst themselves about leaving the union and returning to work. It was whispered that some men, elsewhere, had already done so.

She hung back in the shadow of the trees, so absorbed in what the men were saying that she did not hear someone come up behind her. An arm slid suddenly about her waist, and then she was pulled round and a kiss planted fiercely upon her mouth. She was so startled at first that she did nothing, until she realised it was Jack Marley (who else indeed could it be? She would have known his rough fervour anywhere). She wriggled free of him, laughing but resistant.

The disturbance clearly reached the men, and she heard Adam call, 'Howay Marley, let the lass alone! Come and join us.'

Jack went and crouched down beside the others, where they sat on fallen logs and tree stumps. 'I've a grand piece

223

of news. Had it from your wife. The strangers in my house – they've gone. Fled from the cholera.'

Matty stood very still, her ears strained so as to miss nothing. A dreadful desolation dropped suddenly into her spirit. Tommy had gone; she would never see him again. *That's good*, she thought, trying to jolt herself into cheerfulness.

Then Jack said, 'All but the single one, him that was pestering Matty. He's still there. Tending the sick, so they say.' His tone was sneering. 'Typical Ranter carrion, hanging over deathbeds hungry for meat.'

Adam turned cold indignant eyes upon him. 'Watch your tongue, Marley!'

'Why, would you stick up for a blackleg?'

'No, nor do I wish him well. But there's no cause to mock Christian charity.'

Matty had a vision of Tommy kneeling at the bedside of a dying man, his kindly face full of concern, his deep slow quiet voice soothing to sick ears. She knew what the cholera was like. She had been sick with it herself in December, recovering only to watch her infant brother die. Tommy was deliberately putting himself in danger, staying to face it when his friends had fled. She told herself that if he caught the disease then that was no more than he deserved, while a cold fear churned somewhere in her stomach.

To calm herself, she wandered away in search of distraction. Lately, her old restlessness had returned to her. She had found work for a time getting in the corn on a nearby farm, but that was finished now, well before time because of the good summer. And meanwhile, nothing seemed to be happening. The drama of the trial was over and Adam restored to his wife; they were wrapped up in one another, with no time for anything else, except of course the union. Meanwhile, there seemed no end to the dispute, no hope that they would ever be able to move from the woods back to ordinary houses, with a normal existence to look forward to. The novelty of her present life had worn off some time ago, and Matty simply found it uncomfortable and inconvenient. There was no longer any of the drama of those heroic early days, the struggles and triumphs of last year, the resistance and the evictions of this. There was no longer even the old certainty that they would win, one day.

Not that she was very anxious either to return to her old life, which had as many tediums built into it as this one. She wanted more than a daily routine of housework, cooking, washing, cleaning, casual labouring in the fields, with an occasional diversion – a fair, races, a christening or a wedding – to add a little excitement. She did not want Tommy (of course not; how could a loyal pitman's daughter like herself want a blackleg?), but no one else showed any sign of taking his place. Jack Marley would like to do so, she knew, but she could not bring herself to give him any encouragement. There was simply a great emptiness where Tommy had been.

She was angry with him still that it should be so. That beating at her brother's hands had not been punishment enough, for her unhappiness had not ended with it. Besides, what were those little physical hurts, against her aching heart, her bitter regret?

Eliza had just returned from a visit to her children and was at the door of her shelter, looking over a newspaper that had been left there. Matty wondered if she feared that the children might be endangered by the new outbreak of cholera at Brick Garth, but thought probably not. After all, the Raines household had suffered enough last winter, and Matty had never heard of anyone getting cholera twice. Not that Adam and Eliza had caught it then, but they had lived a little distance from Brick Garth and were perhaps stronger in some ways than most people.

Matty stood looking down at her friend. 'Is there any news?'

'You should learn to read, then you'd find out for yourself.' Eliza was smiling, but there was a hint of reproach in her voice, as if she thought Matty weak-willed.

Stung by the tone, and still more by the memory of what might have come about if only Tommy had not been who he was, Matty burst out, 'Then teach us!' If she could learn to read at last, then perhaps she would find a new purpose and excitement.

Eliza looked regretful. 'I wish I could. But we cannot be private here, and you know your dad would forbid it. Besides, I have so little time.' She saw the disappointment in Matty's face. 'There are other ways to learn, other places you could go, away from here, where your dad would never know. Not,' she added quickly, 'that I'm saying you should deceive him. But he can't be watching you all the time.'

Once there had indeed been others she could have gone to, one other; but that was all in the past, and Eliza had no very concrete suggestion as to where precisely Matty could now find what she wanted, since the Sunday Schools had been severely disrupted by the effects of the strike, most of those who had taught in them having been turned from their homes.

It was only in the early hours of the following morning, when she woke, as she often did, for no good reason and lay looking at the faint outline of the doorway, just visible from her bed of straw and blankets, that Matty knew what she would do. It was so obvious that she was amazed she had not thought of it at once. There was only one person she knew who would be willing to teach her. He had promised to do so, before that dreadful day when she had learned the truth. Why should she not keep him to his promise? If he would not agree freely, she knew ways of making him do what she wanted.

There was, of course, the remaining difficulty that he was still a blackleg and an enemy, but then she would not this time be going to him in any spirit of friendship. On the contrary, whatever his feelings for her now were, he would not welcome what she asked of him. If he hated and feared her for what she had done, then he would know what power she had to harm him again, and yet resent her humiliating use of that power. If he cared for her still, then her going to him would hurt him terribly, for he would be forced into closeness with her while seeing only too clearly how much she now despised him. And she would still get from him the thing she wanted most of all. She would, of course, have to be very careful, for no one must even guess what she was doing, but then she would have had to be careful anyway, whoever she chose as a teacher.

That evening she twisted her hair into some semblance of curls, and put on her brightest skirt and most low-cut bodice and her longest earrings, and pulled a large shawl over her head so that no one seeing her pass would recognise her, and then she set out for Brick Garth.

Since returning from work Tommy had taken food to one neighbour, prayed with three others, cleaned and tidied and washed for another household, so that it was late in the day by the time he reached the now empty house, where his own few belongings looked unbearably sparse, even though he had not even attempted to furnish the front room. A stool and a small table, along with the straw mattress on which he slept, some kitchen utensils, his books and the wooden box in which he had brought most of his personal possessions to Hetton were inadequate even for his simple needs. He did not want to spend much on himself, for it would leave less for Jenny, but when he had time he knew he would have to buy one or two more items of furniture.

Unfortunately, money could not compensate for the loneliness he felt, once back in the house. He thought he would even have welcomed Rebekah's complaining, in preference to the silence. Though the silence might have been more bearable if it had indeed been a complete silence, such as he had known sometimes in Weardale, with only the sounds of wind and water to break it and no human sound to be heard at all. Here, there was noise enough from the other houses, even now when so many had fled. Brick Garth was never free of the sounds of dogs

227

or children, cockerels crowing or feet clattering or men and women shouting and singing and quarrelling; and the incessant noise of builders at work. Even after four months he had not grown used to it; he wondered if he ever would.

He washed and made himself a supper of crowdy (at least that was an improvement on Rebekah's cooking, if less ambitious than her efforts), read a little from the Bible and prayed and then sat down to his studies, neglected for so long when the house was too full of people for proper concentration.

He had not thought to bar the doors. He had no fear of being disturbed by union men, now that the cholera had broken out again, and he wanted anyone in need to be able to reach him easily. After a time, the sounds from outside ceased to trouble him; he grew absorbed in his studies, his mind held and excited by the journey of discovery that lay before him. He forgot that he was lonely and far from home.

He did not hear someone come in by the front door, or cross the next room, or softly open the intervening door and then close it again. He did not hear the quiet steps approaching behind his stool. He heard nothing, until the voice spoke sharply just beside him.

'Stranger!'

He jumped, looked round; and then stared in amazed disbelief, thinking for a moment that his imagination was playing tricks on him.

It was as if she had materialised beside him, a small slight figure with a shawl over her head and her dark eyes intent upon him. But she was not exactly as he would have imagined her, because he had never seen her quite like this, neither glowing with tenderness and laughter, nor fiery with hate. There was no softness in her face, but no anger either, nothing warm at all, only a kind of chilly concentrated seriousness. She laid her hand on the open page before him. 'Teach us!' she said fiercely. 'Teach us to read. You promised once.'

It was spoken so much like a threat that he could not

immediately grasp what she was asking of him. It could not, surely, be as simple as the words implied? As he continued to stare at her, rather stupidly, she went on, 'You're the only one who would do it, and not ask owt in return. If you tell a soul I'll lead them to you, and you'll wish you were dead.'

He had imagined teaching her, on the day he had walked, that last time, to meet her in the wood. He had imagined them sitting side by side under the trees, he with his arm about her, perhaps, while he formed letters for her to learn, showed her the words on a page, watched her make her first struggling attempts at writing. He had imagined them laughing together with all their usual tender intimacy, punctuating the lessons with kisses, turning each one into a celebration. He had imagined how, as time went by, he would watch her grow to fluency, develop skills to equal his own, and he would be filled with pride and happiness that it was he who had guided her first steps. He had imagined how every one of those steps would bind them more closely together.

He had not imagined for one moment that he would teach her in this house, burdened by the knowledge that she came to him only because there was no one else who would give her the one thing she wanted of him – the great gift that, once, he would have given gladly.

He would give it gladly now too, he knew that; or at least willingly, in the hope that one day they might be reconciled. But his heart was heavy that it had to be like this.

She was still waiting for him to say or do something. There were so many things he wanted to say, so many questions he wanted to ask, but he did not know where to begin or how to put them into words, and he was by no means convinced that she would answer them, were he to do so.

In the end, he simply rose to his feet and pulled out the stool and said, 'Sit down then.' She did so, without

229

looking at him, pulling off her shawl and throwing it aside.

He bent over her, acutely conscious of the scent of her hair, her warmth, the glimpse, as she moved, of firm young breasts, the perfection of the long slim neck and the tiny ears so close to his mouth. He ached to kiss them, heedless of those shameless earrings dangling mockingly from them. Had she dressed like this to entice him, or because she hoped it would offend him? . . . As if anything she did could offend him, loving her as he did, desiring her . . .

He forced his eyes to the books and his mind to the supplying of her need. He reached for pen and paper, drew the Bible towards her and opened it rather at random (try as he might he could not think as clearly as he ought); and then he began, slowly, to shape letters and words for her on the blank sheet.

They worked at first by the inadequate remnant of daylight from the small window and later by the light of his one candle, and not once did Tommy think of how time was passing, or of anything but what was happening here and now in the bare little room – because, quite simply, he was enthralled by it, in a wholly unexpected way.

It was nothing like those lessons in the wood he had imagined, but that was largely because she was like no pupil he had ever taught before. It was not just that she learned quickly, as if her mind had only been waiting for some tiny hint for everything to fall into place, so that he wondered that she had any need of a teacher at all, but there was also her endless curiosity, her hunger for knowledge of all kinds. As soon as she had grasped a word, she wanted to know more – what did it mean, not simply on the surface, but in all its implications? – and then her mind would dart off, following all the trains of thought that the one word had set in motion, constantly probing and questioning. The need to answer her taxed his own mind to the limit, set him thinking too about words and ideas he had always taken for granted. The whole process exhilarated him, and would have done so even without the added spice, the added pain of his physical feelings for her.

Not that she gave him any cause, ever, to suspect that her affection for him was anything but dead and replaced by a bitter hate that came out now and then in some passing phrase or glance. She had brought her mind, in all its breadth and perception, to his lodgings, but the rest of her was veiled, apart, beyond his reach, and marked as such by its worldly adornment. He could feed the one, but with the rest he must have nothing whatever to do. Sometimes, delighted by their talk, eager to teach, he could forget the girl in whom the intelligence dwelt, as she seemed momentarily to forget him; at other times, the whole proceess was a potent and painful mixture of torment and delight.

By the time he became aware of an exhaustion temporarily held at bay by the fascination of the evening, it was well after midnight. He suspected that she would have been content to go on for hours yet, but he had to be up for work in the morning and he had spent much of last night by the bedside of a dying man. Besides, since she had the only stool, he had been on his feet for some hours now and every limb and joint was aching with weariness. He closed the Bible and straightened slowly, trying not to show how tired he was.

'That's plenty for one lesson,' he said. 'If you want to come again, then you're welcome.' It sounded very cold and inadequate as an expression of what he really felt.

She rose to her feet with obvious reluctance. He could see that she was disappointed at the dismissal. She stood there, and for only the second time since her arrival looked directly at him. He felt as if he could hardly breathe, seeing that lovely face, beautiful in the candlelight, its bones starkly outlined by the shadows that daylight would have painted out. He almost said, 'I love you!' but stopped himself just in time. Instead, he said, 'You've got thinner.' His voice was soft with concern.

231

'Aye, well, my dad's not in work.' There was no softening there and no wish to bring back what had once been between them.

'I've some bread and cheese, if you'd care to eat before you go.'

'I'd choke on your charity, stranger.'

All the joy and exhilaration of the evening was fast dissolving into nothing. 'Why did you come to me?' he asked, after a little silence.

'I told you: because you promised. And because no one will know. My dad especially.'

'But you might be seen . . . '

'I shall take care.'

'I still don't understand. There must be others.'

He wanted her to say, *Aye, but I don't love them,* or at least hoped to see something of it in her face; but there was not the remotest hint of it there. Her mouth was set in a hard line, her eyes glittered coldly.

'There's no others. Not with time to spare.' She picked up her shawl and pulled it about her, and then turned to go.

Tommy said, 'Matty—'

She swung round. 'I gave you no right to speak my name.'

He felt himself colouring. 'No, you did not. But – I want to say . . . believe me – I am most deeply sorry for the way I deceived you. If I can do owt to make up for it—'

She stared at him as if she could not understand what he implied, though he knew she must know quite well. 'I don't remember you deceived us. You're my teacher and I came tonight for my lesson. That's all.' He knew she had told him in the clearest way she could that, as far as she was concerned, what had been between them once was erased for ever, as if it had never existed. If he had thought her coming to him in this way had meant otherwise, then he was mistaken. She turned back to the door and as she walked away said casually, 'I'll come again, some day.' And then she was gone.

Tommy ran to the front window, but the alley, lit by the glow from one or two neighbouring windows, appeared to be already empty. He went back to the kitchen and tidied the books away with hands that were trembling violently, and then he went to bed. He hardly slept at all.

Chapter Fifteen

Eve had tried, she had really tried. Convinced at last that, in spite of everything, her father loved her, she had been encouraged to try to behave more like the kind of daughter he clearly wanted her to be. She had meekly (on the whole) done as her stepmother told her, the moment she was told, or as soon afterwards as could reasonably be expected. She had tried to do what she was given to do as well as possible, whenever a tendency to daydream did not make her careless. She held in her mind all the frequent strictures of Aunt Jenny and Uncle Rowland about doing well everything that God put into your hands.

It was not easy. She disliked very many of the tasks she was given, finding them tedious or wearying. The other children were at school in the day, her father generally busy with his galloways, and she was left alone in the house with her stepmother who, at her best, disliked her. At first, after her escapade, Phoebe was clearly trying as hard as Eve was to make the best of their mutual incompatibility. But in a very short time too much of one another's company rubbed away at the smooth surface of their good intentions and the old bad ways crept back.

Eve continued to try her best, but she seemed to fail more often, and her stepmother grew daily less patient, reverting to her old scolding ways, the slaps and the carping.

What was worse, her father still refused to allow her to go to White Lea. He went there once or twice himself, but always alone, and when he returned he would answer her questions with sombre brevity, as if he was angry with her for asking. 'Your uncle's bad. You can't go,' was all he would say, when she begged to visit them.

After less than three weeks, the loving father who had so feared to lose her seemed to have disappeared without trace. It was hard to remember that she had once seen how much he loved her. She began to think he was punishing her in some obscure way for some unconscious misdemeanour, by refusing to let her go to White Lea. Uncle Rowland had been sick before, but never before had that meant she was kept away from White Lea. In fact, in the past her father had seen it as an additional reason for her to go there. 'You can give your aunt a hand,' he would say.

At last she could stand it no longer. Following one of the now daily rows with her stepmother, she fled from the house. She longed for Aunt Jenny, for her warmth and tenderness, her ready welcome, for Uncle Rowland's understanding. She ran all the way to White Lea without stopping, and paused only to get her breath before softly pushing open the door. It was early in the afternoon, and her cousins would be out at work and school. She could have her aunt and uncle to herself.

She took one step into the room and then stopped. It was very quiet, and at first, glancing instinctively towards the hearth, she found there was no one there. Then she heard a sound and looked the other way, towards the box bed. Her uncle sat propped on the pillows, his struggle for breath making the horrible unnatural rasping sound she had heard, his eyes closed, his face a mask of suffering. Beside him, Aunt Jenny sat on a stool holding one of his hands in both hers and gazing at him from a white drawn weary face, while, silently, endlessly, the tears ran unchecked down her cheeks. It was, Eve, knew, something she was not meant to see, something no one was meant to see.

She knew, with certainty, that if Aunt Jenny were to look round and see her now she would quickly brush away the tears and smile and come to hug her, and Eve would even wonder if she had imagined what she had seen. But she did not put it to the test. Without a sound or a word she stepped back, out of the room, and very softly closed the door behind her. She knew now why her father would not let her come to White Lea. Uncle Rowland was dying.

She walked quickly away from the house, up onto the fell, where she sat on a rock looking over the dale. Below her the roofs of White Lea – stone-slabbed, lichen-covered – seemed part of the hillside, as if the house was a living thing. In a way, Eve had often thought, fancifully, it was; something warm and safe into which she could escape for comfort and security, with Aunt Jenny's arms at its heart. Today she knew what a precarious thing that sense of safety was.

She sat on the rock for a long time, pondering it all, watching the smoke curl faintly from the chimney into the still summer air, watching the road and the track for signs of coming and going. It would not be very long before her cousins were released from school, and only a little later before William and Em would be home from the washing floor.

She saw few people and little traffic. Two men on horseback, guns on their arms, rode along the fell path a few yards from where she sat and glanced at her curiously. She wondered if they were poachers – lead miners had always supplemented their income with poaching – but decided that they were too well dressed for that, and she thought poachers did not ride. Perhaps they were gamekeepers. She remembered her father saying the other day at supper that a gamekeeper had been accidentally killed the other day on Stanhope moor, by a desperate and drunken poacher. Her father, once something of a poacher himself, had sympathised with the murderer. 'Poor lad, he'd been out of work for months, with nowt coming in. He'll be transported, at the very least. They say his mother's beside herself.'

So much misery; the weight of it seemed to settle over Eve's spirit, adding to the burden she had carried up the hill with her. Were people ever happy?

Yes, for she remembered the moment when she had come out of the mine and her father had found her. She had been happy then, and for quite a long time afterwards. Now, she was ashamed that she had so easily allowed her knowledge of her father's love to be overcome. *Seek not to be loved, but to love.* The words came suddenly into her head. She saw herself sitting beside Aunt Jenny and her cousins in the chapel at Side Head one Sunday while Uncle Tommy was preaching. Afterwards, at dinner, he had apologised a little sheepishly to Uncle Rowland for borrowing his words, and Uncle Rowland had said he had himself borrowed them, from a holy man of long ago, called Francis. Then he had added, 'But their true source is the Gospel. The more they are spoken the better.'

Yet what had she done all her life but seek to be loved, and then resent the fact that no one loved her enough? Yet they did, she saw that now. What she must do was to learn to give from her own store of love. She did already, a little; she loved her father and her aunt and her uncles and her cousins. Starting there, she could go on and love other people, less easy to love. Might it even be possible to love her stepmother? That seemed rather a doubtful prospect, but before the difficulty of it could depress her she saw Mary and the younger children coming into sight from Side Head. She got up and ran down the hill to meet them.

Before ever she reached her, Eve saw the strain and weariness on Mary's face. Even the little ones were quieter than usual, wrapped in their own sad thoughts. She slowed as she came near them, her determination

237

faltering a little. Would they want her at this time? Would she have wanted them if her father had been dying? The thought was so appalling that she came to a halt, and it was Mary who took the last steps towards her.

'I wanted to come,' Eve said, and then stopped again. She knew why she had come, but she was not now going to put her own need of solace first. Yet, failing that, she could see no reason for coming at all. 'I shan't stay,' she added.

Mary slid an arm through hers. 'I wish you would, a bit.'

'Just a bit then,' said Eve. They turned onto the track that crossed the White Lea field towards the house. She could not think what to say, but Mary seemed content just to have her there. The thought of being needed, however little and for however short a time, made her feel happy and yet a little tearful.

Dread seized her as they pushed open the door, but she need not have feared. Everything was calm and orderly, much as she had expected to find it when she had stepped inside this afternoon. Aunt Jenny, who had been stirring something in a pot over the fire, came to greet them, kissing Eve as warmly as she did her own children. Then the others went to kiss their father. Eve hung back, until Mary took her hand. She felt a little afraid, even repelled; he looked so unlike the uncle she knew, scarcely responding to the kisses and hugs of his children, as far as she could see. Her heart thudding, she went and stood by the bed and then quickly bent over and made a kissing noise somewhere near the stretched parchment skin. She was about to turn away when he lifted a hand and took hers in it. His fingers felt bony and damp with sweat.

'Eve—' he said, faintly but quite distinctly. She realised that his eyes had not changed after all. He had always looked at her as if, for the moment at least, she was the only person in all the world in whom he was interested. He smiled, just a little, but at once his face lit up, almost the face she knew so well. 'It's good to see thee, lass.'

On impulse she bent over again and put her arms about him. She felt his hand on her hair, touching it lightly. Then it fell back and she saw his eyes were closed. He looked again as he had looked before, something that was not quite a person. She went slowly to help Mary set the table for supper. She saw, counting quickly, that Aunt Jenny had included her in her calculations; there were eight bowls.

She studied her aunt's face as she moved about the table, seeing now no trace of the tears, of the bitter grief, she had observed before. That was strength, to hide such misery for the sake of others, to bear it with such patience. She would be like Aunt Jenny, she resolved, brave and strong, always giving.

Her aunt had gone back to the bedside, and was now sitting there quite calmly, her hands busy with a piece of knitting. There was a little time to wait before the boys came home from work, so while Mary took the younger ones to wash their hands, Eve wandered in the direction of her aunt, trying to look as if she had arrived there by chance.

Jenny laid down her knitting and put out an arm to draw her nearer. Eve looked gravely down into her face. 'Aunt Jenny, how do you love someone you don't like?'

A passing amusement lightened her aunt's face. 'You mean, when you're supposed to love your neighbour as yourself, but she's your stepmother?'

Eve nodded vigorously, amazed by such instant understanding.

'I think,' her aunt said slowly, 'all you can do is treat her always as if you did love her. Think, *What would I do now, what would I say, if I really loved her? What would I want if I was her?* Then it may be you'll find you do love her after all. But even if that doesn't happen, you're doing the best you can.'

Eve considered the matter. Looking up, she saw that Uncle Rowland's eyes were on her face again, with that accompanying half smile, encouraging her. 'I'll try,' she said, and put her arms about her aunt. She felt then, as

239

Jenny held her in silence, pressing her cheek against her own, that for this she would have promised anything.

Jenny had found it very hard to be patient with Eve, even harder to be tender and welcoming. Seeing her come into the room with Mary, she had shrunk at the thought of what demands must now be made on her emotions and what remained of her understanding and her patience. Her own first instinct was, gently but firmly, to send the child home again at once. But she knew Rowland would not have wanted that, so she did what she had to do and when, after supper, Eve went meekly away, she turned back, with a relief that was not really relief, to the bedside.

The days since the camp meeting had merged into one long black continuum of suffering, of which Rowland was at the heart. In everything, she focused herself on him, living through him, trying to feel as he felt, trying to see the days through his eyes, so that she could meet his every need even when he could not tell her what it was. She hardly slept, because Rowland did not. She ate only what was necessary to keep herself from failing him. As far as possible she left the housework to the children or to any neighbour who came. She had enough to do simply to keep Rowland washed and changed, to shift him in the bed in the hope of preventing sores and easing the ache of stiffened limbs that only added yet more pain to all he had to endure. Morning and evening, without fail, she would read to him from the Bible – what she knew to be his favourite passages, if he was not able to tell her what he wanted – and then she would kneel down and pray aloud, in what she hoped were words that expressed what he wanted to say. When he was able, he joined in. Because she was living through him, she had nothing left to spare for anyone else at all.

Other people became important only as they were useful in caring for Rowland. Because he wanted the occasional company of their children, she encouraged them to do things for him, when possible, and sometimes to talk to him or simply sit by him. Otherwise she was glad when they were at school or with neighbours. There was a constant flow of callers at White Lea, some of whom she welcomed. Nathan Elliott came several times at weekends, and quietly did any outdoor tasks that she had been unable to do – mending a wall, taking the galloway to be shod. Many of their neighbours came to bring food they had prepared, or to do shopping for her. She knew that at times they paid for the goods too, without letting her know what she owed, but she never questioned it. Others came simply to see Rowland – his cousin Lancelot from Chapel, men who had worked with him, fellow Ranters coming to sing or pray or offer spiritual encouragement. Sometimes she was glad of a tiny respite, while some man or woman he cared for kept him company for a little time. Other callers only left him exhausted, and when she could not speed their departure she fidgeted with agitation and anguish until they were gone.

A few days before Eve's visit, Luke had returned to Weardale with his little family. He could hardly make light of the cholera, since it had driven him back to the penury from which he had fled, but Jenny wasted no more than a momentary anxiety on Tommy. More important was the fact that Rebekah now took care of the children, taking them when it seemed best to stay at Side Head with her own family, seeing to their needs; that, and the letter Luke brought from Tommy.

Jenny read it to Rowland as soon as Luke had left the house. It was at the end of a particularly bad day, and he gave no sign that he heard any of it, sitting there with his eyes closed in their deep shadowed hollows, his painful breathing forming a constant background to her reading. But at the end his eyes opened suddenly and rested on her face, and she felt his fingers close about hers. She knew that, if he could, he would have smiled. She leaned over and kissed him. 'So you see, my hinny, it was right that he went after all.'

'Aye.' The word, breathed out, summed it up for them

241

both. That Tommy and Rowland would not meet again in this life no longer mattered, for all was well between them without need of meeting.

A little afterwards, he asked Jenny for his Bible and a pen, and managed to convey to her that he wanted to write something inside the cover. It took some time and a great effort on his part, but with her hand about his he wrote a few words. Afterwards, she added the date underneath the inscription.

September came in with fierce winds and hail and torrential rain, but Jenny scarcely noticed it. For her it was the struggle inside the house that mattered, that and nothing else.

More than once she thought the end was near, yet Rowland hung on, day after day, sometimes apparently a little better, sometimes so ill that the only sign of life was the ceaseless noise of his ravaged lungs.

Now rarely a day passed without one or other of their Ranter neighbours coming to call at White Lea. Jenny knew that, for Rowland as for all Primitive Methodists, the way a man or a woman died was of the greatest importance, the final supreme demonstration of his holiness. To fail in the face of death was the most terrible failure of all, a dreadful warning, as a good death was an example and an inspiration.

So the Ranters came, singly or in twos or threes, to give words of encouragement to the gasping skeleton on the bed that was all that now remained of Rowland, and to watch for signs that he was dying in the Lord.

Some prayed quietly and sang softly and were even prepared to kneel or sit in silence at the bedside. Others were noisy in the extreme, full of loud exhortations and louder singing – *I think our dear brother is convinced the Lord is hard of hearing*, Rowland had said once, to one such preacher; even though a loving frankness between Ranters was encouraged, the remark had not been kindly received. Now, Jenny found the ministrations of such men and women almost unendurable and, though some of them were dear friends, she would have forbidden them the house if she had been certain that Rowland wished it. But here her understanding and her love faltered. She had never shared Rowland's passionate faith and now she could not know for sure what he wanted; and he gave no sign himself.

Emerson and William returned from work one day to find the house noisy with the sound of a hymn. Em slipped between two of the men at the bedside and came to whisper in Jenny's ear; he had to whisper quite loudly, so she could hear above the din. 'Mother, Uncle Joe's out there.' He gestured with his head towards the door.

It was two weeks since Joe had called and she had been thinking it was time she sent for him. 'Then ask him to step in. I wonder he hasn't already.'

'I said to. He won't come.'

Jenny went out into the windy darkness. Joe stood to one side of the door, with his back against the wall, scowling into the night. She laid a hand on his arm and he looked round at her, startled.

'Joe – what's up? Won't you come in?'

'I'll not come in while they're at their caterwauling. Every time I've called, they've been at it.'

Jenny could not, for a moment, find the words or the breath to reply to him. Then she said very carefully, her voice shaking a little, 'Do your feelings matter more than Rowland's? I know he wants to see you.'

'I can't – I want quiet, to see him alone, without . . . It's not something . . . Why, Jenny, don't you understand?'

The pain of that cry cut her to the heart, most of all because it was an echo of her own, stifled within her because her own needs, her own wishes, must not matter. Oh yes, she wanted to be quiet with Rowland, alone with him, to hold him in her arms and share every last moment left to them as closely as she could. She hated to feel, as she did more and more as the days passed, that in dying he had become a kind of public property, a potential hero of the Ranter faith, not simply the man she loved.

She said nothing to Joe, only clasped his hand for a moment and then left him.

When the Ranters left an hour or so later, Rowland having shown no sign that he ever knew they were there, Joe was still outside, hiding himself from the departing men in the shadow of the hay-byre steps. But once they were well down the hill he pushed open the house door and came in.

He crouched beside the bed. Rowland opened his eyes precisely at that moment, and looked at him, though with no alteration in his expression – if it could be called that, when the gaunt bones of his face seemed set permanently in lines of suffering. After a moment, Joe reached out and took his hand. There was a long silence, in which only the harsh sound of Rowland's breathing could be heard. And then the breathing stopped, to be resumed in a gasping croak. Joe realised Rowland was speaking to him. 'I'll hope . . . to . . . see thee . . . one day . . . in Paradise.'

It must have taken a superhuman effort for him to say it, and Joe seemed to have almost as much difficulty replying. After a time, he said huskily, 'Why, I shouldn't bank on it, man. But if there's owt would make me take up the offer, it would be knowing I'd see thee again.'

Rowland was long past laughing, but there was a ghost of laughter in his eyes.

At the door Joe hugged his sister. 'How long, Jenny? Does thou know?' His voice was harsh and anguished.

'It can't be long now.' She made a strange noise, somewhere between a sob and a cough. 'I want it to be over, yet I don't—' She broke off and Joe held her tighter, feeling how she shuddered.

Then he released her and walked away into the night, and she went back to the bedside.

During the next week Jenny knew that Rowland had at last gone beyond her reach. He ceased to speak her name or communicate with her in any way. In the moments when they were alone, she continued to kiss him and put

244

her arms about him, but there was not even a faint movement of his fingers, held in her hand, by way of reply. She thought he was glad of her caresses and her nearness, but it was only instinct told her so, not any sign from him.

By the morning of the following Sunday, he showed no signs of consciousness. Only the dreadful breathing continued, rasping into the quiet room. His eyes were closed, his thin hands motionless on the blanket that covered the skeletal angularity of his body. Jenny sensed that the end was very near. She sat as usual on her stool at the bedside, as close to him as she could be, holding one of those near-lifeless hands.

Sarah Craggs, planned to preach at Side Head that morning, came on to White Lea afterwards and was still there in the afternoon, when Nathan and Rowland's cousin Lancelot came up to the house. They prayed at the bedside, but quietly, and after a time Jenny asked Nathan to read a passage from the Epistle to the Romans that she knew Rowland had often read to the dying. Nathan read quietly, in something of a monotone, but with great clarity. Jenny sat holding Rowland's hand and trying to feel some of the consolation from the words that she wanted him to feel too.

'*For I am persuaded, that neither death, nor life, nor angels, nor principalities, nor powers, nor things present, nor things to come . . .*'

She saw that Sarah was gazing intently at Rowland's face; she turned to look and saw then that his lips were moving, faintly, almost imperceptibly, as if he was trying to join in the familiar words.

'*Nor height, nor depth, nor any other creature, shall be able to separate us from the love of God, which is in Christ Jesus our Lord.*'

There was a long silence. The movement of the lips had ceased and Rowland was still again, his breathing harsher and more difficult than ever.

Sarah fell to her knees, hands raised high, tears in her eyes. 'We praise thee, O Lord!'

At dusk Rebekah brought the children back from Side Head where they had spent the day, and made supper for them all.

Afterwards, the children came to the bedside to say their prayers. Sometimes, in the past, their father had joined in, but not for some days now. They kissed him, one by one, and then went up to bed, Rebekah going with them. They had only just left the room when Rowland suddenly shuddered and coughed and a great flow of blood spurted from his mouth. When it ceased, Jenny, holding him, knew that he was dead.

Chapter Sixteen

'*A*shes to ashes, dust to dust . . . *' The curate of
St John's Chapel, well known as an avid
preacher against the evils of religious dissent,
intoned the words with a certain relish, as if it filled him
with satisfaction that so notorious a Ranter had returned
to the dust from which he was so patently made.

It was over very quickly. Family and friends had
gathered at White Lea this morning to sing a hymn and
say a few brief prayers before carrying the coffin down
the hill to the churchyard for burial. Now earth was
rapidly covering it, rattling on the cheap wood, obliter-
ating the last poor earthly remains of the man she had
loved more than any other person in all the world.

Until now Jenny's chief feeling had been one of thankfulness that the long suffering was over and that his end
had been in every way as it ought to have been. She had
wept, often, but from pride and love and even a strange
kind of happiness. Now, as they turned away from the
grave in silence, she felt cold and numb, cut off even
from Joe's close comforting presence, though he had put
his arm about her as if to shield her from the curate's
malice. It should not have been like this, the ceremony

that marked Rowland's passing – so arid and unconsoling, marred by hate.

They went back up the hill in the rain to the Ranter chapel at Side Head, and found a great crowd gathered there for the prearranged prayer meeting, too many for the sparse seating of the place so that most were standing. Hymns were sung, Joseph Walton gave a short address, full of love for the dead man, and prayed for consolation for his grieving friends and family – which brought many an *Amen* and a *Come down, oh Lord!* from the congregation – and then one after another those who had known Rowland stood up and thanked God with tears in their eyes and a break in their voices for all he had meant to them. Time and again Jenny heard of his generous giving of himself, of his inspired teaching and his exemplary life.

It went on for nearly an hour and even then it was not over, for the whole assembly came back to White Lea, where food and drink in large quantities had been made ready during the previous two days by Phoebe and Rebekah and the White Lea womenfolk. There were too many mourners for the house, so they overflowed into the yard and the field beyond, eating and drinking while the tributes and the memories continued. Jenny had known that Rowland had many friends; she had not until today known how very many they were, or how deeply he had been loved, even by those who had not always agreed with him. The realisation took away the bitter aftertaste of the burial service, replacing it with love and pride and a return, enhanced, to the tearful joy that had followed his death.

It was not until late in the day that the last of the mourners left the house. Joe and Rebekah lingered on, to see the children to bed and tidy up as much as they could. They both offered to stay with Jenny, but she refused. She thought she would welcome a little time of quiet. She had not been quiet for a very long time.

When they had gone, she stood by the fire, not quite knowing what to do. The house seemed vast and silent

248

and very empty. She did not want to go to bed. Though she could not remember when she had last slept, she was beyond tiredness.

After a time she walked about the room rather aimlessly, looking for things to do. She found a tankard behind the settle, and a muffler belonging to one of the children. She washed the tankard and then went to the chest to put the muffler away.

Inside, folded neatly, lay Rowland's plaid. *I'll be wanting it yet*, he had said. But not any more; not ever.

Slowly, she lifted it out. Worn and faded, so that the original pattern and colours had long since been lost, patched many times, it had seemed a part of Rowland. And it was still hung about with the scent of him, for it came up suddenly, catching her unawares, reaching to her nostrils, as if he was there, just a touch away. She felt a terrible wrenching sob rise in her throat. She shut her eyes and pressed the plaid to her face, breathing deeply, trying somehow to feel him through it, as if his body was still warm beneath its rough fabric, as if the smell still came from the living man; as if by some miracle it might bring him back. Nothing in all her life had ever hurt like this. It was like the moment when feeling returned to a frozen limb, only worse, much worse, an intensity of anguish she could never have imagined.

'Mother, I can't sleep.'

She opened her eyes. The candle on the table was still alight, though burning very low. It showed her Mary standing in the doorway, barefoot and shivering in her nightgown. Jenny could see that she had been crying. Other feet pattered down the stairs behind her. 'Nor can I.' It was Em. Then the others followed.

Jenny rose and went to them, the plaid over her arm, and gently steered them to the box bed. She climbed in with them and they gathered about her, arms round each other, all tangled together under the plaid. They cried a little, and sang ragged snatches of hymns, and Jenny prayed with them and joined them in remembering things their father had said and done. Sometimes they even laughed. The little ones soon fell asleep, and then at last William and Em and Mary too.

But Jenny lay very still among their warm sleeping bodies, with one end of the plaid held against her cheek, waiting for the dawn.

Chapter Seventeen

Over their heads the tree-tops rocked in the wind, the noise drowning all the smaller sounds in the wood, even down here near the burn where it was relatively sheltered from the storm. Last weekend's hail had left some of the tents battered and drenched, and had been succeeded by a steady rain that completed their misery.

Matty, shivering in the tent doorway, was peeling potatoes with hands so cold they could scarcely hold a knife, though she was only dimly aware of it. This afternoon, when her father went, as usual these days, to drink with his friends in one public house or another, she would escape to the other life that now meant so much more to her than this; for it gave this all the meaning and happiness it had.

It was increasingly easy to escape now that the end of summer had made the woods much less enticing. The lure of the public houses was all the stronger, even for men with little money to spend. Sometimes Matty's mother went out too, with her own friends, and then Matty would be left to mind the children, which she hated because it kept her from her reading.

For many years now, Matty had wanted more than anything to learn to read, but even so she had not expected to be so overwhelmed and delighted by the experience. It was as if her mind had been sleeping, or only half used. Now she felt that she could do anything. All day long words and ideas ran through her head, delighting her, exciting her as nothing had ever done before.

The progress of the strike still mattered to her, of course, and even took on a larger significance set against other struggles she had read about, and measured by what she had learned already of man's relations with God and his fellow beings; but the fact that it seemed doomed to failure and a trickle of men slid back to work each week was no longer the devastating blow it might once have been. As for Jack Marley's advances, they meant no more to her than the buzzing of an irritating fly; she rebuffed him briskly when he approached her and was otherwise so cold and distant that he seemed to have given her up. She thought she had heard someone say that he was showing interest in someone else, but she had not paid a great deal of attention to the talk. Gossip seemed amazingly trivial and unimportant beside what she read and talked about in the little house at Brick Garth. She was astonished that it could ever have interested her.

If forced to admit it, she would have had to say too that the sense of danger, of doing something wholly forbidden, gave an added spice to her visits to Tommy. She did not believe that she was truly betraying the colliers' cause, for it was only necessity drove her to seek Tommy out, and she knew, because she saw it sometimes in his face and heard it in his voice, how painful he found her presence. She knew quite well that he loved her as much as ever. If anything, she despised him for doing so, after all that had happened. On the other hand she was awed by the impressive self-control that kept him from so much as touching her, through long hours spent in the closest proximity to her; especially that first time, when she had done all in her power to taunt him. She doubted if any other man she knew – with the possible exception of Adam – could have done it.

Not that she thought about Tommy much at all, or at least not as a separate being she had once thought she loved. He was simply the person who could satisfy her hunger for more of the learning so newly acquired, the teacher on whom she depended for that secret sustenance. In that sense, he was an essential part of almost all her thoughts, inextricably bound up with them, because without his books and his paper and pens she would not have been able to make progress, and without his answers to her questions and his counter-arguments, she would have had to find her way alone. As a man, he was nothing.

'Matty, I've spoken to you five times. What's up with you, lass? Your head's always up in the clouds.'

Matty looked up at her father, who stood in the rain gazing at her with irritable affection. She said nothing, largely because her thoughts were still concentrated on more important matters – in this case, pondering the story she had read two days ago, of Jacob wrestling with the angel, and trying to work out what it meant. She had not been entirely satisfied with Tommy's explanation.

After waiting in vain for her to make some kind of excuse, her father went on in exasperation, 'I'm sure I don't know what I've done to deserve such a lass as you. What I said was – if you'd not been deaf as a post – up at Little Eppleton Hall they want workers for the oat harvest. It'll give you work for a couple of weeks, I'd say, at the usual rates. Though they'll not be doing much till the rain stops.'

Her attention fully caught now, Matty felt her spirits sink. Once she would have been glad of the chance to make some money. But farm labourers worked long hours, as long as daylight lasted and sometimes more. That would make it very hard to find time to go to Tommy at all. 'I'll go and see them some time then,' she said vaguely, though she knew her father would not let her leave it at that. An idle unmarried daughter was something he could not abide, as he often said. If she wasn't to marry and get a place of her own, then she must do her best to help keep the rest of them.

Her father wandered away, talking of going for a drink. As the men left the camp, she heard them discussing the cholera epidemic.

'Five strangers dead since this time yesterday, I heard,' Jack was saying with satisfaction. 'Still more of the buggers down with the sickness. We'll soon be rid of them.'

'Aye,' said her father. 'If only our lads would be patient, the owners will be begging us to come back on any terms.'

'Let's hope it's soon then,' Jack retorted. 'Before there's more out of the union than in it.'

Matty finished preparing the supper, putting the broth to cook over the spitting fire, and then went to get ready to go to Tommy's house. In the tent doorway she found her mother just coming out, clearly dressed up for an evening's entertainment. 'Watch the bairns, Matty. I've to see someone.'

Matty, sullen with disappointment, slouched in the tent entrance, until the younger children returned from playing in the wood, muddy and hungry and tired. She gave them their meal (rather early) and put the little ones to bed, ignoring their protests. Then she turned to her sister, 'Maria, I've to go out, to see someone. Watch the bairns while I'm gone.'

Maria looked at her with her head on one side. 'What will you give me, not to tell Mam and Dad?'

Matty scowled, wondering whether to deny that there was any reason why her parents should not be told (but that would have carried the risk that Maria would test her by telling them), or if there was some kind of threat she could use, but she could think of no sure means of exerting pressure. 'You can have my red ribbon,' she said at last.

'The one Jack Marley gave you at Houghton Feast?' Maria asked, looking pleased.

'Aye,' said Matty, who had not in any case worn the ribbon since she had first been given it.

She ran all the way to Brick Garth through driving rain and by the time she reached the house she was drenched; but at least the rain had emptied the streets and she did not have to be as careful as usual not to be seen as she let herself in. Tommy was not there, but then she never told him when she was coming, so he could not know when to expect her. She closed the door behind her and poked the fire into brightness before hanging her wet shawl over the table edge to dry. Then she took the Bible from the shelf near the hearth and pulled out one of the stools (Tommy had bought a second stool now) and sat down to read.

It was a slow business, making out the words as her finger followed them, murmuring them in a soft whisper, over and over until she grasped their meaning; but after three weeks and six lessons she was gaining fluency. More than that, every day her sense of wonder and delight grew and intensified. She was constantly drunk on words, carried away by the singing rhythms of phrases and sentences; they filled her head with images, her whole world with delight. No wonder, she thought, men cared so much for this book, when it had words like this contained within it, words full of passion, anger, tenderness, hate, severity and love, woven together into the most wonderful stories. The colourful earthiness of many of them astonished her, for they seemed a long way from what she had always thought of as pious and proper.

She had told no one – not even Eliza – what she had done. It had been hard to keep it from her friend, who would so have approved of her new skills and who could have shared some of her delight and pride in them, and her enjoyment of the Bible. But Matty knew that her uncompromising friend would not have approved of the teacher she had chosen, would not have been able to understand what had driven Matty to seek his help; not even, perhaps, if she had been told the whole story, from the beginning.

Sometimes she came to Tommy's house when she knew he was at work, because then she could read without interruption, or practise the writing he was now teaching her. She knew where he kept everything in the house, and he did not seem to mind what she did in his absence. Not that she would have had any scruples about it if he had minded. As it was, he spent less time at home than ever, for the cholera had reached epidemic proportions amongst the strangers, and every day there were new cases and new deaths. The sad, furtive little funeral processions met with daily on the road would have grieved any but a union supporter, who saw the whole business as a just reward for strike-breaking.

For Tommy, caught up in the heart of the epidemic, almost the worst thing about it was the fear. It took many forms, had many different effects. It destroyed all the usual ties of neighbourliness, or what few there were in the disparate community at Brick Garth; when the sickness struck, the afflicted household would become almost completely isolated. It added to the torments of the sick, at least until they became too ill to care any more. It deepened the grief and anxiety of their families, not only for their loved ones but for themselves.

It was, Tommy thought, a cause for thankfulness on his part that God had armed him against that debilitating fear, and continued to give him the words that could bring some measure of comfort and calmness to the troubled households. He brought food to the healthy, to keep up their strength, encouraged them to go for walks, to rest while he watched over the victims. He became all too familiar with the way the sick would lie in a deadly apathy, dusky-skinned, dried-up, wrinkled, their eyes deeply sunk, their voices reduced to a hoarse whisper, the bedding around them soaked hideously with the fluids that had drained from them. He learned to see the signs of each stage, the little indications that would signal the approach of death, or, to his great gratitude, a sudden change for the better. He learned, by bitter experience, that an apparent recovery could suddenly be overturned, sometimes several days later, by a relapse that was almost always fatal. For a child or an old man or woman, the hope of any kind of recovery was small; for others, it could go either way. As for himself, he took care to eat as well as he could and to rest when he was able, conscious that if he became ill he would no longer be of any use to anyone. But then he knew he was well placed to escape infection, protected as he was by his orderly and temperate lifestyle.

Orderly and temperate, at least, apart from the evenings when Matty would interrupt his studies with a demand for a lesson; or, as happened more often these days, he would return from a visit to a sickbed to find her already there, seated at his table reading steadily from his Bible. He loved to find her there like that, treating his house as if it were her own; almost, he found himself thinking sometimes, as if she were his wife. Except that in spirit she was as remote from him as ever. She came to him because he could give her what she wanted, and that was all; he could expect no more – so her manner told him all the time they were together. After each lesson, he feared that she might not come back again. He recognised that she no longer had any need of his teaching, for she would have been quite able to take the last few steps towards full literacy without any further help from him. On the other hand, she had no books anywhere but here. He had thought of giving her a Bible of her own, but feared that she would refuse even that gift at his hands – no, he was sure that she would. He still hoped that one day, somehow, he would be able to break through the barrier she had erected against him and find that all her old feelings for him had not after all disappeared; but there was still not the smallest sign of that. The one hope he clung to, encouraged by her enthusiasm for the Bible, was that she would learn from it to know the God he loved, and come to share his faith, if she could share nothing else of his.

Today, coming home a little earlier than usual from his visits to the sick, Tommy did not waste time eating – he was not in any case very hungry – but simply washed enough of the dirt from his face and hands to make himself presentable. 'We shall write today,' he said matter-of-factly, as unemotional in manner as any schoolteacher.

He sat watching as she formed the letters, slowly, carefully, precisely, large letters, with long firm strokes, as if the fierceness of her nature was expressed in them. Tonight they seemed to dance before his eyes and he found it hard to concentrate on what she was doing. He recognised that he was close to exhaustion, after too many sleepless nights (not simply from caring for the sick, but because when in bed he still found it hard to sleep), too many calls upon his emotions. But if Matty noticed that she had less than his full attention, she gave no sign of it.

They had been at work perhaps half an hour when there came a wild, frantic hammering on the door. They looked at one another, then Tommy said, 'I'll have to go. Get in there.' She went, quickly, into the front room and Tommy opened the door. Mrs Raines stood there, her face white and smudged with tears. 'It's the bairns, Mr Emerson – they're sick. Samuel's not home yet; I know he'll be late. Oh, find our Eliza for me, for the love of God!'

He seized his coat, trying to take in her confused instructions as to where to look for her daughter, but before he was ready Matty came in. 'I'll go,' she said, and did not wait for the astonished comment that was taking shape on her former neighbour's lips. She ran off into the night.

Mrs Raines, momentarily forgetful of her anguish, gave Tommy a long inquiring look.

'Forget you saw her,' he said quietly. Then, 'Is there owt I can do?'

'Pray for them, lad. It's all there is left.' She went back to her house.

When she had gone, he set about getting supper, not because he was at all hungry, but because it was supper-time. Besides, it saved on candles to do all that had to be done while daylight lasted, if this dim light could be called daylight. Outside the rain fell in torrents, rattling on the roof, dripping through its weak places. Tommy felt all at once horribly alone, depressed.

He made some crowdy and took it to the table, and then sat looking at it, quite unable to eat. He felt very tired. He was tempted simply to tip it away, but that would have been wasteful. He got up, and then felt the cramping pains in his limbs and his belly. Shivering, he went out into the rain to crouch on the midden at the end of the row. By the time he came in again he was drenched, and the pains were worse than ever. He felt desperately thirsty. He crawled up to bed, not even finding the strength to undress, and lay there shivering. He knew well enough what it was.

Eliza was too dismayed by Matty's news to wonder what chance had led her to meet Mrs Raines, as she claimed to have done. She sent someone in search of Adam, who had gone to a meeting in Houghton, and set off at a run for her mother's house. By the time Adam joined her there, an hour later, the baby was dying and little Ruth was desperately ill. By the morning, the Fenwicks were childless.

The children were buried at once, in the churchyard at Houghton. News of what had happened was brought back to the camp in the woods, but not by Eliza or her husband. They went from the sad, hurried funeral to the chapel at Brick Garth, where their Ranter friends soon joined them. Matty supposed that they found comfort of some kind in the companionship of other Ranters and in the prayers and singing that was their natural response to the tragedy that had happened to them. She longed to go and comfort her friend, but she suspected that, for the moment at least, whatever she could give was not what was needed.

For the first time in many weeks her reading and all it meant to her ceased to occupy the centre of her thoughts. It was not until she had eaten her sparse breakfast of bread and cheese that her father reminded her of what he clearly thought should be uppermost in her mind. 'You'll go up to Little Eppleton the day?'

The rain had ceased and there was a brisk drying wind. It was likely that the harvest would begin before too long. She told him meekly that she would go, and pulled her shawl about her and set off in the right direction – which, initially at least, was the same direction as Brick Garth.

At Four Lane Ends she hesitated. If she went on up the hill she could spend an hour or two reading or writing, and her father would be none the wiser. On the other hand, Tommy would be at work so early in the day and, besides, she must at least make the effort to seek employment. They had need of every penny she could earn, for all but a few of the working colliers had ceased to contribute to the union fund and it had dwindled almost to nothing. If the news of the children's death had not brought her painfully to earth, she might not have found the will-power to take that left fork but, as it was, her reading no longer seemed supremely and exclusively important.

At the Hall they told her they hoped to begin cutting the oats tomorrow, or perhaps the next day. If she came at dawn, there might be work for her. Glad that it was put off for a little longer, she turned and retraced her steps; and this time set off up the hill south from Four Lane Ends towards the houses that crowned the hilltop.

The men were back from the pits by now, and there were a number of people about, so she had often to slip into an alley or take a roundabout route to avoid being seen, but she came at last to Tommy's house and as usual let herself in at the front, where she was less likely to be observed. The house was very quiet, but she had that odd conviction that it was not after all unoccupied. She pushed open the door into the kitchen, which was not quite shut, and then she felt suddenly afraid. A stench –

the familiar, horrible stench that had been so pervasive last winter – struck her nostrils.

And then she did hear a sound, a faint moan in the stillness. She did not at first know where it came from; she began to wonder if she had imagined it, or even if it was caused by some supernatural manifestation. The kitchen looked normal enough, much as it had looked last night, the books spread on the table, a page of her writing, a bowl containing some kind of porridge, cold and solid and scarcely touched. She stood looking at them, thinking that it was unlike Tommy to leave things so untidy, and then she heard the sound again and realised it came from upstairs.

She ran like the wind and as she reached the top of the stairs saw Tommy stretched on his mattress on the floor. He was long past knowing she was there.

Something seemed to catch in her throat. The moan this time came from her. She knew then, as she saw how ill he was and recognised that he might not live, that she had never ceased to love him. All the bitterness she had built up against him was a sham, and in this moment it finally crumbled to nothing. She had not come to him for what he could give her: that had been an excuse, because he had her heart fast in his hands and she could not keep away.

She ran to the room and knelt on the floor beside the bed. 'Tommy! Tommy, my hinny!'

The most bitter thing of all was that she knew he could not hear her and, worse, that he might never do so again.

When she had made him as clean and comfortable as she could, she slipped quickly back to the camp. It was growing dark now and her father was ready to scold her for being late.

'I've got work at Little Eppleton,' she told him, her mind working quickly. 'But I've done better. I'm working in the kitchens. They'll give me lodgings too. I'm to go there the night.'

She knew as she said it that the time would come when

her father would realise that there was no money and that she had lied, and then there would be hell to pay. But for now it was enough that she had found an explanation for an absence that she would have had to explain in some way, somehow; because no power on earth would keep her from Tommy now.

Chapter Eighteen

For Tommy, waking to appalling weakness mitigated by the knowledge that he would live, it had been a shock to see Matty kneeling on the floor beside the bed, watching him, her face full of something like the brightness of the old days, only softened and more tender. For a moment he thought that he had not after all recovered, but was wandering in delirium, of which this sweet vision was simply a passing delusion.

Then she smiled and laid a soft hand on his forehead and he knew she was no delusion. He wanted to ask her for an explanation, but finding the words was too complicated a process for his exhausted resources, so he simply forced a smile from somewhere and yielded to the overwhelming peace and joy that bore him up like a cloud.

Then she bent lower and he felt her lips on his forehead. 'I love thee.'

He could not even say in return, 'I love thee too,' but he was sure he did not need to say it.

After that he drifted in and out of sleep for an indeterminate time, and by some miracle whenever he awoke she was still there, ready to supply his smallest need, with an instinctive understanding of what that was, even if all he wished for was a smile and a soft reassuring word.

At last he woke feeling hungry and more himself than he had feared he ever would again. He ate the food she brought him, appreciating the delicacy with which it was prepared; and saw too that at some time she had washed his clothes and changed the sheets and blankets on his bed. He knew from his own experience what foulness was a part of the disease through which he had passed and felt faintly disturbed that she should have had to do such things for him. Yet he knew he would not really have wished it otherwise, and perhaps she would not either. If their positions had been reversed, he would gladly have done the same for her.

When she had taken his empty bowl downstairs he lay thinking of her and of all she must have done for him. She gave no sign that any of it had been any trouble to her, but he considered the possible implications. She had apparently stayed here all the time (though he was still not very clear how long that had actually been), yet the only bed was the narrow mattress on which he lay – where then had she slept? . . . And there had been little food in the house – to find food and water for the washing she must have left the house, most probably in daylight, and then returned to it. He knew what she risked by coming to live in the house of a blackleg. She must have been cautious enough to avoid detection or she would not still be here, but it could not have been easy.

When she came upstairs again he said, 'Don't they wonder where you are?'

'I told them something to keep them quiet,' she reassured him cheerfully.

A lie, he supposed, and felt uncomfortable that he should have brought her to this, but he recollected his own deceit and said, 'Maybe now you'll accept my apologies for what I did.'

She shook her head, which rather dismayed him (though she was smiling), until she said, 'I know why you did it. It doesn't matter now.' He questioned her a little more, discovering that she slept at night on the kitchen floor in front of the fire and that she took the greatest possible care when she went out. 'I have to,' she added. 'There's a fair few families I know back in Brick Garth, now so many strangers have gone.'

Those days of recovery, merging into one another, were varied only by his progress from bed to stool to walking (with Matty's arm about his waist, as once before) carefully downstairs, and, later, up again; by his increasing appetite and the different ways she satisfied it; by the sound of rain outside, or wind, or passing feet and voices, by night and day. Sometimes Matty left him for a while on some errand, usually while he slept, but she was never absent for long, so that the one constant factor was her companionship and the joy of a love acknowledged and shared and growing.

He almost regretted his returning health, because she would soon have no reason to stay with him. In fact, even when he knew he was perfectly well able to look after himself again, he did not tell her so, for fear that she would leave him. But he recognised how selfish that was, and that for her sake he must let her go.

For three days now he had spent most of the day out of bed, while she cooked for him and did what household tasks there were to be done, and even read to him, with great pride. They talked a good deal, and he made up for all the evasions of the past by answering all her questions as fully as she wished. He felt that now his own life, his own past, were fast becoming a part of hers, though she had never seen his beloved Weardale hills and could only imagine them from her little experience of life.

That evening, about an hour after supper, Tommy grew tired of sitting on the stool and rose to go up to bed, though reluctantly, because he wanted to stay with Matty. She came with him to the foot of the stairs, her arm about his waist, and then he turned to kiss her goodnight; and realised that passion had returned to him.

They clung together, eyes closed, their mouths nuzzling and nibbling. She drew back enough to whisper, 'I'll come up with thee.' And he felt how his body ached and burned for what she offered, how much he wanted it.

'No, my hinny. We mustn't,' he murmured, though quite what part of him it was that put the words into his mouth he did not know, because there was no conscious will behind them. He slid his hands to her shoulders and held her just a little way from him and forced out more words, still more reluctant. 'Matty, you should go back to your people.'

She looked almost indignant, and distressed too. 'You don't want us to go?'

'Why no, how could you think that? But I fear we'll be led into sin . . . ' He broke off then. He knew that this wonderful time had to come to an end. Even without the feelings that they were now fighting, it could not last. But he saw all at once that it did not have to end exactly like this, with her leaving him and – at best – nothing better to hope for than a return to the furtive meetings of the past.

'Matty, we can be wed.'

Even if she had not thought of it until now, he was surprised that she seemed so amazed at the suggestion.

After looking at him in silence for a time, she frowned with obvious distress and bit her lip. Then she shook her head. 'No. I cannot wed a blackleg.'

The chill that settled on him at her words drove out the passion of a moment ago. 'But you've stayed here for days now – all you've done . . . '

'I didn't say I cannot love you. That's not the same. But I need my dad's consent to wed you, and he'd never give it. I don't know even then . . . ' She looked at him earnestly. 'I don't think I could live here with you always, out in the open, after what's happened.'

He tried to understand the curious moral blindness that would have allowed her to come up to his bed, but would not permit her a more permanent and respectable relationship with him; and failed. Seeing his obvious distress, she reached up and kissed him, lingeringly, in a way that quickly blew the flames into life again. 'But I'll stay a bit yet. So long as no one knows.' She realised with regret that inflamed though he might be he was not going to accept what she so clearly offered. 'I'll stop down here the night, if that's what you want.'

It was not what he wanted, but it was what had to be. He went upstairs, slowly and deep in thought. It took him a considerable time to go to sleep.

The next day began well for Matthias Dunn, in spite of the cold and the rain. The recent quarrels among the Hetton partners had reached such a pitch that today he had learned that three of them had decided to sell their shares in the company – and one of the three was a man he particularly detested. He could have wished that several of the others had gone too, in particular those who still found fault with almost everything he did and most of all with his refusal to live at Hetton, but it would do nicely to be going on with.

Better still, the strike was over. Yesterday the union had sent a final delegation to Mr Mowbray, with as little effect as ever, and this morning the men who had remained faithful to the union (which was, it had to be admitted, the vast majority of the old Hetton pitmen) had gathered with their leaders and heard Tommy Hepburn advise them to swallow the bitter pill and return to work. Not having been present at the meeting, Dunn did not, of course, know precisely what had been said, but the upshot was that soon afterwards a long line of skilled and experienced colliers had formed a queue at the office door, ready to sign on for work, on whatever terms were required of them. Since he had no intention of turning any of the strangers out (that would have been grossly injust), there were more men wanting places than he had places to offer, which meant he could take his pick of the best and least troublesome of them. It all seemed thoroughly satisfactory.

But as the morning passed, and he observed the men waiting outside the colliery office, Dunn began to feel progressively more uneasy. They had no particular look of defeat about them; on the contrary, they seemed almost cheerful, talking noisily amongst themselves. It was not what he had hoped for. Furthermore, it began to reinforce certain suspicions that had been growing in him for some time. On first coming here, he had believed that strong support for the union was limited to the most active leaders; that once they were gone, the union itself would crumble. But more recently he had begun to suspect that he might be wrong. The majority of the men had stayed loyal to the union through considerable hardships and for much longer than he had anticipated. So strong had they been until now, that he had been surprised by the suddenness of their final capitulation. Would they really be willing, after all this time, to give up an association that had meant so much to them? Certainly the union had given way on almost every point and openly conceded that membership was incompatible with employment at Hetton. But there could sometimes be a considerable gap, Dunn knew, between what men said and what was in their hearts.

He was right to be uneasy. Very few of the returning colliers had any intention at all, except as a temporary measure, of abandoning the union for which they had suffered so much. Hepburn and the other leaders had promised them that, for the time being, it would demand nothing of them that might bring them into conflict with the owners, so that they could sign the declaration the company required of them with a clear conscience. But one day, when all this was in the past, when the time was right, then they knew that the union would rise again, because it would never have died.

John Grey, taking his place in the queue for work, spotted a familiar figure passing on the road by the colliery. He called out, 'Howay there, Bridget Armstrong!' The woman turned to look at him, but scarcely slowed her pace. 'They tell me you're working up at Little Eppleton.'

'Why aye, so I am. What of it? I slept in. I can't stop now or I'll have no work.'

'Just stop by the kitchen for us, will you, and tell our

Matty the strike's over and she'd best come home. We'll be flitting soon and she won't know where to find us.'

The woman did halt then. She looked a little puzzled. 'Why, is she not with you now?'

'She's working in the kitchens up there. Since a week past Monday.'

'I didn't know. I'll tell her then.'

John Grey was fortunate, for he was skilled and knowledgeable enough for his son's past misdemeanours to be overlooked. By the end of the morning, having waited his turn with unaccustomed patience, he had made his mark on the bond, crossing his fingers under the table as he did so, because of the declaration against union membership; and then he found himself once again a working pitman with a house to go to.

That evening, as the families in the wood were beginning to pack their belongings ready for tomorrow's move, Bridget Armstrong came to find John Grey.

'I don't know what she told you, but your lass isn't up at the Hall. They'd never heard of her in the kitchens, when I asked. Mind,' she added, enjoying the sensation she was clearly creating, 'I don't know if there's owt in it, but Frank Watson's wife, she said she'd seen her talking to Eliza Fenwick, outside the Ranter Chapel up by Brick Garth. Two days ago that was, she said.' She would have gone on, but John Grey had already swung round and gone in search of Matty's friend, whom he had seen with Adam just an hour earlier.

They were standing with a group of other men outside their shelter. Both husband and wife looked grey and weary and haggard, as if they had slept very little since their loss. Grey knew that today Adam had gone with the others to the colliery office to bind himself for work, only to be told that, in common with the rest of the union committee, he would never work for the Hetton Coal Company again, or any other colliery on the Tyne and Wear. Grey supposed that was what they were discussing now, but he did not wait to find out. He grasped Eliza's arm. 'Where's our Matty?'

Eliza turned astonished eyes on him; though there was also, he noticed, a degree of consternation in her expression. She knew something then. 'I don't know,' she said.

'Don't lie to us. You were seen talking to her just two days ago, up by the chapel.'

'She passed by, that's all.' She spoke calmly enough, but he knew she was still keeping something from him.

'Where from, that's what I want to know? Where was she going?'

'I don't know,' said Eliza. It was true, in that Matty had been evasive in the extreme, and clearly alarmed that Eliza had seen her at all. The way she had behaved before Eliza called to her had been strange too, for she had clearly been doing her best to avoid being seen by anyone, a difficult enough procedure in broad daylight anywhere near Brick Garth. The girl had asked after Eliza and Adam, in a rather breathless manner, as if impatient to be away; and at the earliest opportunity she had muttered some excuse and run off – down the hill towards Four Lane Ends, Eliza thought, but she could not be sure.

John Grey gave up and went in search of two of his friends, and summoned his sons and Jack Marley to come too. 'I'm going to find that lass if it's the last thing I do,' he said. 'She's lied to us. Someone must know what she's up to.'

Matty was out fetching water when the man called with the letter. It was part of what they had agreed, that she should see that everything was in order for Tommy and then, tonight, she would go back to the camp. She had heard that the strike was over and guessed that her father might try and send word to her. It was important that she reached him before he found out not only that she was not at Little Eppleton, but that she had never been there.

It was growing dark, and bringing the water was the last thing she had left to do. Tommy, absorbed in gloomy thoughts, was glad when the knock on the door distracted him. He went to answer it and found one of the Cornish-men there, a man called Trevenna whom he knew slightly because of some favour he had done him at the height of the epidemic. 'One of your friends from the village asked me to bring this. Your kin from home sent it with him when he was back there lately. He'd have got it to you before now, but he was taken ill himself.'

Tommy took the letter and thanked the man.

'I see you're well again,' said Trevenna.

'Aye. I should be back at work Monday.' He said goodnight and closed the door, and then he lit a candle.

He saw with foreboding that the letter was in Jenny's writing. He opened it and took it to the candle, tilting it so that the light fell on it. He saw from the date that it had been written more than a week ago.

My dear brother, it said, *Rowland went to the Lord, Sunday. His earthly remains will be buried, Wednesday. I am in good health, and the bairns. God bless you. Your loving sister, J. Peart.*

When he came to the end, Tommy stood very still, staring unseeing into the fire.

So Rowland had gone. He had known that it was possible, even likely, that they would never meet again in this world, but now that it had happened he felt numb, as if the truth of it could not yet quite reach him. He had never felt so far from home as he did at this moment, when he had no one who had known Rowland to speak to him or hear all the things he wanted to say. He would have gone to see Mark Dent, who had known him slightly, but it was unwise to walk so far after dark and by the time he got there the other man might well be in bed.

He knew how he ought to receive this news – with rejoicing that Rowland's suffering was over, that he was at peace, and with gratitude for his life. But all he felt was a dreadful emptiness. He dropped to his knees by the table and laid his face on his hands and tried to pray, but round and round in his head went the words, *He's dead. Rowland is dead.*

He heard Matty come back into the house and slowly rose to his feet, facing her. She must have seen at once that something was wrong, because she put down the pail and came to him. 'What's up, hinny?'

'Rowland's dead.' He felt the tears rush to his eyes, and then her arms were about him and she was holding him tenderly, making all kinds of consoling murmurings. After a time, she made him sit down and sat beside him and listened to him talk for a long time, about his family, and how much he missed them and longed to see them again; and his grief at what he had lost, and his regret that he had not even been there for the funeral.

When he was calmer, she said, 'You go up. I'll stop here till you sleep.'

He had momentarily forgotten that she was to leave tonight, and now he looked at his watch in dismay. It was almost midnight already. 'Why no, my hinny, you must go now. Sharp as you can. You should have been gone long since.'

'You go up first, then I'll go.'

In the end it was the only way he could get her to agree to leave, so he kissed her gently and left her. A little later, as he lay in bed, he heard her fastening the shutters and barring the back door, and then the front door opened and closed again.

He no longer felt numb or empty. The emptiness had been filled – all of him had been filled – with a dreadful ache of grief, and he lay very still, hurting too much to move or sleep. He wanted more than anything in all the world to find himself back at White Lea, to comfort Jenny and share this time with her.

A sound broke into his pain, a creak of the stair. Then a soft step, and another. Then all at once Matty was standing beside the bed, and the next moment she was on it, lying close to him, holding him in her arms. 'I'm not leaving you the night,' she whispered between kisses. 'I'll stay till morning.' And he knew that this was what he had wanted most of all.

If she had thought he would take tonight what she had

offered so readily a few days ago, she was wrong. He was thankful beyond words to have her there beside him, and he wanted her, urgently, with a hunger made sharper by grief. But he felt that to take her now would be in some way an insult to Rowland's memory, a betrayal of all he had learned from his brother-in-law. So he lay quite still, holding her, allowing her to kiss and caress him, but making no move to respond, concentrating all his will on curbing the fierce and growing demands of his body.

They had been lying there for perhaps an hour, and he knew that his resistance was growing weaker by the minute, when there was a clamour of feet in the alley outside and then a loud persistent hammering on the front door. A man shouted, 'Emerson! Open the door!'

Matty shot upright. 'It's my dad, I'm sure it is!'

For a moment they stared at one another. The knocking became a ferocious kicking and banging. 'You'd best go, quickly, out the back!' said Tommy.

Matty scrambled to her feet and moved towards the stairs, while outside the hammering went on and on, louder and louder. Already Tommy could hear how the wood was giving way. They would soon have the door down.

'Get down here, you bastard, open the door! And you, whore – we know you're there!'

'Go on!' he urged her, for she had come to a halt.

'You come too.'

'Don't be stupid, that would only make matters worse.'

'If you stop here they'll kill you.'

'Not if you're not here.'

'They know I'm here or they wouldn't have come. My being gone won't help you. Come on, Tommy! If you don't, then I'll stop too.'

He hesitated only until he realised that she was in deadly earnest. Then he grabbed his clothes and pulled them on as he ran down the stairs behind her. As they slipped out through the back door they heard the front door fall in with a crash. Someone must have remembered the back, just too late, for as they reached the end of the row they heard feet running down the alley towards them. Tommy took Matty's hand and they ran faster, stumbling in the dark on the uneven bumps in the ground, down the slope into the shadows of Elemore Vale, where the bushes along the burnside hid them from view. They could hear the men shouting above them.

He halted and held her close, his mouth on her hair. 'Where shall we go?'

'You wanted to see your sister. Go now, tonight. Stay there till it's died down a bit.'

'What about you?'

'I'll go home, wherever that is.'

'But you'll get wrong.'

'Why aye, my dad'll belt me.' He made a dismayed exclamation. 'He'll sharp get over it, when he sees we're not meeting any more.'

He was silent for a long time, then he whispered, 'I can't bear that, not again.' After a moment's thought, he urged, 'Matty, come with me! We'll go to Gretna, and marry, then no one can part us, ever again.'

She was silent for what seemed a very long time. They could hear the shouting still going on above them, backwards and forwards, setting dogs barking, bringing other shouts from angry households woken by the noise. Glancing up, Tommy saw a lantern swinging its way along the ridge, and the shouting came nearer.

Matty said, 'Howay man Tommy! Now!' And he took her hand again and they ran on, up the slope past the pit, seeking a westward road.

Chapter Nineteen

Tommy and Matty stumbled on in silence through the night, often glancing behind them to make sure they were not being followed. Several times they thought they saw lanterns, or heard shouts; they quickened their pace, not daring to halt to get their breath even after they had put a wood or the brow of a hill between themselves and the signs of pursuit.

They splashed through burns, nearly lost clogs in the mud, tore their clothes and their flesh on brambles, knocked their heads on low branches, unseen in the dim and fitful light of the waning moon. Tommy never once let go of Matty's hand, though after a time it was she who led the way, running ahead of him as he stumbled and panted behind, quickly exhausted by this unwonted exertion so soon after rising from his sickbed. He soon felt he could go no further, but still they ran on, while his head throbbed, his breath came in gasps, myriad specks blurred his vision.

And then at last they scrambled up a steep slope and found themselves, at its top, within sight of a crossroads, with a signpost, the first clear indication they had seen of what direction they were taking.

Tommy staggered to a tree and fell back against it. Matty went to look at the sign, peering at it in the inadequate light. 'Durham!' she said at last, with a note of satisfaction in her voice. Then after a further examination, she added, 'We're four miles yet from Durham. We've not come as far as I thought. I reckon we took a long way round.' When he made no comment, she said anxiously, 'You're not fit for all this.'

'I'll manage,' he gasped. He forced himself fully onto his feet and she took his hand again. They went on at a slower pace, though now that he had lost the momentum of flight Tommy felt more weary than before. Dogged will-power kept him going, not any reserves of strength. He ceased to notice what lay under their feet or to either side of them, concentrating all his attention simply on keeping upright and moving forward. As the sky lightened behind them, it began to rain, not very much, but enough to wet their clothes and set them shivering.

They came to a scattering of houses, quiet and grey in the early light, with an old church and a mill. Some way off they could hear the sound of a river. Here Matty stopped at last. She cast a quick glance at Tommy's face. 'Let's stop here. There's an inn. We'll have a bit rest. They'll not think to seek us here.'

Thankfully, Tommy took a step or two towards the prosperous group of buildings that she indicated; and then he halted. 'We've no money.'

'I've got fourpence,' she said.

It was what she had left from yesterday's shopping, but at the inn it was clear that it was nowhere near enough for food and accommodation, particularly from a landlord deeply suspicious of two dishevelled and certainly not respectable young people arriving at his establishment so early in the morning. Matty's hint that Tommy was not in good health did not help, for sickly fugitives might have the cholera and were thus more threatening than mere vagrants. 'He's not long off his sickbed,' Matty pointed out, hoping that would be less disturbing. Even in his exhausted state Tommy was impressed by what he saw of her considerable reserves of charm, brought forward to impress the man.

Eventually they must have had some effect, for, with obvious reluctance, he showed them to a byre, well away from the main body of the inn, and told them they could stay there for a while. As they settled down on the hay that offered a tempting place of rest, they heard him slam the bolts and bars noisily home again on the door of the inn.

Matty's money had at least provided them with bread and ale, though Tommy was too weary to eat much and his principles would not allow him to touch the ale. He curled up on the hay beside her, watching her in the faint light that came in round the edge of the door, enough to show him the dark tendrils of hair escaping from her flowered kerchief, the curve of long lashes above her lustrous eyes, the eager way she gnawed at the bread – white even teeth on the brown crust, rosy lips hungrily parted. Somehow he was still gazing at her when his eyes closed and he fell asleep.

He slept, deeply and soundly, for a long time. When he woke again there was a depression the shape of her body in the hay beside him, cold to the touch, and the remains of the bread lying close to his head. Matty herself was nowhere to be seen.

At first he thought she had gone outside for a breath of air, or perhaps to check on their route. Pushing open the door of the byre he saw that it was now well into the afternoon, the sun high and quite warm, with a gentle haze over the farther view of a tree-clad slope rising from level stubble fields. There were a few people about, a boy driving cattle, two women talking by a well, a man unloading barrels from a cart into the inn. But no Matty.

He was still not really alarmed. She would be somewhere about. He decided not to go and look for her, in case she were to come back while he was outside and think he had gone on without her. He left the byre door open and sat down again on the hay to wait. He felt much

277

better now, rested and ready to face the remainder of the journey to Weardale, which was where he intended to take her first, before going on over the border to Gretna Green, where they could be legally married without her father's consent. It was not, of course, how he would have preferred it to be. He was too conscious of the duty of children to their parents to be quite at ease about it, but theirs were special circumstances. And whatever his reservations about them, the very thought – coming to him suddenly as an approaching reality – that they would soon be married filled him with a warm glow of happiness. He wished she would hurry back to him.

Time went by – he was not sure how long, because in their flight he had left his watch behind – and still she did not come. He began to feel just a little anxious. It could be, he thought after further consideration, that she had gone to the inn, perhaps to offer to undertake some task in return for food or even money, to help them on their way. It would be like her. He decided to go and investigate.

The cart had gone by now and the landlord was just emerging from his cellar, having presumably been seeing to the storage of the barrels. He looked at Tommy with no great friendliness.

'I'm seeking the lass that's with me. Miss Grey.'

The landlord frowned, and only after a moment or two seemed to remember where he had seen Tommy before. 'Oh, you're the lad who came this morning. Sorry, I've not seen the girl.'

'Not since first thing?'

'No.' He was already turning away, concerned with his own preoccupations.

Tommy stared at him, not really seeing him. Where could she be? A chill of doubt began to creep over him. There were possibilities he had not considered before. He took a step after the man, fast making towards the kitchen door. 'Has anyone been by, that you've seen? Men, lads – colliers, that is.'

The landlord swung round. 'What are you mixed up

in? I want no trouble here. Get away with you, now, and fast.'

There was a gun hanging on the wall, and when the man reached for it Tommy saw no sense in arguing further. He went back to the byre to check that Matty had not returned. It was empty, and the landlord shouted at him again to clear off. He walked on along the road until he rounded a bend. When he retraced his steps, a little cautiously, the man was no longer watching.

He spent some time questioning the few people that were about, but no one had seen any sign of Matty, nor of any gang of rough-looking men seeking her. She had disappeared without trace.

He hung about the place, keeping out of sight of the inn but returning furtively to the byre at intervals, until it began to grow dark. Then he knew he must decide what to do next. He walked a little way from the village into the woods and found a spot which offered him a distant view of the houses and the road and sat down to consider his position.

She had gone, he had no idea why or how or where. Unless some dreadful accident had happened to her (an appalling possibility, but not, he hoped, the most likely) she had probably returned, somehow and for some reason, to Hetton. Either her father had found her (but then, surely, he would have been aware of some kind of disturbance, even in his exhausted sleep?), or, for some inexplicable reason, she had gone of her own free will.

If only he knew what had made her go! When he thought of what she might have to face in returning to her family, his urge to rush back and protect her was almost uncontrollable. Yet that might make everything much worse for her, confirming as it would that there was something between them, if her father still had any doubts on the subject. Besides which, he had no idea whether the evicted colliers were still living in the make-shift camp in the woods, or whether, the strike being over, they had moved back into one or other of the many colliery rows that scattered the Hetton district. If that

279

was the case, he would find it very difficult to discover where the Grey family now were. And even if he found her, what then? She was protected by father and brothers and the other men, all of whom detested him and saw him as a threat. They were not likely to allow him any access to her.

And then there was Jenny, his beloved sister, so recently bereaved. It had not been simply an excuse that he should go to her. Even before they had known there was any reason for flight, he had told Matty he planned to go back to Weardale, for a day or two. He thought it had been Thursday – or was it Wednesday? – when they left Hetton. He had time to go on to Weardale now and still be back in Hetton for work on Monday. Then, after work, he would seek Matty out somehow and ask her for an explanation . . . But then they would be as far as ever from the possibility of marriage, firmly returned to the circumstances that made their love an offence and a stumbling block.

This was just such an occasion when a random opening of the Bible might have shown him what to do, but his Bible, like everything else, was still in the house at Brick Garth. Of all he had left behind, he regretted that most. He felt bereft without it, as if a sure and trusted guide had abandoned him. After a time he knelt down on the damp earth and tried to pray for guidance, but the confused thoughts tumbled through his head and he could not clear a way for the sign he so desperately wanted.

Still undecided, and feeling both chilled and depressed, he left the wood, slipped back to the village for one last fruitless search of the byre and then made his way towards the river. On its banks he halted again. On their way here this morning, he had been too exhausted to notice what path they took, so he could not now simply retrace his steps, even if he had been sure he wanted to. He could see no obvious signpost or milestone to help him and he was reluctant to go back to the village and ask for help. But if – as he supposed – this river was the

Wear, winding its devious way from its source a few miles west of White Lea to the sea at Sunderland, then he could use it as his guide.

In the declining light, he studied it to see which way it flowed. Then he considered the alternatives. If he were to turn left along its bank, walking upstream, he would be sure, very soon, to reach Durham city, from which the road led to Weardale. If he were to turn right, he could follow its seaward journey until he came to a road that cut across to the east, back to Hetton.

He closed his eyes for a moment, 'Show me, Heavenly Father!' When he opened them, as if by no choice of his own, he turned right.

It was just light enough still to make out the path that led along the river bank, through low meadows bounded, ahead of him, by a steep wooded slope. Across the river, further woods covered the far bank. He walked on steadily, not thinking of anything much except that his decision had been made for him, which was a relief, since all he had to do now was to act upon it.

The river curved round in a great sweep between the wooded hills. He followed it for perhaps a mile, and then halted to look about him again and try and estimate how far he still had to go before finding a path away from the river.

Ahead of him houses gathered close on a hill, on the heights of which, black against the last faint greenish glow of daylight, stood the emphatic, unmistakable outlines of cathedral and castle. Something had gone wrong with his calculations. He had reached Durham.

Chapter Twenty

The pedlar came again to White Lea on the second Friday after Rowland's death.

Jenny heard the donkey braying to the galloway as he clopped up the track, and the pony's answering whinny. She went to the door, with the memory of the man's last visit coming sharp and sudden, as such things did, so that she had no defence against them. She stood waiting for him to reach her, bracing herself for his banter and his gossip.

He did not even smile, though the edges of his mouth seemed to soften a little. He raised his hat. 'I heard of your trouble,' he said quietly, 'but I thought I'd drop by all the same, in case there's anything you need.'

Need. Need had nothing at all to do with the bright assortment of buttons and buckles, the ribbons and trinkets laid out before her in his cases and boxes; not even with the more practical items, soap and brushes, fabrics of various kinds. Need was the thing that howled inside her night and day, tearing her to pieces. It was not something for which any pedlar could offer solace.

'There's nowt, thank you,' she said quietly.

He raised his hat again and closed his bags and, just on the point of leaving, added, 'I'm told he was a good man. I'm sorry he's gone.'

She was surprised and touched by his sympathy, but did not quite know how to tell him so. 'Call again next time,' she said.

Next time, six months from now. Another weary six months of her life, but a mere drop in the vast ocean of time that must still lie before her.

She went back into the house and began to do one or two things in preparation for supper, stopping often to try and remember what she had to do next.

She was so tired, so desperately tired. She could not remember when she had last slept, for longer than a few brief seconds of blissful unconsciousness. Not since before . . .

There was an air of unreality about everything. She went through each day in a daze, doing what had to be done, not thinking very much. Sometimes, momentarily, she would find herself believing that it was all a ghastly dream, from which she would suddenly wake with the warm wonderful realisation that everything was as it always used to be; that in just a moment she would hear Rowland's step on the flagstones outside the door, or his voice call from half way up the track, and then she would go out and find he was there, that the past months had all been a nightmare and he was alive and well and had never left her.

But at night she knew it was real. She dreaded the nights. They were interminable, marked by the slow plodding passage of each long-drawn-out second. The nights brought solitude and darkness and howling emptiness, and the endless, endless longing for Rowland, a longing that ached through her veins and her limbs, without respite or ease. She would gather his plaid in her arms and lie on their bed holding it close, her eyes shut tight, trying to feel him there with her, not as the sick suffering man who had last lain there, but well and whole and strong, her lover and friend and companion.

Sometimes she found herself talking to him in a soft reproachful whisper, 'Why did you leave me? Love, I can't bear it, come back, I want you so!' Sometimes she would try to pray, 'Lord, it hurts so much – help me to be strong! Help me! Help me!' But there was never any answer, only silence.

The children would soon be home from school and work. It gave her some relief when they were in the house. Yet even they were beginning to leave her behind. They mourned their father, for they had loved him, but as far as they were concerned he was with Jesus and happy, and though they missed him – desperately at times – acceptance had come with astonishing speed. Already they could laugh again and play and squabble, and even the older ones appeared sometimes to forget their loss for a little while. Jenny envied them that healing simplicity.

Someone was crossing the flagstones outside the house, slowly, not a child but a man . . . On Friday afternoons he used to come home after his week's work at Guinea Grove . . . Jenny stood quite still where she was by the table, trying to bring herself under control, waiting for the knock, which of course would come at any moment. When it did not she swallowed hard and went to open the door.

At first she did not recognise the man standing there. His fair hair was tousled, his face disfigured by several days' growth of beard, he was thin and ill-looking, clearly close to exhaustion. He was staring at her as if she were as much a stranger to him as he was to her. A beggar, wanting shelter and food . . . ?

Then she realised.

'Tommy!' What had happened to the rosy-faced, bright-eyed, healthy young man who had left White Lea little more than six months ago? She took his arm and led him inside and steered him to the settle by the fire. 'Tommy, you look so ill!'

He smiled wanly. 'I've been bad, but I'm better now. I walked a long way, that's all.'

She gazed down at him. 'The cholera?'

'Aye.'

'You should have let us know!'

'I was sick, remember. Besides – why . . . ' His voice tailed off into silence, but she knew what he meant.

She made him some tea and was reassured to see the colour returning to his face. 'I got your letter,' he said at last. 'I wish I could have been here.'

'You're here now,' she said gently. She sat down facing him. 'Luke gave me the money. Thank you.'

'I wish it could have been more. I meant to bring you some this time.' He thought with regret of the leather bag left on the mantelpiece at Hetton.

'We're managing,' she said. 'The boys will be able to go to school this winter.' The washing floors always closed during the winter months, when frost and snow made work impossible; it gave the lads an opportunity to resume their schooling. 'I got Em some new clogs too.'

Tommy laid down his cup and got up and began to walk about the room, looking round as if to reassure himself that nothing had changed. By the bed he stopped and then put out a hand and touched the plaid. 'It feels wrong, without him.'

'Aye.'

Turning round, he saw that her eyes were brimming with tears. She ran to him with her arms reaching for him and they clung together, both weeping, and a little consoled by it. Afterwards, she went to the bed herself and took something from under the pillow and handed it to her brother.

'Rowland's Bible,' he said, not quite sure what was expected of him.

'Look inside.'

He opened the cover and read what was written there. In a neat youthful hand, marking the moment of conversion: *Rowland Peart, new born in Christ, 21 February 1816*; and then, underneath, in a painful scrawl that was scarcely recognisable as the same hand: *For my dear brother Thomas Emerson, 26 August 1832.*

'It was after he had your letter,' said Jenny.

He could not speak. He ran his hands over the book. It had never been as good as his own, and now, after years of daily use, the cover was limp and worn, its corners rubbed away to nothing, the pages yellowing and curled at the edges. For more than seventeen years Rowland had carried it everywhere with him, an essential part of him.

The children came running in, and Tommy was so still and quiet that it was a moment or two before they saw him. When they did, he had to slip the book quickly into his pocket, because there was no peace for him for a long time afterwards.

Brother and sister sat up late that night, talking over the past months – the past months at White Lea, for Tommy said very little about his recent experiences. He found that for some reason he could not do so, other than in a very general way.

He had no doubt that the error that had taken him to Durham, and so brought him home, had been no simple mischance. In such things a man of faith must always see the hand of God. He had been sure that in coming back to White Lea he would find that there was some special purpose for him, other than the loving duty to offer consolation to his sister. He was sure that here everything would be made plain – why Matty had gone and how, what he should do about it. He had thought that at the very least he would be able to talk to Jenny about it all.

But now, in the face of Jenny's grief, his own lesser troubles seemed to shrink to triviality. He knew they were not trivial. The hurt of Matty's sudden departure was very real, the more because he could not be sure that he would ever see her again. Under the ache of grief and pity that was a part of this homecoming, impatience nibbled at him, to be away from here, back in Hetton where he

286

could learn the truth. He did not want to talk about what had happened. He wanted to do something about it.

Later, as he was about to go up to bed, he saw Jenny looking about her. 'What are you wanting?'

'Your things—'

'I didn't bring any.'

She stood looking at him. 'You're not stopping then.'

'No.' He saw the disappointment in her face, veiled just too late.

'The cholera's still bad then?'

'It's past its worst, I think. But – well, there are things I must finish . . . ' It sounded lame and inadequate, but he could not bring himself to say more. Perhaps he was just too tired. He would tell her tomorrow.

If Jenny had been shocked by Tommy's appearance when she saw him standing at the door that night, Tommy was even more shocked by how his sister looked. He wondered if he would have known her, had she not been where he expected to find her. In the months of his absence she had turned from a youthful-looking wife and mother to an old woman. She had never been large – they none of them were – but she had always had a sturdy, healthy look. Now she seemed to have shrunk and shrivelled to a frail white-faced woman, her grey eyes shadowed and haunted, every line of her body expressive of weariness and a complete absence of all her old energy. He lay awake for a long time that night wondering if he did wrong not even to consider returning to White Lea for good, whatever the consequences to his pocket and his heart. How could this broken little woman be expected to go on caring for the house and the land and her six young children without a man to help and support her?

He put some of his worries to Joe, when he called next morning at Well House.

Joe was reassuringly unchanged. 'Have you made your fortune yet, man?' was his first greeting to Tommy, when

287

he opened the door to him. He did not really listen to Tommy's rather confused reply, but invited him to inspect his newborn daughter, before taking him out to the field to admire the ponies running there. They leaned on the wall watching the shaggy black creatures grazing, trotting, nuzzling one another, while Joe commented on their most admirable points. Then he said, 'You're just visiting, I take it?'

Whereupon Tommy told him his anxieties about Jenny. Joe listened sympathetically, but without any particular signs of anxiety. 'She's had a bad few months of it, but she'll come through. She's tough, our Jenny. It's not as if it's the first time she's had to face this kind of thing. She's got over it before.'

Tommy knew Joe was thinking of their father, nursed by Jenny through the same disease that had killed Rowland. 'It's not the same,' he said.

A little to his surprise, Joe gave the observation his serious consideration, and then agreed with him. 'No, it's not. I can't recall two people as close as they were. She loves her bairns, but he was always first. Love when you're young, and it's new, that I can understand. But after all these years . . . I reckon I care for Phoebe, but – why . . . Still, she'll get by, I'm sure of it. It's not two weeks, you know. Can't expect miracles.'

Tommy thought of how much he loved Matty. He did not think it was possible to love anyone more than that, but then he could not imagine what it would be like to have shared years of marriage with her. The worst thing for him at the moment was to fear that he might never find out.

Joe shrugged off his gravity and cast a sideways look at his brother. 'How are you doing then? Any Hetton lass to rival Sister Craggs?'

Tommy coloured, and Joe, seeing it, slapped him on the back. 'Why, our Tommy, I do believe I've touched a nerve! There is someone then.'

'Maybe,' said Tommy, and had some difficulty fending off Joe's eager questions. If he did not at the moment want to discuss Matty with Jenny, he most certainly could not do so with Joe.

It was a strange sensation coming back from the hostility and violence of Hetton to Weardale where, as soon as it was known that he was home, Tommy was overwhelmed by the warmth of his welcome. He had little time alone with Jenny on that Saturday, for there was a constant stream of friends and neighbours coming to call, and he had many calls of his own to make, on others besides Joe. As soon as he could, he went to see Luke.

It was odd to see his cousin back in his old house at Side Head, as if he had never been away, as if their shared experiences of the past months had gone without trace. Even odder was to find that he felt closer to Luke then he had for a long time. It helped, he supposed, that Rebekah was clearly content with life again.

Soon after he arrived she went off to Chapel market, so they had the house to themselves and time to talk. Luke had found work at one of the mines without too much difficulty, but he admitted that only the money they had saved at Hetton enabled them to live on the pittance he earned. Rebekah, thankful to be back in Weardale, had not once complained about the drastic fall in their income, but it was clear that Luke could not take the matter so philosophically. 'There's a canny few mean to sail for Canada next year. Joe Wilson wrote that there's a good living to be made out there. He's not been there much above a year. If he can say that so soon, there must be something in it. I'd go myself, but Rebekah won't hear of it.'

'Maybe by next spring she'll feel differently,' Tommy suggested, though he felt depressed at the thought that Luke might move so far away.

Leaving Luke's house Tommy came face to face with Sarah Craggs. They both halted and he put his hand to his hat and was about to greet her with his old friendliness when he saw that she was overcome with confusion, lowering her gaze while the colour flooded painfully over her face. He had enough experience now to recognise the signs that she cared for him. Joe had teased him often enough about his own supposed feelings for Sarah, but until now he had not considered that she might feel for him what he conspicuously failed to feel for her.

He watched her struggle for control, and achieve it in some measure, managing at last to look straight at him, if with something short of her usual directness.

'You're back for good then?' She hid her disappointment at his reply with a measure of success, then asked eagerly, 'But you'll be here tomorrow, to join us in worship?'

Tommy was genuinely regretful that he could not stay. After the furtive meetings at Hetton, he longed for the old joyful fellowship of the Weardale chapels. But he knew that if he was to be back at work on Monday, then he must put aside all his scruples about Sunday travel and leave early the next morning. Not that fears for his job were the only impetus that sent him away . . .

He studied Sarah as they talked. She was a fine-looking lass, he had to acknowledge – indeed, he had always recognised that. She was not very tall, but sturdy, with fair hair and a fresh rosy face and bright blue eyes. Looking at her, he had much the same feeling as he had when confronted by a healthy child or one of Joe's ponies – pleasure, both of the eye and the heart, but no excitement, no longing, nothing but an easy friendship, marred now by his dismay that she so clearly saw things rather differently than he did. He made his excuses as soon as he decently could and went on his way, feeling a little uncomfortable about it; but what could he do? It was simply a pity that he had not made life easier for himself as well as for her by falling in love with her, so eminently suitable as she was, instead of with a wayward collier's daughter like Matty.

He was ready to leave before dawn the next morning. Jenny got up with him (since she rarely slept much, it was no particular hardship) and gave him breakfast and food for the journey. She said, 'Do you think of coming back here at all?'

'It's too soon to say,' he replied. He left shortly afterwards, still without saying anything about Matty. If all went as he hoped it might, then she would one day know everything, and rejoice with him.

Chapter Twenty-one

In a state combining physical exhaustion with a ferment of hope and fear, Tommy reached Hetton very late on the Sunday evening, after walking all day. It was dark and there was no moon, so he did not do what he longed above all to do and go straight to the wood to seek out Matty. That would have to wait for daylight. Instead, he made his way to Brick Garth. Remembering the circumstances of his leaving and what had happened after, his heart felt heavy.

It was late, so there was no one much about, though he could hear drunken singing some distance away. He passed the chapel, a black shape a little larger than the rows that faced it, and went on towards the place where the alley ran down beside his house. Within sight of the corner, he halted. A man stood there, just visible in the light from a nearby window. He looked innocent enough, leaning casually against the wall with folded arms; yet Tommy had an uneasy conviction that he was one of the men who had attacked him in the wood. Quite what he based that feeling on he was not sure, because he had gained no very clear view of his attackers and it was a long time ago; but he felt the hairs rise on the back of his neck.

He was no coward, and he knew there might be nothing in it, but he guessed that if this man was watching for him, then others would not be far away. He had no particular wish to end up in the gutter, beaten senseless. He retraced his steps and went a long way round, coming to Brick Garth from the south. At the bottom of the alley there was another man, crouching by the wall on his hunkers, as colliers often did. It was too much of a coincidence that two men should be hanging about for no particular purpose at either end of the alley in the middle of the night.

He walked some way along the waste ground near the houses. There were enough lights still burning for him to make out the shape of a third man in the court behind his house. Tommy stood watching for a time, to see if either of the men in his sight would make a move that might indicate their innocence of any ill intention towards him. Both stayed exactly where they were, watching the house and the alley. He had no doubt now. He went on to the furthest row and knocked softly on the window of the Cornishman's house.

It was some time before he roused anyone and he was growing anxious in case any of the watchers should hear him and come to investigate, but at last he heard sounds inside, and then a candle was lit. Trevenna opened the door, just a crack, and peered suspiciously round it. As soon as he saw Tommy he opened it wide and stood back. 'Come you in, quickly now!' It was further confirmation, had Tommy needed it, that the men out there had been watching for him. He stepped into the house and Trevenna set down the candle and barred the door again firmly.

'I think my house is being watched,' Tommy said.

The man nodded. 'I seen them. Been there since yesterday.' He looked rueful. 'Guess I did wrong. Went round to your house yesterday, just to see how you were doing. Found the door down and all. A proper mess, they'd left. I was just leaving – seemed the wisest thing to do – when this big fellow comes round, full of questions, a-shaking of his fists. Said did I know when you'd be back. Should have kept my mouth shut, I see that now, but he'd three more fellows outside waiting for him. So I tells him what you said, about coming back to work tomorrow morning. I knew the moment I'd done speaking I'd made a mistake.'

Tommy wondered uneasily what they had done to the house, not least to his precious books.

'What are they after you for?'

Tommy hesitated. He liked Trevenna well enough, but he was reluctant to explain his difficulties to someone who was not a close friend. Perhaps the man realised that, for after a moment, to Tommy's relief, he shrugged and said, 'Never you mind. 'Tis none of my business. I'll get some tea and we'll think what's to be done.' Later, as they drank, he said, ''Tis not safe for you to stay here, or anywhere in Brick Garth. Is there somewhere else you can go?'

Tommy thought suddenly of Mark Dent, whose two fellow lodgers had moved out – one back to Weardale, the other, having died of the cholera, to a grave in Houghton churchyard. There would be room for him in his house, and it was far enough from Brick Garth to offer the possibility of safety, for the time being at least. It was also conveniently close to the wood, should Matty still be there, though Tommy was beginning to see that finding an opportunity to talk with her might be more difficult than he had anticipated.

He said some of this to Trevenna, who heard it with approval.

'I'll walk there with you,' he said, but Tommy would not hear of it.

'This is my quarrel. You've done plenty already. Besides, I'll go quieter alone.'

That was undeniable, but the other man was not quite satisfied. 'What if your friend won't take you in?'

'He will,' said Tommy.

He was glad that since coming here he had got to know the byways of the district, the most hidden paths. Now he

294

slipped down into Elemore Vale – remembering how he had last run down here with Matty's hand in his; was that really only five days ago? – and then on along the edge of the burn in the direction of Hetton village.

The row where Mark Dent lived was in darkness. Tommy rattled with his fingers on the window of his friend's house. He was afraid to make too much noise and wake the whole row, so it was some time before the window was pushed open and Mark's head appeared.

'It's Tommy! Can I come in?'

As soon as he was inside, he told Mark the immediate reason for his unexpected arrival, but it became clear that this time he was not going to get away without a fuller explanation. 'You can stay here, of course you can, as long as you want,' Mark assured him. 'Mind, I don't see . . . I know they've no love for any of us, but why single you out?'

'There was a lass,' said Tommy, colouring.

'A collier lass?'

Tommy nodded, and Mark's eyes widened. 'You great gowk! You must have known what that would get you into. I hope you've stopped seeing her.'

'I don't know. I may not have any choice about it.'

'Take my advice and forget her. If you do, maybe this'll blow over soon enough. If not, you'll be looking over your shoulder for ever.'

'Not for ever,' said Tommy. 'Things are bad now, I know, but they can't go on hating us for ever.'

'Can't they?' retorted Mark, before turning his attention to where Tommy should sleep.

Tommy had some distance to walk to work the next morning, though it was easy enough to cut across the fields to the pit, avoiding the houses and the streets busy with returning colliers – all of them, that is, who could be found jobs, now that so many of the places were filled with strangers. Nearing the pit, Tommy watched for someone he knew (everyone, strangers and colliers, seemed to be walking to work in groups this morning) and then attached himself to them, for safety. Trevenna was among them and expressed relief to see him safe. 'My wife will get your things for you this morning, while there's no one about,' he promised.

There was no open violence, but it was in the air, in the angry mutterings, the shouted insults, the hatred in the faces of the returning men as they passed the strangers. The constables were out in force, watchful for trouble. ''Tis going to be a mite hot for us down there today,' said Trevenna, nodding towards the pithead.

But for today at least he was wrong. The strangers worked uneasily, watchful for trouble, but the returning men stayed away from them, keeping to the company of their own kind, except when forced into proximity. Then there might be spitting or a brief bitter exchange; otherwise there was much talking in undertones and defiant singing, but though the atmosphere was tense in the extreme nothing happened. Even so, Tommy was glad to return to bank after the shift without mishap. He walked briskly back to Mark's house, glancing behind him all the way to check that he was not being followed.

His books were waiting for him. The woman next door told him that Mercy Trevenna had gone with a number of other women to collect his belongings from his house. They had seen a young girl watching them from the corner, but no men (presumably they had all been at work). The girl had made no effort to stop so large a contingent of women and they had managed to bring out the things easily enough. Tommy wondered at first if the girl might have been Matty, but further questioning told him she was a child – Matty's sister perhaps.

Some of the books had pages ripped out, but Tommy thought he would be able to repair a good deal of the damage. Fortunately, that was his greatest loss. All his crockery had been smashed, but he did not mind that so much. What astonished him most was that the money he had left on the mantelpiece had not been touched, though it amounted to nearly two pounds, a considerable sum. Since his pursuers had destroyed everything else that stood near it (including a pewter candlestick, which they had bent and distorted beyond further use) he knew that they had not simply failed to see it. His watch, too, was intact. It was clear that they saw the destruction as an act of justice and had not wanted to taint it with any advantage to themselves, however great the temptation must have been for men who had received no pay at all for many months. In spite of everything, Tommy felt a grudging respect for their integrity.

He went to the wood at dusk that day, though very cautiously. No one saw him, for there was no one left to see. Nothing remained but the bruised grass, scarred with black rings where the fires had been. He stood for a long time gazing at the clearing, wondering that so many shelters could ever have been contained in so small a space, trying to work out where Matty had lived. Then he slowly retraced his steps.

He had not told Mark where he was going or why and when he returned to the house his friend was explosive with anxiety. Tommy decided that he owed Mark a fuller explanation of his behaviour and told him the whole story. By now, considering what he had found waiting for him at Hetton, he had come to a definite conclusion about Matty's disappearance. He was quite sure that she had not left him of her own free will. He had not heard any sounds of struggle, but if (as was likely) she had for some reason gone outside the byre for a short time, before anyone was about, it would have been easy for her father to surprise her and carry her off with him by force, leaving no trace behind. He did wonder why, in that case, the men had not searched until they found him too, with results he preferred not to think about, but he supposed that Matty must have somehow succeeded in putting them off the scent. In every other respect it was the only explanation that seemed to fit the facts. After all, he could think of no other possible reason for her to have left him. But he recognised that having the mystery explained did not make its solution any easier. His greatest fear was of what she might have suffered at her father's hands; and it was fear of what she might suffer again if he blundered too readily in on her that held him back from doing exactly that.

At the end, Mark said, 'Believe me, Tommy, there's no future in this. If you want a wife, seek one in Weardale. There are fine lasses in plenty there. Lay off this one. She's nowt but trouble, and you should thank God she's gone. Whether she meant to or not she did you a favour, Tommy. Take it that way and forget her.' When he saw hesitation on Tommy's face, he added, 'I'm not risking my neck for you if you keep on with this.'

After that, Tommy had no choice but to cease his search for Matty, openly at least. He continued, nevertheless, to watch for her wherever he went, his eyes sweeping every house he passed, in the hope that he would discover where she lived and then somehow manage to engineer a meeting with her. He wished he was familiar with the appearance of other members of her family, so that he might recognise them even if she were not present at the time, but he had only glimpsed one of her brothers in the middle of an ugly fight, and the rest he had never seen, as far as he knew. Once, near Four Lane Ends, he saw a slight dark youth walking away from the crossroads in the direction of the Blossom pit, apparently on his way to work; the intense darkness of hair and complexion, the slightly foreign look brought Matty strongly to mind, but he had no means of telling if that was only a coincidence, for he did not see where the youth came from and he was quickly lost to sight.

There were other troubles that convinced him that Mark was right, at least in his contention that it was hardly the moment for a stranger to seek out a collier's daughter, for whatever reason. The uneasy truce underground, maintained only because each of the two sides behaved as if the other did not exist, lasted only for a day or two after the bulk of the colliers returned to work. Then the incidents began.

They were never on a large scale, and never entirely overt. One of the stranger hewers would be working alone in his bord when he would hear someone come up behind him. Before he even had time to glance round and see who it was, they would be on him, silently, purposefully. There would be a scuffle, soon over, and then the attackers would slip away into the darkness, leaving behind whatever damage they had inflicted – a split lip, a broken nose, bruises, a cracked rib, though nothing of great seriousness; more often than not they simply stripped the stranger of his clothes. If one of the supervisory officials came to investigate, the attackers (if they could be found at all) would have their story ready; there had been an accident, or perhaps an unprovoked assault.

At other times, it was the putters who caused the problems, though many of them were strangers, since those who had proved ineffective at hewing had been set on putting instead. But where the putters were lads who had been in the union, the stranger hewers would find their corves somehow tipped over, their coal mingled with stones that brought them fines, the trams that trans-ported the corves taken away just when they needed them – small irritations that made life more unpleasant. The strangers quickly found that complaints to officials got them nowhere. Somehow, no one ever believed them and the officials, even when near at hand, never seemed to see any sign of what was going on. It was only when Matthias Dunn became aware of an incident that strong action was taken against the offenders; but, as chief viewer, he spent only about three days a week within the colliery, and even then could not be everywhere. At Moorsley, so Mark said, his influence meant that every effort was made (not always with success) to offer protection to the strangers. But at Hetton it was obvious that when Dunn's eye was not upon them the lesser officials treated his instructions with contempt. The old pitmen were in the majority, and it was their favour that their superiors sought now.

''Twas wonderful how we could do no wrong when we was all they had,' said Trevenna one day, with consider-able bitterness. 'Now they've got the union men back, 'tis all the other way.'

'I'm sure,' agreed Tommy. It did not make him like the work any better. He was involved in the odd scuffle himself, but so far he thought there was nothing particularly personal in it. He suspected that Matty's father and brothers had not yet realised where they could find him, unless it was simply that they no longer saw him as a threat. He did not know whether to be glad or sorry if that was the case. Until he saw Matty herself and heard her explanation of what had happened, he would not know.

Trevenna told him that life at Brick Garth had become intolerable for the strangers. Most of the houses were now occupied again by returning colliers, who did all they could to harass their unloved neighbours. As far as possible the strangers stayed indoors at night, with shutters closed and doors barred, and kept away from public houses, but there were still many fights. The women were as bad, if not worse, for they seemed to have no fear of the intervention of the constables. Men would return from work to find their wives in a state of hysteria after some incident or another while fetching water or at the communal oven. The stranger children would be set upon by colliers' children as they played in the courts and alleys. There was, of course, a good deal of this in Hetton village too, but there the colliery houses were mostly built in single rows, less closed in on themselves than Brick Garth, and the violence could not be hidden so easily from the patrolling constables.

In spite of everything, it was still true that most of the colliers seemed content to ostracise the strangers, rather than fight them. But it was a constricting life, and Tommy, who had more reason than most to avoid any confrontations with the colliers, grew to hate the feeling that after all these months he was even less able than before to go where he pleased. Somehow, now that all the colliery houses were occupied, the strangers felt more isolated than ever. The friendships they had cautiously begun to build up among themselves were suddenly swamped by the return of a community that had existed long before they came to the place, and had been made stronger and brought closer by shared misfortunes.

One afternoon at the beginning of October, sick of caution, Tommy made his escape, setting out alone to walk over the fields and up onto the hill beyond the Hetton pits, from where, above the smoke of pithead and colliery row, he could sometimes see for many miles and even imagine, in his more fanciful moments, that he could glimpse in the distance the dark line of the Weardale hills; though common sense told him that all he ever saw was a bank of cloud gathered on the horizon. Today was bright and sunny, a lovely golden autumn day, with a freshness in the air that warned of the approach to winter. With every step he began to feel more cheerful.

As he reached the top of the hill he passed a substantial mansion with stables and other buildings around it, set in trees and a small park. Beyond it, fields stretched, some bare, some under grass, one busy with labourers – mostly women and children – harvesting early potatoes. It was back-breaking work, but he could hear their songs and talk and long high shrieks of laughter as he passed. Their clothes were bright splashes of colour on the brown earth. There was something so normal and agreeable about the scene that he slowed his pace, watching with enjoyment.

There were two girls working near the hedge that bordered the road, one fair, one dark, deep in some intimate girlish conversation. The fair one, standing up, turned to look at him; she was thin and weary-looking, without the cheerfulness of most of her fellow workers. For a moment she stared at him, as if she knew who he was but did not much like the sight. Then she bent her head again; but at that moment her companion must have realised there was something odd in her manner, for she stood up in her turn.

It was Matty, and she was looking straight at him.

He stood there, not knowing what to do, his head

spinning. Her eyes rested on him, dark and beautiful as he remembered. And then she coloured, so that her face and neck were fiery red.

How could he have forgotten how much he loved her? He had last seen her in the byre, sitting beside him and gnawing at the bread with all the concentrated unself-consciousness of a squirrel. Here she was again, real and warm and alive, perhaps five yards from where he stood. Yet he did not know what to do. Go to her, beg her to tell him what had happened – and, more to the point, what was going to happen?

The other girl grasped her arm. 'Matty – we'll take these to the cart.' Matty jumped, as if momentarily she had forgotten she was not alone. She stammered something incoherent and then stopped and gathered up the basket of potatoes that lay at her feet. Together the two of them carried it towards the cart at the far side of the field. As they went Matty looked back, once, with a swift glance over her shoulder, but her expression was unreadable. Tommy had no idea what she was thinking or feeling. He waited there by the hedge for her to return, as she surely would. But an hour passed and she did not come.

He wandered about near the field until it began to grow dark and the women packed up to go home; then he made his way down the hill until he could see where they were leaving the mansion to take a path across the fields. Searching intently, he saw Matty at last, conspicuous even in the dusk in her red print gown and flowered kerchief, with the fair girl beside her. Keeping to the road, he stayed level with them. Once, he lost sight of them behind some farm buildings, but they soon emerged again, coming out onto the road at the bottom of the hill. He knew it was foolish in the extreme, but he walked slowly, keeping them in sight, even when he came to the first houses near Four Lane Ends, where the road was busy with people. He had no thought at all for his own safety.

The girls reached the crossroads, and he waited there to see which way they went. They turned left, but at that moment a group of passers-by got in the way and he lost sight of them. When he was finally able to see again, he was relieved to find that they had halted in front of one of the first cottages, where they talked for a little longer before the fair girl went on up the hill. Matty disappeared into the little house.

He knew at last where he could find her, if he wanted. But he knew nothing more, least of all what kind of welcome he could hope for from her. He turned to walk slowly home, deep in thought, to be brought to his senses by a scattering of shouts from behind. Glancing round, he saw a group of youths following him, jeering and hurling colourful insults. They were egging each other on, enjoying the game; for the moment, he thought, they were not intent on anything more serious. But he had no wish to find out if he was right, so he quickened his pace, thankful that he was already some way ahead of them. By the time he reached the house, he had lost them.

But he had come to a decision. He could not, in the present state of things, openly seek Matty out, and to do so in secret would only bring disaster on her (not to mention himself), were they to be discovered. It was clear enough that she still felt something for him, from the way she had blushed, though he tried to remind himself that people sometimes blushed from shame. But if he could do nothing about it for the time being, he was able now to see that there was a solution.

He put it to Mark that evening as they sat at supper. Mark had been talking of some trouble in his part of the Moorsley pit that morning, adding, 'I've a mind to seek work at another colliery. There's the new one at South Hetton, nearly won, I heard. Or over Bishop way, maybe. Somewhere all the colliers are new to the pit.'

'It seems to me,' said Tommy, 'that we should be seeking to make our peace with the pitmen here. The strike's over now and the union ended. Things can only get better. It must be right that we should all learn to live comfortably together.'

303

Mark stared at him, a faint derisive smile twitching at his mouth. 'How you can say that after all that's happened in the past year, I don't know. You can't really believe we'll ever be accepted.'

'I don't see why not. Why, I know it won't be easy or quick, but in the end — '

'In the end you hope we'll all be living in such fraternal sweetness that a man you put out of work will give you his daughter in marriage – that's it isn't it?'

'Not all of it,' said Tommy, colouring.

'Would you ever forgive us, if you were them?'

Tommy considered the matter. His difficulty was that, even after five months at Hetton, he was still no nearer being able to imagine what it was like to hate another human being as much as the colliers clearly did. Looking at the matter coldly, he thought he could understand why he should be disliked, but it was beyond him to imagine the intensity of feeling that he must evoke in these men. Mark, reading something of that struggle on his face, grinned and patted him on the shoulder. 'You're past teaching, man. But you're a canny lad for all that. There's one thing, though – even if you're right, you'll have a long wait to win your lass.'

'I'd wait for ever,' said Tommy, and knew he meant it, dreary though the thought was.

The next week it was Houghton Feast. Tommy had heard about the occasion, an annual event enjoyed with great enthusiasm by the population for miles around, with horse races and wrestling and Billy Purvis's travelling theatre and every kind of sideshow and festivity, lasting for an entire week – something like the annual pay at Newhouse, he thought, marked (regrettably) by a good deal of drunkenness and dancing and fighting and other occasions for immorality. As a good Ranter he should have seen it as an opportunity for prayer and preaching. There would certainly be Ranters there; but they would be Hetton Ranters, men like the fair young man who had turned him from the chapel. 'One thing's for sure. We

keep well away,' Mark said, and this time Tommy agreed
with him.

They watched from the window of their house as the
colliers and their wives and families streamed daily along
the road towards Houghton, putting behind them for a
time the cares of the past two years and all their bitterness and disappointment. There was singing and laughter
and much noise; and a company of Ranters singing more
spiritual songs (though with equal vigour and enthusiasm), making their way to witness to a higher form of
celebration. Tommy did not see the young man from the
chapel among them.

Then one afternoon he saw a group of young people
pass the house, laughing girls on their sweethearts' arms,
all in bright clothes, the girls with ribbons in their caps
and swaying earrings and pretty shawls, the lads with
flowered waistcoats and striped trousers and bright
neckerchiefs. Among them was a tall and handsome
young man whom Tommy had an uneasy sense he had
seen before; and on his arm, as happy and carefree as any
of her companions, and as showy in her dress, was
Matty. Just as they disappeared from view, Tommy saw
the young man bend over to kiss her, and she raised her
face to his, as once she had done for Tommy. He saw
their mouths come together.

He had not thought anything could hurt so much. He
turned quickly away, brushing past Mark, and scrambled
blindly up the stepladder to the garret, where he could be
alone. There was no mistaking what he had seen, or its
significance. Until now, he had been able to fool himself
that she might still care for him, but in the little scene just
witnessed he had been confronted with the truth. When
she had blushed on seeing him it had been from surprise
or shame, not passion. If she had ever loved him, it was
over now. *Fickle creatures, women*, Joe had said once, he
could not now remember why. Fickle or not, Matty had
changed, and the man who now had her heart was tall
and dark and strong and one of her own kind.

After a time, seeking an end to the bleakness of his

thoughts, Tommy knelt to pray; and emerged, later, with the bitter consolation that in his wish for reconciliation he now had the purest and most unmixed of motives. He wanted peace for its own sake, not for any end of his own.

Chapter Twenty-two

It was only when Tommy had failed to reply to some remark she had made that Matty had realised that he had fallen asleep beside her, there in the byre.

She had looked down at him, studying his dear and now familiar face, just as she had done, often, when he was so ill. Then, she had learned him by heart as she watched at the bedside or washed him or changed his clothes and sheets. She had learned every feature of that face in all its strong simplicity – almost as wide as it was long, marked by the strong straight lines of brow and nose and the wide mouth, so grave in repose, so ready when he was awake to soften into the sweetest and gentlest of smiles, lighting to brightness those candid blue eyes. She knew the breadth of his shoulders and chest, the narrowness of his hips, the strength of his legs, she knew where the hair curled shining and golden in the places most people never saw, how thick and fair his lashes were over his eyes, how broad and yet gentle his hands.

In the byre in those early morning hours, she had gazed at him with her love for him warm about her heart, and known that she would gladly have given her life for him, had it been asked of her. She had wanted to lie down close beside him and put her arms about him, but she had been afraid of waking him, when he needed sleep so much. For herself, she had been too anxious to sleep.

Some sound outside, she was not sure what, had caught hearing already sharpened by apprehension. She had supposed they had thrown off their pursuers, but she could not be sure. With her heart suddenly beating very fast she had slipped to the door and peeped through the gap where it did not fully close. She had seen only the street, empty except for a woman carrying water. What noise she had heard she did not know, but there had been nothing out of the ordinary within her range of vision.

She had gone back to sit beside Tommy, but found she could not be still. She sat with ears strained for the least sound; hurrying feet or loud voices. As the daylight had grown so had the sounds outside, mostly the ordinary sounds of a village waking to the day, but any noise that was less than familiar had set her hurrying to peep out again.

Still, in the intervals, she had gazed at Tommy, with love, but increasingly with fear. He had looked so peaceful, lost in the untroubled sleep of a child. She had dreamed as a girl of falling in love, but she had not imagined it would be like this, something that filled her so completely, gathering together all her capacity to feel – her passion, her tenderness, her need to be protected and cared for, and her need to protect and to care. There in the byre it was that last quality in her love that had been uppermost. Every unknown sound outside had made her fear for him. She had known that her father would have no mercy if he were to find them. She herself would suffer, of course, but that would only be a passing thing compared with what they would do to Tommy. They might not kill him, perhaps – though she could not take that for granted, knowing how uncontrolled her father and Jack Marley could be in anger – but they might cause him serious injury.

Time passed, and her terror had grown. She had been seized with an urge to shake Tommy awake and hurry him on his way, beyond her father's reach. But she had known that Tommy could not go further without rest, so she had fought the impulse and sat on, listening and listening.

While she sat there, she had thought about all that had happened. Tommy had urged her to marry him, to ensure that they might stay together. Forced to decide quickly, that had seemed to her the best way out. What more did she want than that, after all? But looking back she had found herself wondering, *What will happen afterwards? Does he mean we should come back to Hetton? If we do, then the fact that we're married will make no difference to my father – it might even make things worse.* And if they were to stay in Weardale – would they then be out of her father's reach? He knew Tommy came from Weardale. She imagined the dale as a place much the size of Hetton – a little larger perhaps – where everyone knew everyone else. It would not be hard even for a stranger to find Tommy, given that knowledge.

She had recognised the enormity of what she had done, still more of what she had been about to do. She had seen what shame she had brought on her family by it, how greatly she had offended and would offend. She could not feel the shame of it any longer, because her love for Tommy was greater than anything else in all her life. But she had understood it with her mind; she had after all been born into it.

Then she had seen that there could be no escape for them, ever. Her father would hunt them to the ends of the earth, if he had to. He would make sure, somehow, that Tommy was punished for his temerity in running off with John Grey's daughter. The fact that she had gone of her own free will would make no difference, for to him it would be obvious that Tommy had worked on her will, seducing her into betrayal.

If she could have found paper and pen she would have written Tommy a note. *I don't love you*, it would have said, because only then could she have been sure he would try to forget her.

But it would have been a lie. She had looked down at the thin flushed face, the hand curved under one cheek, the steady rise and fall of his breathing. She had felt her heart turn at the thought that she would never again look on him like this, or in any other way. But it had to be, because otherwise she might one day be looking upon a corpse, knowing that she had killed him as surely as if her own hands had done it.

She had swallowed hard and taken the remains of the food and laid it near his head and then, very gently, so gently that he did not stir, she had brushed his forehead with her lips. And then she had slipped out of the byre, closing the door behind her. There had been no one about in the street, and she had left the village as quickly as possible and soon found the right road and hurried along it. This time she had not avoided the most obvious route, nor had she sought to hide from any passer-by. She had remained watchful for signs of her father and the other men, but now she wanted to find them. They had to know that she had returned, because only then would they leave Tommy alone.

She had come up with them at Rainton Gate, at the toll-house, where they were questioning the gatekeeper. She walked up to them and halted beside her father, who cast a vague glance in her direction without taking in who it was. 'Dad,' she said.

He turned then, and the storm broke about her. John Grey grasped her by the shoulders. 'Where is he then? Where's the bugger who got his hands on you?'

'No one got his hands on me—' But he was not listening. He repeated his question, taking in only her persistent, 'I don't know.' After a time, he gave up and they hustled her back with them to Hetton, to the clearing in the wood, where already the shelters had been dismantled and many families had gone. Matty saw the shocked faces of family and friends as they watched her come down the hill, in a silence louder than any condemnation.

Her father beat her, as she knew he would. It was not

something he often did, but she had never offended so deeply as this. What made her punishment worse was the public nature of it, there before everyone. But then they probably all approved too. She did not cry. She held back her anger and her pain, and submitted, and then went, as she was told, to help her mother pack their belongings on the back of the borrowed donkey ready for the journey to their new house, near Four Lane Ends. From that moment, wherever she went, her father or one of her brothers went with her. No one spoke to her, except to give a command.

Their new house was smaller than the old one, a single-storied building with one room and a thatched roof, facing onto the road just south of the crossroads. They had no difficulty in finding space for their furniture, reduced as it was to a few basic items, and those the least good. Anything of real value had been sold long since, to augment their income during the strike. There was now no mahogany bed, no fine china, no brass candlestick or grandfather clock. Having helped to unload the first items from the donkey, Matty was sent back for the rest, with Maria and Jamie for company.

Already the clearing had a half-abandoned look, the grass crushed and brown and muddied, the earth bare where the shelters had been. There were now only a few forlorn heaps of furniture and cooking pots lying waiting to be transported, and one or two people who had still not got everything together. Eliza was carefully packing books in a box and did not look up as Matty came into the clearing.

Jamie, distracted by seeing a friend, had forgotten his surveillance duties for a moment and gone off to talk to him. Matty made use of old habits of authority and commanded Maria to continue packing the donkey's panniers, while she went over to Eliza.

Her friend looked up, and her eyes were cold. 'How could you, Matty?'

Matty did not waste time asking what she meant. She was not sure how much her father knew, though she supposed that what he knew everyone else knew by now, and it was clear that it was enough to condemn her even in the eyes of her friend. 'I love him,' she said softly. 'I loved him before I knew – well, what he was.'

'But you did know, in the end. In good time.'

'Aye.' She was relieved to see that Eliza looked more sad than contemptuous, which was something. There was still a trace of affection in her eyes. Knowing Eliza's uncompromising attitude even towards members of her own family during the late troubles, she had been afraid she might find herself beyond forgiveness. Not that she had been forgiven yet —

'Where is he now?'

Was Eliza working for her father in this? She said, 'I don't know.'

'In Hetton?'

She shook her head.

'Is he coming back?'

To that she had no answer. How would he react when he knew she had gone? The one thing he must not do was to come seeking her, all in the impulse of the moment. She regretted more than ever that she had not been able to leave him a note, telling him that she did not love him, for then surely he would have stayed away from her. If he came seeking her he would walk straight into the trap from which she had hoped to save him. Suddenly she was anxious that they should all be out of the clearing at the earliest opportunity, so that if he were to come he would not be able to find her, which might at least delay the worst and give her time to persuade her father that Tommy was not to blame. 'No,' she said at last, warily; it seemed the safest reply.

'Then you'll not see him again?'

She found she could not put her answer into words. It was an unendurable prospect, which yet had to be endured. She shook her head, pressing her lips firmly together. Eliza stood up. 'I thought better of you, Matty, truly I did.'

Matty coloured, as if she felt the shame Eliza clearly

expected of her. Weary of talk that was leading them nowhere, she asked, 'What are you going to do?'

'I'm moving back in with my mam.'

'Just you?' Eliza had her head bent again, so Matty could not see her face, but there was a dry harshness in her tone that troubled her friend.

'Adam will seek work where he can. I can get something round here. They'll soon be potato picking.'

Two things, changed beyond her imagining, were contained in that reply. Adam and Eliza, that close and tender partnership, were to be separated, though how deeply and for how long she did not dare to ask; and Eliza, uncompromising in her hatred of her brother's betrayal, was going to share a roof with him after all. 'I thought you wouldn't live in the same house as Samuel.'

'I've got to live somewhere. I don't have to speak to him.'

Her hands were fumbling with the books so that they fell all ways, and she did not seem able to fit them in the box. Matty crouched down to help her, quickly righting them. 'Oh! You've got *The Pilgrim's Progress.*'

'Aye—' Eliza stopped, her hands falling to her lap. She stared at Matty. 'You read that!'

Matty nodded, her face hot.

'Where did you learn? Who taught you?' Then she seemed to see the answer. 'Why . . . The grover. It was him, wasn't it?'

There was an oppressive lump in Matty's throat, so that at first she could only nod. Then she said, 'That's what I went to him for, after I found out he was – well . . . Not owt else.'

'Do you think I believe that?'

'*I* did,' said Matty. 'Then.' Looked at from where she was now, she did not believe it herself any more.

Eliza sighed and shook her head. 'You fool. You should have known it would do you no good.'

'I learned to read,' Matty pointed out, with a tremulous smile.

Her friend came as near to smiling as she had this morning. 'Aye, well, maybe it wasn't all bad then.'

At intervals in their talk, Matty had been studying the titles in the box. Now she laid her hand on one of the books. 'Do you want this?'

Eliza looked at it. 'No, we've other Bibles. You can have a lend of it if you like. Don't let your dad see it.'

'I'll not,' promised Matty.

'I shouldn't be encouraging you to go against him again.'

'Maybe I'll tell him anyway. It doesn't much matter now. He thinks that badly of us anyhow. What difference does one more thing make?'

Jamie came back then, and they had to end their talk. Matty hid the Bible among the cooking pots on the donkey's back and once at the house slipped it out and pushed it under the mattress she would share tonight with her sisters.

She had only just finished concealing it when her father summoned her. He was standing behind the house with Jack and her brothers, clearly just ending a conference of some kind. 'Now, lass, I want some answers from you. We'll find that bastard somehow, but it'll be the better for you if you give us a hand. So, where is he?'

'I don't know,' said Matty, trying to sound genuinely innocent.

'Where did you go with him? Because you did go off with him, didn't you? What brought you back here?'

She decided that some carefully edited version of the truth was the wisest course, and probably the safest for Tommy. 'I changed my mind,' she said. Then she burst out in a flood of pleading, 'Dad, it was all my doing. He was sick and I nursed him. He never laid a hand on us, not once, though I wanted him to. I went away with him, because you were all after him and he wouldn't go without us. But then I knew I'd done wrong and it wouldn't lead anywhere, so I came back. But it was me, not him. He's not to blame, not at all.'

'Not to blame! He's a blackleg, Matty!'

'Aye, I know. But he's not to blame for what I did.'

'You were in his house!'

'Because I went there. He never asked us to. He was sick, that's all.'

'And how did you know he was sick, tell me that?'

She coloured, hesitating. Then she plunged into the rest of it. 'I went to him for lessons, to read.'

There was a burst of derisive laughter from Jack Marley at that, and a further explosion of anger from her father. 'If you think I'll believe that you're more of a fool than I took you for!'

'Believe what you like! I'll read to you if you want, then you'll see. Whatever, it was me that went to him.'

'It was him you got Jack to beat up for pestering you – that's right isn't it?'

She nodded.

'What have you to say about that?'

'Nowt,' she said wearily. 'I know I should have had nowt to do with him, but I never will again, ever. I swear it.'

'You're dead right you won't.' He stared at her in exasperation. 'Where is he? Back in Weardale?' She remained obstinately silent. 'Is he coming back here?'

'No,' she said; but they did not accept her assurance. Later, she heard Jack Marley say in a low voice to her father, 'I asked one of the strangers – he said he told him he'd be back at work Monday.'

'We'll be waiting for him,' was her father's response, and Matty heard it with dread. Had she done all this for nothing?

Two days later Eliza came near her as she went – Maria trudging behind her as usual – to fetch water from the well. 'Thought you'd want to know. His friends fetched his things from his house. The company's put Will Lee into it. So he'll have gone back where he came from.'

It was a relief, because he was safe; and a grief, because she would not see him again. She forced herself to face the future with courage. It was after all for the best; but it did not feel like it.

Her greatest hope had been that Tommy's departure would close the matter as far as her father was concerned, but she soon learned that it had done so only conditionally. He came to her and said, 'Hear me, lass. You make one move to get in touch with that blackleg or go to him or so much as wink at him, and I'll make sure he's no use to any lass in all the world, ever again. And the same goes if he tries it on with you.'

She knew the threat was real and was relieved that she had no possible means of defying her father.

After that, John Grey's vigilance relaxed a little, and she did not have to contend any longer with the constant company of one or other of her brothers. In return, she was careful to act the model daughter, just in case her father should still harbour any wish for revenge on Tommy. Even in the one thing that she was not prepared to give up, she tried not to cross him too openly. She read her borrowed Bible whenever she could, and made no pretence that she was not doing so, but she tried not to read in her father's presence. Once, one of his friends left a newspaper at their house, so she read that too, amazed at the multitude of things going on all over the world and the immense number of trivial events reported. She wished Tommy had been there, so that she could discuss with him what she had read. Few of those around her were interested in anything beyond colliery matters and the union.

There was Eliza of course, but she had troubles of her own. Matty was distressed for her, because she could see how unhappy her friend was. They did not often meet, now that they lived some distance away from one another; besides, Matty knew that her father was still suspicious of Eliza's influence – the more, perhaps, now that she had shown herself to be a neglectful mother, with such disastrous consequences. The fact that she lived with Mrs Raines, whose household was still ostracised by the returning colliers, did not make things any better.

But potato picking started earlier than usual, and Matty found work at Little Eppleton Hall, where Eliza too was employed. There was no one to prevent them working side by side in the field, sharing the same aches and cold hands and hours of companionship during which they could talk.

At first Eliza did not talk much. They would work for a long time in silence, exchanging scarcely a word. Matty was wary of questioning her, since the least hint of probing brought Eliza's defences up.

It was not until after the dinner-time stop on the first day that Eliza suddenly began to talk. What started it was a chance remark from another woman among the group with whom they sat in the lee of a hedge to eat the bread and bacon and drink the cold tea they had brought with them. The remark was not addressed to Eliza, though whether she was meant, from spite, to overhear it, Matty could not be sure. It was addressed to another woman, evidently not wholly familiar with some of the events of the past months, for she had whispered some enquiry to her neighbour, while her eyes were on Eliza. 'Why,' the other woman replied, 'she's the one turned out her bairns, to give her time for meddling in men's business.'

'Why aye, I mind it now!' murmured her companion. 'The bairns died of the cholera.'

Eliza scrambled to her feet and began to walk swiftly back to where they had been working. Matty paused only to tell the women, furiously, what she thought of them, and then hurried after her. She caught her arm, feeling how she trembled. She was very white and fighting back the tears.

'The old bitch!' said Matty. 'Pay no heed.'

'She's right!' Eliza cried. 'She's right – that's the worst of it.'

'No – you did it for the best. To keep them safe. You weren't to know.'

Eliza halted and turned to face Matty, her voice low and quivering. 'If I'd kept them with me they'd be living now, I know they would. I wasn't thinking of them. I wanted to be free of them, to be with Adam. I thought it mattered more than they did.'

317

'It did matter.'

'I don't know any more. I think maybe we were wrong, that it wasn't what God meant us to do.'

'Is that what Adam thinks?'

'That's the worst of it. He thinks it's not us was wrong but—' She broke off, as if she could not bear to finish the sentence.

Not they who were wrong, but the God who had let them down; it seemed to Matty a reasonable enough view, in the circumstances. After all if God was so powerful why had He let the owners win this fight so completely, using the most ruthless methods money and influence could buy?

They walked back to where they had been working and bent again to their task. 'Is Adam away again?'

Eliza nodded. Her face had an odd shut-in expression, as if she was trying both to hide and suppress what lay inside.

'Has he had any luck yet?'

Eliza shook her head. Then she said suddenly, as if she had to speak to someone, 'It should have brought us closer, losing the bairns. But—' Matty studied her, Eliza Fenwick who had been so strong, so single-minded in her passion for the union cause, reduced now to this unhappy wreck of a woman. 'What if we go on for ever like this?' she continued after a time, her voice harsh with misery, 'Like strangers.'

'Maybe it'll be better when he finds work.'

'Maybe.' Eliza sighed, and then straightened for a moment to rest her back. She was upright for so much longer than usual that Matty glanced at her, and saw something odd in her expression; she was staring over the hedge at the road beyond. As soon as she saw Matty looking her way, she bent down again, starting to say something, though Matty did not hear what it was. She had risen herself; and come face to face with Tommy.

It was so unexpected that it took her breath away. She felt swept by a wild confusion of emotions, in which the strongest was a great wave of love and longing that almost

318

carried her onto the road and into his arms. She could see on his face – that open face that could hide nothing – that he loved her as much as ever.

Then she felt Eliza's hand on her arm, her voice encouraging her to carry the potatoes to the cart. It was a ruse to take her out of danger; and Matty saw the need at once.

If Tommy was still here, then the danger had not passed. If she were to give him the faintest hint of encouragement, he might pursue her again, and that could only mean disaster for him. She lifted the basket of potatoes and went with Eliza, though she could not go without one last glance at that forlorn figure watching her from the road.

She felt Eliza's arm slide through hers. 'I wish you'd not stood up then,' said her friend.

'Do you think he's come back for me?' said Matty bleakly.

Eliza studied her face for a little while, then said, 'He never left. We thought he had, for a day or two, that's all.'

Matty turned on her. 'You knew that? You didn't tell me?'

'What was the point? It's no use thinking you can start seeing him again.'

'Is he in the same house then?'

'No. He moved in with another grover. And don't look at me like that! I'll not tell you where he's living now.'

'Do you think my father knows?'

'Why aye, of course he does. But so long as he keeps away from you they'll let him alone, I think. And so long as you keep away from him.'

She longed to return to the place where they had been working, but Eliza led her to the far side of the field. Glancing once or twice towards the road, Matty saw that Tommy stood there for a long time afterwards.

As they walked home she was lost in thought, considering all the implications of what had happened today. She knew that, in spite of everything, seeing Tommy like that

319

had revived hope in her, however furtively. But she knew too that she must suppress it at all costs. Not only must he not be allowed to guess that she loved him still, but she must convince herself too that her future lay elsewhere.

The only sure way to do that was to take a step that would cut her off irreversibly from Tommy, for ever, whatever happened.

Near the house, Matty saw a group of men standing talking on the corner, Jamie and Jack Marley among them. Whatever they were talking about must have given them some pleasure, for they gave a sudden cheer. Eliza glanced sharply at them, but no explanation came.

'We'll hear soon enough,' said Matty.

'Aye.' Eliza's tone was weary. Once, Matty supposed, she would have been the first to know, kept in touch with events by Adam, who did not share the scruples of most men about involving women in serious matters.

Matty saw from the corner of her eye that Jack Marley had detached himself from the others and was coming towards them.

'You know what I think?' she said, very clearly and distinctly. Eliza looked at her in some surprise. 'If colliers can unite to make things better for themselves, why can't women?'

'They don't need to,' said Jack Marley, coming up behind her. 'There's not a woman born doesn't know how to get her way if she chooses.'

Matty laughed and turned to look at him. She saw the change in his expression as his eyes met hers. She let her gaze linger a moment longer than usual and then looked away. She knew he had read the message she had given him.

Her father came out of the house just then and Jack said, 'They're saying Dunn's to be hoyed out, come November.'

No wonder they had looked pleased, Matty thought. John Grey said, 'Who told you that?'

'I heard them at it in the office again, him and Wood

and Robson. There's been meetings in Newcastle, with Dunn not there and Robson plotting with the owners. Or that's what Dunn said. Then Robson came out. The Redhead lad was there and they went off together. I heard Robson say the owners wanted Dunn out, sharp as possible, most of them anyway. His agreement's up, November the first. So we could be shot of him by then.'

'Come in and take a nip of rum, and we'll drink to that.'

They disappeared inside, and Matty said to Eliza, 'Do you think the union would have won, if he'd gone sooner?'

Eliza shook her head. 'It wasn't just Dunn, from what I heard. The coal owners stuck together, all of them, all over the coalfield. We didn't know it, but it seems the ones who kept the union men on, they paid into a fund to help the rest, so they could bring strangers in and pay the soldiers. They say Hetton got thousands from that fund. But all the same it'll be better for us with Dunn gone – for them . . . ' Struck suddenly by a renewed sense of her own losses, she said an abrupt goodnight and went on her way.

Matty went indoors, to continue the process of winning Jack Marley.

Next week was Houghton Feast, when every young single collier wanted the girl of his choice on his arm, to parade before his friends and neighbours and work-mates. It would be a perfect opportunity for a public demonstration of the beginnings of a courtship that Matty intended should end very soon, as such things generally did, in marriage.

Chapter Twenty-three

On the fourth Saturday in January Jenny turned a beggar away from White Lea, without shelter or even a drink.

She watched him trudge wearily back down the track he had come up with such hopes a short time ago and felt only a bleak indifference. She had not wanted him in her house, she had little enough to spare in the way of food; she was tired, so very tired.

Soon afterwards, it began to snow, and she thought of the man – old and sick as he was, his clothes in rags – out in the bitter wind, and she was filled with self-disgust. But she knew that if he were to come back to the house now she would do exactly the same. She had no compassion left in her. Somehow she could not help herself, though she hated this thing she had become – no longer a person, but a wayward mass of impulses blown this way and that. It was as if all that had kept her on the right course, all the things that had anchored her to the earth and those she loved, all that had made her what she was, a person worthy of love and respect, had been cut through, to leave her floating adrift, without sense or purpose, except somehow to get through each day and then the next and the one after that, on and on into an interminable future.

The children, who had been shopping for her at Chapel market, came home soon afterwards, earlier than they might have done because of the snow, which was swirling fast. She was glad that by then the beggar was out of sight, so that they would have no means of knowing what she had done. She saw, with irritation, that Eve was with them. Presumably they had met her on the way. They were chattering together as they came up the track, but fell silent as soon as they were within earshot of her. She said little to them, not even thanking them for their help. She saw them looking warily at her as they set about getting the supper. There was little talk as they ate, and afterwards they quickly cleared away and went upstairs or out in the snow to do their evening tasks. She heard Em playing his fiddle with great vigour up in the bedroom. Its cheerful sound (he was playing one of the more popular Ranter hymns) grated on her nerves unbearably and she went to the foot of the stairs and called to him to be quiet. The silence that followed seemed almost as unbearable.

She sat down by the fire with her mending, and it was there, a little later, that Mary found her.

'Mother—' Jenny turned to look at her daughter. Mary had the guarded look that had become habitual these days, as if she was never very sure what her mother's response would be. With an effort, Jenny refrained from saying anything and simply waited for her daughter to continue. 'When I go into service, can Eve come too? I mean, can we go to the same place?'

The question startled Jenny out of her lethargy. It had been agreed that in the spring Mary would find work as a servant, not too far away if possible. They none of them wanted it much, but though Tommy's money helped greatly, there were too many mouths to feed at White Lea for Mary to be spared the necessity. Jenny glanced at her niece, who was standing in the doorway watching her with imploring dark eyes. 'Does she want to?' she asked, though it was clearly a superfluous question. Mary nodded. 'What would her father say?'

'He'd be glad,' Eve said emphatically.

Jenny wondered. Even now there was a new baby at Well House, no child of Joe's needed to go into service to earn her keep. He loved Eve, whatever the difficulties he had with her. Was this what he would want for her?

'I wish she would,' Mary said. Her voice was trembling a little. Jenny saw then, clearly, how frightened she was at what lay before her, how it must seem like a step into the darkness, hard to take after all she had lost last year. She saw what a comfort it would be for her to share the experience with her cousin, who was also her friend. As for Eve, she was closer to Mary than to her half brothers or sister.

'I'll speak to your uncle,' Jenny promised. 'If he agrees, then we'll see what can be done.'

Eve stayed overnight at White Lea and came with them to worship at Side Head the next morning. Jenny continued to go chapel, from habit and because it was what Rowland would have wanted and because, now and then, someone would speak lovingly of him, but on the whole the services left her feeling more alone than ever. She seemed unable any longer to find consolation in the very real affection of everyone there for herself and her young family.

The preacher this morning was Anthony Craggs. A shy young man, he lacked his sister's spirited and joyous manner. No Ranter preached for very long – short prayers, short sermons and lively hymns were the heart of Ranter worship – but Jenny began to feel drowsy almost as soon as he had begun, so monotonous was his voice. She fought the impulse to let sleep take her over, but with some regret. Even after all this time she was still unable to go through the night without waking more than she slept and she was constantly tired. Three times her head fell forward, and three times she jolted it up again, forcing her eyes open. Then a fourth time . . .

There was a clattering at the back, a creak of the door

and the noise of clogs on the earth floor. Someone had come in late. Heads turned, though not Jenny's. She did not care who the offender was, though the children nudged one another and whispered together. Anthony paused in his sermon, while the latecomer found a seat somewhere at the back. Then, having tried without success to find his thread again, the preacher brought the sermon to an abrupt end. He cleared his throat and raised his hands, 'Heavenly Father, we thank thee for the presence among us again of our dear brother Tommy Emerson.'

Jenny turned her head sharply. He was there, sitting on the bench by the door, looking both embarrassed and happy. Somewhere in her dead soul warmth and affection flickered to life. She wanted to run to him at once, but even in her present ungracious frame of mind she could not bring herself to cause such a disruption to the worship. The praying continued, moving on to other matters, passing from one to another of the worshippers, and then dissolving at last into singing. Beside her the children – like many of the adults – swayed in time to the rhythm of the music, their voices loud and joyous.

It was over soon enough, and the children reached Tommy before she did, pushing through the eager neighbours and friends who had gone to greet him. Jenny stood waiting, not having the energy to force her way to him. Anthony, making his way to the door, paused beside her. 'May I speak with thee, sister?' He gestured to her to come to the small general purpose room that had been partitioned off from the main body of the byre, and there closed the door and spoke very softly, 'Sister, a man came to our house in great need last night. We tended him—' Already she could feel her colour rising. 'He said he had been turned from White Lea. Maybe he misunderstood . . .'

'No,' said Jenny. 'There was no misunderstanding.' She looked up into the regretful face of the young man, feeling a mixture of shame, and irritation that someone so much younger than she was should be rebuking her like a naughty child. 'Why do they always come to me?' It was rather a cry than a question, but he answered it.

'Because they were always sure of a Christian welcome, in the past.'

Jenny bent her head and swallowed hard, fighting tears.

'We pray for you, sister,' he said gently. 'All the time.'

At that her head flew up. 'I don't want your prayers.' She turned from him. 'My brother is out there, waiting.'

He caught her arm. 'Suffering can be for good or ill. Don't let the devil tempt you from the path—'

'Spare me any more of your sermons,' retorted the spiteful demon that had her tongue. 'You've sent me to sleep once already this morning.' And then she left him and marched back to Tommy.

Her brother came to greet her and then halted, concerned by what he saw in her face. 'What's up?' He put an arm about her.

'Nowt,' she said sharply. 'Let's away home.'

She gathered the children together and they went out into the bright snowy morning. She walked quickly, so that he had some trouble keeping pace with her.

'When you weren't at home, I knew where I'd find you,' he said. 'I got a lift with a carrier yesterday, as far as Stanhope, but it was late when we got there and the way the weather was I thought it best to stop over last night.'

He talked on, though she heard little of what he was saying. She struggled to fight back the tears that were threatening her, and it was not until they were almost at the house that she had herself under control again, as far as she could be said to be in control at all, these days.

In the kitchen Tommy's bags lay in a heap just inside the door. Jenny halted, looking at them. 'You're stopping then?'

'Aye, at least until I know what to do next.' There was something rueful in his expression.

'Then you've left for good?'

'Did you not hear what I said? I was telling you, coal

326

prices have hit the bottom. They don't neea the men any more.'

'Yet they took the union men back.'

'Aye, because they were broken. Most of all, because they're skilled men, and they're needed. We're not, not any more. We've served our purpose and now we're nothing to them.'

She did not say, 'Why, you were warned.' She had enough self-control left to spare him that. In any case, it hardly needed saying.

In the next few days, Jenny saw Joe and got his agreement for Eve to go into service with Mary, if places could be found for them together. Any hesitation he might have had was quickly overcome by Phoebe, present at the time, who made little attempt to hide her delight and declared, 'It will be the making of her. It's time she learned what hard work is.' Eve was ecstatic, and spent long hours at White Lea talking to Mary and planning a future of which – fortunately perhaps – they could neither of them know much. Watching the happy girl giggling in a corner of the settle with her cousin, Jenny found it hard to believe this was the same Eve who had given them all so much trouble last year. Now, she thought with weary helplessness, it was she who was behaving like a hurt child.

She called on Anthony Craggs and did what she could to put things right with him. She supposed she should be grateful that he had not made her callousness a matter for public rebuke, as many in his position would have done, but it did not make her feel any better that he was relentlessly understanding about it. In any case, she knew he could not possibly understand, because even she did not.

She had thought it would get easier. *Time is a great healer*, people often said. In the past, faced with other losses – of her parents, her first sweetheart, two infant children – time had never brought forgetfulness, but it had indeed brought healing, an ability to live with the absence of the person who had gone, the replacement of anguish with an endurable regret. Yet now, five months after Rowland's death, she felt as if she were only sinking deeper and deeper into a morass of grief from which she could see no way of escape.

She thought she was glad that Tommy had come home, but his presence made little difference to her, except that there was another adult in the house to carry some of the burdens. She felt quite unable to tell him how lost she felt.

As for Tommy, he was puzzled and dismayed by his sister's withdrawn and irritable state of mind. He thought she seemed rather worse than she had in September, with a harassed look added to the air of exhausted resignation that he remembered. Yet she showed few of the signs that he recognised as grief. She did not weep very much, nor did she spend hours talking of Rowland, as she had when he was last at home. He knew he could not begin to discuss his future with her, as he had hoped to do.

Luke told him that lead prices had shown signs of a slight rise in the past weeks. The improvement was nowhere near enough to offer any early prospect of an increase in the pay of Weardale miners, but it was the first rise for many years and did give Tommy a faint hope that he might after all be able to find work in the dale again. For the moment, there was none to be had, which at least gave him time to consider what he really wanted to do. Meanwhile, he had enough to live on, saved from his earnings at Hetton.

He was learning to put Matty behind him. It was easier now that he was so far away from her to accept that there was not – and never had been – any future for them together. He stopped looking back, with constant regret for what might have been, and began instead to look forward, though without any great optimism. If he could not have love and happiness, there was still a great deal that he could usefully do. After all, earthly happiness was not (except incidentally) a part of God's plan for His children, so to expect or seek happiness in this world was a sure way to lose it in the next.

It was Sarah Craggs who forced him to confront a possibility that he had considered and rejected many times in the past years, always for what seemed to him the most sound of reasons. They met at a routine leaders' meeting at the chapel, to which he had been invited in the hope that he could be persuaded to take on the leadership of a class again. He pointed out at some length that he was not as yet certain that he would be staying in Weardale, but somehow they had their way all the same. As he left the chapel, he said ruefully to Sarah, who was beside him, 'I don't know how that happened. I didn't mean that it should.'

'Why no, but so many of the strongest members have left the dale. We can't afford to let you stand idle.' She looked at his face. 'Have you any plans at all?'

He shook his head. 'The Lord will show me what to do, in His good time.'

She was silent for a moment, while they walked slowly on together. Then she said, with a faintly calculating note in her voice, 'I've often wondered why you've never put yourself forward for the ministry.'

It was a simple enough question and a perfectly reasonable one, but he felt an odd combination of shock and resentment that she should ask it. 'Oh, that's not for me,' he said quickly.

'You'd make a fine minister.'

'So would you,' he retorted, 'but you haven't gone forward either.'

'I have thought of it. For a woman alone it isn't so easy. It takes more courage. I don't know if I have plenty, not for that.'

He looked down at her fresh rosy face with its faintly rueful expression. A Primitive Methodist minister was required to travel from place to place, wherever conference ordered him (or her) to go, ministering to existing congregations and preaching to the unconverted in the places he or she passed through. Many itinerant preachers, crying their message of salvation to hostile crowds, had been beaten and ducked in ponds and even

imprisoned, often with the connivance of local clergy an
magistrates. Not every district was as receptive to th
Ranter message as Weardale. Yet Tommy had neve
thought of Sarah as lacking in courage. As for him
self . . .

Faced with Sarah's admission, he saw only too clearl
why in the past he had rejected the possibility. It had bee
for none of the good reasons he had convinced himsel
stood against it, but simply because he lacked courage
more surely than did Sarah, who had greater cause for i
Not just that, but loving his home dale as he did, he coul
not bear the thought of having to travel hundreds o
miles away from it; perhaps even abroad. Hetton ha
been quite far enough, too far. And as a minister he woul
be committing himself to go wherever he was sent.

It was not a very creditable admission, even made t
himself alone, in the privacy of his thoughts. Nor, h
realised now, was it one that ought to be allowed any par
in his plans for his future.

They had reached Sarah's house and he parted fror
her there, walking on, alone with his thoughts. They wer
thoughts that would not leave him alone through th
following weeks, and crystallised at last into a firr
resolution.

He said nothing to anyone about what was in his mind
even when he became quite sure about it. He did not war
to take any irrevocable step until he was at ease abou
Jenny, who gave no sign yet that she was emerging fror
her disturbing state of mind. There was, too, one othe
complication, which was not really a complication at a
and grew more appealing every day.

He had been perfectly sincere when he had told Sara
she would make a good minister. He firmly believed it t
be true. But he could see how she might shrink at th
prospect, with more justification than he had. Wha
better solution then, for two people afraid of the cours
they both knew they ought to follow, than to take i
together, strengthening and supporting one another a
they went? They would need the approval of the distric

committee for their marriage and for their joint ministry, but he did not foresee any difficulty about so obviously right a course. He did not love Sarah, or not as he had loved Matty; she could only ever be second best. But he had a warm affection for her, respected and even admired her. She would be the most agreeable of companions through life, sharing all his interests and concerns. They would be admirably suited one to another, and he knew she cared for him.

Because of that fact, he was scrupulous about not singling her out or allowing himself to be alone with her more than he could help. He would wait until the right moment, until he was absolutely sure, and then he would approach her.

One afternoon early in March, he returned from a visit to one of his class members and, finding Jenny was not in the house, went out in search of her. He was always a little anxious when she had to be left alone for any length of time.

It was a bitter cold day with a drenching rain sweeping down the dale, though snow still lay in grey unlovely smears on the shady sides of walls and woods. He found Jenny half-way onto the fell behind the house, replacing stones that had fallen from one of their boundary walls during the worst of the winter storms. She looked very small out there in the rain, a thin black figure, drab and old, working with a dogged determination. *How can I even think of leaving her?* he thought. But he realised he had no idea what she would feel about it, and remote as he was he did not know how to set about finding out.

He went to help her, saying nothing. She glanced at him with no change in her expression and then bent again to pick up the next stone. With his help the task was soon finished and, still in silence, they began to walk back down to the house. He saw that she did not even bend her head against the rain but let it lash her face with all its icy force. She seemed indifferent to it.

He was startled when she said suddenly, in something

approaching her normal voice, 'Have you thought any more what you'll do?'

He wondered if she was genuinely interested, or if she was simply seeking something to say, no matter what. Certainly she did not look as though she cared very much what his reply might be. After a moment's thought, he decided to tell her what was in his mind. He could not see that he would lose anything by it, and he might even catch her interest after all.

'I have thought,' he said carefully, 'that I might offer myself for the ministry. Not at once, not yet, but before long.'

He succeeded better than he had expected. He saw her face visibly brighten, like the momentary parting of clouds on a wet day, so that there was, briefly, a glimpse of the old Jenny.

'I'm glad,' she said. 'It's what Rowland always wanted.'

He had suspected it, but his brother-in-law had never openly expressed his hope. Now he said, 'I often wondered why he never went as a minister himself . . . He didn't want to leave you, I suppose.'

There was a hint of a smile about her mouth. 'That wouldn't have stopped him, if he'd thought he was called to it. No, he believed he was meant to stay here and live as a miner, and witness that way.'

'Then you don't think that's what I should do?'

All the light had gone again from her face, leaving it as bleak as ever. 'I think he believed he'd failed.'

'Failed! How could he think that?'

'There were things he dreamed of, things he hoped would come about through his preaching, and they never did. Though I hope—' She broke off, biting her lip. What her hope was he never heard, for they were almost at the house and she said suddenly, 'There was a letter for you. Did you see? The carrier brought it.'

He had done no more than glance into the room, so he had not seen what lay on the table. The letter was so stained and crumpled that it looked, he thought, as if it had come from the ends of the earth. He did not recognise the writing, though there was something about it that tugged at his memory. While Jenny went to take off her wet clothes and put the kettle on the fire he broke the seal and unfolded the single grimy sheet.

Dear Tommy — He felt the colour flood his face. How could he not have known it at once, the writing that he had coaxed from the small brown hands, day after patient day? This carefully inscribed letter – with a crossing-out here and there, to correct some misspelling (though she had missed some) – how long had it taken her to write? Not that the time was of any significance, set against the thing that had made her do it, in spite of all the obvious inevitable difficulties she must have faced.

He read on, and his colour rose and rose as he did so.

Eliza give me a Bible. I have been readin in it. There are many beutiful words. This I red the day. It is what I would say if I was lernd.

There were no errors in the sentences that followed, for she had copied them, laboriously, word for word, from the Bible. He could almost see her, seated at a table, working by candlelight, scratching away with her pen (where had she found pen and paper in her father's house?), her face a mask of concentration. Or would there be something else on it, considering the nature of what she was writing?

'*I opened to my beloved; but my beloved had withdrawn himself, and was gone; my soul failed when he spake: I sought him, but I could not find him; I called him, but he gave me no answer . . . I charge you, O daughters of Jerusalem, if ye find my beloved, that ye tell him, that I am sick of love . . .*'

He had always been taught that the Song of Solomon, that most passionate of books, was a poetic expression of God's love for mankind. It was quite clear that Matty, her mind not as yet illuminated by religious perceptions, had read into it a much simpler and more direct message; and it was that she wanted to pass on to him.

He was trembling so violently that the letter shook too

much for him to read any more. He pressed the page down on the table so that it was still, but even then it was a while before he took in the little that was left of it – *Dear Tommy*, again, as at the beginning, but now standing alone, like a caress; and then *Thine, Matilda Grey*.

Still trembling, his whole body on fire, he read it again, and then again. Jenny, conscious of something strange in the way he looked, said, 'Is it bad news?'

He raised his head, blinking, because his eyes seemed to have some difficulty in focusing on her face. He shook his head, rather as if to clear his brain than in denial. 'No – no, I don't . . . I don't know.'

'Tell him, that I am sick of love . . . ' Bad news? No, for the words were singing in his heart. She loved him, she had always loved him, she wanted him to go to her. It could not be clearer.

Yet if it was so simple, why had she not put it simply, so that he could have no doubt about what she was asking of him? He stood staring vaguely in Jenny's direction, trying to make sense of it.

'Who's it from?' Natural curiosity seemed to have overcome her usual apathy. Tommy supposed he should be relieved. The trouble was he did not know how to begin to explain – or to end, come to that.

'A . . . someone. They call her Matilda Grey—'

Jenny's eyes widened. 'A lass? From Hetton?'

He nodded, colouring. 'I thought, you see . . . Her father was in the union. It didn't . . . '

By some miracle Jenny seemed to grasp the essentials. 'You thought nowt would come of it, and now she's written?'

He nodded again and felt a foolish grin spread across his face.

'What will you do?'

Suddenly it was obvious. 'I shall go and seek her.'

There was a little silence, then Jenny said, 'To wed her?' There was an odd note in her voice, which he could not place, though he did not try very hard.

'If she'll have me. There's her father . . . I don't know yet.' Then, struck by a new thought, he said with sudden joyfulness, 'I see now, it couldn't be better! You won't be alone after all. If I go as a minister, then she'll be here, to keep you company. You will love her, Jenny. I know you will.' She was standing very still, and her face had that expressionless look again. He felt ashamed that he should have intruded his happiness and his love on her so thoughtlessly; though indeed it did seem to him a perfect solution to the problem of caring for Jenny. It would not solve that other problem of his own fears about the ministry, but he thought that if he had Matty as his wife he would find courage for anything.

The children came home from school then and he had to put the letter aside and talk of other things. It gave him time, though, to think further about its implications. He realised that it promised nothing, and he could not believe that its obliqueness was simply a matter of chance. She had a reason for ambiguity, and he would not find out what it was until he had seen her. On the other hand, she would not have written at all had there not been some point in it. That she wanted him to come to her he had no doubt at all.

By the time the children were in bed and he found himself alone with Jenny again, he was sufficiently coherent to explain the whole thing to her at greater length. She sat facing him across the table while he talked, her hands tightly clasped, her bleak grey eyes fixed on him, and she said nothing all the time he was speaking, until at the end he said again, 'So you see, if it all turns out well, she'll come and live here. You won't be alone—'

Jenny suddenly swept to her feet and stood looking down at him, her face very white, her eyes burning. 'I don't want a stranger here! She never knew him – I couldn't bear it! Can you not see?'

It was a howl of pure anguish, and it took his breath away. He sat staring at her, not knowing what to say. She turned from him and pressed her head against the

335

mantelpiece and began to sob, harsh dry sobs that seemed to be wrenched from her one by one.

He got up and tried to put an arm about her, but she shook him off. 'Go away, let me be, let me alone!'

He stood gazing at her for some time longer, distressed and helpless. Then, not knowing what else to do, he did as she asked and left her there, sobbing by the hearth. He went to see Luke.

When he had gone, Jenny fell to her knees and hammered on the wall with her arms like a mad creature, weeping with bitter desperation. Why – why had this happened to her? She was all wrong, all astray, her life a bleak bitter chaos, without meaning or hope, a chaos that crept into the lives of all those she loved and cared for, infecting them too with her misery. She could not even accept their happiness, allow them to love, as she had loved, as she had been loved. If only she still had that love, it might have been different.

Exhausted at last, she fell forward, resting her forehead on the wall. How long she knelt like that she did not know, nor was she very clear what precisely happened next, though she knew she heard no door open or close, no sound of footsteps. There was only the sensation of hands upon her shoulders, holding her firmly, yet with a caressing tenderness. And then a voice spoke just beside her ear, soft and low. *Jenny, my hinny, this isn't like you. Come now, my lass, my love!* He was so near that she could feel his breath on her cheek, like the ghost of a kiss.

She did not move, or open her eyes. She only felt the warmth of those hands, the tender resonance of that voice, filling her like liquid poured into an empty vessel. A moment only, and then they were gone, yet the warmth lingered, and an inexpressible sense of consolation.

Very slowly she stood up. She was crying again, but softly, gently, tears that had something in them that was very close to joy and brought only relief. She went to the mat before the fire and sat there, gazing into the glowing peats. After a moment the cat came and settled himself, purring and kneading with his paws, on her lap, and at last curled up and went heavily to sleep. Jenny sat on, drowsiness filling her, and a warmth that had nothing to do with the fire or the cat.

Chapter Twenty-four

'Well, we're shot of them at last,' her father had said, jubilantly.

'Not all of them,' Jack had pointed out. He had called for Matty, bringing with him news of the departure of a large number of the strangers. 'We'll see the back of the rest at the binding, now Dunn's gone.'

'We're shot of the ones that matter, anyhow,' her father had said, with a glance at his daughter. She had avoided his gaze, trying to look as if the conversation had nothing to do with her and wondering when she would find a moment to slip away and see Eliza, who might be able to tell her more than it was likely her father would. Adam had still not found work, but he spent more time than before in Hetton, involved with a monthly publication that several of the old union leaders were putting out. *The Spirit of the Tyne and Wear*, they called it, filling every page with articles and verses recounting recent struggles, pointing to future ones. Even John Grey had been impressed by it, so much so that he had bought a copy and demanded that his daughter should read it to him. 'First time I've seen a use for reading,' he had observed. 'Maybe you could learn us.' It had been no more than a passing thought, not mentioned again, but it had marked a turning-point in his acceptance of her shamefully won skill.

But before she could go to see Eliza, Matty knew there was something else she must do. It was not something she looked forward to, but she knew it must be faced; that not until then could she enjoy the sense of release that the news of Tommy's departure (however obliquely given) had brought her.

It had come just in time. She had known she could not put Jack off much longer, that he was impatient to be married and was already puzzled by her constant evasion of the subject. To keep Tommy safe she would have gone through with the marriage, telling herself that since she could not have Tommy it did not much matter who she wed.

But with Tommy gone, she realised that there was an alternative to marrying another man, and that was not to marry at all, at least not for the time being. It was not something she had ever seriously considered before, marriage having always been held before her as a natural and essential part of every woman's life, as inescapable as grey hairs or death. To question that certainty seemed presumptuous in the extreme, but the more she thought about it the more she saw that it was a choice she could make. The thought exhilarated her, at least for the time being, when the only alternative offered to her was Jack Marley.

He had come to take her for a walk, as he often did. Lately, much of their time together had been spent by Matty in trying to fend him off. She told herself she would let him have what he wanted some day soon, but not yet. But with Tommy gone, she felt elated by the knowledge that the time need never now come.

She told him as soon as they were alone, away from houses or people, and she put it as bluntly and unequivocally as she could. She wanted him to be in no doubt at all of her meaning.

'Jack, listen: I cannot wed you. I don't love you.'

He did not at first believe her. After all, she had gone about with him openly and apparently happily for nearly four months. She could hardly blame him if he found it hard to believe that it had all been pretence. 'I wanted to love you,' she said.

'How can you want to love someone, and not love them?' he demanded. 'Stop playing with us, Matty.' He pulled her to him, bringing his mouth forcibly down on hers.

She wriggled and freed herself, retreating a little way off, and relieved that he did not immediately come after her. 'I know I've wronged you, Jack. I'm sorry. I tried to love you.'

She had not thought he was capable of being hurt to any great extent (except in his pride), but she saw then that she had been wrong. 'I'm sorry,' she said again, and meant it.

'Who is it then, tell me that?' he burst out. 'Have you been seeing that blackleg again?'

'No, not once since I came home. There's no one else. I don't want to be wed, that's all. Not to anyone.'

'Don't want to be wed?. What the hell's wrong with you?'

'Something must be,' she conceded with a sudden wintry smile, 'if I cannot love you.'

He did not give in at once, but tried to talk her out of it, as if he thought it might simply be a passing mood. But in the end she convinced him. He was furiously angry, and stormed away leaving her alone in the wood where they had been walking, hurling abuse at her until he could no longer see her, and even then she heard his voice echoing its anguish into the night. For she recognised his pain for what it was. She had hurt him perhaps as much as she herself had been hurt, though not by him. And for that, because it had been her doing, however unwittingly, she was sorry.

She went home, and found Jack had already been there and told John Grey what he thought of his daughter. Her father was almost as angry as her thwarted lover, and there was a brief and noisy exchange between them until her mother burst into tears and begged them to shut up.

A moment's silence followed, before John Grey said, wearily, 'She's expecting again. I thought at least with you wed there'd be one less in the house.'

Matty stood looking at him, and found herself feeling sorry for him too. She seemed unable to please anyone today; not even herself, at the moment. In the end, she found herself saying, for no good reason she could think of, 'I can't wed where I don't love.'

'Beats me what's wrong with Jack Marley.'

She felt her eyes fill with tears. 'I love someone else.'

'Damn you, lass, you've not been seeing that blackleg again?'

'No, I haven't. But I can't stop, well . . . '

Her father's reaction to women's tears could not always be predicted. It would depend on his mood. Occasionally they roused him to fury, but on the whole he was softened by them, and this time he put an arm briefly about his daughter's shoulder.

'I'd have thought wedding a lad like Jack Marley the best cure for that sort of thing.'

'I thought so too, but it isn't.'

He shook his head. 'God, what a mess. Still, nowt we can do about it. You know he's gone, your grover?'

'I heard. It makes no difference. I know I cannot have him.'

The days passed. Matty was touched and surprised by her father's concern at her unhappiness, which she seemed unable to throw off. Her momentary relief at Tommy's going had fast disappeared. It had been easier to face the loss of him when her first concern was to protect him. With him gone, she simply felt very alone and empty.

'Plenty more fish in the sea,' her father said more than once.

'They're a long way off, then,' she retorted and he grinned kindly.

A month passed, with the worst of the winter weather

making life in the crowded little house uncomfortable in the extreme, since they spent so much time indoors. Her father came home as little as possible, spending his time with his friends, sometimes at furtive meetings, where they talked over directives from Tommy Hepburn or Charlie Parkinson, still meeting in their old haunts in Newcastle, planning for a future that seemed increasingly bleak, with the fall in coal prices putting all the cards in the owners' hands. But he could not always be at meetings, or out drinking. One day, falling over children, the cat and a pile of mending as he came in the door, John Grey glowered at Matty and exclaimed, 'You should have wed that grover, then we'd have a bit space here!'

Matty caught her breath; and held it for a moment before releasing it, resisting the impulse to make some instant reply. Then she said carefully, 'He's not a blackleg now, then.'

'Once a blackleg, always a blackleg,' her father said, but rather automatically, not as if he felt it with any passion.

Two days later Jack Marley let it be known he was to marry one of Matty's friends. The girl seemed ecstatic at the prospect, as (to Matty's surprise, remembering his hurt) Jack was; though she wondered if he was simply showing the world, and herself in particular, that he could be perfectly happy without Matilda Grey. Three weeks later, the wedding was celebrated with all the usual noisy and uninhibited rejoicings. Finding her standing alone in a corner of the barn where the dancing was going on late into the night, her father – good-humouredly drunk – put an arm about her. 'Having second thoughts, flower?'

She shook her head. He put a hand under her chin. 'I'd give a lot to see you smile again.'

She smiled then, and he patted her cheek. 'All these canny collier lads, and not a one takes your fancy. I cannot credit it!' He gestured towards the room, misted with the dust thrown up by the dancers, whose perspiring happy faces glowed in the hazed lantern light. 'My own lass, and she hasn't the sense to see what's best for her.'

'You didn't wed a collier lass.'

'Aye, you're right there.' He glanced across the room at the seaman's daughter whose dark prettiness had caught his eye so long ago. 'Give it time. You'll see sense.'

As he turned away from her, she said suddenly, 'Dad—' He looked back at her. 'If he came back to Hetton now, what would you do? Not to work, I mean, but . . .'

It took him a moment or two to grasp whom she was talking about; then he said, 'Some days, I'd hoy you into his arms and be glad to see the back of you . . . ' Then, seeing how she had coloured, he said more seriously, 'Matty, I want no daughter of mine wed to a blackleg.' But there was no anger in his voice, and no threat.

'If I was of age and chose to?'

'Then I reckon I'd have to bear it. But you'll have thought better of it long before then, you mark my words.'

It was after that, conscious of the risk she was taking for both of them, that she asked Eliza for paper and pen and wrote to Tommy. She did not write directly, stating in bald terms what she thought. She had no means of knowing if he still wanted her, and even if he did, she did not want him to come rushing to her without thinking of the possible consequences.

She sent the letter on its way, and then she waited.

Tommy walked from Weardale in brilliant sunshine as soft and sweet as any summer day. The birds had been singing since long before sunrise, there were flowers, white and gold, along the roadside, in the woods, under hedges. His spirits were high, full of hope and happiness. He was going back to Matty, and this time he would not lose her again.

He stayed overnight in a cheap lodging house in Durham, ready to set out early next morning, so as to reach Hetton not long after her father and brothers had left for work.

He would come to her in the early light, while the birds still sang to greet the morning. Lying awake through the long night before they were to meet again, he had imagined their meeting and words had lilted through his head, companions to those lovely words she had written to him:

Rise up, my love, my fair one, and come away.

For, lo, the winter is past, the rain is over and gone;

The flowers appear on the earth; the time of the singing of birds is come . . .

He got up to a raw cold mist, swirled by a bitter wind and shot through with rain. It seemed like a warning, not to hope, not to be happy. Nothing was certain yet, and might not be. After all, the letter had promised nothing.

He felt sick with apprehension as he came within sight of the houses strung along the ridge and took the road into the valley and then on, to Four Lane Ends.

The house looked as he remembered it, small, built of rough stone, exactly like its neighbours. He crossed to the other side of the road and stood there, staring at it, trying to pluck up courage to go across and knock on the door.

What if her father and brothers were not after all at work? What if she had changed her mind about him, in the three weeks since she had written?

He shut his eyes, searching for words of prayer, but none came. He swallowed hard and stepped across the street and raised his hand, heart thudding wildly; and then he knocked.

He realised he had never seen Matty's mother before. He supposed that was who opened the door to him, a tired-looking woman with a child clinging to her skirts. Large dark eyes gazed at him without great interest from the pale careworn oval of her face. He took off his hat. 'Mrs Grey?' Her expression did not change. Perhaps the formality of the greeting bewildered her. 'I should like to speak to Matilda, if I may,' he said, with great care.

There was a flurry of movement from somewhere

beyond his vision, and then Matty stood by her mother's side, poised on her toes as if for flight – or rather, as if she had just that minute touched the earth. Her eyes were glowing, her face warm with colour, her lips parted. Tommy felt his heart turn over. He was quite incapable of saying anything. All he could do was look at her.

Someone spoke, and the words, repeated, eventually reached his brain. 'You'd best come in.'

He took a step forward, and then Matty suddenly moved, passing her mother. 'I'll come out.'

She was there, beside him, smiling still. 'Howay then.' He went with her, dazed, feeling as if he were walking in a dream. They walked on over the crossroads, up the hill, on into the woods where they had first met, almost a year ago. And there, once out of sight of the houses, he felt her hand slip into his.

He halted and turned to face her. 'Matty—'

She reached up and put her arms about his neck, and he held her and kissed her and could not believe it was real. When there was a pause (which he regretted) he said, 'Your father . . . '

She looked at him gravely. 'I don't know,' she said. 'I think he'll accept it now. But I don't know.'

'Do you want me to take a chance?'

'If you're willing.'

He was still not thinking clearly. There was so much he ought to say, but he did not know where to begin. He began to stumble into words, saying too much too quickly. 'I'm not in work, Matty. I've no money. There's none to be made in Weardale. But I've thought, these past weeks, I'd go as an itinerant preacher, if they'll have me. The pay's enough to live on, if you live simply – more than a grover earns anyway. Not that money's important, but you must have something to live on. If you stayed with my sister, while I was away—'

'She might not want me.'

'She will when she meets you.' He was sure of it, though he could not forget Jenny's outburst, which to his relief had burnt itself out in his absence that evening.

Returning home, he had found her calmer, more like herself than she had been for a long time. The improvement had seemed to be continuing.

Matty did not share his certainty. She would be an outsider, a stranger. She would face it, for his sake, if she had to, but – 'Could I not come with you?'

To take with him a fellow preacher, someone who shared his faith and longed as he did for the salvation of souls, that would be one thing; to have a wife at his side who must be cared for and protected could only be an added anxiety. 'Ministers can be sent anywhere, even overseas.'

She grinned and her eyes sparkled. 'I'd like that.'

He realised she meant it, that where he shrank at the thought of going so far from home, her adventurous spirit was exhilarated by it. Perhaps, after all, with her at his side, he would find himself welcoming the unknown as she did.

Then she said, with sudden gravity, 'I'm not religious, not like you.'

He smiled faintly, 'If I can't win you over, then I'll not be much of a preacher.'

She thought that for him she would blithely have followed any religion he cared to mention, but she knew that was not what he meant or what he wanted. 'I'm not holy or learned,' she warned him again.

'You are you. That's all I ask.'

They walked on through the wood, stopping now and then to embrace before moving on again. As they went, she told him at last, in full, why she had abandoned him that morning in the byre near Durham. He had thought until then that he had reached the limit of his capacity to love, but after that it seemed to grow still more. He held her for a long time in silence, ashamed that he should ever have doubted her. Then, as it drew near the time when her father would be back from work, they made their way towards the house, slowly, reluctant to face what might be a difficult reality.

*   *   *

John Grey was already there, washing himself before the fire, while his wife hovered in attendance on him. Matty held Tommy's hand tight and led him forward, or he was not sure that he could have found the courage to step into the room.

Her father lowered the towel that had been at his face and studied him, his eyes running up and down, as if making some kind of not very flattering estimation of the young man. 'You've got a nerve, coming back.'

Tommy heard a sound from Matty, as if she was about to speak, but he squeezed her hand, in warning. 'I know what you think of me. I understand—'

'Why aye, you do, do you?' The man's eyes were sharp and combative.

'I came here last year because there was no work and no way to live. I saw no wrong in it then, though I was warned not to come. I wouldn't listen. I only saw the truth too late.'

'Small comfort that is, now we've lost. And it didn't stop you chasing my lass.'

Tommy glanced at Matty, who seemed once again to be about to speak. He decided it was time he got to the point. 'I love her. We'd like to be wed. I don't expect you to welcome me. I only ask that you give your consent. Then we'll go away. But I give my word that as far as it lies in my power she'll never have cause to wish she'd not wed me.'

'What makes you think I'd want to lose my daughter to you, under any circumstances?'

'I don't think it or expect it. I hope, that's all.'

John Grey pulled a clean shirt over his head, and then stood tucking it into his trousers, his eyes still on Tommy. 'If it wasn't for one thing, I'd send you packing. But for some reason that's beyond me she's set her heart on you—' In a rush Matty was on him, her arms about him, kissing him. He laughed ruefully, fending her off. 'Now, lass, I've not said yes yet.' He stood with his arm about her shoulder and said sternly to Tommy, 'You can have her, but I want it done properly, in the new church at

347

Hetton, so there's no blot on her name. But you needn't think to have dancing at your wedding, or more spent on it than has to be, for I'll not give a penny towards it. Decent, quick and quiet, that's what it must be. And afterwards, go away, right away, so no one can point the finger for what my daughter's done.'

With Matty's fingers caressing the palm of his hand, Tommy said earnestly, 'I'll ask for nowt, so long as I have her. That's plenty for me.'

'Aye,' said her father drily, but with a faint smile. 'More than plenty, I'd say. You needn't think you've got yourself a quiet obedient little wife. She'll never be that. She'll run circles round you, I can tell you. You'll have not a moment's peace with her. But if that's what you want, then good luck to you.'

'It's what I want,' said Tommy, unafraid.

A THREAD OF GOLD

Helen Cannam

A compelling tapestry of rivalry, passion and one
woman's undying devotion . . .

In 1865, when beautiful Laure Frémont marries Philippe
Beynac, she believes the course of their love will flow as
smoothly as the golden wine at their chateau in the
Dordogne. But beneath the gaiety and splendour, a
terrible blight is threatening their cherished vineyard. And
then, with the outbreak of the Franco-Prussian War,
Laure finds she is losing everything she holds most
dear . . .

So begins one woman's struggle for both herself and her
child's survival in an alien world, and a fight to restore
the estates which are her heritage. She faces agonising
choices, and conflicting demands: Henri Séguier, the rich
neighbour who offers her a love which she can never
return; Jean-Claude, the romantic painter, who loves with
a passion that will haunt Laure forever; and the solemn,
kindly Charles De Miremont, whom she realises she can
use for her own desperate ends.

And even when the dark clouds of war again intrude and
the threads of Laure's life are once more pulled apart, her
spirit will never be broken . . .

A KIND OF PARADISE

Helen Cannam

A passionate saga of one man's dream, and the woman
who shaped his destiny . . .

Sarah Wedgwood was only a child when she first met her
cousin Jos, but even then she knew their lives would be
irrevocably intertwined. It was his hands which fascinated
her. Broad yet sensitive, shaping clay as it spun on the
craftsman's wheel as miraculously as a conjurer's palm.
Drawn together by their mutual passion for the pottery
works, in time their friendship was to blossom into
love . . .

Determined, quick-witted Sarah cherished and nurtured
his restless quest for perfection – his dreams became her
dreams. And as they fought to establish the name of the
Wedgwoods, their lives would be full of turbulence,
drama, triumph and sadness. For just as the Wedgwoods
were on the brink of a phenomenal breakthrough, Sarah's
heart was being torn in two by her love for another man,
a kind of paradise that threatened the very foundations of
a lifetime's achievement . . .

'A graceful and successfully naturalistic tale which
recreates its period vividly'
Oxford Times

	A Thread of Gold	Helen Cannam	£3.99
☐	A Thread of Gold	Helen Cannam	£3.99
☐	A Kind of Paradise	Helen Cannam	£3.50
☐	A High and Lonely Road	Helen Cannam	£3.99
☐	The Last Ballad	Helen Cannam	£4.99
☐	The Dream House	Fiona Bullen	£4.99
☐	Painted Birds	Fiona Bullen	£4.99
☐	Child of Awe	Kathryn Lynn Davis	£4.99
☐	Too Deep for Tears	Kathryn Lynn Davis	£4.50
☐	The Rising Storm	Suzanne Goodwin	£4.99
☐	A Change of Season	Suzanne Goodwin	£4.99

Warner Books now offers an exciting range of quality titles by both established and new authors. All of the books in this series are available from:

Little, Brown and Company (UK) Limited,
P.O. Box 11,
Falmouth,
Cornwall TR10 9EN.

Alternatively you may fax your order to the above address. Fax No. 0326 376423.

Payments can be made as follows: cheque, postal order (payable to Little, Brown and Company) or by credit cards, Visa/Access. Do not send cash or currency. UK customers and B.F.P.O. please allow £1.00 for postage and packing for the first book, plus 50p for the second book, plus 30p for each additional book up to a maximum charge of £3.00 (7 books plus).

Overseas customers including Ireland, please allow £2.00 for the first book plus £1.00 for the second book, plus 50p for each additional book.

NAME (Block Letters) ....

....

ADDRESS ....

....

....

☐ I enclose my remittance for _____

☐ I wish to pay by Access/Visa Card

Number ☐☐☐☐☐☐☐☐☐☐☐☐☐☐☐☐

Card Expiry Date ☐☐☐☐